The
Midas
Murders

**Penny Spring and Sir Toby Glendower Mysteries
by Margot Arnold**

MARGOT ARNOLD

The Midas Murders

A Penny Spring and Sir Toby Glendower Mystery

A Foul Play Press Book

W. W. Norton & Company
New York • London

First published as a Foul Play Press paperback 1997
Copyright © 1995 by Margot Arnold

ISBN 0-88150-394-0 pbk.

Printed in the United States of America

Library of Congress Cataloging-in-Publication Data

Arnold, Margot.
    The Midas murders : A Penny Spring and Sir Toby
mystery / Margot Arnold.—1st ed.
         p.   cm.
    "A Foul Play Press book."
    ISBN 0-88150-340-1
    1. Glendower, Toby (Fictitious character)—Fiction.
2. Spring, Penny (Fictitious character)—Fiction. 3. Women
anthropologists—Greece—Fiction. 4. Archaeologists—
Greece—Fiction. I. Title.
PS3551.R536M53   1995
813' .54—dc20   95-20829
                                                              CIP

W. W. Norton & Company, Inc.
500 Fifth Avenue, New York, N.Y. 10110
W. W. Norton & Company Ltd.
10 Coptic Street, London WC1A 1PU

1 2 3 4 5 6 7 8 9 0

**To all my good friends,
past and present,
on Cape Cod**

WHO'S WHO

GLENDOWER, Sir TOBIAS MERLIN, 1st Baronet [created 1992], Archaeologist. O.M., F.B.A., F.S.A., Kntd. 1977; b. Swansea, Wales, Dec. 27, 1926; s. Thomas Owen and Myfanwy [Williams] G.; ed. Winchester Coll.; Magdalen Coll., Oxford, B.A., M.A., Ph.D.; Fellow, Magdalen Coll., 1949–; Fellow, All Souls Coll., 1990–; Emeritus Professor Near Eastern and European Prehistoric Arch., Oxford U., 1 dau., Sonya Danarova, m. Dr. Alexander Spring, 1991, 2 gr.ch. Mala & Marcus. Participated in more than 30 major archaeological expeditions. Author of several books, including *The Age of Pericles,* 1993; also numerous excavation and field reports. Clubs: Wykehamists, Athenaeum, Wine-tasters, University.

SPRING, Dame PENELOPE ATHENE, D.B.E. [Civil] 1992, Anthropologist. b. Cambridge, Mass., May 16, 1928; d. Marcus and Muriel [Snow] Thayer; B.A., M.A., Radcliffe Coll.; Ph.D., Columbia U.; m. Arthur Upton Spring, June 24, 1953 [dec.]; 1 son, Alexander Marcus, M.D., 2 gr.ch. Marcus & Mala Spring. Lectr. Anthropology Oxford U., 1958–1968; Mathieson Reader in Anthropology, Oxford U., 1969–1993; Extramural Lectr. Oxford U., 1993–; Fellow, St. Anne's Coll., Oxford, 1969–. Field work in the Marquesas, East and South Africa, Uzbekistan, India, and among the Pueblo, Apache, Crow, and Fox Indians. Author of over 20 books including anthrop. classics *Sex in the South Pacific,* 1957; *Feminism in the 20th Century Muslim World,* 1978; *Modern Micronesian Chiefdoms,* 1989; and *The Fijians,* 1992.

Chapter 1

Sir Tobias Glendower came out of a light doze with a start and wondered lazily at the cause of this unwelcome awakening to the cold light of a grey March morning and to the rain that cascaded against the windows, whipped by an unrelenting northeasterly gale. The peal of the front doorbell, followed by the scurrying steps of Mrs. Evans, his housekeeper, answered his question. He looked at the clock on the mantel above the cheerfully glowing log fire, which was adding its warmth to his cozy, centrally heated study, saw it was eleven o'clock, and muttered with a yawn, "Must be that perishing nuisance, Godolphin. Well, I'll show *him*."

With some caution he twitched aside the plaid cashmere rug that enshrouded his legs, exposing his left foot, which was swathed bulkily in a rather inept cocoon of bandages and propped up on a footstool. He groped for the book that had dropped from his hand as he dozed, opened it, pushed up his round glasses, which had slipped askew, and settled back in his comfortable easy chair with a small sigh of satisfaction as the murmur of voices in the hall grew louder.

The door opened and a small, plump figure surged in, only to recoil with a "Good God, it's like the tropics in here! What are you trying to do, Toby, roast yourself?"

"Oh, it's you," Toby said, none too graciously. "I was expecting my editor from the OUP."

"Ah!" Dame Penelope Spring said, advancing again and shutting the door behind her. "Still after you to do some work, is he? No wonder you're hiding out."

"I'm not hiding out, I'm ill," he said plaintively, and gave a convincing wince as he eased himself up in his chair. "This gout attack is extremely painful."

"You've been beating *that* drum for the past week, which means that you are either not taking your medicine as prescribed, or you've gone on drinking. You know damn well Dr. Croft said if you stick to the colchicine tablets and stay off the booze the pain will be gone in two or three days and you'll be as good as new. And what's all this?" She waved at his enshrouded foot. "He told you *not* to bandage it, it'll only make it worse."

"I find the warmth of the bandage very helpful," Toby hedged, and added waspishly, "Is there any particular reason for this impromptu and unexpected visit of yours, or are you just here to badger me?"

She plumped herself down in the easy chair on the other side of the fire and grinned delightedly at him. "I have a very good reason and wonderful news: news that will allow you to escape from your editor and anyone else who is trying to put you to work, and to literally sail away into the sunset—away from this terrible winter we've had and the equally awful spring we're having. And what is more, you will be surrounded by your nearest and dearest: Sonya and the twins, me, and even Alex when he can get away—we've all been invited."

Toby's silvery eyebrows rose and his round blue eyes widened. "Oh? By whom?" He reached for his pipe and tobacco and proceeded to light up.

"Jules Lefau! He has invited us for a three-week cruise on his yacht to the Greek islands. Just imagine all that sunshine and what fun it will be touring around your favorite country!"

His eyes narrowed. "Lefau? He must be up to something. Anyway, it's out of the question. I'm in no shape to go sailing and am far too busy."

"What! This isn't some piddling *little* yacht like you bounced me around in all over the Hawaiian islands, this is a luxury yacht complete with crew and all the fixings I'm talking about. You wouldn't have to do a damn thing other than enjoy yourself," she exclaimed. "And as to busy, what at, pray tell? Other than apparently trying to drink your way through the entire supply of vintage port in the All Souls cellars with your cronies—which has got you into your present sorry state, I might add—I haven't seen any signs of work going on since you finished *Pericles*."

"I am compiling a very important paper for the Society of Antiquaries on the Dorchester henges," he said stiffly.

"You've been saying that for the past eighteen months and it's beginning to sound mighty thin." Her tone was severe. "Good Lord, Toby, what's the matter with you? I thought you'd jump at this. How can you resist the chance to show the twins the glory that was Greece?"

He was silent for a moment and her hopes rose, only to fade when he said slowly, "You've always been dazzled by Jules Lefau's surface charm, but I think he is one of the most devious men I have ever come across, and if he wants us both along it is probably for a purpose. I don't trust him and I don't fancy my whole family being a captive audience, which, on a yacht, is just what we'd be."

"Oh, it's not like that at all. He didn't even initiate all this," she cried. "I can see I'd better explain the whole thing. The invitation initially came from Juliette Schuyler, who is a great friend of Sonya's."

"Who?" Toby said blankly.

"Oh, for heaven's sake, Toby, don't you ever listen to family news? Sonya must have told you about all this. Jules's daughter, Juliette, who is married to a New York plastic surgeon. You know she went up there to go to art school after the Voodoo Doll affair? Well, she met and married Dr. Richard Schuyler up there and has two children; the boy is eight, the girl is the same age as the twins, six. Juliette kept her contacts in the art world and became an illustrator of children's books. That's how she and Sonya met. You *do* remember that Sonya is now a published author with three children's books out and two more in the works?" she added sarcastically.

He snorted and refilled his pipe.

"Anyway, they became collaborators and close friends, as are the kids," she went on. "So it was she who suggested all this, so that her kids would have someone to play with at this family gathering. You see, there is nothing at all sinister about this trip; its main object is to celebrate the engagement of Vincent Lefau to Melissa Marolakis, granddaughter of the Greek tycoon Demetrios Marolakis. A merging of millionaires, as it were, and it's to be on Marolakis's private island off Hydra. Jules wanted the whole Lefau family on hand to meet all the future in-laws for a few days, so Juliette and her family are coming, and Benedict and Mimi Lefau will also join them on the island. After the celebration, Jules thought it would be fun to go off and cruise in the Cyclades. If there has to be a *motive,* well, he probably wanted you along because you are such an expert on the area."

Toby was apparently lost in his own train of thought and so missed that dangling lure. "That child Vincent is getting *married?*" he queried in amazement.

"That 'child' is now twenty-four years old and has just passed his bar exams," Penny said drily. "You forget how swiftly the years have fled since we first met the Lefaus."

"Talking of children," Toby said loftily, "unless the Americans have completely reversed the school year in one of their crackbrained attempts to 'improve' their educational system, shouldn't the twins be in school at this time?" It was a very sore point with him that all his attempts to have them educated in England had been stoutly vetoed by the rest of the family.

"Oh, good grief! Do you really think taking them out of first grade for a month to go on a tour most Americans would sell their souls for will doom them to everlasting failure? Both of them can already read and write at some astonishing level for their age, and with their IQs, what the hell does it matter anyway?" she retaliated.

The IQ tests had been Alexander Spring's idea while the education battle was being waged within the family. No one had been too surprised when the loquacious and precocious Marcus had tested out at the near-genius level of 160. What had surprised everyone was when his generally silent and apparently uninterested sister, Mala, had tested out at 165. "She must do it by osmosis," her mother had faltered in dismay. "It was quite obvious to *me* all along," Toby had commented smugly, although in reality he had been just as surprised as the rest of them.

The upshot had been a compromise between the egalitarian-minded Sonya and Penny, who were in favor of public school, on the one hand, and the traditionally minded Toby and Alex on the other, when the latter had pointed out that the twins would both be bored out of their skulls by the standard ABCs and picture books of the average first-grade curriculum. As a result, they now attended a small private school for gifted children in Pelham Manor, where at least they found some competition.

"In any case," Penny continued, "the school is a great one for encouraging individual 'projects' and, if I know Marcus, he'll come armed with enough of them to last a year, let alone three weeks. You know, if you went along you could *really* teach him something worthwhile."

The doorbell chimed again and Toby said with alacrity, "That'll be Godolphin for his appointment. I'm afraid you are wasting your time; my answer is still no. I will not be a party to this, and my advice to you is to keep a sharp eye on Jules. Just ask yourself—why does he want *us* along?"

She got up with some reluctance. "Well, I won't be leaving until the beginning of April, so there's still some time for you to change that increasingly paranoid mind of yours. Just let me know." And she stamped out as the young OUP editor rushed in, eager expectation writ large on his shining, morning face.

"I just can't understand him," she grumbled over the transatlantic phone to Sonya that afternoon. "It seems that anything I am for these days, he is automatically against. How about you having a go at him? And if he gives you any piffle about being too sick, don't believe a word of it. He could be up and about in a couple of days if he were really motivated."

"Oh, believe me, I will," Sonya said. "Why is he so anti-Jules?"

"Probably because I've always been pro," Penny said acidly. "Actually, I think he has always blamed him for causing several unnecessary deaths by not being completely honest with us. He has never been able to understand Jules's side of it—and there *was* a very strong side. So over to you on it. Now, what's your update on the plans?"

"Just as I sketched out the other day. I'll go over three days early with the kids to get them settled down and over the jet lag before we join the main party. I'll show them around Athens if they are up to it. So if you would join us at the hotel in Athens on April second, we'll rendezvous with Juliette on the third—she's doing the same thing with her two, but in Paris, so they'll be flying in that morning and Jules will pick us all up that afternoon. I can hardly wait to see some real sun, it's been just *miserable* here. We even had some snow last night."

"Just as bad here." Penny looked out at the rain that was still pouring from a grey heaven. "Oh, how about the clothes?"

"Olga will have them all done by departure time. She's made you two 'dressy' outfits with lots of interchangeable accessories and two smartish daytime ditto. You said you found a formal?"

"Yes," Penny said with a grin. "Picked it up in an antique shop in Woodstock. I think it must be Turkish, but very dressy:

black slathered with gold embroidery. Amazingly, it fits me."

"Well, I think you'll like what Olga has whipped up for you. She is the ultimate treasure and I've managed to keep her the best-kept secret in New York. Everyone thinks I spend a fortune on designer clothes; little do they know it all comes from a refugee ex-couturiere from my old ballet company. Juliette is so intimidated by the company we'll be keeping that she'll be spending a fortune in Paris, but as she has a fortune to spend, why not?"

They talked clothes for another couple of minutes, then Penny asked, "How's your Greek coming along?"

"Fair to middling. It wasn't one of my languages, you know," Sonya sighed. "I've been listening to a set of language cassettes, but I think Marcus has learned more already from them than I have. Must be getting old. Surely we won't need much, will we? Won't they all speak English?"

"I hope we won't need much because I don't know any," Penny said dismally. "I was depending on your father, damn his stubborn hide!" And on that downcast note they rang off.

When Sonya reported back a few days later it was to announce an equal lack of success. "Just no talking to him!" she fumed in a fine Slavic rage, reminiscent of her late Russian mother, that did nothing for her English. "So let him stew in his stupid juices, I say. I tell him *we* are going to have a marvelous time, and Alex too when he comes. Alex says he thinks maybe he come after the first week, just before we go off to the Cyclades. My father, he goes on and on about the devious Jules and says at the first sign of any funny business I must leave with the children. I ask you, what danger can there possibly be? So, poof, I say to him—is ridiculous! Am I not right?"

"I certainly hope so," Penny replied.

Chapter 2

"Oh, how heavenly! Just feel that warmth." Sonya turned her face rapturously sunwards as they stood outside their hotel, while their mound of luggage was loaded aboard a rather ramshackle taxi under the vociferous supervision of Marcus, who was trying out his Greek on anyone he could find who would listen to him. His sister stood tranquilly by, her hand firmly clasped by her friend the doorman, whom she had enslaved in three days and who was interjecting the odd Greek sentence or two when Marcus's Greek failed him.

"While we're en route to Piraeus, you'd better fill me in on the background of all this before we meet up with Juliette," Penny said. "We've been so busy that we haven't had time to go into it, and I don't want to put my foot in my mouth. How did the young couple meet? What's the girl like? What do the respective families think about it, and so on?"

They all climbed into the taxi, where the cabdriver, who had been bearing patiently with Marcus's Greek, said in a broad Australian accent, "It's the Black Goat at Piraeus yacht marina—right, missus?"

"Right," Sonya agreed with a grin at Penny, and settled back. "Well, it has all been rather sudden, I gather. Vincent met Melissa Marolakis during a skiing holiday at Aspen last Thanksgiving and it caught fire from there. She's just twenty-one and is in her senior year at Wellesley. I've not met her, but they did spend the New Year's holiday with Juliette, and she seems to think the girl's okay: bright, not bad-looking, and not as spoiled as one might expect with her background. Juliette tends at times to be a bit waspish about her father and, for that matter, Vincent, but she says the very name of Marolakis brought a gleam to Jules's eye. Apparently the name of Lefau brought an answering gleam from Demetrios Marolakis, who is the patriarch of the family and Melissa's grandfather, so there's no opposition that I know of. This engagement party will be the excuse for the two fathers to hammer out a marriage settlement, Lefau telling Marolakis what he plans to do for Vincent and Marolakis what dowry settlement he's making for Melissa. I think it's all very old-fashioned, but Juliette tells me the old Creole families like to do things this way and the Greeks always do it. The wedding won't be until sometime this summer after Melissa's graduation. The date will also be settled while we're here."

"What about her parents?" Penny prompted.

"Her mother is long dead and her father Georgiou is actually old Demetrios's younger son; the older one was killed years ago at the age of twenty in a mountaineering accident. Melissa and her brother Alexander—who is just about to graduate from Harvard Business School and so can't come—are the products of this first marriage; their mother died when they were quite small. Their stepmother is a power in her own right—Olympia Ribotis. She's half-sister to Lysander Ribotis, the current head of the Ribotis empire, and their family headquarters is on the island of Nisos Speria . . ."

"Nisos *means* 'island,'" Marcus interjected, looking proudly at his grandmother.

"Yes, dear," Sonya said, and continued, "This Ribotis-Marolakis marriage seems to be another megamerger. Olympia has just one child, a teenage daughter in boarding school in Switzerland; I don't think she will be coming either."

17

"And does patriarch Demetrios have a wife?" Penny queried.

Sonya shook her head. "A widower—his wife died just after Melissa's mother, so Olympia Marolakis will be our hostess for the functions, although we'll be staying on the Lefau yacht. I must say I'm rather glad about that. I'm not sure I approve of millionaires *en masse*."

Penny grinned at her Communist-born-and-bred daughter-in-law. "It will all certainly be a change to see how the other half lives, although they sound a pretty innocuous bunch, and if they aren't we can always retreat discreetly back to the yacht."

The jolting taxi came to a rattling stop and their driver announced, "This is as far as I can go. See—the Black Goat is farther down the quay there. If you want to go on down I'll bring the baggage. Best leave the boy with me to keep an eye on things while I'm away from the cab."

"Are you sure this is right?" Penny said, collecting the smaller hand baggage. "It just looks like an ordinary restaurant to me—I thought it would be an inn."

Sonya gave a helpless shrug. "Well, this is where Juliette *said* to come. Maybe I'd better go ahead to check and see if we're expected. You stay with the twins and I'll wave you on if it's okay." She set off, her tall, slim, elegant figure contrasting with the short, stocky cabdriver beside her, while Penny looked anxiously around at the mass of small yachts bobbing at their moorings all along the quay and at the other white sails dotting the surface of the inner harbor like a swarm of butterflies. There was no sign of any large boat.

Sonya disappeared inside the taverna but reappeared shortly and waved gaily as the taxi driver scuttled back towards them for another load.

"Right, kids, on our way!" Penny ordered, and taking a couple of tote bags in one hand and Mala in the other, she proceeded along the busy quay.

Sonya came to meet them. "All set. Table for nine reserved

for the Lefau party, and they're stashing our luggage inside. I said we'd like one of the tables outside since it's such a lovely day."

Penny did some quick arithmetic. "There's four of us and three with Juliette, Jules presumably, but who is number nine?"

Sonya shrugged. "No idea. Maybe he thinks Father came along with us after all. Our cabdriver is back here after eleven years in Australia and said he'll go back there once his young son is sufficiently in touch with his Greek heritage—isn't that amazing!"

"Not really," Penny said, handing over her luggage to an attentive waiter. "According to Toby the Greeks have always exported themselves but kept their strong home ties."

They had settled at a long table overlooking the harbour and had just ordered cold drinks all around when Sonya exclaimed, "And here's Juliette and her bunch, right on time for a change."

Penny looked up to see a svelte, chestnut-haired figure advancing on them, flanked by a dark, curly-haired little girl and a solid, towheaded boy and followed by a squad of luggage carriers. Apart from the striking hair she would not have recognised this poised, serene young matron as the volatile and emotional young girl she had known.

Greetings over, Juliette declared, "Father says to go ahead and order lunch and not to wait for him." While they settled down the children and decided who would eat what, Penny was amused to observe the interaction of the two families. Mala and Emily had silently and fiercely hugged each other, so that dark curls entangled with golden ones, whereas the boys had exchanged sly grins; then Marcus had started to talk a mile a minute at the mostly silent John.

Juliette noted her amusement and smiled at her. "You can see our families are perfectly matched—two talkers and two listeners: Mala never talks and my Emily never stops, and my John never talks and Marcus never stops."

While the mothers indulged in a brief mutual admiration of each other's chic outfits and the children began to tuck into their lunches, Penny relaxed in peaceful contemplation, lulled by the warmth of the day and the excellent Hymettus white wine she was sipping. How pleasant this is all going to be, she reflected, and wondered how Jules Lefau had weathered the years since they had met. She was jerked out of her reverie when she heard Juliette say, in a sharper voice, "Oh, my dear, I haven't caught you up to date—Father just sprang this one on me. I might have known there was more to this than just a simple family gathering. There have been some major additions to our megabucks crowd." Her tone was bitter. "In addition to the two Marolakis and Olympia's brother Lysander Ribotis, there'll be an Argentinian millionaire, one Hans Kepplik, and another that will really make your eyes pop . . ." Seeing that she had caught their full attention, she paused dramatically. ". . . *Kristos Theodopolis.*"

Her dramatic declaration fell flat as they both stared at her blankly. "Er, I'm afraid I'm not too well informed on millionaires," Penny volunteered. "Who is he?"

"You've never heard of mystery magnate Theodopolis?" Juliette cried. "Good heavens! Not only is he a billionaire but nobody has even set eyes on him in years: He's a complete recluse."

"You mean he's batty like what's-his-name Hughes?" Sonya demanded.

"No, I don't think so, he just doesn't like the common crowd. He sits on *his* island in the Caribbean and makes money—lots and lots of it. No one knows anything about him, but if he has been lured to this gathering there must be something *very* big in the works."

Penny felt a faint thrill of unease. "And this has just happened?"

"This is the first I've *heard* of it," Juliette corrected. "And I can't believe it has anything to do with the engagement, even if nothing is too good for Daddy's darling Vincent."

"Oh, come on, Juliette! Not that again," Sonya said. "Jules has done just as much for you and Benedict, but you are both settled and happy, so now it's Vincent's turn."

"It *is* true," Juliette cried, twin spots of color flaming on her magnolia cheeks. "He's never much cared for Benedict, who took after his Yankee mother's family, or for me, because I rebelled against the Creole code and also married a Yankee. But Vincent's all Lefau and the most like him—daddy's little darling."

Her venom shocked Penny into hastily revising her first opinion—the old Juliette was still there, and not too far beneath the polished surface, either. "And who is this Hans Kepplik?" she asked quickly.

The wild light died out of Juliette's dark eyes and she controlled herself with a visible effort. "I've no idea. Doesn't sound like a Spanish name though, does it?"

"And do all these tycoons have wives along?" Sonya queried, evidently doing a quick mental check of her wardrobe.

Juliette shook her head. "No, Theodopolis isn't married; Ribotis is between wives but has his twin nine-year-old sons with him and . . ." She glanced quickly at the children and dropped her voice. "Kepplik apparently has his mistress along—some French woman. Other than that it'll just be Olympia Marolakis and us. And by the way, she and her brother don't get on at all well."

Marcus, who had finished the baby octopi he had insisted on having and which he had been exhibiting one by one to the politely appalled squeals of Emily and the total indifference of his sister, had begun to fidget. "May John and I be excused to go and see the boats?"

The mothers duly conferred. "All right, but don't either of you go out of sight, don't touch anything, and come back pronto when we call you," Sonya said.

The boys raced off with joyous whoops, and Mala looked

21

after them with a faintly offended air. Sonya looked at her, smiled slightly, and whispered to Penny, "John is the only male Mala has ever come across who is totally impervious to her charms. She'll probably end up marrying him out of sheer frustration."

Juliette chuckled. "What a blissful prospect that would be! A completely peaceful haven to which we could beat a retreat in our old age and get away from our noisy ones."

"Emily has a resemblance to your mother, hasn't she?" Penny said cautiously. A shadow crossed Juliette's mobile face. "Yes, she's a Duchamps all right," she said quietly, "and a bossy one at that. Your Marcus looks like Sir Toby, doesn't he? While Mala has her mother's fine features, but where does her spectacular coloring come from?"

Penny looked at the gorgeous spectacle of Mala—the lustrous golden curls, the peach-bloom skin, and the enormous, dark blue, golden-fringed eyes—and shook her head helplessly. "Must be from the Spring side; Alex's father was a 'golden boy.' One thing for sure, she doesn't turn after me, thank God!"

"And John is the spit and image of his father," Sonya broke in tactfully.

Again Juliette chuckled. "Oh yes, solid original Manhattan Dutch to the core and as stubborn as a mule. I don't know where my Richard got his charm from; it certainly wasn't from the Schuyler side . . ."

She broke off with a little gasp as a pleasant tenor voice said from behind Penny, "Ah, there you all are!" Penny glanced over her shoulder to see the well-remembered, slight, elegant figure of Jules Lefau. His hair was now a sparkling silver, but other than that his thin, fine-featured face was little altered. Though he was clad in the standard yachtsman garb of blue blazer, white slacks and shirt, and a nautical cap, there was about him that exotic, slightly dandified air that almost three hundred years of living in America had not banished from the Lefau stock. He looked down at her, his thin, sensitive lips parting in a wide grin to reveal his small white teeth. "And here at long last is my dear Penny Spring." She got up and he embraced her with a fervent hug. "It is wonderful to see you again, my dear."

"The years have treated you well, Jules," she replied.

"The life you gave back to me has treated me well." He smiled back and advanced on Sonya, his hands outstretched. "And this is your beautiful daughter-in-law I have heard so much about. Ah! I see you have your father's eyes!" He gallantly kissed Sonya's hand in true continental fashion.

He turned and embraced Juliette, who said, "We've eaten, Father—you did say to go ahead, so we did. What will you have?"

"Oh, nothing. I had a quick snack on the yacht, and I think it best if we get everyone aboard and settled, so that we can get away from this shipping madness as quickly as possible. We're sort of double-parked or whatever they call it in the outer harbour. Bags inside?" He turned and signalled to a couple of seamen who had been standing watchfully behind him. "They'll pick them up and load them while you gather the children. Aren't you missing some?"

"I'll fetch the boys—I see they're almost out of sight," Sonya said quickly, and went off in hot pursuit. Juliette went with the girls to superintend the baggage pickup.

"Will Toby be joining us later?" Jules asked, a shade too casually.

"No, he's not coming. He's laid up with gout at the moment and is very busy," she said shortly.

"I'm sorry to hear that, very sorry," he said.

"Juliette tells me there have been some unexpected additions to your proposed gathering, a regular massing of millionaires." She looked at him enquiringly.

He shrugged. "I was surprised by that myself, but I suppose, since we'll only be staying a short while until the marriage details are settled, that the Marolakis have seized the opportunity to kill several birds with one stone, particularly as Ribotis

will be making one of his rare visits to his native land." With
a sudden change of tone he went on, "I hope to God that
Benedict gets here on time so that we can get things over and
done with and go on about our vacation."

"Just him, or will his family be coming?"

"Just Mimi—you remember her? The children are in boarding school now, so they won't be coming. Benedict is on a
business trip to North Africa and they'll come on from there.
They are both yachting fanatics now and they've been cruising along the North African littoral in *The Dancing Lady,* with
which I believe you are only too well acquainted." He grinned
slyly at her.

"Yes, and she certainly *did* dance," Penny retaliated. "I hope
in the interests of my ageing anatomy that your own is a lot
more stable."

"Oh, you'll have to see it to believe it. Everything super
deluxe. Sleeps twelve passengers, has a crew of six, and is as
steady as the *QE II,*" he assured her.

"Sounds impressive." She hesitated a second and then, to
put her mind at rest, took the plunge. "There's a question I
have to ask, Jules. Since this is not exactly our scene, why
were you so keen to have Toby and me along?"

He looked at her in hurt astonishment. "How can you ask a
question like that? I've been trying to get together with you
for years, but have never succeeded in catching up with you.
When Juliette suggested asking the Springs and their children
along—an excellent idea, by the way—I thought that you and
Toby could enjoy your own family gathering along with mine.
Besides," he added with a disarming grin, "when touring the
Greek islands, I thought having one of the greatest living au-
thorities on Greek culture along wouldn't hurt, either."

As usual, she succumbed to his overwhelming charm: She
wanted to believe him, so she did. The group reassembled;
children, luggage, adults, and crewmen were somehow all
packed into the gleaming white launch that stood bobbing at

the quay, and they inched gingerly out between the massed boats. While rounding the point to the outer harbour Jules, who was crammed in beside her, nudged her and pointed. "There she is, the *Silver Spray*—the big white one."

Penny peered and gasped. "Good Lord! It's like a miniature cruise ship; a mini 'Love Boat.' Somehow I never connected you with that sort of thing, Jules."

He grinned. "Right as usual. The Lefaus have not so well survived French colonial rule, Spanish ditto, the War between the States and Reconstruction—not to mention the boll weevil and sundry floods—by indulging in costly follies like that yacht. It's not mine. It belongs to a friend of mine who runs a fleet of Caribbean cruise ships and has this as his expensive toy. He ran into a cash flow problem recently, so I loaned him the money and took this as collateral, with him paying the expenses of the crew and the upkeep. Not only will we get a free vacation, but I'll probably make some money out of the deal." He chuckled. "I needed something to impress my love-smitten Vincent's prospective in-laws, and this seemed to fit the bill. A striking example of how to 'keep up with the Joneses' or, perhaps . . ." momentarily his face hardened ". . . of holding a candle to the devil."

Chapter 3

The spirits of the whole party rose visibly as Jules toured them around the luxury yacht, for—in miniature—it had everything, even to a mini swimming pool on the aft deck, which currently stood empty and covered with a tarp. "I thought, since it doesn't have a shallow end and is about eight feet deep, that in the interest of the children's safety it had best be kept this way, at least for the moment," Jules explained. He went on to point out the shuffleboard court marked out adjacent to it, the deck quoits, and even some skeet-shooting equipment at the stern. Just off the main lounge was a smaller one containing a well-stocked bar, a large screen with an elaborate VCR attached, and a library of films, as well as a cupboard filled with games of all kinds.

By this time the children were round-eyed with delight, and their mothers exchanged satisfied grins as Jules led them down the main companionway to the sleeping quarters. Here the first hitch occurred, and from an unexpected source.

"There are four double-bed staterooms and two double-bunk cabins, and when the whole party arrives we'll be more than full, but until then we have some breathing room," Jules explained. "For the moment I have one stateroom, Juliette can have another, and I thought you, Penny, could maybe go in with Sonya—that would leave the spare for Benedict and

Mimi. However, I think it might be as well to settle the children down in the double-bunk cabins, where they can stay the whole trip—Emily and John in one and Mala and Marcus in the other . . ."

A small, clear voice interrupted him. "I won't share with *him*," and to make her meaning quite clear Mala pointed an accusing finger at her brother.

"But whyever not?" her mother cried. "You've shared with him before."

Mala shook her golden curls vigorously. "No!"

"Won't it be fun to share with your big brother? He can look after you," Jules coaxed.

The dark blue eyes widened in outrage at this terrible gaffe. "He may be my taller brother but he is not my *big* brother. In fact," she said grandly, "I am older than he is."

Jules looked in amazement at Sonya, who said, "By fifteen minutes—they're twins. It's just that Marcus has grown so . . ." She turned sternly on her daughter. "Mala, this is silly. You'll share with Marcus and that's that."

The blue eyes flashed fire. "I won't. He has bugs and I *hate* bugs."

Sonya turned to her son. "What's this about bugs?"

He gave a convulsive wriggle at becoming the center of attention. "It's one of my collecting projects—for school," he said. "They're quite safe and can't get out. I've a box for them."

"Well then, how about the boys in one cabin and the girls in the other?" Jules said brightly.

The two mothers looked at him as if he had grown horns. "No way!" they said in chorus.

"I tell you what," Penny broke in. "Why don't I go in with Marcus for the trip and Mala go in with her mother for the moment? Marcus and I have been roomies before, haven't we?" He grinned and nodded.

"But a bunk will not be as comfortable for you," Jules protested.

"I'll get the bottom one and this budding scientist here can go on top," Penny said. "I'm small enough that bunks don't bother me, and I'd rather stay put than bedhop during the trip—and I *am* the odd woman out."

"Are you sure?" Jules said feebly.

"Quite sure," she said, taking Marcus's hand. "But hear me plain, young man, no *spiders* in your collection, is that clear?"

"I am collecting insects," Marcus explained with heavy patience. "Spiders are arachnids, not insects, so you have nothing to fear, Grandma."

"And you are a true chip off your grandfather's block," she muttered, as the party dispersed to unpack. Closeted with her grandson, she brought up the subject again. "Now, before we settle in I want to see this collection of yours and the box they're in."

He dived into his suitcase and, to her surprise, produced a metal box with holes in it that she recognized as an entomologist's professional kit. "Where on earth did you get that?" she demanded.

"My science teacher loaned it me for the trip." Marcus flipped it open to reveal a series of small clear plastic boxes with tiny airholes and whipped off the top of one of them to reveal a large black beetle that clicked angrily at them. "I'm trying to find out what they all eat and how long they'll stay alive in captivity," he said with ghoulish relish.

"Let's see the rest of them."

He carefully recapped the beetle and started an enthusiastic recital of where and when he had captured his prey, as a large cockroach, a dung beetle, and an exotic-looking ladybird were revealed in turn. "But *these* are my prizes—I found them yesterday in the ruins," he said with pride, as he uncapped a larger container holding two large black scorpions and a small green one.

Penny recoiled in horror. "Those are *dangerous,* Marcus! How on earth did you catch them without getting stung?"

"Tweezers." He pointed to a pair that were slotted along with other tools in the lid. "I'm afraid I squished one when I tried it first, but now I've got the knack of it. And I know what they like to eat." He put the lid back on, rummaged through his small backpack, and produced a jam jar with holes in its metal top, in which a bunch of depressed-looking flies buzzed aimlessly. "Though how I am going to get the leaves and stuff the other bugs like to eat on this boat I *don't* know," he sighed.

"What *I* know is that if you are bent on keeping your scorpions that box is not going to stay in this cabin." Penny was firm. "There's a metal locker just outside the door and that's where they'll all stay. And if I see you being at all careless, they will *all* be disposed of. Clear?"

"Yes, Grandma," Marcus said meekly. Carefully latching the box and gathering up his fly bottle, he trotted out to the locker, and on returning informed her, "There was plenty of room—nothing in it but a bunch of life jackets."

By the time they had finished stowing their things in the built-in wardrobe and drawers, the powerful diesel engines were throbbing and they were gliding across a mercifully calm sea. "Can we go and see the engines?" Marcus asked eagerly.

"Not now—let's go on deck and see where we're going," Penny said. They made their way up through the forward hatch to find the rest of the ship's company already assembled along the bow. To her surprise the yacht appeared to be heading into the Saronic Gulf, and not directly south to their destination as she had anticipated. As they came up to the group Jules turned and asked, "Everything okay?"

"Fine," she assured him, "but where are we heading?"

"I thought the children might like to see some famous sights on the way." He looked down at Marcus. "That's Salamis dead ahead—the Greeks fought a big sea battle with the Persians there, you know."

"Four hundred and eighty B.C. the Greeks made the Persians flee," chanted Marcus happily, wriggling in between John and his mother at the rail. Sonya looked down at him, turned, and cast her eyes heavenwards. Detaching herself from the rail, she indicated to Penny by a slight inclination of her sleek head a need to consult. They moved a little apart from the rest as she whispered, "For some reason we don't seem to be in any hurry to get to our destination. The plan is to cruise around this gulf and spend the night anchored off Aegina. Tomorrow we're scheduled to go on to Palaia Epidaurus and then make a land trip to Epidaurus itself on the Peloponnese. We won't get to Marolakis until the day after that. Don't you find this a little odd for a man bent on impressing his prospective in-laws?"

"Not really," Penny said. "He may be stalling a little to allow Benedict to get here. Despite what Juliette says, I know Benedict is his right-hand man as far as business is concerned. Also, he may not want to appear too eager; he might want to 'make an entrance' after the rest of the tycoons have gathered."

Sonya smiled faintly. "Yes, he is a bit theatrical, isn't he? You're probably right. I just thought I'd mention it."

"Has Mala settled down?" Penny looked around in sudden alarm. "Where is she?"

"Why shouldn't she be settled down? She got her way, as usual," Sonya said glumly. "And she is busy captivating the rest of the crew—the captain is already a gone goose. Want to see?" She led Penny off towards the glass-enclosed bridge, and as Penny peered inside she could see Mala hoisted up in the arms of a tall, burly, dark-haired man, who was pointing out all the instruments on the bridge to her rapt attention. An even taller flaxen-haired man grinned at them from behind the wheel, and a small dark man leaned in at the open door, a wide smile on his thin, olive-skinned face.

"The burly one is the captain, Tom Andersen from Corpus Christi. The man at the wheel is his number two man and engineer, Leif Ohlsen—a Norwegian, I believe—and the man at the door is Ramon, from the Philippines," Sonya explained. "He's our steward, waiter, and general gofer, I gather,

so I imagine she'll make a special effort with him."

"Is that the lot?" Penny asked. "Not many of them to handle the boat and all of us."

"There's a couple more. A Greek hand they just took on at Piraeus to replace another American who had to go home on a family emergency, and Ledoux, a French cook—from Marseilles. I'd better go and reclaim Mala before she makes a nuisance of herself." Sonya went up to the door; Ramon stepped aside as she poked her head in and said, "Come on now, Mala, you mustn't get in the way. Let's go and look at all the sights you're missing."

"I'm learning how to work the bo . . . ship," Mala said with a wide-eyed glance at Andersen. "It's *very* interesting."

"She's no trouble at all, ma'am," the big Texan drawled. "And we can show her the sights even better from up here until she gets tired of it. I'll bring her back to you."

Thus dismissed, Sonya remarked as they sauntered back to the bow, "I often wonder how that child ever learned how to walk—men seem to cart her around automatically. Her father is just as bad and my father is worse."

"It's because she's still so tiny and cute," Penny said, "though I do hope she isn't going to turn after me as far as height and figure."

Sonya smiled sideways at her. "Well, good things in small packages, you know. In one thing, for sure, she *does* take after you—she's a 'people person' already, just as Marcus is already a miniature 'think tank.'"

They joined the others to find Jules reading out of a guidebook and pointing out ancient Eleusis, which showed up as a dreary industrial complex with no evidence of its mystical past. With obvious relief he yielded his place as guide to Sonya, who had studied archaeology, and as they headed towards the Isthmus of Corinth to see the canal, Jules came over and sat down beside Penny, who had subsided thankfully into a deck chair. "I must congratulate you on your ship," she said. "She's

as steady as a rock and a real beauty. Did you come all the way across in her?"

"Oh my, no!—I couldn't spare that much time." Jules stretched luxuriously. "The crew sailed her over and I flew out and joined them here just a couple of days ago. A competent bunch, I'd say. Same with Benedict—he hired a crew to bring *The Dancing Lady* to Tangier and flew out there."

"And we are sightseeing until he gets here?" she asked.

"That's what we're here for, isn't it?" he said, but did not answer her question. "And that reminds me, in spite of the holiday there are some business calls I have to make, so if you'll excuse me for a bit?"

By the time the canal had been inspected and they were heading for Aegina, light was dimming and a brisk evening breeze had sprung up, so by common consent any further sightseeing on Aegina was vetoed. After an exquisite epicurean dinner prepared by the as-yet-unseen French chef, to which Penny, after a day in the fresh air, did ample justice, she was so sleepy and euphoric that she retired to bed shortly after the children had been settled down for the night, leaving Sonya and Juliette deeply engrossed in sketches for their next children's book. Jules had disappeared again after dinner, ostensibly to make more business calls to the Far East, where already it was tomorrow's business day.

She slept like a log; her euphoric mood continued as she wakened to another perfect day and an equally delicious English-style breakfast. "Really, it's like being on a personalised luxury cruise. I intend to make your father green with envy when I tell him about this," she told Sonya as they sped across the calm sea in the launch towards the small port of Palaia Epidaurus.

"Yes, I must say if this is *la dolce vita,* I'm in favor," Sonya said. "Too bad about Emily, though. She got miserably sick during the night, so Juliette has asked us to keep a sharp eye on John, as she's staying on board with her."

"Seasickness?" Penny asked.

"No, I don't think so; after all, it's been dead calm. Juliette thinks Emily just pigged out on that rich dessert last night. Anyway, she isn't all that keen on ancient ruins, so she was just as glad to have an excuse to stay aboard and get in some sunbathing."

Jules was piloting the launch under the supervision of the largely silent Greek deckhand, watched with avid interest by the two boys, and it was not until they were about to dock that he handed over the controls to the seaman with a "Here you are, Preftakis, docking backwards Greek-style is beyond me." The Greek took over the wheel with a slight smirk and deftly whisked them sternwards into their slip. He cut the engine and, leaping ashore, had the boat expertly moored in a trice.

They all crammed into a taxi waiting on the quay and began the steep climb up the fragrant pine- and cypress-clad hills towards their goal. "It's about eighteen kilometres to the site," Jules informed them, "and I've booked us in for lunch at the Xenia hotel there—about one-thirty, I said. Afterwards we can do some more sightseeing or, if everyone's had enough by that time, we can get a taxi on to Nauphlia, where the *Silver Spray* is heading. The port there is large enough for Andersen to moor right at the quay. Then tomorrow, if you like, we can get another taxi and go to see Mycenae, Tiryns, and Argos."

"What's to see here, Grandpa?" John asked.

"The great healing shrine of Aesculapius, the Greek god of medicine. It has a very neat museum, I've heard, full of parts of all the people who were cured here—arms, legs, livers, eyes, kidneys . . ."

"Real ones?" John said in awe, looking at Marcus.

"No, just replicas, and there's a great theatre where you can hear a whisper from the stage all over the theatre."

"*That* we have to try out," Marcus informed his friend.

"*I* can tell you all about Epidaurus, John," Mala cut in with a baleful glance at her brother. "I can show you where they kept the healing snakes—my grandpa told me. We may even find one," she tempted.

Sonya looked apologetically at Jules. "I'm afraid it's Father's version of bedtime stories—instead of telling them fairy tales he tells them about ancient sites. And, Mala, we are not here to look for snakes." Mala retreated into offended silence.

"So, shall we start at the theatre?" Jules urged as they reached their destination and decanted from the taxi. "We'd best all stick together, I think, at least until we get our bearings."

"Suits me," Penny said, and there was a general murmur of agreement as they began to move towards the great frozen cascade of grey marble just discernible through the trees.

"Luckily, it is so early in the season that it isn't crowded—in fact it looks as if we have the place more or less to ourselves," Jules said as they strolled towards their goal. Then, with a sudden start, he exclaimed, "But not quite! Good Lord, how amazing! There's Demetrios and Georgiou Marolakis—what are they doing here?" And he hurried forward to meet three men who had detached themselves from the shadows of a young oak and were advancing towards them.

Sonya looked at Penny, her dark eyebrows lifted in enquiry, and Penny's euphoria took a sudden nose-dive as Jules came hurrying back to say, "Extraordinary coincidence! They've run over from Marolakis with Theodopolis, who is of Peloponnesian origin but has never even seen this site. Do come along—they're anxious to meet you.

"Demetrios, may I present my very dear friend Dame Penelope Spring," Jules said, "of whom you have heard so much from me already. And we hope her famous partner, Sir Tobias Glendower, will be joining us shortly."

Penny's spirits sank even further at this blatant lie as she looked at the grizzled Demetrios. He was huge for a Greek—about six feet in height and very broad of shoulder. His face, seamed and craggy and as grey as the ruined masonry around them, was marred by a livid white scar that ran from the corner of his left eye almost to his tight mouth, where his bluish lips and the hoarse, weak voice in which he acknowledged the introduction signalled to her either emphysema or a severe heart condition. "My son Georgiou," he wheezed, indicating the much smaller, dark-haired, plump and pallid man who, unlike his two nautically clad companions, wore a three-piece dark business suit of heavy Italian silk that looked totally out of place. "And this is our honored guest, Kristos Theodopolis," the old man wheezed on.

Unlike Georgiou, who had pumped her hand vigorously with his slightly sweaty one, Theodopolis kept his hands clasped behind his back and gave her a stiff little bow. Although almost as tall as the aged giant beside him, he appeared much slighter and smaller, and his own expensive nautical outfit had a faintly rumpled and uncared-for look about it. The hair under his cap was white and in startling contrast to his darkly tanned, seamed face; he gazed at her with deep-set, hooded dark eyes. There was something about him that struck her as faintly off-key, but she could not pinpoint what it was. As the introductions went on she continued to watch him carefully.

But a further surprise was in store when they got to Mala, who stationed herself directly in front of Theodopolis, looked up at him with her most winning smile, and said, "My grandpa has told me all about this place. Would you like me to show you where they kept the snakes that healed people?"

To her further surprise, after a quick glance at Sonya he sank down on one knee, took Mala's small hand in his thin, dark one, and said in a deep baritone, "If your mother permits I would be most honored if you would show me around."

"Now, Mala, you mustn't bother Mr. Theodopolis," the equally startled Sonya stuttered.

He straightened up, still holding Mala's hand and with an urgent appeal in his dark eyes. "Madame Spring, I would be delighted if you would allow me to escort her. I will take good care of her."

"Oh, good," Mala chirped and tugged at his hand. "It's over this way, by the temple." And they started off as the group gazed after them in stupefaction.

Penny came out of hers. "Go after them," she hissed urgently at Sonya. "He may be a billionaire but he may also be a first-class nut!"

"Don't worry, I will—at a discreet distance," Sonya whispered back. "But you know, it's funny, but Mala always seems to *know* about people; she's never picked a bad one yet. You ride herd on the boys, then . . ." She sauntered after them, guidebook in hand.

The trio of millionaires seemed as startled as they had been at this development, but now drew together in low-voiced discussion. The two boys, who had been hastily stuffing their pockets with sundry leaves, flowers, and grasses to feed the insect collection, pounced on Penny before she could interpose herself into the group. "Grandma, would you go right up to the top there and see if you can hear us down here? We want to see if it's true about the sound," Marcus asked eagerly.

Penny looked up at the towering, vast semicircle of steeply tiered rows of marble seats and uttered a fervent "No way!" but seeing the deep disappointment in their faces, she added hastily, "Tell you what, you two go right up to the top, John to the left and you to the right, and work towards each other, and I'll walk slowly across the stage down here saying, 'Can you hear me' in a whisper, and then you wave at me if you can. Then you come back here and we'll go and see all the bits of people in the museum."

"Great!" They raced each other up the precipitous aisles and waved wildly from the back row.

"I'll start now," Penny called. She took a pace towards the men, who had gathered in the shade of an olive tree, Demetrios propped against the trunk, the others flanking him and oblivious to anything else. "Can you hear me?" she said in a normal voice, and was answered by two waves.

Slowly she advanced towards the men, repeating herself over and over as the boys came closer together, but her mind was racing in a very different direction. By her side stalked a tall and spindly shade whispering, "Keep an eye on Jules; he's up to something."

All euphoria vanished; she was now prey to raging doubt. She did not believe for a second that this "meeting" was a coincidence, and yet she could not for the life of her understand what part she was playing in it. Of only one thing was she certain—Jules *was* up to something; the trouble was that she had not the faintest idea what it could be.

Chapter 4

The events of the remainder of the day did little to soothe her unease. Sonya and Mala had caught up with her and the boys at the museum with the news that Theodopolis had been reclaimed by his hosts and Jules after a heated exchange in Greek that Sonya had been unable to follow, and that Jules had called to her that he would meet them back at the hotel for lunch. The lunch itself had been a hurried affair, with Jules on the jump to get on to Nauphlia; and when they had arrived to find the *Silver Spray* anchored at the quay, he had been visibly annoyed to hear that apart from Ramon and Leif Ohlsen on the bridge, the crew was dispersed on various errands on shore.

Having ordered Ramon to go hunt them down and bring them back at once to ready the ship for departure, he admitted that plans had changed and that Marolakis wanted them at the island as soon as possible. "Everyone's there, so he is anxious to get things started. Unfortunately, our Mycenae trip will have to be postponed until later," he apologized with a rueful grimace. "There will probably be time to look at the Venetian fort here in Nauphlia if you feel like a climb." He jutted his chin upwards to indicate the towering, crenellated mass of masonry that spread itself across the hilltop, dominating the town. "I'm afraid I must stick around here to see that the crew gets cracking with the refuelling and supplies once they are rounded up, so you'll be on your own."

Mala took one look at the towering hill and shook her golden curls with a definite "no."

Penny was not far behind her. "I think I'll stay with Mala," she said hurriedly, as the boys clamoured to get started. She looked at Sonya. "Do you feel up to it on your own?"

Sonya grimaced. "What else is a mother for? Besides, if this doesn't wear this pair out, nothing will." She consulted her guidebook. "Right then, boys, to your left and then straight up." She strolled off in their wake down the gangplank.

"We should be ready to leave about seven, so you've plenty of time," Jules called after her, and turned back to Penny. "Sorry about this, but Marolakis was very insistent, and I'm sure you understand that I don't want to make any waves until everything is settled."

Penny gazed steadily at him. "So you aren't going to wait for Benedict?"

He did not meet her gaze. "Unfortunately, no." Then on a brisker note he said, "Now, is there anything I can do for you before the crew turns up?"

"Well, yes, there is. I'd like to know more about both our hosts and this unexpected company they seem to be having. Got any reference books handy? I'm feeling somewhat underinformed and more than a little puzzled," she said bluntly.

"I do have a biography of Marolakis," he admitted, avoiding her implied question. "Not much on the others, I'm afraid, unless you can use a computer. I've a program on disk that has all the major reference books on it."

"Let's start with the book and I'll try my hand at the computer later," she said. "But if I can't manage it, Sonya can—multitalented is my daughter-in-law."

"Fine! One book coming right up, if I can find it." His heartiness had a hollow ring to it. "Where will you be?"

"I'll get Mala settled and be right here on deck," she assured him and, while he disappeared below, retrieved Mala from the bridge where she was in earnest converse with the big Norwegian. She deposited her beside the recuperating Emily, who was on a couch in the small lounge watching *Who Framed Roger Rabbit* with rapt attention; her mother, it transpired, was taking a nap. "There's *The Little Mermaid* after this, if you like," she informed Mala, who nodded a grave assent and settled down beside her.

The book duly delivered, Penny settled in a deck chair in the sun on the port side and began to read. To her surprise, she found that Marolakis was a northern Greek from Macedonia and not—as she had supposed—from the southern island that bore his name. "Well, anyway, that explains why he's so big," she said to herself. The early part of the book, dealing with his teenage activities with the Greek freedom fighters against the Nazis, she found very interesting. The livid scar he bore was the product of a hand-to-hand fight with an SS officer, who did not survive the bout. Ironically, he had got his start on the path to fame and fortune by selling surplus German arms and equipment after the tide had turned against the Nazis; but when the book went on at tedious length into his early business wheelings and dealings, her interest began to flag, for she was mainly interested in his personal life, about which the book said very little. To her vexation it did not have an index, being a translation from a Greek original into English, and so she became increasingly distracted by what was going on around her.

First she became dimly aware of a shouting match going on between Juliette and her father; then, as the crew started to straggle on board, by arguments between the glum-faced men and the impatient Jules. Captain Andersen had brusquely squelched Jules's hopes of an early departure, since they had had to book a time at the refuelling dock of the busy port and there was no possibility of moving that time up. And they were still one man short, since Ramon had been unable to locate the Greek seaman Preftakis. "Going by your former orders, I gave all the men not on watch shore leave until ten tonight," he pointed out sternly. "So he probably won't show up until then."

Jules was not used to being thwarted and would not accept this, so poor Ramon was again sent out to comb the town for the missing seaman. By this time Penny was hopelessly distracted so, abandoning the book, she went in search of the computer. She found the right disk, but one look at the bewildering operating instructions was enough. "I'll wait for Sonya," she thought, and after checking on the girls, who had moved on to *Aladdin,* she regained the deck and doggedly went on with the book.

Shortly thereafter Sonya and the boys straggled on board, all evidently worn out from their mountaineering, so she hadn't the heart to put the weary Sonya to work again. She filled her in on what had been happening.

Sonya grimaced. "I'm beginning to appreciate Father's 'captive audience' comment," she said. "Still, there's nothing to be done about it. Any idea what's up with Juliette? She seems to be in an absolutely foul mood."

Penny shrugged. "No, I was too far away to hear what the argument with her father was about."

Sonya yawned. "About Vincent, I expect. She's almost paranoid at times about him. You'd never think he was her full brother." This recalled another Lefau brother-sister relationship, and did nothing to soothe Penny's unease.

In spite of all Jules's efforts, they were still at the dock when they all retired for an early night after a strained and subdued evening. Penny awoke briefly when the diesel engines started to throb. Looking at her watch, she saw it was well after midnight. So much for an early start, she thought, and drifted back to sleep. When she awoke it was daylight; Marcus was still fast asleep so, slipping quietly into her clothes, she went up on deck to find Sonya already at the rail, guidebook in hand, gazing out at a large and precipitous pine-clad island on their starboard side.

"Is that it? Are we there?" Penny demanded, joining her.

"No, that's Hydra," Sonya informed her. "Sounds neat, too—the only motor vehicle allowed on the island is a garbage truck; otherwise it's donkey carts or Shank's mare. Well worth a visit, says the guidebook."

"Well, if the Marolakis setup turns out to be under- or overwhelming, maybe we can borrow the launch and one of Mala's devotees and take refuge there," Penny said with a grin. "Feel up to taking a crack at that computer?"

"Yes, let's grab a cup of coffee on the way. Juliette is all sweetness and light this morning—she certainly is into mood swings—and she's keeping an eye on Mala for me. Where's Marcus?"

"Still recharging his batteries," his grandmother said. "By the way, has Juliette any idea what the programme is for today? Things were so grim last night I didn't like to ask."

"Latest update on that is that we're expected for lunch. Which is why, I surmise, we are going the long way around: Instead of heading north around Hydra we're heading south, and will have to turn north again to get there when we reach the tip. Kids are included at lunch and it's informal. Tonight we are asked for dinner, formal, kids *not* included. I wonder how informal one is meant to be. I'd hate to turn up in shorts and a tee shirt to find our hostess decked out in St. Laurent's latest," Sonya commented.

"I think the Spring family should take them at their word. After all, *we* aren't out to impress them, that's a Lefau headache. Anyway . . ." She grinned suddenly. ". . . with your legs in shorty shorts the men should be impressed as all get-out."

Sonya chuckled. "Perhaps you're right, and we'll dress Mala up in that gorgeous smocked dress that friend of yours made for her. She never gets dirty and she'll be an eye-catcher."

"When isn't she?" Penny said dolefully, as they helped themselves to mugs of coffee from the buffet-style breakfast table and settled themselves before the computer. "And is it my imagination or has it suddenly turned much warmer?"

Sonya was busy clicking away in expert fashion as the screen sprang into life. "Yes, it has."

"I'm going to roast in that damned Turkish robe," Penny groaned. "I should have brought my 'dinner at high table at St. Anne's' dress. At least that's sleeveless."

"I shouldn't worry about that because a) they'll probably be air-conditioned and b) in this part of the world they don't eat until some ungodly late hour, so it should be cooler anyway. We'd better stoke up at lunch or we'll die of hunger," Sonya returned. With a triumphant gasp she added, "Here's the info on the Ribotis clan."

Penny peered over her shoulder. "Also Macedonian!— regular southern migration went on, didn't it? No mention of Olympia do I see, except for her birth."

"Terribly sexist, these reference books," Sonya snorted, and having absorbed what there was on the Ribotis, went on to Theodopolis.

"Sixty years old! He certainly doesn't look it," Penny said. "But not a word about his private life, other than that he was born in Sparta."

"If he's as reclusive as they say, he's the sort to pay reference books *not* to put him in," Sonya replied. "I can't find anything on Kepplik—maybe he's another of the same ilk."

"Don't you find it a little odd that someone as paranoid about privacy as Theodopolis doesn't have some hulking bodyguards in tow?" Penny mused.

"If no one knows what he looks like and no one knows where he is, why should he bother? And maybe he has some but just didn't bring them along yesterday—"

They were interrupted by a voice behind them, causing them both to jump. "Find what you want?" Jules enquired from the doorway. He was looking extremely dapper and appeared to have recovered his good humour.

"Yes, fine, thanks." Penny was not about to enlarge on that. "What is our programme for today?"

"We should reach the island about twelve-thirty. Lunch, to which everyone is invited, will be at one-thirty, so if you're ready to go ashore about one, that'll be fine. I have to go off for a preliminary meeting with Melissa's father as soon as we dock, so I'll see you all there, shall I?" He started to turn away but then turned back. "Oh, one more thing, as you disembark I believe there's some kind of security check—pure formality in this case, of course, but they have to be very careful—don't let it upset you. I believe even Theodopolis has to go through the drill, and with this horde of VIPs such a tempting target for any terrorist group, they are being super careful."

"Ah, the price of riches!" Sonya said after he had gone. "Birds in a golden cage, we'll be."

"But not sitting ducks, we hope," Penny returned. "Find anything else of interest?"

"Marolakis has only owned this island for about twenty years: 'Formerly the volcanic island of Medeos,'" Sonya quoted. "So he changed its name. Oh well, not the first time the Macedonians have invaded southern Greece, is it?"

"How about the Ribotis island?" Penny asked.

Sonya checked back. "Oh, they bought that back in the sixties. At least they kept its old name—Speria. Villages on both of them—I wonder what the inhabitants think of it all."

"Probably they all work for the owners. It must take a small regiment of them to keep an island going. What is Ribotis into?"

Sonya busily clicked away. "Shipping mainly, it appears. Has a whole fleet of them, but does have other industrial interests as well—just like Marolakis. Aha! here's a possible link with the mysterious Mr. Kepplik—has plantations and ranches in Argentina."

"Is the fleet oil tankers?"

"Just says ships and shipping lines, and spread wide—Black Sea, Mediterranean, and Atlantic."

"How about Theodopolis?"

Sonya peered at the screen. "About everything from arms

to zebras, but mainly he just plays the market: the true 'Midas touch.'"

"Well, enough of this, let's go and have breakfast," Penny said firmly. "I'm famished."

"Me too," Sonya said, exiting and turning off the computer. "And after that, let's get changed. I'll see to Mala and you see that Marcus is presentable—leave changing him to the very last minute because he can get dirty quicker than the speed of light."

As indeed it proved, for when the islands hove into sight, Penny had run Marcus to earth in the engine room, where he had managed to cover himself with oil. By the time she had cleaned him up and seen him into a long-sleeved white tee shirt and black shorts, the rest of the party was already assembled on deck and peering eagerly at what lay ahead.

"It must have been one whopper of a volcano," Sonya observed as they approached her. "Look!—both islands seem part of the rim of the caldera." She handed Penny the binoculars.

As the two islands sprang into sharp definition she saw that they were shaped like half-moons facing each other across a strait half a mile wide. Marolakis to the north was the larger and flatter of the two, and she could make out a small village on the eastern horn of its crescent, and what had to be the mansion and its compound on the western horn. A landing pier jutted out from this into the bay formed by the arms, and nestled snugly within the bay were three yachts, two large and one small. Speria, by contrast, had a hilly barrier all along its southern side but flattened out to the north into its crescent. In this case the tiny village was on the western end and she could just make out the mansion to the east, buried among a grove of trees; a very large white yacht was moored at its pier.

"Grandma, I've forgotten something I need, may I fetch it?" Marcus said, squirming in her grasp.

"All right, but you come right back and don't you *dare* get so much as a spot on you," she said absently, letting go of him.

As they made the final turn that would bring them into the sheltering bay, he wriggled back in beside her and she glanced down to see he had put on his backpack. "Oh, do you have to take that thing?" she protested. "It makes you look like a hunchback."

"I *need* it," he repeated, then with a hurried change of subject, "Grandma, I'm very puzzled about something."

"What?"

"Well, about that castle we saw yesterday—the Venetians are Italians, aren't they?"

"Yes, so?"

"So what were they doing building a fort in Greece?"

Penny sighed, for she had only the vaguest knowledge of modern Greek history. "I expect it may have been put up during a war of some sort, but I don't really know."

"Grandpa would know," he said wistfully. "I wish he was here."

She looked down at his bowed, mouse-colored, knoblike head. "So do I," she said grimly.

A small silence fell; then Marcus looked up at her, his hazel eyes, so like her own, troubled. "I don't know what's wrong with me, but I've had the funniest feeling since yesterday—I think we are in some sort of trouble. Do we have to go to this place?"

"Oh, my," she said faintly, "I'm afraid we do, dear, and I hope you aren't right, but just keep your eyes open and look after Mala, will you?"

"You can count on it," he said grandly.

Chapter 5

As the engines cut out and they glided to a stop at the long pier Sonya gave a little gasp of astonishment. "Will you look at that! The same kind of security whatchamacallit they have at airports!"

On the other side of the gate stood a large man whom Penny at first took for Demetrios Marolakis, but as the gangway rolled out and Preftakis and Ramon hurried down to secure the mooring lines, she saw that he was a middle-aged man who had the same stature and build. Two smaller men stood behind him, one of whom gave a hand with the lines while the other stood scanning the deck. As Ramon gave an "all clear" signal, Captain Andersen said behind them, "Okay now to disembark whenever you're ready."

"Where's Jules?" Penny asked Sonya.

"Left in the launch about half an hour ago while you were still below," Sonya murmured back, as Juliette gathered her two children and started down the gangplank. "There's just us," she added, and followed Juliette. As they descended John came rushing back up, clutching his mother's camera. "No pictures allowed—Theodopolis," he informed Marcus as he sped by.

Sonya and Mala passed through the gate to join Juliette, who was looking extremely chic in a white heavy-silk trouser-suit, but who was also looking extremely annoyed. Penny followed them, but as Marcus passed through the gate it went off with a resounding scream, and the big man sprang forward and extended his hand. "Hey, youngster, what's in that knapsack?" He had a heavy American accent.

Marcus went beet-red. "Just my collection," he stuttered. "I was going to find food for them." He reluctantly extracted the metal box.

"Let's have a look." The man flipped it open and peered in as John raced back down the gangway and stood shoulder to shoulder with his friend, glaring at the big man. "What's this, live bugs? Good God, scorpions! Sorry, son," the man growled, "but you can't bring this ashore." He turned to Penny, who was hovering protectively by the gate. "I'm Pappas, Mario-lakis's head of security, ma'am, and I'm sorry, but the boss is so allergic to insect bites of all kinds because of his heart condition that we can't take any chances. Preftakis will take it back." He turned towards the seaman behind him, who was gazing raptly at the spectacle of Sonya's legs in her white shorts.

"That's not necessary," Penny said quickly. "Marcus, go put these back where they came from and get rid of that backpack at the same time."

Marcus retrieved his box, and the crestfallen boys marched together up the gangway. "What's up?" Sonya demanded, strolling back with Mala.

"Marcus was taking his insects for an airing," Penny said drily, "and the importation of bugs is forbidden."

"My, my!" Sonya turned a frosty gaze upon the security man. "No photos, no bugs, no metal objects—I'm beginning to feel right at home; it's just like the USSR customs in the good old days."

Pappas winced. "Just following orders, ma'am." To break the tension he sank onto one knee and regarded Mala, who was indeed a sight to behold in her cream sundress, its straps and yoke embroidered in multicolored smocking. "And who might you be, lovely little lady?" He extended his hand.

Mala took it. "I'm Mala Spring, and Marcus, the boy you caught, is my younger brother," she informed him gravely, which only increased his confusion.

The boys marched back through the gate, this time with no effect, and he got up. "If you'll just follow me?" he said formally, and led the group through a steel-mesh gate at the end of the pier and then through massive double doors penetrating the high walls that surrounded the compound. "I am sure Mrs. Marolakis will inform you of all these things, but I should warn you that if the children . . ." and he looked meaningfully at the two boys, ". . . should go off by themselves, they should not go outside the compound or, if on the beach, beyond the protective fence that runs down into the water. The area outside the walls and between here and the village is patrolled and has large guard dogs on the loose, and I wouldn't want the children to get hurt or scared."

Juliette gave an angry snort of "What next!" as Penny and Sonya exchanged long looks, and Sonya murmured, "Hydra is beginning to look positively beckoning to me, how about you?"

They crossed a wide, marble-paved courtyard, and Pappas indicated French doors that stood wide open. "Mrs. Marolakis is waiting for you in the salon, please go in. I will leave you here," he said, and marched away.

Crossing the threshold from the bright sunlight into shuttered gloom, it took Penny a few seconds to adjust her eyes to see a slim, tall, dark-haired woman rising from a high-backed chair and advancing towards them across the vast room. As the woman took on clearer definition Penny saw a strong, tightly drawn, large-featured face, dominated by magnetic dark eyes; a faint smile touched the full-lipped, wide mouth. "I am Olympia Marolakis, welcome to our island," she said in heavily accented English; her voice was a deep and beautifully soft contralto. Although she was dressed in a simple white linen shift it was enhanced by a heavy necklace of solid gold. Both hands glittered with red, blue, and white fire from her many rings as she came into the sunlight. After introductions had been made all around, she said, "We'll be ready for lunch shortly, but in the meantime would you care for something to drink?" She waved her hand at a well-stocked bar. "We are very informal here, so please help yourselves to anything you like. There are soft drinks of all kinds in that cooler, if you prefer."

As the mothers sorted out their children's orders, she turned to Penny. "Ah, Dame Penelope, I have heard so much about you, but where is your famous partner? Will he not also be joining us?"

"Not so far as I know," Penny said cautiously.

"A pity. My brother, who will be here shortly, has come upon some remains on his island that we thought Sir Tobias could shed some light upon. May I help you to something? A glass of champagne, perhaps?"

"No thank you, but a glass of Hymettus would be nice."

Her hostess filled a slim glass and held it out to her. "I think you'll find this good—a white wine from our own vineyards. Then I thought you might like to join the others on the north patio by the swimming pool until lunchtime." She waved a hand at the open glass doors at the other end of the enormous room. "I'm afraid I must wait here for my brother and his two boys. Two more for you to play with, won't that be nice?" She looked down at John and Marcus, who were still subdued. The boys exchanged looks and sank into deeper gloom. "Juliette's brother is out there, so he'll introduce you around," she said rather hastily, and thus dismissed, with glasses in hand, they straggled out into the sunlight and another large marble patio, in the middle of which stood an untenanted Olympic-sized pool.

Two figures detached themselves from the chaise longues beside it and came bounding towards them hand in hand.

"Vincent and Melissa," Juliette said redundantly, as the small, dark-haired young man came up and pecked her on the cheek with a "Hi, Sis, thought you'd never get here—you remember Mel?" He turned with a charming grin to Penny. "And I remember Dr. Spring very well, great to see you."

As he shook hands and she introduced him to her family, she thought, "He's Jules all over again—no wonder Juliette's jealous."

"Father's still huddled with Mel's dad," he grimaced at his intended, who giggled. "And Demetrios is in a huddle with Theodopolis, but come and meet Kepplik and his fancy lady— both *very* boring." Mel shushed him quickly, then giggled again; her small, lively face was overwhelmed by a disproportionately large nose that destroyed its potential prettiness, but Penny noted her nicely rounded, petite figure and her shapely legs.

As they walked towards the pool Juliette murmured in Penny's ear, "I saw you looking at *the* nose. Richard can hardly wait to suggest an op, once all this is settled. He could make her into a stunner, if they'd let him."

A stocky, broad-shouldered, fair-haired man rose out of a chaise longue as they approached, followed more languidly by a very petite red-haired woman in shorts and a halter. The man looked expectant, the woman bored.

"Hans Kepplik from Argentina," Vincent said solemnly. "And Mademoiselle Michele Dubois from France."

The unlikely Argentinian was eager and hearty in his greetings, the French redhead markedly unresponsive and faintly hostile: She looked in quiet horror at the small crowd of children, who by this time were looking as bored as she did.

Quickly sizing up their growing restlessness, Vincent said, "How about a quick look at the compound before we eat? I know Olympia is planning to take you on a grand tour around the island after lunch, but this'll give you an idea of the inner layout."

They trailed dutifully after him, as Kepplik and his unhappy mistress sank back into their chairs. Everything was on a grand scale: twin helicopter pads, devoid of helicopters; twin hard-top tennis courts, where the boys promptly fell upon a couple of stray tennis balls and started to play catch; and beyond a strand of stunted trees was a beach of black volcanic sand interspersed with lava boulders, with several small cabanas, an open-air shower, and a couple of small boats drawn up on the sand. Mala broke her tranquil silence. "I've never seen a *black* beach before," she observed. "However . . ." She pounced on something that glittered in the sand and held it up for Emily's inspection. "This one might be interesting—obsidian, volcanic glass." She examined it critically. "But unworked, I think."

Sonya cast her eyes heavenwards. "The things she picks up from her grandfather—unbelievable!"

The boys were racing away towards the eastern end of the beach, where Penny could make out the junction between the high wall of the compound and the steel fence. "Boys!" Vincent yelled after them. "You can explore later. I think we'd better all get back now—lunchtime." Marcus and John skidded to a stop and came loping back. "Not that Ribotis is ever on time," Vincent added quietly. "I think he does it to bug his sister."

"And wouldn't be the first brother to do so," Juliette observed acidly.

They retraced their steps to find a small crowd assembled on the patio by the pool—all peering around anxiously. Olympia came surging from the group towards them. "Ah, there you are—now we are all here we can go in." She was looking a little wild-eyed. "Theodopolis will not be joining us after all, and Demetrios is not feeling too well, so he'll be resting. If you would follow me? It is buffet-style, which I thought might be easier."

The dining room was almost as vast as the salon, and three long tables, one loaded with an elaborate buffet, ran parallel. Two were set formally with place cards, a quick inspection of which showed the startling fact that all the women and their children had been seated at one, all the men and Ribotis's sons at the other. "I rather feel we should have worn veils," Sonya whispered to Penny. "Where, oh where, are the dancing girls?"

"I'm beginning to yearn for Alex to get here—or even Benedict at a pinch. How the hell are we ever going to find out what is *really* going on here?" Penny whispered back.

"Do we care?" Sonya asked. "Well, at least the food looks good. Don't forget to eat hearty, we aren't expected for dinner before nine-thirty tonight, and probably won't eat until much later."

"I care. If we're being used as some kind of front, I'd damn well like to know why," Penny hissed.

She found herself seated at Olympia's right hand, across the table from Juliette and with the petulant Michele on her right. At the bottom of the table was Melissa, glaring at her stepmother, with the two girls on either hand; beyond Michele were Sonya and Marcus, and John was seated beside his mother and opposite the silent Michele; neither she nor their hostess appeared to have much appetite.

"I thought that after lunch you might all like a drive across the island to the village," Olympia said graciously. "I imagine Melissa will look after the children, if you think this might tire them too much."

As Penny was quite certain that this would be the last thing the love-smitten Melissa would want, she said, "That sounds splendid, but the children would also enjoy it. Do you spend most of the year here?"

"Oh no, Georgiou and I move around a lot: winter in our house in Athens, spring here and . . ." Olympia's expression softened ". . . summer and autumn on our estate in the mountains of Macedonia. We also have a house in Paris and, while my daughter is in school there, a chalet in Switzerland. Because of his uncertain health Demetrios spends the bulk of his time here now, surrounded by his faithful band of retainers." There was a slight edge in her voice. She turned to Juliette. "I believe your father moves around a lot, does he not?" And the conversation became general, although Penny noted that her hostess pointedly ignored the glum Michele, so she was quietly relieved when she heard Sonya start chatting in French to her and getting some response.

It came as no surprise to Penny when Olympia rose and ushered all the women and children back to the salon for coffee, where a small, stolid, middle-aged woman was presiding over a silver coffeepot and a Turkish-style tea urn. "Zehra is my father-in-law's housekeeper." Olympia indicated the wooden-faced woman. "We couldn't keep going without her." And it struck Penny that this was the first servant she had seen.

"I wonder where all the servants are?" she asked Sonya, when they wandered to a remote sofa with their cups.

"On strike maybe? I certainly would be in this setup," Sonya declared.

"I can't see our hostess laboring over a hot stove to provide that buffet, and it must take a regiment of them to keep this place up," Penny said. "Apart from the sullen Zehra we haven't seen a soul."

"Maybe it's catering to the paranoia of the revered Theodopolis—though he isn't even here, so that doesn't make sense." Sonya shrugged. "You've got me, I don't know."

They were interrupted by the irruption into the salon of the Ribotis twins. With single-minded determination they advanced on Mala, who had followed her mother to the sofa and, after her hearty lunch, seemed to be settling down for a quiet doze. The black-haired, black-eyed, slightly tubby twins were identical, and as they stood gazing hungrily at Mala, Penny was irresistibly reminded of Tweedledum and Tweedledee. "I'm Theo Ribotis," announced the slightly taller of the duo. "And I'm very rich."

"I'm Leo Ribotis and I'm very rich too," his brother said quickly, with a glare at Theo.

Mala opened her half-closed eyes by a fraction. "That's nice. And I'm Mala Spring," she said with a yawn.

"Are you rich?" Theo demanded.

"Rich enough, I suppose. My daddy's a doctor, which is what I think I'll be when I grow up," she said. "It's very interesting."

"I'm going to be a doctor," Theo said hastily.

"Me too," Leo chorused.

"Or maybe I'll be a sea captain," Mala went on reflectively. "That's interesting too."

"I love boats—we have a great big one," Leo managed to get in first. "You could have it."

"That boat will be mine," his brother growled. "I'm the older one—but I'd give it to *you*," he added quickly to Mala.

Mala slid a sly glance at her amused mother. "Or maybe I'll be an archaeologist like my grandpa."

This floored them, for they clearly hadn't the faintest notion what that was. They stood jostling each other, getting steadily redder in the face as Mala nestled up against Penny and closed her eyes, the audience clearly over. They were saved from utter rout by their aunt, who came up with a "Now run along, boys, and amuse yourselves. I'm taking our guests to the village."

"Can't we come?" they pleaded.

"No room for you," Olympia snapped. "Go back to your father." Crestfallen, they retreated.

The group was rounded up and shepherded out to where a large station wagon awaited them; to everyone's surprise Olympia got behind the wheel. As they drove slowly out of the gates on the other side of the compound, Penny, who was in the back seat with Sonya and Mala, witnessed an intriguing scene. A white-faced, blazing-eyed Vincent, his arm around the equally white-faced Melissa, was apparently yelling at his very perplexed-looking father. As she watched, Vincent shook his fist at Jules and more or less dragged Melissa back into the house. Mala, who was kneeling and looking out the back window, started to wave gaily. "Mala, what are you doing? Turn around and sit down," Sonya said sternly.

"I was waving at Mr. Theodopolis—up there." Mala pointed at an upstairs window. Penny could see no one.

"You must be mistaken, he's not here," Sonya said with a quick glance at Penny.

"Yes he *is*," Mala insisted. "He was looking out the window and waved back at me."

"Curiouser and curiouser," her mother murmured, and settled back.

Although Olympia drove at a painfully slow pace, there was little to see along the arrow-straight, tarmacked road but low scrub, the occasional goat, and, in the distance on both sides, the sparkling blue of the Mediterranean. On a more somber note, they passed at spaced intervals three khaki-clad armed men, each with a brace of large guard dogs on leashes, who solemnly saluted the car. As they reached the village, Penny was surprised to see that it was also guarded on its land side by a new-looking high wall. Just inside the great gates she was further surprised when Olympia got out and announced, "I have some domestic business to take care of, so please wander where you like. Shall we meet back here at, say, four-thirty?" She handed Juliette a camera. "Also, I do apologize about your own camera—this ridiculous business of kowtowing to Theodopolis—but this one is fully loaded, and if you'd like to take the whole roll I'll see it's developed and in your hands before you leave the island. I'll see you back here, then?" She walked gracefully away down a side alley.

A little nonplussed, they straggled through the village, peered briefly into the tiny whitewashed church, and ended up on the beach looking out on the seawards side of the island. Here a couple of fishing boats were drawn up on the shore and several more white sails dotted the horizon, giving a clue to the village's economy and suggesting that it was not entirely at the mercy of its owners. "May as well settle here," Juliette, who had been snapping pictures of them en route, said. "At least the kids can let off some steam. All pretty boring, isn't it?"

They settled, as the boys raced off to commune with the fishermen mending their nets and the girls began an elaborate sand castle. Juliette wandered off along the beach, snapping more pictures.

"Did you find out anything interesting from the redhead at lunch?" Penny asked when they were alone.

"Not much, except that she and Kepplik have only been together a very short time and that she thought they were going for a long romantic cruise. She seems both puzzled and upset about this stopover; not her usual scene, you can tell," Sonya said.

After a while the hot, bright sun, combined with the wine she had had at lunch, was too much for Penny. She got up and stretched, feeling more than a little dizzy. "I think I'll head back for the car. This sun is a bit much for me. Can you cope alone?"

"Sure." Sonya looked at her anxiously. "Will you be all right?"

"Oh, yes, once in the shade I'll be fine." Penny wandered back, smiling and nodding at the curious stares of the villagers and cursing herself for her ignorance of Greek. She rolled down the windows of the car and tried to settle for a nap, but her mind was too active, and after a while she got out again and decided to explore some more on her own. She made for the beach on the bay side and was just about to emerge from the sea-lane onto it when she heard something that stopped her in her tracks: two voices speaking in Spanish—a language she did understand. Cautiously she peered around the corner to see two figures in the shadow of a fisherman's shack—her hostess and Hans Kepplik. He was clasping both her hands in his, and Olympia was looking at him with an expression that was both yearning and triumphant. He was very red in the face and obviously excited. As Penny observed them, Olympia glanced down at her watch and gave a little moan of dismay, drawing away from him. "It is almost time, I must go. Be careful, *querido*." He nodded and headed back for a small motorboat drawn up on the beach.

Well, well! Penny thought as she scuttled back to the car. *That* was interesting. She arrived to see the beach party coming up the road, as her hostess emerged from another lane that ran parallel to her own.

"Pretty little place, isn't it?" Olympia said, settling in behind the wheel. "Shall I take you directly back to your ship?"

Taking that as a signal that the party was over, Juliette replied, "Too kind of you," somewhat acidly, and the journey back was accomplished in drowsy silence.

When their thank yous and goodbyes were said at the gangplank and they were safely back on board, Sonya said with a stifled yawn, "Well, if that was a sample of the *dolce vita,* they can keep it. If the dinner party is equally thrilling, I'll probably fall asleep into my soup plate. Maybe a miracle will occur and we won't have to go."

"Actually, I'm rather looking forward to it," Penny said, hugging her secret discovery to herself for the moment.

But Sonya's wished-for miracle arrived in the shape of a haggard and tight-lipped Jules, who burst into the dining saloon as they were overseeing the children's supper. "Tonight's dinner party is off," he announced. "I'm afraid a tragedy has happened. Demetrios Marolakis is dead."

Penny gazed at him in stunned amazement. "How?"

He looked at her grimly. "Apparently he died in his sleep during his afternoon siesta. And believe me, it could not have happened at a more inopportune moment."

Chapter 6

"Grandma, Grandma, please wake up, something bad has happened!" Penny came groggily awake to see Marcus's anxious little face peering into hers.

"What is it?" she croaked, sitting up.

"It's my bugs—they're all gone! Come and see." His mouth was quivering and he tugged at her. She fumbled into her bathrobe and followed him barefooted into the corridor to the metal locker. Lifting the lid, she peered inside.

The metal box was open and upside-down, the plastic boxes scattered, and there was no sign of any insect. "Oh, really, Marcus, this is just too careless and naughty of you," she fumed, slamming back the lid and turning on him. "When you took it back yesterday you must have flung it in and not even bothered to shut it—very naughty of you!"

He drew himself up in outrage. "That's not true! I shut it, ask John, he'll tell you. I shut it and put it back right-side up. Someone else must have done that."

She looked at him searchingly. "Are you telling me the absolute truth? What about later on?"

He shook his head definitely. "No, I didn't touch them last night. We didn't find any food for them on the island, so I just left them quiet. Ask John—they were locked up tight."

She looked at the locker with a grimace of disgust. "Well,

they must all still be crawling around in there, so I'm not going to tackle that alone. Go see if your mother's awake and bring her back here."

He ran off, while she hastily scuttled back into the cabin and donned her clothes and shoes, determined that this would be the end of Marcus's collection. That Sonya was of the same opinion was evident from the stern tone of her voice as she returned with her anxious son. Penny armed herself with another shoe, for squishing purposes, and went out again. "How do you think we should go about this—what really worries me are those damn scorpions," she said.

Sonya was peering gingerly in at the overturned box. "Why don't you hold this lid up while I get the box and the plastic doodads out, and then I'll get the life jackets out one by one and whatever I see crawling I'll swat."

Penny handed her the shoe as Marcus groaned in protest. "Marcus, you assemble the plastic boxes back in the big one, and when we move on from here you can start again," his mother said sternly. "And I don't want another word out of you about this, clear?" He nodded as she handed him the box and its contents one by one; one of them was still capped and contained the ladybird, which he received with delight. She had begun cautiously on the life jackets when he exclaimed, "There's a box missing—see!" He held it out for their inspection.

"Must have slipped further down," his mother said, and went on with the removal and shaking out of the life jackets. But there was no sign of it, and when the locker was emptied they gazed down at what remained of the beetle, the cockroach, and the dung beetle, all of which seemed dismembered; of the scorpions there was no sign. Exchanging a puzzled look with Penny, Sonya said, "Now, you go and get dressed, Marcus, and I want you to go and ask John if he had anything to do with this. If he says no, I don't want *either* of you to say a word about this to anyone. Understand? Grandma and I will try and find out what happened." He nodded and went back into the cabin, while they started to pile the life jackets back in. Sonya shook her head. "I don't like this one little bit. It is such a funny, mean little trick to play—and who could have done it?"

"What mainly worries me is that missing box and the missing scorpions," Penny mused. "That looks deliberate."

"The only people besides ourselves and Juliette who were aware of this are Pappas, the other two men on the dock, and Preftakis and Ramon," Sonya pointed out, "and they had no means of knowing *where* it was stashed, unless . . ." She paused. "Unless they deliberately searched for it—but why should anyone do that?"

A cold feeling was growing in Penny's heart. "You missed out on the explanation of the 'no bugs' policy," she said quietly. "Pappas said it was because of Demetrios Marolakis's allergic reaction to insect bites: He fairly trumpeted it. And now Marolakis is dead—let us hope he *did* die of natural causes in his sleep."

Sonya looked at her with dawning horror. "You don't think he . . .? Oh, my God, I've just remembered something . . ." She appeared to go off on a tangent. "Alex gets a lot of calendars and such from drug companies. We have one of the one-page-a-day kind right by our kitchen phone and I often read snippets of info and the headings when I'm on the phone." She closed her eyes as if conjuring up an image and quoted, " 'Myocardial damage from scorpion stings'—there was a whole bit about it—'although impairment is usually temporary, ventricular arrhythmias can lead to cardiac arrest and death.' I remember thinking at the time how scary that was." With a gasp she opened her eyes. "I've simply got to get off this boat and phone Alex in private to see that I'm not imagining this."

"I hope we *are* imagining this whole scenario, but one thing I do know is that we'd better keep very quiet about it until we know more," Penny said, and was startled by the sudden throb of the ship's engines. "What now? Good heavens, are we leaving?"

They hurried up on deck to see what was going on and saw Jules in heated consultation with his daughter, as the ship drew slowly away from the pier. He turned away from her as they approached and said, "We're just pulling out and anchoring in the bay for a while to make room for a launch that will be coming from Athens to pick up Marolakis's body. I'm afraid there's been a hitch in the funeral arrangements—something about the doctor they helicoptered in last night not being entirely satisfied and insisting on an autopsy. Georgiou and Olympia are understandably furious and upset. Apparently his own retainer is the one who started all the fuss—Demetrios Pappas."

"The security man?" Penny queried.

"No, that's Constantine Pappas, his younger brother." Jules lowered his voice. "Surely you noticed his likeness to the old man? The brothers are apparently the offspring of one of his youthful affairs. Their mother died during the war. He has always looked after them and they him. It was Demetrios who found him yesterday. I don't know any of the details—just that they want us out of the way pronto."

"Then are we leaving?" she demanded bluntly.

He sighed, his lean face etched in lines of worry. "That's just what Juliette has been urging, but I simply can't leave immediately—there are still too many problems to resolve with Georgiou. We hit an unexpected snag yesterday . . ." He stopped and shook his head in perplexity. "All the business arrangements were going fine, but then Georgiou said they'd like to have the wedding in September up at their mountain estate. He said Demetrios thought it more fitting than the early June date Vincent and Melissa had planned. I found it a little strange, since I didn't think Demetrios was all that involved but, as head of the family, I supposed he had his reasons and I couldn't see any objection to it, so I said fine. But when I told Vincent . . . well . . . he just went ape! I've never seen him so furious. I just don't understand it: Both he and Melissa completely lost it, and insisted that *I* insist on a June wedding. I was just taking it up with Georgiou, who seemed equally set on September, when the news came about Demetrios. So nothing is settled and I can't leave before it is. However . . ." He looked hesitantly at her. "If you would all like to leave and go back to Athens, I quite understand. What I could do is send you all in the launch to Hydra and you could get the ferry back from there."

This put Penny in a quandary. "Well, we certainly don't want to add to your problems," she temporized, "and this may all get quickly resolved. But it would be nice if you could let us take the launch this morning for a quick trip to Hydra. It will get us all out of your way, and Sonya wants to contact Alex to see when he is arriving."

"I'm afraid I can't let you have it this morning. While we're moored out here I'll need it to get to Georgiou," he said slowly. "But possibly this afternoon, if we're able to go back to the pier; then it'll be free. And Sonya can phone directly to New York from the ship—I'll have Tom Andersen set it up, shall I?"

"Oh, there's no need for that. She's in no hurry," she said hastily, knowing that a third party on the line would be the last thing Sonya would want. She could not resist adding, "I suppose this means that Theodopolis and Kepplik will also be leaving, since whatever negotiations were going on will now be on hold with Demetrios gone. Or will they just move over to Ribotis's island?"

He looked at her with sudden suspicion. "What on earth are you talking about?"

"Oh, come on, Jules! It's pretty obvious to me that there is more going on here than just a merry get-together in the sun, and *they* certainly aren't involved in Vincent's wedding. I'm not a fool, so don't treat me like one," she snapped.

"I'd never do that," he said sternly. "But I have no idea what they are doing." He turned with relief to Ohlsen, who came up saying, "The launch is ready for you, Mr. Lefau."

"I must go now," Jules said, turning back to her. "But I'll

set up the Hydra trip for this afternoon. Bear with me, Penny. When I can I'll tell you more."

In no way consoled, she made her way back to Sonya, who had gone below to have another search through the locker and its vicinity. "Jules has offered to have the launch take us to Hydra this afternoon, and we could get a ferry back to Athens from there. Want to do that? Otherwise we could be stuck here for quite a while. The news on Demetrios isn't good. There's going to be an autopsy—reasons unknown.

Sonya sat down heavily on Penny's dismantled bunk, which she had been searching. "Until I've talked to Alex and until we know more about Demetrios's death, I don't feel like making a decision about going," she said. "If Alex tells me my medical imaginings are a lot of nonsense, then maybe we should go. But just to cut and run now I don't think would be a good idea. What if someone did deliberately wreck that box and take the scorpions for some malicious reason? If we are not here it would be very easy to pass it off as the carelessness of a small child, and I'm damned if I'm going to have a stigma or burden like that put on Marcus."

Penny nodded her approval. "Then we stay?"

"For the moment I vote yes. Look, would you mind very much staying on board this afternoon to keep an eye on the kids? I know Juliette is hell-bent on going and calling Richard. For some reason *she* does not want to talk on the ship's phone either, so coping with her and coping with the Greek telephone system will be all that I can manage."

"Okay, and maybe I should have another crack at getting Toby; I wouldn't mind doing that from here," she replied.

"Fat lot of good that would do!" Sonya snorted. "You can't tell him the whole story so all he'd say is, 'I told you so' and 'Get out of there.' No, I shouldn't bother. I'm getting Alex here ASAP, and if I know solid Richard he'll not be far behind. With them around I'll feel a whole lot better." She got up and started to remake the bunk. "One thing for sure, you'd better be damn careful in here from now on—not a sign of the scorpions, but they could be lurking in a crack."

They straightened things up and went up on deck again to find no sign of the children but delighted squeals and splashings wafting to them on the hot breeze. They tracked down the sound to the swimming pool, whose tarpaulin was now off, and peering down into it was a grinning Ohlsen. They peered also and saw all the children bobbing around like corks in about three feet of water; an amused Ramon in swimming trunks was standing by the metal ladder that ran up the side and keeping a watchful eye on them.

"Mala complained that she was very hot," Ohlsen explained earnestly, "so we filled the pool for them. It's very shallow, so they won't come to any harm, and Ramon and I will keep an eye on them at all times until they've had enough."

"Just be sure when they come out that the covering goes back on," Sonya said. "You know how the boys race around, and that's about an eight-foot drop to the water."

"Oh, we certainly won't leave it open," Ohlsen assured her. "And they are such bright kids that they understand they mustn't go in it unless one of us is on hand."

At lunchtime the launch returned as promised, but its sole occupant was Preftakis, and there was no sign of Jules. After lunch Sonya and an eager Juliette, this time piloted by Ohlsen, set off for Hydra. "They won't get back before seven," Tom Andersen told Penny, "so I thought it might amuse the kids if we went on a voyage around the two islands." He indicated the bow. "I've set up a couple of small telescopes there—I thought that might keep the boys occupied."

"That's very thoughtful of you, Captain; yes, that would be very nice," she said, and quickly checked to see if the pool was covered. It was. "I wonder if I might put a call through to England on your radio telephone some time this afternoon?"

"Sure thing. Want to do it now, before I have to take the wheel?"

She checked her watch. "Let's see, we're an hour ahead of them, so, yes, this should be a good time. The person I'm ringing is housebound anyway, so he'll be there." She followed Andersen below to the tiny radio room, which was nonetheless packed with elaborate equipment; the only thing it lacked was privacy. She handed Andersen the Oxford number, and within minutes he had her connected. He passed her the phone and said, "When you're done, just put the phone down, give me a shout, and I'll come and sign off," and went outside.

The phone rang and rang, but to her increasing perplexity, there was no answer. "Captain," she called, "are you sure we are through to the right number? I'm not getting an answer."

He came back in, went through the same sequence, and this time stayed put as the ringing started again. "Sure you've got the right number?" he queried. "We're not even getting an answering machine."

"Positive about the number, and the party I'm calling won't have such a newfangled gadget in his house," she said wryly.

"Well, there's evidently no one home." He signed off. "We can try again later, after our round-the-islands trip. I'd better get underway."

She was worried. Where can they be? she fretted to herself. Even if he is out and about, where is Mrs. Evans? She never goes anywhere.

Her preoccupation continued throughout the trip, which was as perfect as it could be, the azure sea a flat calm under a blazing blue sky. She sat on deck, keeping an eye on the children: the boys engrossed in their telescopes, the girls, more languid after their morning swim, nestled in deck chairs at the bow in which they presently drifted off to sleep.

Absentmindedly she noted a launch going from Theodopolis's yacht to Kepplik's humbler vessel and a launch docking at their vacated spot on the pier. Out of it emerged Ribotis and Constantine Pappas, who were joined by a third man of such similar build and appearance to Pappas that she assumed this was Demetrios. Momentarily diverted from her worry, she wondered what their status would be now with the senior Marolakis dead. If Jules were right and they were Marolakis's bastards, it could be an unenviable one especially if their younger and legitimate half-brother Georgiou was not a generous man; somehow she had got the impression that he wasn't, that he was in fact a little man in all senses of the word.

As they completed their tour of Marolakis and then made a wide sweep to take in the craggier island of Speria, she, too, dozed off for a bit, but was again awakened by Marcus, who was bouncing up and down with excitement. "Now what?" she yawned.

"When do you think we can go back to Marolakis?" he asked eagerly.

"I thought you didn't like it there."

"Yes, but John and I have seen things—lots of caves! Maybe they're full of pirate treasure. You know, there were lots of pirates here in the Mediterranean long ago, Grandma. And could we go to Speria as well?—*that* has caves, too, on the hilly side of it. Volcanic tubes, Captain Andersen says. Could we?"

"My dear, I don't know, and we can't ask just now with poor Mr. Marolakis dead and everyone upset," she evaded.

"But *after* he's buried, then can we go?" he persisted.

"Perhaps when your father gets here; until then no more fuss about it, right?"

"Okay, when's he coming?" Marcus said; in single-mindedness he was his grandfather's equal.

"We'll find that out when your mother gets back," she told him, and he rushed off to confide the glad tidings to John.

As soon as they were back at their mooring, she had Andersen try the Oxford number again and this time, to her relief, the call went through. "Mrs. Evans? This is Dr. Spring calling from Greece. I need to speak with Sir Tobias."

"I'm afraid he's not here. He's away," the housekeeper said cautiously after a short pause.

"Then he's better? Where did he go?"

"Well, he's somewhat better," Mrs. Evans agreed. "And he's gone to Maidenhead."

"Maidenhead!—whatever for? And when will he be back?"

"I don't know, he didn't say. Shall I give him a message?"

Penny controlled her impatience and looked at Andersen. "Is it possible for someone to call directly here?"

He nodded. "Safest way is to leave us a message," he indicated a tape recorder, "and have us get back to them at a specific time. Here's how." He scribbled a series of numbers on a scrap of paper and handed it to her.

She got back to Mrs. Evans. "Yes, please tell him as soon as he gets back to leave a message at this number as to what *time* I should call him." She read off the numbers.

Mrs. Evans read them back and said, "I'll do that, but I really don't know when he'll be back." She sounded forlorn. "Is it important?"

"Yes, it is. Tell him there's been a most unfortunate death," Penny said grimly. "Thank you, Mrs. Evans." She handed the phone over to Andersen. That should give Toby a jolt, she reflected, but what on earth was he doing in Maidenhead of all places?

Her worries soothed, she was further comforted when the obviously elated Sonya and a composed Juliette arrived back from their outing. "Alex will be on tonight's plane to Athens, and Richard will be coming on tomorrow's, so all is well," Sonya announced. "Did you get in touch with Father?"

"No, I didn't. He's on the gallivant somewhere, probably hiding out from his editor," Penny said wryly. "Anyway he's better—and who needs him?"

Chapter 7

"I have always despised all this 'cloak and dagger' stuff you go in for, so I hope you have some damn good reason for being in this benighted place. Why the devil couldn't we have met like civilised people in the Athenaeum?" Sir Tobias Glendower said peevishly.

"Because far too many people know us both there and this is not a meeting I want noted or advertised," his elderly companion returned. "Not that I am here in any official capacity—in fact, I no longer have one—I'm here as a friend." He could have pointed out that his companion had little to complain about, since they were settled in a cozy, warm nook of an ancient hostelry, whose low-beamed ceilings and mullioned windows, shining horse brasses on the walls, and dark oak furnishings had appeared on many a picture postcard sent home by American tourists as the typical "olde English pub." Beyond the mullioned windows, a greensward dipped away towards the swollen Thames, surging savagely on towards the sea; it was still raining. "And because, as a friend, I am about to break every rule in the security book," Toby's host continued.

He was interrupted by the arrival of the barman for their orders. "Whisky and soda," he said.

"Er, brandy and soda for me, and light on the brandy," Toby ordered with a guilty twinge.

While they waited for the drinks to be served, Barham Young went on. "I retired last year, you know, but I still have my uses—knowing where so many bodies are buried, as it were—so I'm consulted quite often, and through my sources know in general what is going on." Again he fell silent as the drinks arrived and were paid for.

Toby stirred. "Yes, I heard. So, how does this concern me?"

Young did not answer him directly. "I received a message the other day from your old pal Cordelia in Rome. She had had an unexpected visit from another old friend of yours, who appeared to be under the impression that you and Dame Penelope were off on a Mediterranean cruise with some American multimillionaire. He seemed quite concerned and had a message he wanted passed on to you: Be very careful, for something very big is brewing and there could be danger. He advised retreat."

"Who was it?" Toby interrupted.

"Gregor Vadik."

"Never a friend of mine!" Toby exploded. "Gregor is a murderous thug—you must know that."

"Ah, but a very well-*informed* murderous thug," Barham replied. "He's worked for so many countries and in so many capacities by this time that he usually knows what he's talking about. Anyway, Cordelia was very anxious for me to use my influence to get the message to you and Penny Spring somehow. When I checked, I found you were still here—incapacitated, I heard; gout?—and so here we are. But I take it that Dame Penelope has gone?"

Toby controlled his mounting anxiety with an effort. "Yes, together with my daughter and grandchildren. So what did Vadik say?"

"That's all he *would* say, though Cordelia did press him for more specifics. However, I did some enquiring myself and got a little more. Tell me, who is this American millionaire you were to accompany?"

"Name of Jules Lefau, out of New Orleans, he . . ." Toby was about to go into his usual spiel on Jules, but decided against it. "He supposedly was going to meet with the Marolakis family on their island to make arrangements for the upcoming wedding of his younger son to Melissa Marolakis and then to go on an extended cruise around the Med."

"Hmm. Well, I think there may be a little more to it than that. Our people didn't seem to know much, but they do know the Americans have been keeping a wary eye on a billionaire who is also there—Theodopolis. Have you heard of him?"

"Isn't he a recluse?"

"Not at the moment," Barham said dryly. "What is more, in addition to father and son Marolakis, the son's brother-in-law, Lysander Ribotis, is there, along with an Argentinian millionaire and your American friend—a small multitude of Midases, you might say. I wondered if you'd been invited for the same reason or for some other reason?" It was a definite question.

"I'm scarcely in the same bracket as the rest of them, am I?" Toby parried. "Penny thought Jules wanted me as Greek expert and guide, and I'm no businessman." He did not mention his own forebodings.

"So what is this Jules Lefau into? And is he an old personal friend or did you meet him in the course of one of your murder investigations?" Barham was blunt.

"He's from old Creole money in Louisiana and into a multitude of things. I can't be specific, I just don't know. And, yes, that's how we met him years ago—a very complicated murder case. I haven't seen him since."

"Ah, and yet he suddenly invites you both for a cruise," Barham said blandly. "Didn't the thought cross your mind that maybe *he* was expecting trouble of some kind?"

"My daughter and her family are close friends with his daughter and her family; it was therefore only a family affair," Toby retaliated.

71

"And have you heard from them?" Barham persisted.

"No, and I didn't expect to," Toby said. He decided it was time to get off this uncomfortable subject and go on the attack. "Why are the Americans after Theodopolis?"

Barham sighed. "Since we aren't directly involved, none of our people seems to know. And they aren't exactly *after* him. The thing is that, apart from the fact that they are all filthy rich, there does not seem to be a common bond of any sort amongst these millionaires—so why are they all gathered there? I must say I'd like to know, particularly in view of Vadik's message to you; and with your family there I should think you'd like to know also."

"So *finally* we get to why you're here," Toby said acidly. "You want me to go and snoop on behalf of Her Majesty's government—well, no thanks! So far as I know Lefau has already finished his business at the island and they are all blissfully cruising around the Med; they don't need me and I'm not about to put myself out on behalf of MI5, MI6, or any other faceless organization."

"My dear chap, it's not that at all!" Barham protested. "I was merely passing all this on and wanted to add that *if* you felt like going, we'd be happy to back you up—unofficially, of course." He finished his drink and stood up. "If you should change your mind on this for any reason, you know how to reach me. Always glad to hear from you. Busy on another book, are you?"

Toby flinched. "Not at the moment." He hesitated. "Er— by any chance do you know or could you find out where Vadik is?"

Barham gave him a wry smile and shook his head. "No one *ever* knows where Vadik is—a regular will o' the wisp. Cordelia tried to contact him, thinking *you* might want to contact him, but he'd already disappeared from Rome." He shrugged into his heavy macintosh and couldn't resist a parting shot. "With all this appalling weather we've endured, I'm amazed you did not jump at the chance of a cruise in the sunny Med, particularly in the bosom of your family."

He shambled off, leaving Toby gazing gloomily into his empty glass. He pondered having another, but prudently decided against it; driving back to Oxford in the endless rain did nothing to lighten his spirits, and it was with relief that he reached the cozy warmth of his own home and made a beeline for his study, calling out as he went, "I'm back, Mrs. Evans."

She emerged from the kitchen, an anxious expression on her plump, round face. "Oh, Sir Tobias, I wasn't expecting you back so soon—I haven't prepared any luncheon."

"That's all right." He was rewarding himself with another brandy and soda. "Just bring me a ham sandwich and some cheese and biscuits, will you? And I'll be dining at All Souls tonight."

"There's just been a telephone call for you—Dr. Spring. She said would you ring her back to tell her what time to ring you. I've got the number." She fumbled in her apron pocket and produced a scrap of paper. "Said to tell you there's been an unexpected tragedy."

He stiffened. "Who?"

"She didn't say."

"Where was she telephoning from?"

"I think it was that boat they were going on. Wasn't like an ordinary phone call. Leastways, there was some man on the line with her at the beginning and end."

He reached automatically for the phone, then checked himself. "Well thank you, Mrs. Evans, I'll take care of it. Nothing to worry about, I'm sure. If it had been anything to do with the family she'd have told you." As she scurried away to get his belated lunch, he consulted his watch; Barham Young should have reached his own home by now. He picked up the phone.

"Barham? Toby Glendower here. All right to talk on this phone? Apropos of our recent conversation, would you check with your contacts in Athens to see if anything untoward has happened on the island of Marolakis and get back to me on it? Had a message from Dr. Spring about some tragedy—unspecified. You will? Good, talk to you later."

He munched his way absently through lunch, dipping into sundry reference books as he ate, but without any great enlightenment. He began to pace restlessly, deep in thought. When the phone rang again, he sprang for it.

"Just got the word from Athens," Barham informed him. "Demetrios Marolakis died in his sleep yesterday afternoon. However, there is to be an autopsy." He paused. "Does this alter your thinking?"

"Yes," Toby said shortly. "But I'm going to need a lot more information before I make a move. If I drive down to the Athenaeum this evening, can you get all the bumph you have on all the principals we talked of to me there? And another thing—any chance of your being able to find the whereabouts of Benedict Lefau, Jules's older son?"

"On the files, can do. On Lefau, don't know but will try. Why him?"

"I've had an idea," Toby said. "But to bring it off I'll need someone who is not directly involved out there as yet . . ." He elaborated.

"I see—sounds promising. And yes, we can back you up on that. When necessary we *can* get things done in a hurry," Barham agreed. "Shall I meet you at the club and we can discuss it in depth?"

"Yes, dine with me there tonight. I think I will need at least a couple of days before I take off; by that time things may be clearer. See you there—eight o'clock? Right!" He put down the phone and leapt for the door. "Mrs. Evans, would you get out two suitcases and start packing? I'm going away for a while. I'll tell you what I need."

As she trundled obediently up the stairs, she looked back at him. "Then you've talked to Dr. Spring? Not bad news, I hope."

"No, I haven't yet; some other rather urgent business has come up. And if she calls again, tell her I've had to go away; that you don't know where I've gone or when I'll be back; and that you were not able to relay her message."

She gave him a puzzled look. "But I did give you it."

"I know," he said gently, "but it is *very* important that I did not get it. Trust me, I have my reasons."

"Well, if you say so." she muttered. "Such goings-on!" And went on her way, shaking her head.

Their dinner meeting at the club had been well orchestrated by the two professionals to look like a chance meeting between old acquaintances, and it was only after their public dinner that Barham murmured, "I've the files in the boot of my car. Shall I meet you in your room in, say, twenty minutes?"

"Yes." Toby picked up a large folder he'd been toting. "I'll make a show of checking some references in the library, and then go on up with some books." He slipped his key across.

Barham had settled in the small room's single comfortable chair and was sipping brandy from Toby's silver flask as his host rapidly scanned the contents of the files. Finally Toby said with a sigh, "Well, you're right. I can't spot a single common bond among them. There are several interlinks, as it were: Kepplik and Ribotis with their Argentinian interest, or Ribotis and Marolakis both from Macedonia, but that's as far as it goes. And the only remote link with Theodopolis is that, like Ribotis and Marolakis, he was Greek-born, although he is now an American citizen. They don't appear to have any common business interests, either."

"Nothing other than their riches," Barham agreed.

"Even there, there are differences. If we include Lefau, he is from very old money; both Kepplik and Ribotis are second-generation money; and only the late Demetrios and Theodopolis are self-made millionaires. The things I find interesting are these psychological profiles on each of them and their kin—very well done. Any chance of my keeping them for further study?"

Barham shook his head. "Sorry, no, but a chap called Bennett did them and you could meet him tomorrow, if you like. Interesting fellow—has a future, I'd say." He paused. "You could take him along, he's been dying for a field assignment."

"Does he sail?" Toby demanded.

"Haven't the faintest idea. Is that important?"

"For what I have in mind, yes."

"Well, he's a very quick study and, like you, is blessed with a photographic memory."

"My memory isn't what it was," Toby groused. "Otherwise I wouldn't have asked for the files. So, yes, set up a meeting as quickly as you can."

Barham looked at him curiously. "What made you change your mind so suddenly?"

"Penny's call," Toby said heavily. "She would never have made it unless she was worried about something. And that something has to be connected with Marolakis's death. Otherwise, why ring at all? She wasn't even speaking to me when she left."

Barham looked amused. "Is that why you haven't rung her back?"

Toby gazed sternly at him. "No, that's not the reason, and you know it."

Barham chuckled and got up. "Well, it's getting late, so if you've finished with the files I'd better take my weary bones home. Call me tomorrow at the usual number, and I'll tell you the rendezvous time with Bennett and also about any line on Benedict Lefau."

Toby handed him the files and he started to amble out, but turned at the door. "Oh, by the way—a couple of other things that slipped my mind. Cordelia called again. While she wasn't able to track Vadik's onward movements, she does know where he came to Rome from—it was the Ukraine. Also, she said that if you were puzzled by Kepplik's non-Germanic name, it's because his family originally came from Croatia."

"Oh," Toby said blankly.

Again Barham chuckled. "Two more things for you to chew on, eh? Good night," he said, and was gone.

Chapter 8

Thunk-thud, thud-thunk—thud, thud—Penny stirred out of sleep and lay there irritated and wondering what on earth was making that infuriating and semicontinuous banging.

A small, drowsy voice wafted down from above. "I can't sleep, Grandma. What's that noise? It woke me up."

"Me too," she said with a wide yawn, and struggled up to look out of the porthole. They were still anchored out in the bay, but there was no sign of movement from any of the other yachts, and her angle of vision was so constricted that she couldn't make out anything close to their own hull. "Sounds like something banging against the boat, but I can't see anything." She flopped back on the bunk.

"I wish it would stop," Marcus said grumpily. "I'm tired."

"So am I. Try to ignore it and think of something else and then you'll go back to sleep," she said firmly and closed her eyes. She really was tired, for it had been after midnight when the happily reunited Spring family had gone to bed. Alex had not arrived at the *Silver Spray* until late afternoon, despite his early-morning arrival in Athens. He had had to take the ferry to Hydra and then search for someone willing to take him out to Marolakis, as the ship's launch had not been available to pick him up. The excited children had not been bedded down until long after their usual bedtime; Mala moved temporarily into the cabin reserved for the still absent and unheard-from Benedict and Mimi, where she had been joined by a determined Emily. And it was not until Juliette had gone to bed that they had been able to get to the issue that was on all their minds.

After he had heard the whole story, Alex had been his usual reassuring and soothing self. "I grant you it's all very odd, but you've erected a large edifice on very little foundation," he pointed out. "Until the autopsy results are in we have no reason to suppose it's anything other than the natural death of an old man with a bad heart condition. And granted that Sonya's recollection of scorpion stings being *possibly* toxic in cardiac cases is correct, if it's murder you have in mind, I can think of at least a dozen more likely and surer methods of offing a heart patient than the very *unsure* method of scorpions. Anyway, I don't see how anyone could point the finger at Marcus, since his unfortunate collection no longer even exists. I suggest that we just get on with the vacation and, if Lefau has to stay on here beyond the next day or two, that we just quietly slip off to Hydra and places west and enjoy ourselves."

At that point Penny had made up her mind: He was right, and whatever strange thing was happening on the island was none of her business; she would butt out. She had given Jules every opportunity to open up to her and he hadn't, so to hell with him!

Thud, thud, thud—this time the rapping was louder and more consistent, and it startled her out of her semidoze; it was too insistent to ignore, so she had to do something about it. With a sigh, she got up.

Marcus peered accusingly at her from the upper bunk. "I tried doing what you said but it doesn't work," he stated.

"I know. Want to put some clothes on and come and investigate with me?"

"Sure thing!" He clambered down.

When they had both scrambled into their clothes they went

up on deck and peered over the rail. A small powerboat, its painter trailing in the water, was nudging up against the yacht like a baby whale nuzzling at its mother, as it rose and fell on the slight tide. "Oh, honestly!" Penny said crossly. "How careless of someone!—must be from one of the other yachts."

"It looks like one of the boats we saw on the black beach," Marcus observed. "See, on the back there—M2? *I* said it must stand for Marolakis, but *John* said it just meant motorboat. I think I was right."

Penny paid him scant attention, as she was looking to see if anyone was on watch. But there was no one on the bridge. "Let's go find someone," she said. "It's getting on for breakfast time, so Ramon should be around."

They started back down the companionway and ran into Jules, who was fully dressed in his usual dapper fashion but whose strained face and dark-circled eyes indicated a bad night. "You're up early," he said curtly.

"We couldn't sleep—there's a drifting boat banging against the hull and creating a tremendous racket," she snapped.

"Really?" They retraced their steps and indicated the boat. "How odd!" he said, then yelled down the companionway, "Ramon, get up here!" As Ramon's head popped out he continued, "Get a crewman up here to get this drifting boat made fast and find out how it got here. And then we'll be in for breakfast." He turned back to them. "Sorry about that, just one damn thing after another. Let's go on down, there should be something ready."

When they were settled at table with their coffee and Marcus had been supplied with hot chocolate and cold cereal, she remarked, "Looks as if it woke you too—or was it just a bad night?"

He shook his head. "No, I'm on the other side, so I heard nothing, but yes—a bad night: No word from Benedict and, most maddening of all, Georgiou never showed up last evening to finalise our business. He and Olympia went back to Athens yesterday afternoon to make funeral arrangements, but he was supposed to come back last night to try and get everything cleared up before the funeral. He never showed and never called. Absolutely infuriating! Sorry I wasn't on hand to meet your son or to be more helpful about getting him here. Everything all right, is it?"

"Oh yes," she said, wondering where he had got to the previous evening. "But we thought that we might get out of your way until things have settled down and move over to Hydra until you are ready to move on."

"No need to rush off, but if that's what you'd prefer I quite understand." He looked somewhat relieved as Sonya, Mala, and Alex joined them. Alex was introduced, and breakfast arrived, along with Juliette and her offspring.

"I've just told Jules about our Hydra plans," Penny said. "Now it only depends on when we can have the launch."

"Oh, don't go yet!" Juliette cried. "Richard is arriving today, so why don't we wait until he gets here and we'll all go." She shot a venomous glance at her father. "After all, he's far too involved with his precious Vincent to want *us* around, and Benedict is a no-show, and who can blame him?"

There was a small, awkward silence, finally broken by Jules. "You can do whatever you like, Juliette," he said evenly. "If you are all going I'll have Captain Andersen take you over in the *Silver Spray,* and I'll stay on Marolakis until he returns."

After a quick glance at Alex, Sonya said, "We're not in any rush. We could easily wait for Richard and then go off tomorrow. It'll give Alex another day to get over his jet lag."

"Then I'll arrange it for tomorrow afternoon," Jules said.

Another silence fell, as the sound of raised voices came from the deck, followed shortly by the clatter of feet on the companionway. A ruffled-looking Tom Andersen came in, closely followed by the burly figure of Constantine Pappas. "Sorry to disturb you at breakfast like this, Mr. Lefau, but Pappas here was very insistent on seeing you right away."

"That's all right." Jules waved a hand towards an empty chair at the table. "Sit down and join us, Pappas. What can we do for you?"

The big man did not accept the invitation, but stood staring at them, his dark eyes hard and wary. "I'm looking for Georgiou—if he's on board I must see him immediately."

Jules looked at him, his fine eyebrows raised in surprise. "Georgiou? I don't think he is back on the island, and he certainly isn't here."

"Then what's that Marolakis boat doing tied to your ship's ladder?" Pappas growled.

"Oh, that! We found it adrift just now and had it tied up. I supposed it must have drifted on the tide from one of the other yachts," Jules said easily.

The concern on Pappas's craggy face deepened. "Marolakis *is* back on the island. He 'coptered in about nine last night, had some dinner with the young couple, said he'd see them in the morning but he had some business to finish off. My brother went to wake him at seven as he'd ordered, and his bed had not been slept in."

The concern on Jules's face now reflected his own. "That certainly is strange. I was expecting him last night, but when I didn't hear from him I naturally thought he had stayed in Athens. Have you tried the others?"

"Theodopolis wasn't available, but his crewman on watch said no one had been near them all day. And Kepplik said the same."

"Maybe he went to see his brother-in-law?" Jules suggested.

"Unlikely. He didn't fly to Speria, and the only boat missing is the one tied up to you." Pappas was abrupt. "So I'd like to search your ship."

Jules started to bristle. "What are you implying, Pappas? I told you, we found the damn thing adrift."

"I can verify that," Penny cut in quickly. "My grandson and I were awakened by it thumping against the hull at just after seven this morning; its painter was just trailing in the water. We notified Mr. Lefau."

Pappas grunted and scowled as Jules went on sarcastically, "Do you seriously think I'm hiding Marolakis or holding him captive here—with all my family and their friends on board? But go ahead, search to your heart's content, we've nothing to hide."

"I'll do just that." Pappas turned to go, then turned back and pointed a finger at Marcus. "What happened to that boy's collection of bugs?"

"We got rid of them," Sonya said sweetly. "Actually, I did allow him to keep one—the harmless ladybird. Would you care to see it? You probably already know where they were stored."

He glowered at her but went out without another word, as she stared hard at Marcus, who was wriggling in his chair and looking as if he were about to explode into speech.

Jules looked uneasily at Penny. "This is all very strange," he said. "You don't suppose Georgiou *did* try and reach me here last evening, and something happened to him on the way?"

"Well, I don't know much about currents, tides, and such, but it strikes me that if the boat was heading here from the island, it would have ended up on your side of the boat and not mine," she replied. "My first thought was that it had drifted from either Theodopolis's yacht, which is the closest, or Kepplik's—both on my side."

"Maybe I should go and have a word with them," he fretted. "They may be more inclined to tell me things that they did not care to confide in Pappas."

"Because you know what's going on here and Pappas, being only the hired help, doesn't?" Penny suddenly felt intensely irritated with him. "If so, I should get right on to it." He looked at her in hurt silence, as she went on, "And if Georgiou fails to show up shortly, is there any reason for you to stick around here? You obviously can't finish your business with him, so why don't we all go to Hydra and meet Juliette's husband off the ferry?"

"Vincent would not dream of leaving Melissa during the present upheaval, and I can't just go off and leave him," Jules said unhappily. "I must make some calls." He got up, and the breakfast party broke up and straggled out after him, Juliette, again in a sulk, collecting her two children and going below.

As the Springs came out on deck they saw Pappas at the ship's ladder with Preftakis and Ohlsen, the latter saying loudly, "You've searched every inch of the ship and found nothing, and Preftakis has told you about the boat, so what the hell more do you want?"

Pappas muttered something and started down the ladder. The Spring family, *en masse,* wandered over to the rail to see him depart in a large launch, the errant motorboat in tow. "Come and see my telescope, Daddy," Marcus said, tugging at Alex. "It's real neat. Maybe Captain Andersen'll take us on another tour now that you're here, and I can show you the pirate caves. Maybe we could even explore some?"

"Ever hopeful, that child," Sonya said, as they all moved up to the bow and Alex bent down at his son's bidding to scan through the telescope. Penny noted a launch putting off from Theodopolis's yacht and heading for the island.

Alex straightened up with a grin and beckoned Sonya over. "Here's a sight to cheer my jet-lagged eyes!" He indicated the Kepplik yacht.

Sonya looked and chortled, "You're just a dirty old man." She handed over the telescope to Penny, who saw the luscious form of the red-headed Michele, clad only in a string bikini, clinging to a rope ladder as if her life depended on it, while Kepplik's burly form could be seen shaking the ladder and evidently trying to entice her into the water; the redhead was looking very unhappy. She continued to scan until she picked up the village on the opposite side of the crescent. On the beach where she had observed the strange encounter between Olympia and Kepplik she saw, to her surprise, a large launch drawing up at a short fishing pier she had not previously noted. Emerging from it were a number of people, among whom she recognized Lysander Ribotis; they all quickly disappeared up a sea-lane into the village.

Straightening up, she handed the telescope back to Marcus, who said wistfully, "I can't see any pirate caves from here. Want to look through my telescope, Mala?"

"No," his sister stated. "I'm far too hot to do anything."

"I'm hot, too," Alex said. "Could it be that our northern blood has not yet adjusted to this southern warmth?" He eyed Sonya's lithe form appreciatively. "How about emulating our neighbors and having a swim off the boat? Got a string bikini?"

She snorted her derision, but looked interested as the twins chorused, "Oh yes, let's!"; then she shook her head. "It's too dangerous for them, I wouldn't want to risk it."

"Why not? They can swim, and we'd be there to fish them out if they got into trouble," he demanded.

Sonya was still shaking her head. "No, I've seen jellyfish around the boat, and there are strong currents out there. I don't mind for myself, but not with the children."

"Tell you what," Penny put in hastily, seeing the gleam of marital battle dawning in their eyes. "The pool here is still set up for the children, I think, so why don't I keep an eye on them there and you two go for a sea-bathe? That way everyone will get to cool off."

"Sounds reasonable," Alex agreed. "But how about you?"

"This sun feels good to my ageing blood." She smiled at him. "Why don't you all go and get changed and I'll find someone to take the tarpaulin off the pool?"

They all clattered off and she went to the bridge, where Ohlsen was chatting to Andersen. She had a surefire opening line to get their attention. "Mala's very hot again. Could we perhaps use the pool for the children?"

They snapped to attention. "Sure thing—poor little mite,"

Andersen said. "And maybe later on we could go on another cruise around and stir up some breeze; beats sitting here doing nothing."

She followed them back to the pool, where they systematically undid all the fastenings of the heavy tarpaulin and, stationing themselves on either side of the smaller end, on Andersen's signal started to roll it back. Ohlsen looked down and with a choked cry dropped his end. "Oh my God, there's a floater! How the hell . . .? Who the hell . . .?"

Andersen stood like a frozen statue on his side, his face drained of color, as Penny, her heart pounding, peered over. Floating face down was the dark-suited, pudgy figure of a dark-haired man, the sunlight glinting from a ring on the little finger of a flaccid, floating hand. She reeled back, her mind whirling, for she recognized the figure: Georgiou Marolakis was no longer among the missing, but he would do no more business.

"Quickly, before the children get here, put the damn tarpaulin back," she snapped at the frozen men.

They reacted instinctively, beads of sweat starting out on Ohlsen's freckled forehead. "But who is it?" he gulped. "And how the hell did he get in there?"

"Georgiou Marolakis, unless I'm very much mistaken— and since he surely didn't fall in there and then tidily cover himself with the tarpaulin, it looks as if he's been murdered," she hissed. "Captain, you'd better notify the police—if there are none on the island, get in contact with Athens. Then notify Mr. Lefau."

Andersen was recovering quicker than his ship's mate. "What about Pappas?"

"He's not the police. But if Mr. Lefau okays it, notify him *after* you've called the official police," she said. "And Ohlsen, head off my family, but don't tell them what's happened yet. Tell them the pool's not ready and take them over to the village beach in the launch. Just get them *out* of here and stay away as long as you can."

He looked at Andersen for confirmation and the Texan nodded grimly. "Just do it, I'll take responsibility."

As soon as Ohlsen had rushed off, he turned to her. "You're sure it's no accident?"

"Captain," she said gently, "unless you can explain how that tarpaulin rolled itself up to let someone fall in, and then rolled itself back again and fastened itself down, it can't have been an accident. It's murder all right—and, if I'm not very mistaken, it isn't the first. I hope it will be the last."

Chapter 9

Penny felt there must have been some time in her life when
she had been this weary, but she certainly couldn't remember when. The initial rush of adrenaline on the finding of the
body and the confirmation of her own worst fears had long
since passed, leaving her limp and increasingly worn by the
confusions, repetitions, and histrionics that had followed in
its wake.

The news of the murder had hit the Lefaus like the prover-
bial thunderbolt, but their reactions had been markedly different: Jules had appeared stunned and had lapsed into a quiet
stupor, whereas Juliette had promptly had hysterics and had
demanded that she and her children should leave for Hydra at
once, if not sooner. Since this was impossible, a compromise
had been reached. Tom Andersen had very sensibly taken
charge; had up-anchored and taken the yacht to be moored at
the Marolakis pier; and had commandeered Theodopolis's
launch, which was still there, to take Juliette and the children
to join the Spring family in the village. Penny had bestowed
on John—the only calm member of the group—a haversack
containing extra clothes for them all and Alex's wallet.
Theodopolis had arrived back at the pier in the middle of all
this and, to her surprise, had volunteered to take them himself. Everyone except herself had thought this extremely nice

of him, but it seemed so out of keeping with his image that she suspected his real reason was to keep out of the way of the police—who were due to arrive at any moment—as long as possible. This suspicion was confirmed when Ohlsen arrived back in the launch shortly thereafter and all alone, with the news that Theodopolis had told him that he should return to make his statement to the police, and that he himself would bring the party back in due course.

Her next surprise had come with the arrival of Constantine Pappas, from whom she had expected an explosion of rage and accusations. The opposite had happened: He had calmly viewed the floating body and confirmed it was Georgiou's, and the only remark he had made in her hearing was to say that it had not occurred to him to check the pool, since he had tried the tarpaulin fastenings himself that morning and found them secure. Apart from telling them, unnecessarily, not to touch the body, he had asked nothing and done nothing except make a quick departure to inform the new widow; he had seemed smugly satisfied.

While the wait for the police—which seemed endless—continued, she half-expected a distraught Olympia Marolakis to appear, but there was no sign of the bereaved. She was not altogether surprised when she saw Hans Kepplik arrive—without Michele—and hasten into the compound. A large police helicopter finally appeared, hovered over them like a sinister dragonfly, and settled down in the compound. Shortly thereafter Pappas reappeared, followed by a small horde of policemen, who immediately collected all their passports. Jules and herself, along with the entire crew, had been shepherded below into the main saloon under the supervision of a young uniformed officer, while the forensics team had gone to work on deck. In these close quarters she had not dared to say too much but, while the crew and their guardian were having a hasty lunch, she did manage to draw Jules aside and whisper, "This is not the time to go into a state of shock, Jules, you must keep your wits about you. And there's something I must know if I'm to be of any help. *Did* you see Marolakis last night?"

Dull-eyed, he gazed at her. "I swear to you that I neither saw him nor had any idea he'd reached this boat. And besides, what earthly reason would I have to do him harm? His death is a tremendous blow to me."

"Is it?" she demanded. "You'd better think hard about this, for the first thing the police are going to look into is *cui bono.* Three days ago your son was only going to marry the daughter and granddaughter of two very rich men; today he is going to marry an extremely rich heiress in her own right. And that, combined with the difficulties you both had admittedly been having, could be construed as one hell of a good motive."

"Don't you think I know that?" he sighed. "But I'm afraid it's not that simple." He walked away from her.

One by one they had been summoned up on deck to make statements, and she had been pleasantly surprised by her interrogator. He had waved her into a deck chair set up by a small table at which he was sitting along with another policeman armed with a notepad, and had introduced himself as Major Nicholas Karras of the Athens prefecture.

"Ah, I see you are an American, Dame Spring," he said in excellent, American-accented English. "Two years I spent in your country with the NYPD studying their methods. But you do not live in America?"

"No, for many years I have been a lecturer in anthropology at Oxford University, and so my home is there," she stated. "And I prefer to be called just Dr. Spring."

"Ah yes, this title 'Dame,' it is English, no? I did not think Americans had such things. May I ask how an American lady comes to have an English title?"

There was no sense sidestepping the issue, for the police would find out easily enough, so she took the plunge. "It came out of a murder investigation in Rome I was involved in some years ago. My partner and I were credited with saving the life of the English prime minister and so rewarded. My partner is Sir Tobias Glendower, of whom you may have heard, for he is a great authority on your country."

"Yes indeed, of him I have heard," he nodded. "So that explains why you do not seem very shocked by what has happened."

"It is always a shock to find a dead body," she said drily. "But let's say that, over the years, I have become inured to it."

"There have been others?"

"Eleven to be exact; all brought to a successful solution, I might add."

He pursed his lips in a silent whistle. "Then you indeed will make a witness most admirable." And step by step he had taken her in meticulous detail through the finding of the boat to the finding of the body, but at the end of it he said, with a wry grimace, "This was indeed excellent, but I'm afraid it is only the first time of asking. My superior, Colonel Vassos, who commands the plainclothes and intelligence division of the Athens prefecture, will be arriving shortly and you will have to go through it all again for him." He dropped his voice confidentially. "The Marolakis family is very important, you understand, and with so many other important people here we have to be extremely careful. I, however, will much appreciate any help you can give us."

Her second interview had been much more exhausting; for one thing, the grizzled, dour Vassos spoke little English, and so everything had to go through a highly nervous young interpreter, which made the whole process seem never-ending. On top of this, Vassos appeared suspicious of her and consequently of everything she had done, particularly her swift despatch of her own family and then Juliette's, and he had sent orders for them to be brought back from the village. Mercifully, before that could be brought about the body had been fished out of the pool, encased in a body bag, and taken off to the helicopter; she had managed to corner Karras and ask, "Is the cause of death apparent?"

He shook his dark, curly head. "Apart from lividity, there's not a mark on him. No means of telling until after the autopsy but, off the cuff, I'd say he didn't drown—no froth in the mouth."

"Any idea of the time of death?"

"Not yet, and it's not going to be easy to establish, either. It was hot under that tarpaulin and the water warm. The medical officer's first guess is that it could be any time between ten last night and two this morning."

"But surely it must have been *after* midnight or we'd have heard something," she protested.

"Would you?" he queried. "Don't forget, by your own statement you were all in the saloon well away from the pool area, and no one came back on deck. The crew also heard nothing, and no one had been left on watch. Three of them, namely the captain, the mate, and the French cook were up until after one in the morning playing poker in Andersen's cabin."

As the crowded launch from the village had approached, Vassos had peremptorily ordered Karras to the rail to help the interpreter, and was obviously taken aback by the first boarder: Theodopolis, firmly clutching Mala. There was a rapid interchange in Greek that brought a dull flush to the colonel's dark cheeks, and Karras muttered to Penny, "So that is the great man? He does not want the children to be questioned, he wants them to be kept out of it entirely—and I think he's winning."

He evidently did, for, collecting all the children, he disappeared below and was not seen again for a considerable time, while a thunderous-looking Vassos turned on the others. Alex had swiftly crossed to Penny, given her a hug, and whispered, "Are you okay, Ma? You look all in. Thanks for the reprieve today, that was quick thinking."

"I'm tired, but otherwise okay. Has Juliette calmed down? That may be important."

"Yes, Sonya's got her in control," he said, as a small constable, over whom he towered, came and grabbed him by the arm to tow him back to Vassos. "See you later!"

While Vassos questioned him, then Juliette, Theodopolis reappeared and went over to Sonya, who was sitting under a constable's watchful eye awaiting her own grilling. "They are all settled down watching a movie," he informed her, a twinkle in his dark eyes. "I had some trouble with Marcus, who is most anxious to help with investigations up here. I bribed him into silence with the promise that when it is allowed I will take him in my yacht to look at the pirate caves he seems so set on."

She smiled faintly up at him. "Thank you, you've been very thoughtful."

"My pleasure." He turned to leave, but Vassos, who had been watching the exchange, roared out something in Greek. At the top of the ship's ladder Theodopolis swung around and snapped in English, "If you want to see me, Colonel, you may come to my yacht." And pushing aside the constable guarding the ladder, he descended out of sight.

With an angry growl Vassos dismissed Juliette, who immediately fled below, and summoned Sonya; but she had scarcely settled in the chair when the constable at the ladder cried out, and Karras, who had been sitting with Penny, leapt to his feet. "A boat under sail coming in at speed on the starboard bow," Karras translated. "Now what?" He moved swiftly to the rail.

"Probably Benedict Lefau at last!" she said thankfully, and began to follow him as a voice hailed, "Ahoy there, *Silver Spray,* permission to come aboard requested!" This stopped her in her tracks, for it was a voice she knew only too well. She joined the general rush to the rail and when she got there her jaw dropped in amazement. The tall and now massive figure of Benedict Lefau was indeed at the wheel of the sleek sixty-foot white yacht; a smaller fair-haired man was at the stern preparing to drop anchor; but standing beside the helm was an unmistakable tall, spindly figure. Toby had not merely arrived out of the blue, he had arrived in style: For once in his life he was resplendent.

His perfectly cut black blazer bore the gold insignia of the Royal Yacht Club of Cowes, as did his gleaming yachting cap; his fine white flannel trousers were immaculately creased, and into his open-necked white shirt was tucked a silk Wykehamist cravat. His overall and astonishing elegance was slightly marred by the fact that he was propping himself up on a massive, knobby stick, which she recognized as an ill-advised gift their mystery writer friend Jocelyn Combe had sent him from Ireland, while laboring under the delusion that the shillelagh was an emblem for all Celts.

Sonya, along with Vassos, had also rushed to the rail, and her jaw sagged equally in amazement. "Father?" she gasped.

Penny chuckled suddenly. "Yes, not exactly his usual style, but the cunning old fox is evidently holding a candle to the devil. Rich as the others may be, he is flaunting symbols from which, even with all their money, they are barred: the Royal Yacht Club, Winchester College—I'm amazed he didn't throw in his Order of Merit and tote his heraldic banner."

Karras had got his wits back first and was shouting, "I regret, sir, but you and your party cannot come aboard. The vessel is temporarily under the jurisdiction of the Athens police and no one may embark or disembark. Who are you and what is your business here?"

"We are all invited guests of Jules Lefau. May I introduce Mr. Benedict Lefau, Mr. Lefau's son, and," he waved a hand at the stern, "Dr. Richard Schuyler, Mr. Lefau's son-in-law. And I am Sir Tobias Glendower. My family are already on board and I intend to see them. Who is in charge here?"

Karras indicated Vassos. "Colonel Vassos, head of the Athens prefecture, but I assure you—"

"No!" Toby interrupted firmly. "I assure *you* that we are coming aboard and I am taking my family off your yacht and onto this one." He reached into his inside breast pocket and produced a paper. "I am sure your Colonel Vassos will recognize the signature of your minister of the interior that is appended to this document, allowing me and my party free access to *any* place at any time. So kindly fetch Mr. Lefau, wherever he is."

Karras looked helplessly at Vassos, who evidently had understood little of what was said and looked ready to burst. "I'm afraid the colonel speaks little English."

"No problem," Toby boomed and repeated himself in fluent Greek.

As Sonya sighed wistfully, Penny felt an overwhelming sense of relief. "*Now* we should get somewhere," she said, under her breath. "God knows why he's here, but I'm glad he is."

Karras and Vassos had been in muttered consultation, and Karras went below, emerging not only with the dazed Jules but with Juliette and the entire contingent of children, who rushed to the rail in wild excitement; the confused situation became even more so as a shrill chorus of "Daddy, Daddy!" and "Grandpa, Grandpa!" rose in frantic crescendo.

Jules was clutching the rail, white-knuckled, and staring at his eldest son with pleading intensity, as a constable was despatched to pick up Toby and the document. His dignified approach to Colonel Vassos was somewhat hampered by the fact that the moment he set foot on the deck, Marcus and Mala clamped themselves to a leg each, Marcus shouting excitedly, "Grandpa, there's been a murder right here—can we solve it?"

Toby stiffened slightly at the news and, detaching him, said, "Not just now, Marcus."

Mala looked up at him. "You took a *very* long time to get here," she said reproachfully. "How about a hug?"

"Later, my pet," he said. She relinquished him and ran back to her father, as Toby, disencumbered, joined the two harassed policemen in long and grim discussion.

Penny went back to her chair and, leaning back, closed her eyes, feeling totally relaxed; the rumbling of their voices a comfortable counterpoint to her semidoze. She must actually have dozed right off, for the next thing she knew was Toby's voice in her ear: "Well, that's settled. They wanted to interrogate you some more, but Alex intervened and said he would not stand for it—that you were worn out. Sonya is about done, so we can go soon. Er, no one has mentioned yet *who* got murdered—was it Theodopolis?"

She opened one eye and squinted sideways at him. "No, Georgiou Marolakis—and I think Demetrios may have been offed as well, but no one has got on to that as yet."

He pursed his lips. "My word! No wonder Jules is looking like death warmed over. I thought he'd burst into tears when Benedict came aboard. Juliette *did* when Richard arrived— still very hysterical, isn't she? We'd better get over to my yacht and we can get down to cases."

"Your yacht? I thought it was Benedict's," she queried.

"Well I'm not actually *paying* for it," he admitted, "but no, it's mine. I picked up Benedict in Athens and we found Richard on Hydra. I'll explain it all when we get away from the police."

"Not now you won't," she said with a yawn. "I'm dead on my feet. My first priority is a nap—a very long nap, so I'll be over later. Sonya can fill you in."

"But . . ." he protested ". . . after I've come all this way, aren't you even glad to see me?"

"I'll think about it and tell you later," she said, and tottered off to her bunk.

Chapter 10

"Alone at last!—this has been some day, are you sure you want to go into everything tonight?" Penny said, looking across the small table at Toby, who, having shed his blazer and cravat, was more like his usual crumpled self and was absorbedly working through a small pile of notes, while puffing contentedly away on his pipe.

He grunted and looked up. "Since we're stuck here for the moment we might as well get on with it, just to get some idea of what we're into and where to start. God knows when we'll get time alone again."

Things had not worked out exactly as he had hoped. The police had vetoed a wholesale departure of the Spring family, and with the new arrivals there had been a major upheaval in the sleeping arrangements on the *Silver Spray:* Mala had dispossessed Penny, going in with her now bugless brother, and Emily returned to John. Sonya and Alex had also elected to stay there for, as Sonya had averred, they would be more likely to hear of any fresh developments than if on Toby's yacht. They had all dined aboard the Lefau yacht, but with the return of the police promised for the morrow, it had scarcely been a festive occasion. Afterwards Penny's baggage had been transferred under the watchful eye of a guardian constable onto Toby's vessel, where the family would join them for breakfast in the morning.

"So this is what I got from Sonya," Toby said and went over the notes.

"That covers it pretty well, except for a couple of things," Penny said. She went on, telling him about the strange rendezvous between Olympia and Kepplik, and Ribotis's descent on the village, ending with, "What's more, there is something very wrong about Theodopolis."

"How so?" He looked at her curiously.

"I don't know, I can't put my finger on it, but there's something that simply doesn't ring true to me. He's up to something."

"Any idea what?"

"Haven't a clue! Jules knows a damn sight more than he's telling, but I've tried again and again and he's closed up like an oyster. I could throttle him."

"Maybe someone will," he said. "If you're right, there have been two murders in the past three days and it may not stop there; but with the way things are shaping in this last murder, if he isn't actually involved himself, the finger of suspicion is certainly pointing his way. But, as usual, he appears to be as devious as hell."

"Ah, I was waiting for the 'I told you so' bit," she sighed, "but, nevertheless, I appreciate your taking my baited lure about Demetrios's death."

"Wrong again," he lied. "What sparked me into action was a message from an old nemesis of ours, Gregor Vadik—relayed to me through an impeccable source, I might add, namely Barham Young."

"What!" She gaped at him.

"Yes, and this is strictly for your ears only. I'm not even telling Sonya, but this is the situation . . ." He related his interview at Maidenhead and its aftermath.

She groaned at the end of it. "Here we go again! At least I was right about Theodopolis. And here I thought you were rushing to the rescue of your beloved family."

"I am—in a sense. My short-term goal is to get Sonya, Alex, and the children away from here. And we don't *know* about Theodopolis—he may even be the next target."

"You're not going to get rid of Sonya that easily," she countered, "particularly if you don't tell her the rest of this. And if she won't go, neither will Alex or the children; Lord, what a mess!"

"All this breast-beating is getting us nowhere," he rumbled. "We've got to find a starting point, and as I see it we have such an assortment of possibilities that it's difficult to know where to begin. One: that Jules *is* involved in the murders as a way to the fabulous Marolakis fortune, or equally that Vincent is involved and his father knows it. Two: that Olympia Marolakis is romantically involved with Kepplik and has seized the chance to get rid of an unwanted husband, becoming even richer in the process, while putting the blame on an unwanted prospective in-law."

"She couldn't have offed Georgiou, she was still in Athens," Penny interrupted.

"Kepplik was here—how about him?" Toby said and sailed on. "Three: that some big business deal involving all the millionaires had either been finalised or gone sour, so that the Marolakis were expendable. Four: that some wild-eyed fanatic is at work polishing off millionaires on principle. Five: that someone with a particular grudge against the Marolakis has taken the opportunity afforded by this meeting to murder them, banking on the fact that the police will be so intimidated by the assembled company that they won't do their job properly— and I could go on and on with combinations of these. Yet I have this gut feeling that if we can only put our finger on the true motive, we'll be almost home. The question remains— where the hell do we start?"

"Well, as you've pointed out, we don't know for certain that the old man was murdered, so why don't we start with Georgiou? Sadly, I don't know much about him, except that he struck me as not at all of the same calibre as his father: a 'little' man, nervous, somewhat slippery, and not a strong character."

"I know a little more," Toby said. "Apart from his business wheelings and dealings, at which he seemed able enough, he was a notorious womanizer—mistresses all over the place. Strong suspicions that Wife Number One may have committed suicide because of that, though Wife Number Two appears to be made of sterner stuff."

"And that could explain Kepplik," she retorted. "Olympia beating her husband at his own game. And the old man wasn't exactly a saint along those lines either. Sonya told you about his two bastards in the household?"

"Yes, and probably no love lost between them and the legal heir. Yet another scenario . . ." He sighed. "What if Georgiou hastened his father's end, they realized it and took care of him? I wonder if they profit at all from this."

"But why dump him on Jules?" she asked. "They'd have nothing against him and many more opportunities of getting rid of Georgiou on the island, I'd have thought."

"Constantine Pappas probably knew that Lefau was planning to leave the island shortly. He could have hidden the body there, thinking it would not be found until Jules had taken off and banking on the fact that when it was discovered Jules would panic and quietly ditch the body at sea."

"Sounds a bit thin," she commented.

"It does, doesn't it?" he sighed.

"The thought that nags at me," she went on, "is that whether Georgiou was actually killed on the yacht or killed elsewhere and dumped, you'd think that someone aboard would have heard *something*. For one thing, although one person may have killed him, it would take two to manage that tarpaulin—which leads me to think there may be a snake, or snakes, in the grass among the crew."

"But aren't they all accounted for?" he queried. "Three playing poker and two asleep in their bunks."

"Suppose Preftakis or Ramon merely feigned sleep and crept out while the other slept? Or, alternatively, suppose Andersen and Ohlsen were in on it and set up that alibi with the cook—for money, of course."

He sniffed. "Sounds even thinner to me."

"I suppose so," she sighed in turn. "Anyway, I can't believe it of Andersen and Ohlsen, they were too shocked when the body was found—so that leaves the other two."

A small depressed silence fell as they cogitated, then Toby roused himself. "Since we aren't getting anywhere this way, let's set some priorities. First, to persuade the family to take off in this yacht; second, you seem to be on Karras's good side for a change, so keep at it and try to pump him for all the bumph on the autopsies, time of death, and so on; third, I'll try to keep the pressure on Vassos, who doesn't like it but in the face of my high-level support can't do much about it, so I'll try to keep him off our backs as much as possible; and fourth . . ." he paused ". . . we've simply got to get closer to the principals in all this, which means getting on to the island *and* meeting Theodopolis and Kepplik. *That,* at least for the moment, I don't see how to bring about."

"Perhaps if I feed Karras a couple of items I've withheld up to now I may get him sufficiently on our side to let me see the statements of the others, or maybe even set up something for us on the island," she mused.

"Like what?"

"Olympia's secret rendezvous, for one. For another, Lysander's visit to the village with all those people—I can't think what that could have been about. And . . ." she hesitated, "another odd thing about our first trip to the island. I told you about the singular lack of servants? We ascribed that to Theodopolis's presence, and yet he didn't show up for the lunch and Olympia indicated that he'd gone. And yet later Mala saw him at an upstairs window on the same floor where Demetrios was subsequently found dead. I didn't see him, but Mala swore he was there. It would be interesting to know what he has said about his movements that day."

"But the police aren't as yet even interested in that day, are they?" he pointed out.

"Maybe I can get them interested in it."

"And possibly open up an even bigger can of worms?" Toby got up stiffly and helped himself to a brandy. "Wasn't it that day you saw Vincent screaming at his father about the wedding date? He seems as hysterical as his sister—I mean, what odds if they marry in June or September?"

"I can think of one good reason for it," she said drily. "And a reason that would not sit well with either of the families. Young people don't exactly wait around anymore for the honeymoon, and accidents do happen. Melissa may be pregnant and that would be one hell of a good reason to want the wedding in June. You know, Greeks are quite fussy about their daughters being virgin brides."

"Good Lord! You think so?" He looked at her, round-eyed.

"It was the first thing that occurred to me when I heard they were both so opposed to the later date. Unfortunately . . ." she paused ". . . it would also make a very good motive for Vincent to want both of the Marolakis out of the picture. And we already know that the Lefau family is capable of murder . . ." She trailed off unhappily.

Toby was off on his own train of thought. "If only I knew if there was any significance to Vadik's having come from the Ukraine when he passed that message—there doesn't *seem* to be any."

"Ribotis has shipping lines that go to it," she pointed out. "But then he has shipping lines that go everywhere, so that may not signify."

"Ribotis *and* Olympia," he said thoughtfully. "I discovered they were co-heirs to that estate. Lysander got two-thirds, Olympia one-third. She's quite a businesswoman in her own right. I wonder how much of a cut she'll get from the Marolakis estate. Could be she's trying to move in on her brother's empire; they've been at odds for years. Something else to look into . . ." He drained his brandy and stood up. "I've been going flat-out round the clock for three days and, not having had the benefit of a long nap, am all in. Let's call it a night." Thankfully, she called it a night.

The morning brought more surprises, when only Sonya and Alex showed up for breakfast. "Theodopolis wanted to get off to an early start on his promised trip for the children around the islands," Sonya explained. "And Juliette was so agog to get a firsthand glimpse of how a billionaire lives that she and Richard volunteered to look after the whole group. Benedict went along, too, 'to get his local bearings.' His wife isn't coming; apparently she went off to Paris instead." She looked enquiringly at her father, but he said nothing so she went on. "Anyway, I could use a break from the kids and wasn't about to miss out on our other surprise—guess what? We've all been invited for lunch on the island by the widow Marolakis!"

"Who is 'all'?" Toby said, brightening.

"Everyone: all of us, Jules, Kepplik and his fancy lady, and I suppose the rest of them, if they get back in time. It fits in beautifully, because the police want us all off the *Silver Spray*—crew included—so they can go over it with a fine-tooth comb."

Penny was worried. "Do you think it was wise to let the children go off with Theodopolis like that?" she fretted. "With this early start I'd say he is up to the same thing he was yesterday—dodging the police."

"Poor man! You really have it in for him," Sonya cried. "He may be a little odd, but for a billionaire I'd say he shapes up as a nice human being. You should have seen him in the village yesterday, he really seems *fond* of children. And what possible harm could come to them with the Schuylers and Benedict Lefau along?"

"I still don't like it," Penny grumbled.

Seeing his wife begin to bristle, Alex hastily stepped in,

saying, "Besides, we thought it would be a good idea to accept Mrs. Marolakis's invitation and give Toby a chance to meet everyone and look the situation over." Since that was precisely what Toby did want, Penny subsided—for the moment.

Lunchtime arrived with no sign of Theodopolis and his party, so they duly trooped off to the compound and to a scene that was vastly different from their first encounter. This time there were swarms of servants in evidence under the command of Constantine Pappas, who appeared to be serving as an unlikely majordomo. When they were all assembled, drinks in hand, he announced solemnly, "Mrs. Marolakis bids you welcome, but in view of the recent bereavement will not be joining you until later. I am sure you will understand." He ushered them to their seats.

This time there was only one long table set up, but he firmly steered the trio of women to the bottom of the table, grouped around an empty place at the end obviously reserved for Melissa, of whom there was no sign. Sonya and Michele sat across from Penny, who had an empty seat beside her that she assumed would be Vincent's; but then she saw that he had been seated next to his father. Toby, she noted with satisfaction, had Kepplik as a partner and was already deep in conversation, while Alex was on the other side of Jules with another empty seat beyond him and no one heading the table. Just as the serving began the black-clad Melissa arrived with a plump little man, whom she introduced as "*Avocati* Demos, my lawyer," and who, to Penny's surprise, seated himself in the empty seat by her. Not that they were to keep Melissa for long, for she had only taken one or two mouthfuls of the excellent moussaka when she went very pale, sprang up with a muttered, "Excuse me, please," and rushed out of the room.

Penny tried her neighbor out in English only to be met with a rueful smile and a shrug, whereupon Sonya, who hadn't been making much headway in French with the glum Michele, switched to halting Greek to the little man's obvious delight. Penny, having tried out her own French on Michele with a singular lack of success, was left to her own thoughts. These were interrupted from an unexpected quarter as a brown hand deposited her dessert before her and a voice whispered in her ear in very broken English, "Madam, I have message." She looked up to see Zehra's solemn face. With a wary eye on Constantine, who was overseeing the men's end of the table, Zehra went on, "Demetrios, he must see you—after, later." Noting Penny's shocked and puzzled expression, she added, "Pappas, Demetrios Pappas."

Greatly intrigued, Penny nodded assent. "Where?" she whispered.

"He find you," Zehra breathed and moved on.

Melissa rejoined them, looking a little wan and apologetic. "A stomach upset, I'm afraid—you must excuse me." But she made no further attempt to eat.

Demos got up, muttered something to Melissa, nodded at the company, and headed for Constantine, giving Penny a chance to move next to Melissa. She expressed her condolences and added, "It's very brave of you to be here at all after two such terrible shocks. I hope you will extend our condolences to your stepmother."

Melissa gave her an enigmatic look. "I shall miss my grandfather very much," she said softly. "We were always close. My father . . ." Her face tightened. "I never got to know. We saw little of each other, even when I was growing up, and in the past few years the gap became wider. But he was not a bad man, I think, and did not deserve a violent end. As to my stepmother," her lips curled in scorn, "there are others who will miss him far more than she, and you may extend your condolences to her in person, for she will undoubtedly make one of her grand entrances shortly."

Even as she spoke there was a scraping of chairs, and Penny looked around to see the men getting to their feet as Olympia swept into the room on the arm of a man so like Constantine that it had to be Demetrios. She was clad in a very chic black dress, the watery gleam of diamonds flashing blue from a large brooch in the vee of its neckline, and wide bracelets on each black-clad wrist. She appeared calm, but her eyes gleamed with inner excitement as she positioned herself at the head of the table and waved a slender hand. "Gentlemen, please be seated, for I have some things to say now as head of the Marolakis family that concern all of you in one way or another." She scanned the table and a faint wrinkle appeared between her dark brows. "I see Mr. Theodopolis is not here, so I will inform him later, but no matter . . ." She fastened her gaze on Jules. "In view of what has happened, you must know I have decided there will be an indefinite postponement of the wedding, and so, as soon as the police say you can go, I suggest you take your family and their friends on the cruise you were planning. Your party, I feel, should also include Vincent, in the interests of propriety."

Expecting an angry protest, Penny was surprised to see Vincent look down the table at Melissa and grin. Olympia switched her attention to Kepplik. "The same applies to Theodopolis and you, Hans, although you are welcome to use the harbor any time you wish on your own cruise . . ."

"Just a minute, Olympia!" Melissa's small, clear voice rang out, and Penny looked up to see her on her feet, leaning on the table, her little fists clenched, her eyes blazing, and twin spots of color on her olive cheeks. "You cannot claim to speak as head of the Marolakis family; that right now belongs to my brother, Alexander, who should shortly be with us. Nor can you speak as owner of Marolakis . . ." She paused, a gleam of triumph in her dark eyes. "This morning I have been apprised by my lawyer of the disposition of my grandfather's and father's estates. My grandfather has left the island and all it contains to *me* outright. The estate in Macedonia and the Swiss chalet go to you and your daughter, and Alexander gets all the rest of the family properties. But it is for me to say what happens on Marolakis and who goes and who stays, and I say all our guests may do as they please. However . . ." she looked questioningly at Vincent, who nodded encouragement. "You, Olympia, may stay on here for as long as you please, for I shall be leaving shortly. You see, as long as my grandfather and father lived I did not wish to upset them, and so went along with these outdated marriage plans of theirs, but I wish to announce that I have been married since last Christmas to Vincent Lefau. We married in Maryland, and as we are of age, my lawyer informs me that the marriage is equally valid in Greece. I, of course, will be returning to America with my husband after this business is settled and plan to make my home there." Her color flared. "And I can now proudly announce that the next Lefau-Marolakis heir is on its way."

There was a stunned silence and Penny quickly scanned the assembled faces. Jules was looking at Vincent in horror; Kepplik at Olympia with lively concern; and, as Olympia turned without a word and left the room, Penny saw her face, which had settled into rigid impassivity during Melissa's startling announcement, twist momentarily with a very different emotion—one of pure hatred.

Chapter 11

"In the circumstances, I felt that was a very unwise statement on the part of the new Mrs. Lefau," Toby said. "For when it comes to the ears of the police, as it undoubtedly will, it will be another nail in the coffin Jules seems to be bent on building for himself."

"Several nails," Penny agreed absently, for she was still wondering how to make contact with Demetrios Pappas. At the urging of the new mistress of Marolakis they were all still on the island, Melissa's lawyer in solemn converse with Jules. Sonya and Alex, at Kepplik's urging, had joined him and the now animated Michele for a dip in the pool, while the newlyweds had temporarily vanished. "What did you get out of Kepplik?" She was hoping that Toby's presence would not deter Pappas as they wandered by the tennis courts, heading for the beach; on the other hand, she thought that if Demetrios's English was on a par with Zehra's she might need Toby.

"Nothing of any great significance. Luckily, he didn't have the faintest idea of who I am, so I put on my 'stuffy old English gentleman' act, which seemed to soothe him. One thing for certain, he does not appear to have the slightest intention of *leaving* here. If the situation between him and Olympia is what you think it is, it may have been going on for a long time. He knew her pre-marriage in Argentina, where she spent a year or so on a Ribotis ranch. He's playing the 'old family friend' bit to the hilt, but really I think he may be sticking around because Theodopolis is here. Maybe he's afraid the new widow is looking with an acquisitive eye at the eligible billionaire; she strikes me as a 'femme fatale' type."

"Um," Penny said; they had reached the beach and she was looking anxiously around for some sign of life: There wasn't any.

"Oh, and we may have to scrub Demetrios Marolakis as a murderee. He told me that the old boy's heart was in such a bad way that his doctors had only given him a few months more at best. Also he'd heard—I suppose from Olympia—that the result of the autopsy was 'death by natural causes.' "

Penny's brow furrowed. "If the old man only had a short time left, it doesn't make sense that he'd want the wedding of a favored granddaughter in September instead of June."

"As I recall, that information came to Jules from Georgiou. It may not have been true," Toby observed mildly. "And judging by Olympia's eagerness to have it put off, *she* may have prodded him into it. Er, why do we seem to be heading straight into a steel-mesh fence?"

"I'm supposed to be meeting someone," Penny said, approaching it and peering through the small gap between the fence and the wall. "Beyond this point is out of bounds, and I thought it might give him a good excuse to come and warn us off."

"Who?"

"Demetrios Pappas. He wants to see me—I've no idea why."

She tried to insert herself into the gap, but it was far too narrow. Her stratagem worked, for a figure emerged between two of the cabanas, yelled, "*Stamata!* Stop!" and advanced towards them, eyeing Toby suspiciously. "You spik Greek?" Pappas demanded of her.

She jerked her head at Toby. "No, but he does."

The two men looked at each other; Toby launched into a

long explanatory spiel; Demetrios replied with an even longer one; and then, to her mounting frustration, they calmly marched off side by side in earnest conversation. "Well, really!" she fumed, "this is a bit much!" And trailed after them. When they reached the shelter of the cabanas they calmly sat down on the wooden steps of one of them and lit up pipes, talking vigorously all the while. She was just about to explode when Toby made a furtive "get lost" gesture with his free hand, and, still seething, she left them to it.

She started back for the house, intending to see what the grieving widow was up to and hoping to find her in a talkative mood, but on the way ran into Major Karras, in civilian clothes, wandering in disconsolate fashion by the tennis courts. His face lit up as he spotted her. "Ah, just the person I wanted to talk with," he exclaimed.

"That makes a nice change," she grumbled. "Nobody else seems to want to." At his puzzled look she added hastily, "Don't mind me. What can I do for you?"

"I wondered if you had remembered anything else that might help us with this murder," he asked confidentially. "The way things are going it looks as if our only hope of clearing it up will be through its motive, for the means and even the *modus operandi* have given us little work on."

"I do have a couple puzzling things to pass on, but first, do you mind telling me what the means were?"

"Not a bit. The search of the *Silver Spray* yielded nothing—we still don't know whether he was murdered on board, or elsewhere and dumped on board, although there was one thing I was just on my way to check out. There were traces of black sand on the shoes and clothes of the dead man. Isn't there a black beach here?"

"Yes, I'll show you later." She hastily steered him to a spectator's bench by the courts and sat down. "But first, why don't you tell me the results of the autopsy?"

"That, too, is most frustrating. If it hadn't been for excellent work by the forensics coroner we'd still be groping: He was killed by, first, a blow to his windpipe that silenced him and probably knocked him out, and then one to the base of his nose that paralysed his brain; he was still alive, though barely so, when he was thrown in the pool, for there was only a little water in his lungs."

"And the water was from the pool of the *Silver Spray?*" she asked.

His eyes narrowed. "I did not think to ask that, but yes, you're right; it could have been the pool here or the sea, for that matter—that I must see to. It was because of the lividity of the floating body that we did not spot the bruises at first."

"What was the weapon?"

He sighed. "The doctor thinks there was no other implement used but a human hand: in other words, karate chops."

She brightened. "Well *that's* a lead! Find a karate expert and you may have your man."

He shook his head. "Or woman or even a child. With all the movies and martial arts classes and such that abound now, it would not take an expert knowledge or even great strength to do it, only an element of surprise and quick action. So we have no murder weapon, no fingerprints, nothing . . ."

"The boat that ended up by the *Silver Spray* was originally parked on the black beach, so that would explain the sand on the body," she pointed out. "He could have picked it up when launching the boat himself to go to any one of the yachts in the harbor, including his own."

"We have searched them all to no effect; all we have is that he was found on the *Silver Spray* and that there was trouble between him and Jules Lefau. And with this latest news it begins to look very bad for Lefau."

"Oh come now!" she cried. "I was there when Melissa Marolakis made her announcement of her marriage, and Jules Lefau was absolutely dumbfounded by it. You could tell he was as unaware of it as the rest of us."

Karras looked at her curiously. "I was not talking about that. In fact I only just heard of it. I was talking about the other bad news."

Penny's heart sank. "And that is?"

"This morning we were informed by the Boston police, with whom we have been in contact concerning his father's death, that Alexander Marolakis was run down by a hit-and-run driver last evening as he was entering Logan airport to come here. The driver got clean away. He is not dead but is in very serious condition. Eyewitnesses to the accident state that it was a deliberate run-down—in other words, a professional 'hit'—and who would be in a better position to arrange such a hit than the only *American* millionaire in this group?"

"Theodopolis is an American citizen," she said desperately.

"*Cui bono?*" Karras was grim. "With all three Marolakis dead, who would remain as sole heir? Melissa Marolakis, now Lefau. If that is not a good motive I don't know what is. It does not end there, either. So far Lefau has not given us a satisfactory account of his movements that night and appears very evasive."

"But why on earth would he do such a stupid thing as to dump the body in his own swimming pool?" she cried. "Why not in the sea?"

Karras shrugged. "Murderers do stupid things, but I agree that it seems absurd. In fact it is the only thing that is staying Vassos' hand from arresting him." He stood up. "Shall we go to the beach? You can show me exactly where the boat was."

"Wait! I have a few things yet to tell you," she said quickly, hoping that Toby and Pappas had not settled in for an endless cozy chat, and she rattled through her own observations, to which Karras listened attentively.

At the end he remarked, "These things indeed bear looking into, but as to Theodopolis, I think, given his reclusive reputation, that it is not surprising he is keeping out of our way.

He is terrified of publicity of any sort, and you must not forget that *he* has no motive for murdering Marolakis."

"None that we know of at present," she said doggedly. "Look, I appreciate your confidences, so please, before you do anything precipitate, let me have a go at Jules and see if I can make him open up. I promise to be just as open with you as you have been with me."

"Fair enough, so let's get on to the beach," he said, and they reached it to find it devoid of occupants and equally devoid of clues. "Very frustrating," Karras sighed. "Well, I can't put it off any longer, I must get back to the house and break the unhappy news of Alexander to the Marolakis."

She was startled. "They don't know yet?"

"No, we told Boston we'd take care of it, and I want the Lefaus to be there also. Their reactions should be interesting."

"Juliette and Benedict are off with Theodopolis," she said.

He dismissed them with a shrug. "It is not in them I am interested."

They walked back towards the house, and she was not too surprised to find Toby lurking by the tennis courts. "Oh, there you are!" he exclaimed testily. "I've been looking for you everywhere. Let's get back to the yacht. Good afternoon, Karras, investigations going well, I hope?"

"Not very," Karras groused and continued on to the house.

"You've got a nerve!" she fumed. "What was I supposed to do—stand there like a ventriloquist's dummy while you yammered away without the grace to translate a word?"

"Once I'd established contact, the last thing I wanted to do was break it by interrupting every few seconds to translate," Toby retaliated. "*And* it was well worth it. You were right, Demetrios is convinced that his father's end was speeded up. The only snag is that it can never be proved as a murder. He found a bite on the old man's upper arm. He later found the culprit, a small green scorpion—they're even more venomous than the black ones—and he killed it."

"What did he do with it?" Penny said, her spirits sinking.

"After consulting with Constantine he threw it out. Constantine convinced him there was no use bringing it up with the police and said that he'd take care of the matter."

"Did he indeed," she said thoughtfully. "Then why did Demetrios want to see me?"

"I don't think he altogether trusts his younger brother," Toby observed. "They may look alike but they are very different types. Demetrios is what I'd term an 'old-style' Greek—honest, upright, moral, rigid, and set in his views; Constantine is more like his late half-brother, very much into wine, women, and gambling. While Demetrios was obviously devoted to the old man and satisfied with his humbler lot, Constantine was more resentful, particularly of the younger generation. Deme–trios's home and family are here; Constantine moves around and has none. It was Demetrios's wife who urged him to tell you."

"His wife?"

"Zehra, the housekeeper—a very forceful woman by the look of it."

"Do they benefit from the old man's death?"

Toby shook his head. "They don't—nor do they need it. Marolakis set up a million-dollar trust fund *each* for them years ago, of which they can only touch the interest, not the principal."

"You mean they are millionaires?" she gasped. "That's incredible!"

Toby looked at her quizzically. "It's a mere bagatelle when you consider the staggering figures involved with the Marolakis fortune. I got a damn sight more out of Pappas on that than I bet the Marolakis lawyers will ever disclose to anyone. The old man's estate is worth approximately three hundred fifty *million* dollars. Under the will it was simply split three ways—a third each to Georgiou, Alexander, and Melissa. Georgiou's estate is worth another one hundred fifty million dollars, one-third of which goes to his widow and her daughter by law, the other two-thirds split evenly between his son and elder daughter. So, with these two deaths, Melissa and her brother stand to split close to a half a *billion* dollars."

"And if Alexander should now die, she would get it all," Penny groaned. "Dear God, what a motive!"

"What do you mean 'if he should now die?' " Toby demanded.

She told him and he groaned in turn. "Things are looking worse for the Lefaus by the minute."

"But why on earth should they want it?" she cried. "Jules is a multimillionaire already; his fortune must at least equal Georgiou's, maybe even the old man's."

"Power," Toby said simply. "The more money, the more power—the thing that puzzles me is the power to do what?"

She pounced on that. "Exactly! Jules is 'old' money, don't forget. He is so used to money that it doesn't mean much to him, so—apart from keeping the family flag flying and living like a king in New Orleans—he's not ambitious. He has no political ambitions, no burning desires—all it would mean to him would be added burdens."

"Can you say the same for young Vincent?" Toby asked quietly, and this silenced her: It would explain much about Jules's attitude, and it would not be the first time he had put his own neck in jeopardy for his children.

They were interrupted by the appearance of Alex, who waved and called out. "Hi! Thought you'd like to know, Ma, that the kids are back—all safe and sound and everyone had a great time. Come and join us at the pool. Benedict has some observations on Theodopolis that might interest you, Toby."

They followed him back to find Juliette in full flood of excited description of the billionaire's yacht to Sonya. "Just imagine—all the bathroom fittings are of gold and Samian marble! It was fabulous: He's got a Cézanne landscape *and* a Chagall in the saloon. Everything was in surprisingly good taste," she added with unconscious arrogance.

Benedict Lefau drifted up to Toby and muttered in his ear, "I can't say the same for the seamanship of his crew. We saw at least six seamen and I'd say that only two of them had the faintest idea of what they were supposed to be doing. I suppose they could be bodyguards, but they certainly aren't yachtsmen. Even Theodopolis seems vague. I made a technical reference to one of the riggings and he didn't even seem to know what I was talking about."

"Is he here?" Toby murmured back.

"No, he took one look at the police launch moored at the quay, dropped us off, and headed back for his own yacht."

Penny had been distracted by Marcus, who was vainly tugging at his father's trousers trying to get his attention and piping, "We saw lots of pirate caves and, guess what, I saw a real *pirate* in one of them."

"No you didn't," John Schuyler said stolidly.

Marcus whirled on him. "I did so!"

"Didn't," John repeated. "I was next to you and I didn't see anyone."

"I had a telescope, you didn't, so I *saw* one. I did, I did, I did see a pirate!" Marcus was working himself up into a tantrum. He stamped his foot and shouted, "Why doesn't anyone ever *listen* to me!"

"Now that's enough, Marcus, be quiet for a change," Alex said sternly.

Marcus glared at him, his lips quivering, then wheeled around and ran off towards the beach.

"We'll get him," Penny said, and set off after him, Toby in her wake. They caught up with Marcus by the tennis courts, where he was leaning against the wire enclosure, his narrow shoulders slumped in despair. "Now, Marcus, no need for that," Penny soothed, rubbing his back. "Grandpa and I would love to hear all about it, so don't take on so, there's a good boy."

"Nobody ever listens to me," he sobbed. "They always listen to Mala—it's not fair!"

"Well, it's a bit like the story of the boy who cried 'wolf,'" Penny pointed out. "You talk all the time, so everyone tends to tune you out after a bit. Mala hardly ever says anything, so when she *does* speak people are so surprised by it that they listen to her—it's that simple."

The sob gurgled into a giggle and he turned around, rubbing his eyes. "John's a rotten liar," he stated. "I did see a man in a cave. Just ask . . ." He bit his lip and blushed.

"Just ask who?" she prompted.

"It's a secret," he muttered. "You're not supposed to tell secrets."

"Oh, it's all right to tell *us*," she persisted. "We're family and we love you, so your secret is ours too."

He looked up at his grandfather doubtfully and Toby nodded. "Well, I did see a man in one of the caves. He sort of popped out of it and then popped back in quickly, but Mr. Theodopolis saw him too. I was so excited that I wanted to go after him, but Mr. Theodopolis said it might be too dangerous, as he could be a *bad* pirate, so he'd take care of him later and tell me all about it. He said it would be our special secret and not to tell anyone."

"Did he, by Jove," Toby rumbled, looking hard at Penny. "Very interesting man, Mr. Theodopolis. Now, it's fine that you've told us, but don't tell anyone else about this, all right?"

"Okay. But you do believe me, don't you?" Marcus said anxiously.

"We most certainly do," his grandparents assured him.

Chapter 12

There followed a bitterly combative twenty-four hours, during which the Greek police managed to antagonize and infuri-
ate practically everyone involved. First they had categorically
refused to allow Melissa and Vincent to fly off to Boston to be
with Alexander, and when Kepplik had made a similar request
as an "old family friend," that also had been vetoed. As a
compromise they had allowed lawyer Demos to go to Boston
on the family's behalf to oversee the situation there. They had
equally infuriated Georgiou's widow by refusing to release
the body for burial "until the case was further advanced," but
somewhat surprisingly had indicated that the Schuyler family
and Benedict Lefau were free to leave if they wished. When
Juliette discovered they were taking her father off to Athens
"for further questioning," though, she had refused to go, so
that was that. No such offer had been made to the Spring family, which aggravated Toby but obviously suited Sonya, who
was in full investigative fury.

"As I said before, unless you tell Sonya the whole truth of
why you're here and convince her that the children might be
at risk, you're not going to get rid of her," Penny told him.
"Even if you still don't know what we're involved in I think
you should do so, and to hell with what Barham Young wants."

"The risk to the children would appear to be minimal compared to the danger there is to Melissa," he replied. "There seems to be a wholesale abolition of Marolakis going on and she's about the only one left intact. Assuming the Lefaus are *not* the guilty parties, I would say she is the next prime target, and if I could trust Jules I'd tell him just that. I managed to have a word with Pappas before we left the island yesterday to alert him and everyone he can trust to keep a sharp eye on her."

"Why don't you tell Jules anyway? What harm can it do?" she urged.

"Because if either he or Vincent, or both, are involved, it would be very easy to arrange for something nonfatal to happen to her in which they could not possibly be involved, and which would conveniently get them out of their present jeopardy," he mused. "And there is also another very nasty possibility. I know much of ancient Greek law but I'm not up on their modern law, although I presume it may be as in other western democracies: A murderer is not allowed to profit from his crime. As it stands now, if the Lefaus are indicted and something does happen to Melissa, I imagine Olympia's daughter would scoop the Marolakis pool, although if Alexander pulls through, I suppose it might all go to him—I'll have to check. But it would give Olympia one hell of a motive."

"I just can't buy that; she'd have to be an absolute monster, and she doesn't strike me like that," Penny said stoutly.

"Not a Medea of Medeos?"

"What?"

"Before the island was Marolakis, its original name was Medeos," he explained. "The island of Medea."

"Oh. Well, I think there's a far more likely suspect, and what worries me is that *he* knows my grandson saw something that he probably should not have. Granted, not too much weight can be put on the observations of a six-year-old, but Marcus *was* definite that the man he saw was tall and fair, 'like Ohlsen, only fatter,' he said, and was not in uniform. That rules out all the Greek security guards and village fishermen, who are the only people likely to be in those caves. And that leaves us with someone from Theodopolis's or Kepplik's boats. I checked with Karras on Kepplik's crew—only two of them, both dark and short. That leaves Theodopolis and his," she finished triumphantly, "and a couple of those were blondes."

"Who were *on* the yacht," he pointed out.

"Doesn't mean to say they were all there."

"Or the man could be part of our unknown factor X," Toby said. "If only we knew what that was! As our university motto puts it, *Dominus illuminatio mea*—O Lord, enlighten me, and the quicker the better."

"Well, here comes Sonya and by herself, so I do wish you'd tell her," Penny urged. They were now tied up to the *Silver Spray* for easy access both to it and to the pier, and Toby was still shaking his head when his daughter jumped down on the deck and said brightly, "We Glendower-Springs are a popular lot: yet another invitation, very pressing and for this afternoon—lunch. Lysander Ribotis wants us to visit him on *his* island. His twins are seemingly yearning for another sight of Mala, and I think he wants you to look at some ancient Sperian ruins, Father."

"Being on the outs with his sister, it's more likely that he just wants to find out what is going on from a disinterested party," Toby sniffed, "but that can work both ways, so it's fine with me." He looked enquiringly at Penny.

"Fine with me, too, but what about the police?"

"Karras was here to take Jules off to Athens and he said it was okay so long as we took Ari along," Sonya said.

"Who?" they chorused.

"Mala's latest conquest—a very young constable and a nice lad."

"Good, then he can help me with the sailing and mooring," her father said promptly. "Is everyone coming?"

"No, Marcus wasn't taken with the Ribotis twins, so he's staying with old pal John, whom he has now brainwashed into believing he also saw Marcus's pirate," Sonya chuckled. "An added attraction is that Ohlsen has promised to show them how to service the engines while in port."

"So the Schuylers aren't coming?" Penny asked.

"Weren't even invited—just us. They'll probably go to the compound later on for tennis and swimming with Vincent and Melissa. See you in about an hour then?" And with a flash of long legs she was gone up the ladder.

"You should have told her," Penny chided.

"Not yet," her partner returned, and seeing the stubborn set of his jaw she let it go for the moment.

On the short trip across the strait to Speria the oppressive mantle that hung over Marolakis fell away and her sagging spirits rose, but after they had moored on the opposite side of the pier from Ribotis's luxurious yacht, she collected Toby and marched him up to the smooth-faced young constable. "I want you to tell him to keep an eye on Mala at all times," she insisted. "Where she goes, he goes. I don't think we should take any chances."

Toby meekly conveyed the message, which was received with a wide grin and an enthusiastic nod of understanding. Her grandmotherly duty done, she prepared to absorb the Ribotis realm. Predictably, it was on as vast and magnificent a scale as Marolakis although, unlike the Marolakis mansion, which was determinedly modern in its furnishings and appurtenances, the Ribotis mansion was stuffed full of antiques and paintings from every corner of Europe, so that it bore a faintly museumlike air. On closer inspection its owner was far less impressive than his surroundings. About the same height as his half-sister, Lysander lacked Olympia's striking features; he also bore little resemblance to the founder of the family fortunes, whose huge portrait and craggy features loomed menacingly over the main salon. Although a more forceful character in person, she concluded, if he resembled anyone, it was the late Georgiou.

As a host he could not be faulted, extending himself to be

both charming and attentive as he toured them around the mansion and compound, and his amiable facade did not even crack in the face of the unheralded and evidently unexpected arrival of Olympia, accompanied by Kepplik, just before luncheon was announced. But Penny was mildly amused when he carefully seated his sister at the opposite end of the table from himself, with Alex on one hand and Kepplik on the other. Only when they were all seated, with Penny on his right, did he turn to her and confide quietly, "There are times when family bonds, however strained, must be maintained, and although you have doubtless heard that my sister and I are not on the best of terms, she is going through such a hard time just now that, as head of the family, I must give her whatever support I can. I did not anticipate her visit here today."

"Oh, I quite understand," Penny murmured back and, seizing the opportunity, went on. "But you often visit Marolakis, don't you? I saw you at the village the other day."

"Oh that!" he said easily. "Part of the ritual when I am on Speria. You see, over the centuries and because of the closeness of the islands, there has been much intermarriage between the two villages, so practically everyone here is related to everyone there. I operate the launch almost as a ferry service for visits while I'm around. You have visited the village, then?"

"Yes, and I was amazed—it's not often you see a walled village these days."

His face tightened. "That wall is new and not very popular with the villagers, I might add. It was only put up some six months ago, when all the security on the island was tightened. Myself, I find it rather ridiculous."

"Then yours isn't walled?"

"No, and never will be," he snorted. "If someone is out to get you, killer dogs and walls aren't going to help, as present events have shown."

She would gladly have pursued this avenue, but he rather pointedly turned to Toby on his left and started to plan an after-lunch inspection of his "ruins." Sonya, who was sitting next to her father, grinned across at her and jerked her sleek head towards the bottom of the table. Penny followed her cue and saw her son's handsome face, transfixed by Olympia's hypnotic eyes gazing languishingly into his own slightly panic-stricken ones as she talked animatedly; the ignored Kepplik glowered at her uneasily and in silence.

Alex was finally rescued from this embarrassing *tête-à-tête* by his daughter. Mala, having steadily polished off everything that had been put before her, and growing tired of the yearning stares of the Ribotis twins across the table from her, calmly got up, trotted down to her father, and climbed up into his lap. She settled back comfortably and stared icily at the gesticulating Olympia, who was completely put off her stride and dried up in a hurry as the luncheon party began to break up.

Not that Olympia was to be deterred from her own agenda, for to her brother's obvious dismay, she insisted on going with them "to see the ruins." He had clearly wanted Toby all to himself, but she was so insistent that in the end everybody, including Kepplik, the Ribotis twins, the Spring family, and even Ari were piled into a trio of station wagons and transported up the mountainous outer edge of the island. Even there the increasingly irked Lysander could not shake off his sister as he and Toby prowled among the ruined walls, with Toby swooping down upon the scatters of pottery, Olympia swooping after him—Kepplik dogging her steps—Mala trotting after her grandfather, the twins following her, and the attentive Ari bringing up the rear.

The view of the Mediterranean from the top was spectacular, and the Spring family, after amused grins at the antics of the others, closed ranks and prepared to enjoy it. Alex put his arm around Sonya and exclaimed, "Whew, that was a close one! Saved by a six-year-old. It may be all the stress, of course, but I think the widow Marolakis may be a little off her rocker."

"I noticed you made quite a hit," Sonya said, with a grin at Penny.

"You'd better believe it! She kept going on and on about Alexander the Great and how much I resembled him; and the greatness that was Macedonia and would be again; and how I must come and visit her in 'my former homeland' and see all its wonders; and did I know Olympia had been one of the major forces in Alexander's life. It really was quite scary. Kepplik was obviously fit to be tied, but every time he tried to interrupt the flow she bit his head off."

"She certainly seems more than a little hyper," Penny observed, for Olympia was now yelling like a fishwife at her brother, as Toby stood by looking extremely uncomfortable. Finally, Kepplik interposed himself bodily between her and Lysander, snapped something at his host, who nodded, and, putting his arm around Olympia's shoulders, urged her away from the group and down towards the waiting cars. Lysander motioned the twins to follow them, and Toby said something to Ari, who was now carrying Mala; then he, too, began to descend. "Looks as if the party's over. Shall we leave Toby to it and join the retreat?" Penny said. They joined the retreat.

By the time they got down the mountain in the second car, Olympia and Kepplik had disappeared, the Ribotis twins were wandering forlornly around the large paved forecourt of the mansion, and the Ribotis butler was outside the main door peering anxiously at their approaching car. As it slid to a stop he came over and peered. "Ah, Dr. Spring?" he said to Alex in halting English. "Your son, he is here. Mr. Theodopolis, he say to come at once."

"Marcus! Here?" Sonya gasped. "Dear God, what's happened to him?" In full alarm they all rushed into the house to be greeted by an odd spectacle. The tall figure of Theodopolis was seated on a large leather couch, a small towel-enshrouded figure on either side of him; both boys were white-faced, tight-lipped, and slumped in despair, but apparently all in one piece.

Theodopolis rose as the family rushed in, his face grave, and looked down at Marcus. "Will you tell them or shall I?"

Marcus looked imploringly at his mother. "We were just exploring," he muttered. "We weren't doing any harm and it would have been all right, only . . ." He gulped, looked frantically at John, and dried up.

Theodopolis sighed and shook his head. "Then I will. The boys apparently took two of the rubber rafts by the swimming pool, sneaked away to the beach, and paddled them around the steel-mesh fence and along the beach for some distance. Luckily, I happened to be cruising along that side of the island, and when I first spotted them they were paddling inshore and beaching the rafts. I immediately readied the launch and had it in the water when I saw them racing back down the beach, piling onto the rafts, and paddling frantically away . . ." He looked expectantly down at Marcus.

"It was the dogs," Marcus confessed. "We heard the dogs coming and barking, so we thought we'd better get out of there."

"Knowing how strong the currents can be, I was afraid they might get swept away in the rafts, so I picked them up and brought them to my yacht. When I got them calmed down and learned where you were I thought I had best bring them directly here. One of my men will already have informed John's parents that he is safe," Theodopolis explained.

Alex drew a deep breath. "We cannot thank you enough, Mr. Theodopolis. Your quick thinking probably saved their lives." He glared at his son. "I only hope you've scared some sense into their addled little heads."

"No thanks are needed, I am glad to have been useful," Theodopolis said stiffly. "Now that they are with you and I am here, I would like a word with Mr. Ribotis—is he around?" He looked meaningfully at Penny.

"He's up on the ridge with Sir Tobias," she said quickly. "There's a car and driver just outside who could run you up there. I'll show you." They went out as Sonya went over to the sofa and wordlessly hugged both boys to her.

Outside his face lit up as Mala spotted him and ran to him, squeaking, "Theo, Theo!" He scooped her up in his arms and looked at Penny. "I don't know how you are going to do it, Dr. Spring, but it is imperative that you get these children away from here," he said softly. "There is danger, much danger. Murder has been done and there may be more to come. Get out of here as quickly as you can. This, too, I shall say to Sir Tobias." And handing Mala over, he stalked away to the car.

"Well that tears it," Penny informed her startled granddaughter. "If Toby won't, then I damn well will." Hurrying back into the house she called out, "Sonya, Alex, let's get back to the yacht pronto, I have something extremely important to tell you."

Chapter 13

The Spring-Glendower clan were thoroughly on the outs with one another: Toby with Penny for what he termed her "premature and uncalled-for" disclosure; Sonya with Toby for a variety of reasons, but mainly because she had been kept in the dark; and Alex with Toby just on general principles and with his mother because she had announced that, though she would be thankful to see them and the children gone, she had no intention of leaving until the matter had been resolved one way or another.

"Why, for heaven's sake?" he fumed. "You've no obligation to the Lefaus, still less to the Marolakis, and if Toby wants to play cloak-and-dagger for the British government, that's his business. As soon as possible we should get out of there, you included."

"Because if I had listened to Toby's advice in the first place, I would have bailed us out as soon as I heard about this meeting of millionaires. In the second place, because Theodopolis is so anxious to get rid of me, and I don't trust him an inch," Penny returned.

"Good God!" Sonya cried. "You're not still on about him? He probably saved Marcus's life and he *warned* you of danger here."

"It sounded more like a threat to me," Penny said. "*Leave*

or else something worse could happen to my family. And once you are away and out of danger, I'm damned if I'm going to leave your father to cope with whatever is going on here alone. And that's my final word on it."

"But we just can't go off and leave you!" Alex protested.

"Enough of this wrangling," Toby suddenly boomed out. "We're getting every bit as bad as the Lefaus, continually sniping at each other. It's up to me to get you out of here, and that I will do as soon as possible, but I suggest a compromise. Namely, that you take off with the children in this yacht and tour around the Gulf of Argos and the Gulf of Corinth for, let's say, six days. You can keep in daily touch with us if you wish by ship's radio to the *Silver Spray* where we, perforce, will be. If at the end of that time nothing has been resolved, we'll both pack it in and you can come and pick us up. Fair enough?"

Alex and Sonya looked dubious. "Not being sailors, I'm not sure we can cope," Alex said.

"Maybe we could ask Jules for Ramon's help for a week," Sonya suggested. "He's good with the children, and I've seen him lend a hand with mooring and things like that."

"If you stay in those two gulfs you shouldn't run into any trouble," Toby persisted. "And you could power along most of the time if the sails are too much for you. Or you could just dock in some handy port like Nauphlia and explore the Peloponnese by car—there's plenty to see. But first I've got to get you out of here." He stood up. "And before that I have some checking to do in the village and then in Athens, so I'd best get cracking."

"Checking on what?" Penny asked.

"Lysander's 'fishing' expedition yesterday started me thinking along a different line, but I need a lot more information before I know if it's a possibility. Once he got me alone he kept asking me what appeared to be totally unrelated questions, like what parts of Greece I was most familiar with; what did I think of all the regional nationalist movements that have started up since the splintering of Yugoslavia; and most curious of all, had I noted any unusual amount of shipping passing the islands? Of course, I pointed out to him that although Marolakis is so flat you can see clear across it, the view from this yacht is completely cut off from it by the other yachts, so that I hadn't seen any passing ships to the north, and so that his own island cuts off any view to the south. At this he seemed relieved and returned to his archaeological queries—and I found that odd."

Sonya, now recovered from her Slavic snit, said, "What exactly did you find out about those ruins?"

He shrugged. "The pottery was a mix, Byzantine overlying what appeared to be very crude late Mycenaean. By the position of the site I imagine it might have been some kind of watchtower or signal tower with a house attached—a primitive lighthouse, in other words. In olden times it would have been on the natural southern route for ships from the Cyclades to the Gulf of Argos."

"Of any interest?" she queried.

"Very minor. I just suggested that if he did want it dug he should get qualified archaeology students from Athens University to do it, but I don't think he was any more interested in it than I was. He just wanted to get me alone. So if no one has any further thoughts, I'll be on my way." No one had, so off he went.

Sonya looked at Alex. "I suppose it would be the most sensible thing to do. And with the Schuylers going, it won't be much fun for the children cooped up here."

"The Schuylers are leaving?" Penny exclaimed in surprise.

"Yes, today sometime. Last night when her father came back from Athens, weary and worn but intact, Juliette had one of her violent turnarounds. She was all set to battle to the death when she thought he was going to be arrested, but as soon as she found out he wasn't going to be, she went all waspish and said that now that he had his precious sons around him, he obviously had no further need of her and so she'd be leaving. I must say, Jules seemed more relieved than upset, so she could be right."

"So Benedict is staying?"

"Oh yes, but he looks worried. I don't think Jules has opened up to him either. I wonder how much Father told him about this other mysterious business."

"Damn all, I imagine," Penny sniffed. "Well, I'd better try to see Jules, and you'd better start packing up and moving your stuff over here so that you can get away as soon as Toby clears it. We'll have to move onto the *Silver Spray*, but Jules can scarcely object to that. Where are the children, by the way?"

"Marcus and John are confined to barracks under Richard's stern eye," Alex said with a faint grin. "And Mala and Emily are working their way through the yacht's video collection— they've gone through all the Disneys and have now moved on to *Star Wars* and *Indiana Jones*. When last seen, Ramon and Ari were watching with them."

They helped Penny up the ladder to the deck of the *Silver Spray* and went their separate ways, but when she enquired of Ohlsen on the bridge where Jules could be found, she learned he was with Karras and so currently unavailable. "Then I'll wait," she said, and settled herself in a deck chair in the shade.

After a while Karras emerged from below, looking grim, and came over to her. "Anything?" he enquired.

"If you mean from Jules, I haven't had the chance," she said sharply, "since you whisked him away to Athens. But I do have some other items for you. I take it you haven't arrested him?"

He sat down heavily beside her. "No, and as long as he and Vincent stick to the same story—and due to the lack of concrete evidence to the contrary—I don't think we will. The time of death for Marolakis has now been established as firmly as possible and that is around one AM. Lefau's story is that, not having heard from Marolakis, he went over to the compound where he found Vincent alone—Melissa having gone to bed early because she wasn't feeling well. Vincent told him of Georgiou's arrival and they went to look for him in his study, but since he wasn't there, they thought he, too, had gone to bed and so left it until the next morning. Jules returned to the *Silver Spray* about midnight and went straight to bed. He says he was almost asleep when he heard your son and daughter-in-law go to their cabin near his at quarter past twelve—and this fits in with their statements. He claims he did not wake up until six-thirty AM. We can neither prove nor disprove this, and the same with Vincent. Says he went to bed as soon as his father left, looked in on Melissa and found her reading, kissed her good night, and went to bed himself, sleeping until eight AM. And we can't disprove that either." He paused. "So what else have you got?"

She related the incidents of the day before and ended with, "After all that, I'm sure you can understand that I'm more anxious than ever to get my family away. Is there anything you can do to help?"

"I can try," he sighed. "Vassos has let the Schuylers go, so I don't see much point in keeping your family here. We've got their statements, and they don't seem to have any conceivable motive—so why not? You're not going?"

"No, and neither is Sir Tobias," she said. "We still think Theodopolis is up to something."

"For a recluse he certainly does seem to get around—and hang around," he said drily. "Yesterday, when we informed him and Kepplik that we still could not grant them permission to leave, his lofty reply was that he had no intention of leaving, permission or not. So what's keeping him here? He's not chasing the widow Marolakis, is he?"

"Not that I know of." She was amused. "Although he did go to see her brother yesterday, so I suppose it is a possibility."

Karras wagged his head sadly. "It's very difficult for the likes of me to understand these people—with so much money among them that it almost becomes meaningless as a motive, and not into politics or dope or any of the usual things leading to homicide. Passion seems to be the only thing left, but passion for what or for whom? It beats me."

Penny looked at him thoughtfully. "You've just said a very big mouthful, Major. And you're right, I think passion will be at the bottom of this, but not in the usual sense of male-female relationships; it will be more complicated than that. All we can do is keep digging until we find it."

"Yes, well, I'd better get on with it then," he sighed. "I'll put in a word with Vassos about your family." They parted, he to the police launch and she below decks to find Jules.

He did not appear overly pleased to see her. "If you've come to grill me, Penny, I'm not in the mood for it," he snapped. "Having spent twelve hours at it with the police yesterday, I've had enough. For the moment what I need is some peace and quiet."

She was equally sharp. "I came on some matters of business. Since the Schuylers are leaving, we are anxious for my son and his family to leave also. Toby intends for them to take the yacht and get on with their vacation, but they need an extra hand to run it. Could they borrow the services of Ramon for a week or so? Your crew has little to do while you are just sitting here in port. Toby and I would therefore like to move onto the *Silver Spray,* if that's all right with you. If it isn't, we'll find somewhere else to put up."

He looked suitably abashed. "I'm sorry—forgive me, I'm afraid I've been so preoccupied with my own worries that I'd forgotten how miserable this must be for the rest of you. Yes, of course they can take Ramon if they need him, but why don't you all go? There's nothing you can do for me and I assure you that I'll be all right."

She gazed stonily at him. "Toby never wanted to come here,

but now that he's here he'll stay. He doesn't like murder or murderers, so he won't stop until he finds the truth. And if he stays, I stay."

"I wish you'd leave it alone and go," he said. "No good can come of it, and possibly much harm."

"Veiled threats do not become you, Jules," she snapped. "I've had enough of that already from Theodopolis."

His jaw dropped in amazement. "*Theodopolis* threatened you? That's unbelievable!"

"Believe it. I may not be as swift as I once was, but I know when I've been threatened." Seeing his confusion, she pressed her advantage. "Look, Jules, can't you see that you are letting history repeat itself? You are doing exactly what you did last time—holding back, even confusing the trail, and all for nothing."

"Do you have to rake that up?" he groaned. "This isn't the same thing at all."

"Isn't it?" She looked at him searchingly. "One thing I did learn last time is that the Lefau family is hellishly bad at communicating with each other on a meaningful level, and I think it's still going on. Let me do some heavy supposing, and then you just think hard about it. You and Vincent alibi each other for that night with a very innocent seeming alibi that can be neither proved nor disproved. And I think it's moonshine. I don't think you were with him that night, so he's covering for you. And equally, you don't know where *he* was that night, so you're covering for him; and now you know, or think you know, that he had one hell of a motive. And both of you suspect the other, but are willing to accept whatever may happen to protect the other. All right, you may get away with it—the police may eventually throw in the towel and let you go—but do you honestly want to go through the rest of your life thinking he might be a murderer, and with him thinking the same about you? You told me you had no hand in Georgiou's death and I believe you, but have you told Vincent that? Have you

133

asked him that question? I bet you haven't, and I'd also bet that he'd give the same answer. But for once in your lives, be *honest* with each other. You don't have to answer me, just think about it."

He looked at her, his eyes wretched. "I will, but I can't yet, any more than I can tell you—it's just not that simple."

She got up. "Then there's nothing more to be said. When Toby and I come on board we'll keep out of your way as much as possible. Will you make the arrangements about Ramon?"

"Of course, and there is no need to keep out of my way, I shall welcome your company as I always have," he said stiffly.

"At the risk of sounding ungracious, I can't say the same for the moment," she snapped, and stamped out.

She found Sonya in the children's cabin packing up and relayed the news on Ramon to her. "Good," Sonya said absently, sorting out dirty laundry, "I've already asked Ramon if he'd be willing and he seems quite keen to get out of here."

"Then I'll leave you to it and see you later on the *Silver Spray,*" Penny said.

Marcus, who had been sitting in silence on the top bunk, jumped down and followed her out. "You come right back here, young man, you're still grounded," his mother called.

"I just want to say something to Grandma. I'll be right back," he piped.

"What is it?" Penny gazed down at the little, round, woebegone face that made him look like a miniature of a depressed Toby.

"Everyone is so cross with me that I haven't been able to tell you something," he whispered. "Something important. Before the dogs came John and I saw something on that beach— footprints, lots of them." He paused dramatically.

"Well, that's not surprising," she pointed out gently. "I expect the dog patrols go along there as part of their beat."

"No!" He shook his head. "The footprints weren't going *along* the beach—there were some of those too—they were going from the *water* and heading for one of the caves. We were just going to explore it when we heard the dogs."

"I see, and did you tell Mr. Theodopolis about this?" She tried to sound casual.

"Yes, it was part of our secret, wasn't it? He said it was very good observing and that I was a great help," Marcus preened.

"Was that all?"

"Yes, except that he said it would be another secret just between us. He said I ought to be a detective when I grow up, and I said if I decide not to be an astrophysicist then I probably would be that. So you will keep it a secret, won't you, Grandma?" he asked anxiously.

"Well, I'll tell your grandpa, but no one else, I promise," she assured him. "Now you'd better get back and help your mother."

She waited with increasing anxiety until Toby returned late that evening, after the family had gone to bed in their new quarters. From his smug expression she gathered he had had a good day. "Everything's set," he informed her. "They can leave tomorrow, if they're ready."

"Good," she said emphatically. "Not a moment too soon for my liking." She related Marcus's latest revelation.

"After what I found out today I'm not surprised, for it has been a day of surprises," he said blandly.

"Well?" she demanded.

"Oh, not tonight, I'm far too tired. Tell you in the morning," he yawned, and sauntered off to bed.

Chapter 14

Toby's revelations were long postponed, for the departure of the Spring family—in the nature of all family outings—was delayed by sundry minor glitches. They had acquired a last-minute addition to their party in the person of Benedict Lefau, who had surprisingly volunteered to come with them as far as Nauphlia and give them a crash course on handling the yacht. "Not that you aren't extremely welcome, but how are you going to get back here afterwards?" Sonya asked.

"Oh, I can get a hitch over to Hydra easily enough, see how Juliette and company are getting on, maybe go with them to Athens for a day or so, and then come back to Hydra; Vincent can pick me up from there," he said casually.

"Apparently Benedict has got no further with Jules than you have and is taking a breather," Alex whispered in Penny's ear as he passed by with some supplies.

"So Juliette is abandoning the sea?" Sonya went on.

Benedict grinned. "I think she's had more than enough of it. Plans are to spend several days in Athens—shopping, I gather—then to proceed to Delphi by car and carry on up to Macedonia."

At this Toby, who was propped against the rail of the *Silver Spray* in moody introspection, perked up and started to pay attention. Noting her father's sudden interest, Sonya pressed on. "Why Macedonia?"

Benedict shrugged. "I guess she wants to see what's so terrific about the birthplace of her new in-laws—Olympia doesn't talk about much else. They'll have to come back to Athens eventually, as the Greek police are still hanging on to Juliette's passport. Issued her a traveller's ID instead, which miffed her considerably."

At this juncture Vincent appeared, bearing a couple of small packages and some letters and looking somewhat crestfallen. "Would you mind sending these from Nauphlia?" he asked his half-brother. "They go quicker from there."

Benedict nodded at the small holdall at his feet. "Shove them in there and I'll take care of it."

"When will you be back?" Vincent asked, sounding forlorn.

"No idea, since there's nothing for me to do here. I'll give you a call from Hydra when I get there," Benedict said curtly. "Not planning on going anywhere, are you?"

"Would that I could." Vincent turned his attention to Penny, who was handing the supplies down to Alex on the yacht below them. "Why don't you and Sir Tobias come and join us in the compound this afternoon—drinks by the pool? Mel and I would certainly welcome the change. The house is like a morgue with Olympia still sulking in her tent, and Michele and Hans are not exactly lively company."

She looked over at Toby, who had lapsed back into his brown study. "We may just do that," she agreed. "About three?"

He cheered up instantly. "That'll be great! I must go and tell Mel the good news."

"You'd never think he was a Harvard magna cum laude, would you?" Benedict observed, as his brother scurried away. "Still acts like some addled teenager." He stooped down and hoisted his bag. "Well, I'd better get on board or this show will never get on the road." He suited the action to the word.

After a flurry of hugs and kisses all around, the Spring family were finally ready. "See you in six days, then, if not sooner," Alex called sternly from the deck. But it was Mala who provided Penny with her only surprise. Breaking away from her mother's firm grip, she looked up at her grandmother and stated with gracious firmness, "You are quite wrong about Mr. Theodopolis, you know. Think of Obi-Wan Kenobi and then I'm sure you'll get it right." And with a dazzling smile of farewell, she leapt down into her father's waiting arms.

Think of Obi-Wan Kenobi? Penny wondered, as she and Toby waved them farewell and the yacht got underway. What on earth is she talking about?

"What is Obi-Wan Kenobi?" Toby said blankly.

"Oh, never mind! For heaven's sake let's go and sit down somewhere and you tell me about yesterday before I burst with frustration. It never occurred to me until after you'd gone, but how on earth did you manage to get to the village and then to Athens and back?"

"The very cooperative Pappas," he said, as they settled in chairs by the stern where they could watch their family retreating over the horizon. "Zehra drove me to the village, as I needed to get a better idea of the lie of the land, then after we'd finished there Demetrios drove over in the big Marolakis launch. I went to Athens in that and he went back with Zehra."

"Why her and not his brother?"

"Because Zehra is a 'local' and just what I needed to get the villagers talking. It comes out as an interesting little anthropological study. This island is rigidly divided into the Macedonians on the one hand and the villagers on the other, and it's only because Demetrios is married to one of them that they partially accept him. The local staff in the compound are nearly all kinfolk of Zehra's, and on the whole dislike and distrust 'the Northerners' with whom the old man surrounded himself and who all live *in* the compound. What is more, they particularly dislike Constantine and his security guards—all Macedonians, and all imported during the past six months. Having a wall built around the village was bad enough, but there was a very nasty incident just after its erection when a local child, who had heretofore roamed free and so ignored all the dire warnings, got badly mauled by the dogs. The villagers got the message after that tragedy, but relations have steadily deteriorated since then."

"You don't suppose they could be behind these murders," Penny put in. "Revenge?"

He shook his head vigorously. "No—let me go on. They are not that active or organized, but what they are is keenly observant of what goes on, and *that's* been a great help." He paused, his brow wrinkling. "What they told me convinces me that *something* is definitely going on on the north side of the island, although I still have no idea what exactly that is. It boils down to the following: More ships are passing close to the island—especially during the night—than the locals ever remember. These ships don't appear to stop, yet the time it takes them to pass between the village and the compound is an hour longer than it used to be. A night fisherman who specializes in catching octopi for local consumption was particularly helpful on this, for he claims that some months ago, when his underwater light to attract the octopi was on, a ship tried to run him down and swamped him. Since then, when he has heard ships approaching, he has doused his lights and lain low by the rocks until they've passed, and has taken note of the ships' names when those were visible by moonlight. One thing he was sure of, and which upset him considerably, was that they were all flying the *Ribotis* house flag—and, as you know from my previous findings, there are strong ties between the village and Lysander's Speria. Unlike Olympia, whom they don't like, they do appear attached to Lysander. And you were right about him; his visit to the village was very much a pumping expedition to find out about this shipping."

"Indicating that he is involved in whatever is going on and is getting nervous?" she put in.

"Not necessarily, let me go on," Toby said. "Armed with all this, I took off for Athens, but by the time I got there, found the right offices, and softened up the people in them enough to talk to me, I only had time to get a tithe of the information I need. I have to go back and dig some more. Anyway, what I did find is very suggestive. They are Ribotis ships right enough, but all but a couple of them fall under Olympia's aegis, not Lysander's. Unfortunately, I could not find any kind of pattern to them, as I had hoped. Some of them came from the Ukrainian port of Odessa, and I got very excited about that, considering Vadik's starting point. Others came from the Bulgarian port of Varna, but the puzzling thing is that their ultimate destinations were Brindisi in Italy, and Sicily and Spain. The rest of the ships were local freighters coming from the Cyclades into Athens and Thessalonika and occasionally to Trieste in the Adriatic . . ."

"Isn't Thessalonika in Macedonia?" Penny interrupted.

"Yes, it is, but only a couple ended up there during all those months, and the bills of lading for all of them were as innocent as you please—olive oil to Trieste, for example."

"Well, they would be, wouldn't they?" she said absently. "I mean, you don't put contraband on a bill of lading, and I assume you are thinking of smuggling of some sort? I'm not sure where you're heading with it."

"As yet I'm not sure myself," he confessed, "but putting things together—the rigid security precautions here and the ships that perform this 'slow-down' as they pass the island—what if they are using those 'pirate caves' of Marcus's for storage? The scenario being that the big ships from the Black Sea ports would slow down enough to allow motor rafts from them to take off cargo and dump it in the caves, and that this cargo is then picked up in the same way by the local freighters and carried on to their intended destinations."

"Yes, but why go to all that trouble, and for what?" she cried.

"If my scenario is right, it can't be anything too bulky—like planes or heavy machinery. I thought of diamonds, industrial or otherwise, since the old USSR was so rich in them, but that doesn't make sense. They are *so* small that it would be simpler just to hide them in a big ship and chance it. So it has to be something easily portable and medium-sized. I've discounted drugs, since none of the ports of origin produce any of them in quantity . . ."

Penny's eyes narrowed suddenly. "Arms!" she exploded. "Tell me, how many of those freighters ended up in Trieste?"

Toby consulted his notebook. "Four from the Cyclades in the past six months."

"Then that's probably it!" She was excited. "Arms, ammo, maybe even missiles. I read somewhere not too long ago that Croatia is the largest arms buyer in what was Yugoslavia. Even though things are supposedly settled down, the Croatians are still as mad as hell about the Serbs' land grab—and *Kepplik,* remember, has Croatian roots. Still . . ." Her brows knitted. "That doesn't explain Theodopolis, does it?"

"Well, the only thing we are certain of about him is that he *is* interested in making money—lots of it," Toby said mildly. "And I imagine there would be a lot of it in illegal arms sales."

"In one year Croatia bought over three hundred million dollars' worth—and that was *during* the embargo, according to that article."

He whistled softly. "As much as that! It would also do much to explain his continuing presence here and his almost daily trips around the island—maybe protecting his investment?"

"Though I'd be happy to embrace this theory, since it lets Jules off the hook very nicely, I still don't see how it links up with the murders of the two Marolakis," she reflected.

"*Does* it let him off?" Toby demanded. "What if he is in on the deal?—whatever it is. And what if the Marolakis initially embraced the deal and then got cold feet, or wanted a bigger slice of the pie?"

She shook her head in perplexity. "I think we're missing something, there's more to it than that. Why should they get cold feet or even have wanted a bigger share?—it was an on-going enterprise. No one except us, thanks to Vadik, was suspecting them of anything. And their murders have brought the police to the island, which must be the last thing that anyone involved would want. No, it just doesn't add up. As Karras so rightly says, millions beyond a certain point become meaningless, unless there is something more involved. Why don't you pass all this along to him? The police have much better resources than we have. Let them sort it out."

"My dear, all we have at the moment is *theory*—not one single proven fact," Toby said with heavy patience. With a groan he heaved himself out of his chair. "And I'm not going to gather any facts sitting here. I have to get back to Athens right away."

"Today? I said we'd go to the compound this afternoon," she cried. "I thought it would be a good opportunity to find out how the young couple fit into this situation."

"Then you go. I simply must get more information. In fact, I'll stay overnight and may not be back until late tomorrow. Will you be all right here alone or do you want to come along?"

"Of course I'll be all right," she said crossly. "The last thing anybody wants around here is another murder."

"Let's hope so. Well, I must go and look for Demetrios," he said, and went ashore.

Bereft of companionship, she wandered down to the dining saloon to console herself with some lunch. It was buffet-style, for the French cook had, with the myriad comings and goings of the group, long since despaired and given up on his epicurean feasts. She helped herself to a shrimp-and-egg salad and some iced tea and settled in for more lonely contemplation, but was presently joined by a downcast Jules, who stated, as he filled his own plate, "I seem to be on everyone's blacklist these days. I've just been dressed down by Tom Andersen for letting Ramon go. It appears we are now desperately short-handed."

She looked at him with raised eyebrows. "Oh?—how so?"

"Preftakis has seemingly jumped ship—cleared out, bag and baggage. Must have been during the night."

"Surely Ari was on guard and saw him?"

"Apparently Ari was taking his duties lightly and spent the night on a couch in the saloon." Jules smiled slightly. "One can scarcely blame the lad, he must be bored out of his skull."

"You'd better notify Karras of this, pronto," she observed. "It's very odd."

"I will. He's due shortly to give me another going-over," he sighed. "Maybe this will get him off my back for a while. He may want to see you, too—will you be around?"

"I told Vincent I'd go over to the compound this afternoon. If Karras wants me, he can find me by the swimming pool. Will you be joining us?"

"No, I'm not supposed to leave the ship, and since it beats sitting in an interrogation cell in Athens I'm complying. I just hope it doesn't last much longer."

"I'd say that is very much up to you," she said curtly and left him to his thoughts.

She found her young hosts and Michele playing in the pool with a huge, brightly colored beach ball, which Vincent was hurling with gay abandon at the squealing, giggling Michele, who hurled it back. Kepplik was sprawled in a chaise longue, watching the proceedings with an indulgent grin. Vincent waved at her and shouted, "Won't you join us?" and when she shook her head, "Be right with you then." Hurling the ball to his wife, he swam over and surged out of the pool, dripping and slicking back his dark hair. "Whew, I'm glad of a breather," he gasped, as he escorted her to a chair shaded by a beach umbrella. "Those energetic young things have worn me out. Just like dear old Dad, I guess I'm not the athletic type—not the build for it. What can I get you?"

"Nothing for the moment, thanks, Vincent. So you're not into sports?" she queried.

"The ultimate nonjock—swim a bit, ski a bit, fence a bit, play a fair game of tennis, and that's it," he said cheerfully, and indicated Kepplik, who had now plunged into the pool and taken his place as ball hurler. "Not like old Hans there—a fifty push-ups before breakfast type, if ever there was one. No, Benedict's the superjock of the family, and, of course, Juliette is our martial arts expert."

A small cold shock went through her. "Juliette!" she exclaimed.

"A late-blooming passion. When she went off to New York and art school she decided she need protection in the big bad city, so she took up karate. Got through quite a few belts, or whatever they call them, before she grew tired of it. Both her kids are in classes, too," he chattered on. "I guess I'll have to enroll mine when he comes so he can protect himself from his cousins . . ."

His flow was momentarily interrupted by the appearance of a wooden-faced Zehra. "A telephone call for Kirios Hans."

Vincent waved at the pool. "He's there—help yourself." He got up as Kepplik left the pool and hurried into the house. "Better get back on duty," he sighed, but the young women had evidently had enough and emerged from the pool, pulling off bathing caps and grabbing for towels. "I'll get Melissa," he announced and went off.

Penny was surprised to see Michele making purposefully for her and then settling down in Vincent's vacated seat. The redhead leaned forward and said urgently, "You speak French, *n'est-ce pas?*" Her face was alive with excitement, her eyes slyly triumphant. Penny nodded. "Then I must speak with you most urgently," Michele went on in rapid French. "I have something of great importance to tell you . . ." Her eyes widened at something behind Penny and she spat out, *"Merde alors,* it cannot be now! I will contact you later." She hurried back to the pool.

Penny looked over her shoulder to see Karras bearing down

upon her, his face grim. He stood looking down at her and his barely controlled anger was palpable. "Dr. Spring, I have a most important question to ask you. Has Sir Tobias Glendower been using his influence to stop this investigation?"

She looked at him in amazement. "Why, certainly not—quite the opposite!" she cried. "What on earth makes you think that?"

He dropped heavily into the seat beside her. "There is great pressure on us from high government circles to do just that. One thing I will say for Vassos is that he is not a man to bend under such pressure, but he is angry—and so am I."

Penny looked squarely at him. "Well, I can assure you it is not from Sir Tobias, who at this very moment is pursuing a very important lead in the case. And if it isn't him, I think there is only one other person it is likely to be, don't you? A man with great power?"

"I agree," he growled. "It has to be Theodopolis."

Chapter 15

No sooner had Karras taken his stormy departure than Kepplik reappeared, his face tight with anger, and more or less dragged Michele away with little ceremony. Left alone with the young couple, Penny tried to seize the opportunity to sound them out, but to her dismay there seemed little in the way of hidden depths in either of them to plumb. They were still so much in the "honeymoon" phase, so intensely wrapped up in each other, that switching their interest to other matters she found to be extremely hard going; as the afternoon wore on, she felt increasingly in the category of "three's a crowd."

The only useful nuggets of information had come from Melissa. Her brother was out of danger and well on the mend. "That one has a hard head like my grandfather," she informed Penny with a giggle. "I talked with him today in the hospital and he said not to get any ideas about running things, since he was the boss now and would do it for both of us. Such a relief! Who'd *want* to run things? I can hardly wait to get out of here and back to America, away from Olympia and her 'causes,' and big business, and running all these places—who needs it? All I want is to settle down in this nice house we've picked out in Boston and look after my baby . . ." She looked at Vincent and giggled again. "No, lots of babies, and my Vincent."

"Boston, not New Orleans?" Penny asked.

"I've been offered a job in a very good Boston law firm," Vincent said with a touch of pride. "And I'm taking it. I'll leave New Orleans and all that Creole aristocrat crap to Dad and Benedict."

"Does your father know this?"

He looked at her in amazement. "About the job? Of course he does—all in favor of it, too. Time the Lefaus branched out, says he, and I'd better make it big up there—or else! Naturally, he was a bit miffed that we didn't tell him that we'd got hitched on the quiet, but he'll get over it. After all, it's not like Benedict's first ghastly mistake, is it?"

"Hardly," she said drily, and turned her attention back to Melissa. "So you've no career plans of your own?"

Melissa gave a delicate shudder. "No, not me. Just the good life with Vincent, the babies, and . . ." She added after some thought, "I might get my nose fixed."

"I like your nose just the way it is," her husband said promptly. "Don't you listen to Richard, he'd say anything for a buck."

"Well, I'll think about it." They gazed adoringly at each other.

"Er, what sort of causes does Olympia champion?" Penny said, trying to get back to something substantive.

Melissa tore herself away from rapturous contemplation and looked at her vaguely. "Oh, you name it, she's embraced it. I think it was one way of getting back at my father for his endless succession of bimbos. Spends oceans of money. I think she sees herself as a latter-day Joan of Arc or something, The past year it has been Macedonia *über alles,* egged on by her old flame, Hans. Next year it'll probably be something else, or maybe she'll go on the hunt for another husband. Let's hope so!"

"So Kepplik is interested in Macedonia?" Penny persevered.

"I doubt it, but who knows?" Melissa shrugged. "More likely he's trying to rekindle that old flame, with a sharp eye on the Ribotis millions for himself."

"If so, he's going about it in a rather odd fashion, isn't he?" Penny observed.

"You mean Michele?" Vincent put in. "I think she's just window dressing to show what a macho German type he is. He spends most of his time with Olympia. Poor old Michele must be fit to be tied, or maybe . . ." he looked at his wife ". . . he brought her along to attract and distract your father's lecherous eye while he and Olympia played footsies, and she's now redundant."

To Penny's surprise, instead of flaring up at his outrageous statement, Melissa gave it serious thought. Finally she shook her head. "No, for one thing, Michele wasn't his type. He liked the tall, emaciated model type or large blond Brunhilds. Wasn't into pocket Venuses at all. Amazing how short men seem to favor tall women, isn't it?"

"Not all of them," Vincent retaliated amiably. "Look at me— picked a mini–pocket Venus, didn't I? At this rate we'll probably produce midgets."

"Oh, you!" Melissa punched him fondly on the arm. "At five-eight you're *tall* for a Greek."

"But small for an American," he said. "Still, what's it matter? Look at tiny Napoleon, look at teensy Attila the Hun! I have inches on them, so should do a lot better at ruling the world." Melissa gurgled with laughter.

Feeling she had had about all she could stand of love-smitten, gilded youth at its most fatuous, Penny got up. "Well, my young friends, thank you for having me, but I must get back to the yacht and wait for a phone call from my family."

They made polite dissenting noises, but got up themselves. "Lovely seeing you, come again tomorrow," Vincent urged, his arm around Melissa, and as Penny walked away she saw them hurry into the house.

As she walked out of the compound gates and across the quay to the pier, she mentally scrubbed them off her list of viable suspects. Unless they were the world's most consummate actors—which she doubted—she could not envisage either or both of them plotting and carrying out the cold-blooded murders of the Marolakis. It was a thought she would definitely pass on to the worried Jules in hopes of shaking something loose or, at least, easing his mind . . . At that juncture another horrible possibility struck her. What if all this time it wasn't Vincent he had been worrying about, but *Juliette*? No one had even considered her as a possibility because of the apparent lack of motive. And yet a case *could* be made: She was skilled at karate, she had known of Marcus's collection, and she had no alibi other than being asleep in her cabin alone during the period of Georgiou's murder. She was emotionally volatile and her motive, although unusual, was not unknown in the annals of murder—naked jealousy and spite towards a favored brother and an uncaring father.

Having made her case, Penny proceeded to make holes in it. For Georgiou's murder Juliette would have needed help— so whom could she have had for an accomplice? With money no object she could have bribed someone, but that seemed unlikely, unless . . . She grimaced as she realized that Preftakis's hasty departure had come quickly after Juliette's own; had he gone in search of a promised pay-off?

Her musings had taken her back on board the *Silver Spray*, and spotting Tom Andersen on the bridge, she made for him. "Any word on Preftakis?" she enquired.

"None that I know of, but Major Karras is with Mr. Lefau now, so he may have an update," he said. "And there was a phone call for you."

"From my son?"

"No, Sir Tobias. Wanted to let you know he would be returning this evening."

"Oh," she said flatly, not knowing whether that boded well or ill. "Well, I am expecting a call from Dr. Spring, so be sure and fetch me, will you?"

"Can do," Andersen said, and returned to working up the log.

She hung around the deck hoping to catch Karras, and was shortly rewarded when he appeared on deck looking far more amiable than during their previous encounter. "Any sign of Preftakis?" she again enquired.

He steered her to the bow and leaned on the rail facing her. "No luck on Theodopolis's or Kepplik's yachts; no one admits seeing him, but I searched the vessels anyway, as well as the Marolakis yacht, which only has a security guard on board—nothing! Just to cover all bases I'm off to check the village and Ribotis. Preftakis doesn't appear to have stolen anything; in fact, Mr. Lefau says he has some wages coming that he did not pick up."

"How frustrating for you," she sympathized.

"Not entirely. It gave me another excuse for seeing our two millionaires out there." He jutted his chin at the inner harbour. "And to try out a bright idea Colonel Vassos came up with. In view of the pressure from on high I was to dangle the prospect of an early release from Marolakis before them—not that we have any such intention—and to note their reactions. They both reacted in the same way: Neither wants to go and both said so vehemently. How does that strike you?"

She pondered. "It's as if they are waiting for something to happen here?"

He nodded. "Exactly what I thought—now if only we can find what that is. Any ideas?"

"Ideas, yes; facts, no," she said slowly. "I told you Sir Tobias was off on a hot lead? Well, he may have something definite by the time he gets back tonight. Will you be back tomorrow?"

"Probably," he sighed, "unless the powers-that-be have their way. Can't you give me something now?"

"The only thing I can safely say at the moment wouldn't be of much help to you in your case, since it rests on the observations of a young child," she parried. "But would it be possible for you to get permission to search the whole island? You could use the missing Preftakis as an excuse, couldn't you?"

He looked at her curiously. "Search where, and for what?"

"Primarily the caves along the north shore, but for what I don't know exactly at this point."

"That would need one hell of a lot of men and a lot of organization. I could put it to Vassos, but I can't see him going for it unless I give him a good reason. With things as they are, an AWOL seaman wouldn't warrant it," he pointed out.

"Exactly, so come back tomorrow and maybe Sir Tobias can give you the reason," she urged.

"Would this have anything to do with Theodopolis?"

"Very much so. You see, the observer was my young grandson, and Theodopolis made a great point of trying to keep him quiet about it."

"Theodopolis seems to be making a great point of keeping everybody quiet," Karras said grimly. "Well, I'd best collect Lefau and then get off to Speria. See you tomorrow, then?"

"You're taking him *again!*" she cried.

"Vassos wants the pressure on him kept up until he feels like talking," he said with a tight smile, "because we know damn well he has something up his sleeve, and until he comes across with it we aren't about to let up."

"Poor Jules!" she sighed, and was left alone with her gloomy thoughts.

She dined in solitary state with the chef Ledoux acting as waiter. He had prepared an excellent coq au vin and after she had praised it enthusiastically he seemed inclined to linger. Seizing the chance, she said, "Seeing it's only us, why don't you sit down and have some wine and keep me company for a while?"

He didn't need a second invitation, but filled a large glass with red wine and sat down, looking expectant. "So difficult for you with all these comings and goings," she sympathized. "And now being so shorthanded as well."

"*On arrive quand même*—one gets by," he said.

"What can you tell me about Preftakis?" she went on. "It may help with the search for him."

"*Pas grand-chose*—not much. He speak Greek and not much English, I French and not much English," Ledoux said. "He do his job well. He not—how you say?—mix much. But a lot better I think than Watts."

"Watts? Who's he?"

"The Yank he take the place of. No-good, lazy bum," Ledoux snorted. "Do anything for a buck. Sick mother—bah! Get a pocketful of money from somewhere and cannot wait to take off. Maybe he steal it and is afraid of getting—how you say?— pinched."

She looked at him with mounting interest. "And how did Captain Andersen find Preftakis to replace him?"

"Watts find him. Show telegram about sick mother, say, 'Gotta go but I find this replacement.' Captain look at his papers, see he's okay seaman, and has no time to look around— Mr. Lefau coming the next day—so he say okay. Must have known Watts lying, 'cos he not even ask for airfare and he always a mean son of a bitch . . ." They were interrupted by the arrival of a poker-faced Toby. Ledoux drained his glass and leapt to his feet. "Ah, Sir Toby! You like some coq au vin? *Et après, les fromages et fruits?*"

Toby slumped wearily into a chair next to Penny and nodded. "Sounds splendid, Ledoux. Any Bordeaux?"

"A good bottle I bring you—St. Emilion?"

"Very good." As the chef sped away, Toby looked at her quizzically. "Consorting with the hired help?"

"To good purpose," she replied. "Looks as if Preftakis, or someone behind him, *paid* to get aboard the *Silver Spray*— which leads to all sorts of interesting possibilities. And now he's flown the coop—mission maybe accomplished?"

They fell silent as Ledoux returned with the wine, Toby's dinner, and the cheese and fruit platter. "Anything else you wish?" he asked anxiously.

"No, that'll be all, Ledoux. This is excellent," Toby said. "Thank you, we'll just help ourselves."

As soon as the chef was out of earshot, Penny said, "Someone's trying to shut down further police investigation here—Karras thinks it's Theodopolis."

Toby's face tightened as he poured wine for them both. "That doesn't surprise me in the least. The doors I had so carefully opened yesterday were firmly shut in my face today. No one knew anything or would give me access to anything."

"But that might be Ribotis at work," she said quickly.

Toby grunted. "I doubt it. The only cooperation I received today was *from* Ribotis's office. They share the same building with Olympia's outfit but not the same staff, so I got nothing on her end of it, but I did find that the one ship of his apparently involved had an explanation for its delay near the island—engine trouble. Anyway, it didn't stop me. I went to the embassy, got through to Barham, filled him in on our theory, and he's having some of the local operatives zero in on it. One of them's meeting me in Hydra tomorrow. I can't go trailing into Athens every day, it wastes too much time."

"Damn!" she said, "I hoped you'd have something for Karras tomorrow."

"Oh God! You didn't *tell* him about this, did you?" he exploded.

"Simmer down! Not in detail, no. Just enough to stimulate his growing interest in Theodopolis." Rapidly she went on to relate her own findings.

When she got to her suspicions about Juliette he snorted in derision. "Poppycock! You're forgetting she speaks no Greek, and from my own observation Preftakis spoke very little English. I doubt whether anyone could arrange a complicated frame-up without communicating in depth, and you've just said yourself that Preftakis was a plant from the word go, so how does that fit in? It doesn't. No, we've got to concentrate on the main issue . . ."

"Oh Lord!" she interrupted. "I've only just remembered about Michele. She was supposed to contact me, and how on earth is she going to do that if I'm cooped up down here? What do you think I'd best do—go and lurk on deck or on the pier?"

He shrugged. "I doubt whether she'll try it tonight, particularly if, as you've indicated, Kepplik was in a foul mood. Maybe you should make yourself visible on the quay tomorrow morning and hope for the best. Any idea what it was about?"

"None, that's all she said. Oh, by the way, Alex called to announce safe arrival and all well. Benedict left them and has gone to Hydra, so they're staying in Nauphlia and taking day trips around Argos for the next few days."

"One less thing to worry about," he said and stifled a yawn. "I'm all in favor of an early night—how about you? Tomorrow promises to be hectic even as far as the weather is concerned. We're supposed to be in for a storm."

"Oh rats!" she grumbled. "But at least we're fairly sheltered here and this yacht's pretty stable, not like *The Dancing Lady*."

They finished their dinner and sought their cabins: Toby had inherited Benedict's and Penny the adjacent one that had been Sonya's. As she settled down in the comfortable bed she thought of Mala's last Delphic utterance. What on earth could she have meant? she thought drowsily. Her memories of *Star Wars* were admittedly vague, but she tried to remember Obi-Wan Kenobi: an old man posing as a hermit, the last of the Jedi warriors. Gave his life for the cause, a "good guy . . . So thinking, she drifted off into a deep sleep.

She was awakened, totally disoriented in the darkness, by the thudding of feet on the deck and confused shouting. There was a thunderous knocking on the door, then Toby's knoblike head was outlined by the corridor light. "You'd better get up. There's a bad fire on one of the yachts and it could spread. There's a gale blowing."

Chapter 16

Throwing on her clothes, Penny raced up on deck, where the gale-force wind snatched her breath away and sent her scuttling back down for a warm jacket. Emerging more cautiously the second time, she made for the stern and, clutching the rail to steady herself from the bucking of the ship against the angry sea, looked out on an infernal, Dantesque scene. Dark clouds, lit by the occasional lightning flash, scudded overhead before the gale, all but obscuring the full moon; she saw the dark bulk of Theodopolis's yacht apparently getting underway and turning towards the fitful glow beyond it, from which fiery fragments were shooting into the sky like fireworks. So it was Kepplik's yacht that burned!

As she watched, the floodlights of the Marolakis compound came on, illuminating the quay and pier, and she saw Toby's tall figure about to board the *Silver Spray*'s launch, which already held the life-jacketed figures of Ohlsen, Andersen, and Ari. She leaned over the rail and screamed down at him, "Toby, for heaven's sake, don't *you* go! Leave it to the young men."

He looked up, waved, and bellowed back, "This is a bad one. Going to need everyone. See you later," and hopped smartly aboard as the launch plowed into the waves. To add to the confusion of the scene, she was startled to see the slim silhouette of Ribotis's yacht, under full power and spuming water

from its bow, cut across Theodopolis's bow and head for the
flickering light beyond. How on earth did he get here so
quickly? she thought in stupefaction.

Theodopolis's yacht effectively cut off her own view of what
was going on beyond it, so she transferred her attention to the
floodlit quay, where figures were now popping out through
the compound gates. She made out the Pappas brothers, both
fully clothed and apparently arguing furiously, then behind
them the slim, pyjama-clad figure of Vincent Lefau and a bur-
lier figure, also in bathrobe and pyjamas, that set her pulses
pounding: It was Kepplik. A chill went through her that had
nothing to do with the howling gale, for there was no sign of
Michele.

Instinctively she looked towards the mansion, and was again
riveted by what she saw. On the brilliantly floodlit upper balcony, framed in a large French window, stood a white-clad,
statuesque figure. It was Olympia. Her hands were clasped
loosely in front of her, her stance was relaxed and tranquil as
a kore statue, and, to add the final touch to this impression, on
her impassive face was the enigmatic Etruscan smile of the
Mona Lisa.

Penny stood gripping the rail convulsively, her mind a whirl
of chaotic thoughts, as what seemed an eon of time rolled by.
A dull *crump* of an explosion brought her attention back to
the harbour scene, and when she next looked at the balcony,
Olympia was gone and the windows closed. The group on the
quay had also disappeared back into the compound. She shut
her eyes, trying to clear her thoughts, and when she opened
them again it seemed that the flickering light had grown fainter.
With relief she saw the ship's launch fighting its way back to
the quay with Toby's round head clearly visible, and at the
same time heard the throb of a helicopter overhead and saw it
settling down on the pad in the compound: the police already?

As the launch docked, Toby and Ari sprang out and hurried
towards the gangway, as the captain and Ohlsen moored the

boat. Toby came up to her, his face begrimed with smuts from the fire.

"Well, it's under control, thanks mainly to Ribotis's quick action, but it looks bad. Not a sign of life from it, so it seems as if our murderer has got his third millionaire."

"You're wrong there," she managed to get out. "Look!" She pointed to the quay where Kepplik, now fully dressed, and Constantine Pappas had reappeared and were running towards Andersen and Ohlsen.

Toby's jaw dropped. "Well, I'll be damned! How . . ."

"He was sleeping at the house. Came out a while ago in pyjamas. But there has been no sign of Michele."

They looked at each other in quiet horror, and he said tightly, "That fire was no accident, that I'd swear to—it was too fierce and spread too quickly, and there was an explosion that took out part of the hull."

"Then it's sinking?"

"No—thanks again to Ribotis's and Theodopolis's quick action. They've got grapples on either side of her, and that should keep her afloat until she cools down enough to get on board and see what the hell has gone on. With Kepplik out of it that means there are two crewmen and Michele still unaccounted for. What the devil was he doing in the compound?"

"I can think of one thing. The widow Marolakis appeared in a very fetching negligee to watch the scene. She seemed to view the fire with relish," she said grimly. "Look, here come the police!"

A dishevelled and blue-chinned Karras, flanked by a small squad of police, shot out of the gates and raced over to where Kepplik and Pappas were engaged in what appeared to be an angry exchange with the crew of the *Silver Spray*.

"Just as well they are here this quickly," Toby said, "although no one will be able to get aboard for hours. We may as well pack it in and try and get some rest."

"I couldn't after all this! Let's go and see if we can find

some coffee in the galley. I can't rest until I find out about Michele—oh *why* didn't I follow up on that? If anything has happened to her, I'll never forgive myself," Penny cried.

"You can't blame yourself," he said quickly. "It was up to her, if it was that urgent."

They went in silence down to the galley, only to find that a tousled Ledoux had anticipated them and that coffee and cognac were already ready in the saloon. They were shortly joined there by Tom Andersen and Ohlsen, both even more begrimed than Toby. "At least they can't blame this one on Mr. Lefau," Ohlsen said cheerfully, as they settled around the table with mugs of steaming coffee. "Though it leaves a lot of other people with a hell of a lot of explaining to do. Just as well Karras gave Ari hell yesterday so that he really was on watch tonight and can give us all the 'all clear.'"

"How did the police get here so quickly?" Penny asked.

"Ribotis. According to Karras, Ribotis's captain got worried that his yacht would suffer storm damage moored where it was, so headed for open water to ride out the storm; Ribotis went with him. They spotted the fire just getting started below decks on Kepplik's, headed straight for it, and radioed the Athens police. Ribotis even had the forethought to get his pumps primed so that they could start hosing the minute they arrived, and, to give him his due, Theodopolis wasn't too behind him on that. Still, if they hadn't got their grapples out fast, she'd have gone for sure after that explosion, and that would have been the end of her; the water is bloody deep in this crater."

"What were you arguing with Kepplik about?" Toby demanded.

"Oh, him!" Tom Andersen snorted. "Wanted us to take him and Pappas out to the yacht. Got all bent out of shape when I told him it was useless and that Theodopolis and Ribotis had things in hand; that she'd be too hot for hours to get aboard but she was in no danger of sinking. I was thankful when the cops turned up; things were turning real nasty."

"Did he explain why he was on the island and not on his yacht?"

"First thing Karras asked. Kepplik said he was expecting an important early-morning business call from South America, so Mrs. M. had invited him to stay, since he'd been having problems with his own communications system. All very innocent *sounding*." Andersen gazed steadily at Toby. "Also, according to him there were only two people on board—his fancy lady and one crewman; the other he'd let go to Hydra that afternoon on family business. That explains why his launch wasn't there. Pappas ferried Kepplik to the compound in one of theirs."

They looked at him in horror. "Meaning the others were *stuck* out there?"

"Unless they had a spare life raft, yes. And that we'd have seen, even if it had capsized on launching," he said flatly. "Theodopolis had his launch out searching, and now the police have commandeered all the Marolakis boats and will do their own searching. But it doesn't look good."

"Then there is nothing to be done?" Penny said.

"No, not until the yacht cools down." He got up. "I, for one, am going back to bed, and I suggest everyone else do the same. By morning this storm will have blown itself out and the wreck should be boardable. Then we should find out what the bad news is, and I have the feeling it may be a very long day."

Reluctantly they followed his suggestion and, despite her protestations, Penny fell heavily asleep, her dreams flame-filled and chaotic. When she finally awakened, it was to find that Andersen had prophesied truly, for the sun was blazing from a cloudless sky, although the ship still heaved on the sullenly subsiding sea. Going on deck she saw that the launch was gone, and on further investigation found that she and Ledoux were again alone.

"What horror!" he exclaimed with a certain amount of relish, as he brought her a fresh pot of coffee. "The others, they go to the wreck. The chief of police, he say for you to stay put. He must speak with you later. Oh, and Mr. Lefau, he comes back today."

Having finished her coffee, she found she had no appetite for anything else, so went up and roamed restlessly around the deck. The compound, apparently devoid of life, drowsed in the sun; nor was there any sign of activity on Theodopolis's yacht, although she could see the white stern of Ribotis's craft sticking out beyond it. She scanned the skies anxiously for signs of a police helicopter bearing Jules, longing for someone with whom she could share her anxieties, but as the morning wore on there was nothing. It was only when the launch returned and Toby stalked on board, looking like a thundercloud, that she could relieve her pent-up feelings. "For God's sake, what's *happening?*"

He came up to the rail and grasped it, his knuckles white. "Karras will be along later, and I think we'd better tell him *all* we have so far, and I do mean all. They aren't letting anyone—not even Kepplik—on board the yacht, but they have recovered three bodies from it. That's all I can tell you."

"Oh my God, *three!*" she cried. "But who . . .?"

"There is one person missing the police did not find, isn't there?"

"*Preftakis?* But Karras searched those boats yesterday. How could it be Preftakis?"

"Karras searched them yesterday afternoon. Plenty of time for Preftakis to have slipped aboard later before the storm. One thing the searchers did find last night was a floating raft like the one Marcus used for his escapade. Preftakis could have used that to get to the yacht from the island or from another boat." He fell silent for a moment. "It does rather alter the picture. What if Kepplik was the target after all? Preftakis gets on board, sets the ship on fire, and then gets caught in it himself?"

"But *why?* What possible motive?"

"Because he'd been paid to—just as he was paid to kill

Marolakis," Toby replied. "Possibly even the old man—you said yourself he was with the group when Constantine Pappas made all the fuss about the insect collection. Which, I believe, brings us back to Theodopolis."

"I just can't believe it," she said flatly. "It seems poor Michele has to be one of the dead, and she had something to tell me without Kepplik being around, so he has to be in on it in some way."

"Until we know what's what, it is useless speculating." Toby looked at his watch and sighed. "I hope Karras gets a move on, I'm supposed to meet Young's contact in Hydra at two o'clock."

His wish was shortly granted, as Karras came on board while a cortege carrying the three body bags made for the helicopter. Apart from his unshaven blue chin, his face was a pasty white even to his lips, and the first thing he said was, "I need a brandy—badly." They quickly got him down to the saloon and supplied him with a large tumblerful, which he gulped down with a trembling hand. "I have seen some terrible things in the gutters of the slums of Athens, but nothing to compare with what I have just seen on that millionaire's yacht," he stated, and looked at them, his dark eyes hard as chips of obsidian. "Now I want *all* you know, down to the very last detail. This must be the end of the killings."

Toby looked at Penny and became spokesman. "And that we will most surely do. But first, Major, it is rather vital that we know what you found on that yacht. I assure you that whatever you tell us will go no further."

Karras gave a furious bark of mirthless laughter. "What we found? Oh yes, I'll tell you. One Greek seaman, dead in the stern, shot in the head. The fire started amidships, so his body was only partly consumed. Two heavily charred nude bodies in bed in the main sleeping cabin where the fire apparently started; one male, one female. They will take some identifying, but we presume the female body to be Michele Dubois.

161

As to the male body—since we know it is not Kepplik and we have contacted the other Kepplik seaman on Hydra—we are assuming it is the missing seaman, Preftakis."

"Were they also shot?" Penny quavered.

"Hard to say, owing to the state of the bodies; only an autopsy will reveal that. One thing we can say is that the fire was no accident and the boat was meant to sink. Now it's your turn. Sir Tobias, you first."

"You have to understand that the same hand that attempted to close down your investigation also succeeded in cutting off mine," Toby began. "However, I have opened another channel and hope to have something substantive from a meeting on Hydra that I simply must get to this afternoon. But this is what we have thus far . . ."

When he had finished, Karras looked at him in stunned silence. "Arms smuggling? And not an atom of proof? What is this?"

"No proof as yet. But I'm banking on the fact that our millionaires are hanging about for a further shipment, which must be due shortly—of what it consists I have no idea at present. But even now a search of those caves may yield some tangible evidence of activity," Toby urged.

"But what the hell has that got to do with this present horror?" Karras bellowed. "That had to have been aimed at Kepplik."

"Not necessarily," Penny broke in. "You haven't heard me yet. The target could well have been Michele. You saw her talking to me yesterday at the pool? Well, she was about to tell me something very important, very *urgent,* she said, but then became scared when she saw you coming and said she'd contact me later. Someone made very sure she didn't." She had a hard time getting her voice under control to tell him the rest of it, ending with, "Although I still think our main suspect is obvious, I also think—in view of what I observed last night—that Kepplik has some heavy explaining to do. Something Vincent Lefau said yesterday keeps running through my mind—that Michele had become redundant to whatever is going on here. And when something or someone becomes redundant—it is disposed of."

Karras looked at them in growing frustration. "But Kepplik has a reasonable explanation and an ironclad alibi, backed up one hundred per cent by Olympia Marolakis. According to them, both he and Michele were invited to dinner at the mansion, but Michele begged off, saying she wasn't feeling well. And it was only *after* dinner that the suggestion was made for him to stay at the house and Pappas sent out to get his overnight things and his briefcase. Pappas confirms that Michele and the crewman were both alive at that time and that, if anything, she seemed relieved rather than upset by his staying away overnight. If she were expecting Preftakis, that would make sense. As you suggest, I will indeed make further enquiries about all Kepplik's telephone calls, but there is one man who has a lot more explaining to do—Theodopolis. It was a small miracle that Ribotis's yacht happened to spot the fire at its very onset; his prompt action, in both tackling the fire and securing the yacht so that it did not sink, saved it. Otherwise it would have sunk beyond recall and we never would have known what happened on it.

"But where was Theodopolis? Supposedly he had a man on watch. He was right next to the yacht. The fire must have been as evident to him as it was to Ribotis but, as you have testified yourselves, he did not move into action until Ribotis's yacht got there. True, he had a hand in saving the yacht from sinking—but what other option did he have once Ribotis was on the scene? No, our billionaire and his American millionaire partner have much explaining to do."

Penny looked at him, astounded. "You don't mean Jules? He wasn't even here."

"Just because he was in Athens, doesn't mean he wasn't

involved," Karras replied. "We have considerable evidence now that he and Theodopolis were in constant touch even before the murder of Georgiou Marolakis."

This thunderbolt struck her silent, but Toby, who had been sunk in deep thought, roused himself and said quietly, "Of course, there is another possibility about this present atrocity. You and all your men, Major, will no doubt be concentrating on this to the exclusion of everything else?"

They both looked at him in amazement. "You can damn well bet on it," Karras roared. "Nobody is going to stop us now. What the hell are you getting at?"

"That, seeing you were not going to be pressured into giving up on your investigation, our murderer needed a diversion—a gigantic red herring, if you will—to focus your attention away from the real cause of all this: the cause that may be on its way to the island at this very moment. So may I have your permission to go to Hydra and continue with *my* investigation?"

Karras looked as if he might explode. "You can go where you damn well please, but three murders a red herring? I think your idea is nuts—you're crazy!"

"No," Toby said softly, "I'm not crazy, but I'm beginning to think our murderer might be."

Chapter 17

"I have an acute case of cabin fever and if I find the returning Jules in his usual tight-lipped state after Karras's latest bombshell about him and Theodopolis, I might just murder him myself, so I'm coming with you to Hydra," Penny declared.

"I will gladly *take* you to Hydra," Toby agreed cautiously, "but you can't hang around me or it may scare my contact off. You'll be on your own."

She snorted. "I'm quite used to that, and it'll be a relief after the past few days. I can make myself useful by seeing if the Schuylers did what they said they would and are therefore off the hook on this latest horror. Then I can sightsee. We'll rendezvous back at the launch whenever you say."

"Fair enough, let's make that five-thirty then. I'd like to be back by seven, because Karras thinks the preliminary autopsy results might be in by then, and that may clarify things about the sequence of events last night."

She didn't enjoy the trip across, for the sea was still roiling from the storm, but once safely moored to the stone quay in Hydra's small harbour, she cheered up and set off up the steep hill beyond with mounting spirits, leaving Toby still mooring the launch. Her investigative errand was soon done; knowing Juliette, she made a beeline for the ritziest hotel on the island—the Hotel Miranda Hydra—and hit pay dirt right away.

Yes, the Schuyler family had been there, had been joined by a large, fair man called Lefau, and had gone on to Athens two days previously. "So that shoots down my Juliette theory," she told herself, and in a moment of reckless exuberance hired a horse-drawn carriage, which had been sitting before the hotel, and its elderly English-speaking guide for the "grand tour" of the island at an exorbitant price.

He showed off the elegant "showpiece" mansions, the monasteries and convents in approved tourist style, and she discovered as they chatted that he had owned a Greek restaurant in Miami Beach for many years. "And you gave it all up to come back here?" she exclaimed.

"Ah, Miami nowadays is no place to be," he said. "Too violent, too unpleasant, too many murders." He went on at considerable and disparaging length about the "Cuban invasion" of Florida. "Ruined it," he snorted. "So I come back to my birthplace. My children are still in America—my son a lawyer in Shreveport, my daughter a dentist in Atlanta. Do very well. They come for holidays here every year. I show you my house . . ." They drove past an impressive stone mansion, almost buried in cypresses, in the upper town.

"You live there and yet you drive a carriage!" she exclaimed in surprise. He grinned back at her. "Ah, we Greeks like to keep busy and to make money. I only work when the weather is fine and when I feel like it, but I give you a good tour."

"Could you go right to the top so I can see the view to the east?" she prompted.

"Whatever you wish, but you will have to walk a little to get the best view. I'll show you." He was as good as his word. The northeast wind was still strong and snatched at their words as they stood looking over the spectacular scene. "You wish to see the islands of the millionaires, eh?" He grinned and produced a pair of binoculars from a pocket of his capacious overcoat.

She focussed the glasses on the islands and saw that there

had been some rapid changes. The Ribotis yacht was back at its Speria mooring; the Theodopolis yacht was on its daily cruise around the island; and the Kepplik wreck was now beached by the village on the inner part of the crescent. Two helicopters stood on the pad in the compound. She handed the glasses back and remarked, "Greece, too, is not without its violence and murders," hoping to pick up some local opinion.

"In Athens, maybe, but not here in the islands," he said with pride. He waved an expansive hand around. "Here we are crime-free."

Her interest quickened, as evidently the news of the Marolakis murders had not reached its nearest neighbour—and that would explain the singular absence of the media, which, up to now, she had not even considered. To keep anything that quiet did indeed indicate some mighty forces at work.

"So now I take you back to the hotel?" he asked.

She looked at her watch and let out a gasp of dismay; it was already after five o'clock. "I had no idea it was this late. No, please take me to the harbour and as fast as you can." And at breakneck speed they careered back down the mountain and through the narrow streets of Hydra. "There at the quay, that launch!" She pointed to where she could see Toby pacing anxiously up and down, his face a study in dismay.

"You pay in dollars and I give you a ten per cent discount," her guide said grandly. "And come back soon, you're a nice lady."

Meekly she handed over most of her dollars and rushed up to Toby. "What is it? You look as if you've been run over by a steamroller."

"Get in and I'll cast off," he replied. "We've got to hurry. Tell you on the way back, but it's much worse than I thought. In fact, it's bloody terrible."

He roared away from the quay at a speed that took her breath away, but once free of the harbour he shouted, "Cling on to something and stay near me. I can't shout all the way back to

Marolakis, and we have to decide what to do before we see Karras. You'll soon see why."

She did as she was told and yelled in his ear, "Get on with it."

"With the info I gave them, Barham's network has done miracles, but the news is all bad," he said in a more normal voice. "Trouble is that they have the beginning and end of the story but not the middle bit, which is where we come in. They are almost certain that the shipments that came out of Varna are Russian missiles from Afghanistan that were never recovered by them after the war there. Those coming out of the Ukraine have been mainly smaller arms like high-power automatic weapons, antitank bazookas, and the like—again, apparently stolen Russian surplus—that is, up till now. But I'll get back to that later. Word in Trieste is that none of these arms has shown up there, but they do report fairly consistent tardy arrivals of the Ribotis Cycladic freighters, which may indicate a drop-off stop along the Croatian coast. Word is that in Croatia there is an arms buildup backed by *German* neo-Nazi groups. Similarly, there is an extremist Greek separatist group operating in Greek Macedonia, the objective being to unite with the rest of what was Yugoslavian Macedonia. It is basically an anti-Serb movement—indeed, the Croatian movement is, also—and they are being supported by Moslem and Albanian elements there. Our people can't trace the source of the buildup there, but it looks very much as if the Croats may be about to launch an onslaught on the Serbs, with Macedonia as a second front; that would literally put Serbia between two fires. Worst of all is the latest development. You remember quite a while back that the Ukraine agreed to dispose of all its long-range nuclear missiles, but that they had to be shipped back to Russia for the warheads to be deactivated?" Penny nodded mutely. "Well, in a recent shipment they came up one short—and *that* may be what our millionaires have been waiting for."

"Oh, my God!" She was aghast. "But surely a huge thing like that couldn't be *hidden!* Why not just stop all ships en route or something?"

"It can apparently be broken down into much smaller and easily disguised elements—except for the warhead itself. I have the feeling that Gregor Vadik may have been working for the Russians on this one, because they are fit to be tied and are sabre rattling at the Ukraine like crazy. Being Slavs themselves, they are fundamentally pro-Serbs—also Slavs—and that the Ukraine has let one slip away from them, probably for use against Serbs, is panicking them."

"But they'd ruin the whole of Yugoslavia if they exploded it there!" she cried. "It doesn't make sense."

"Their civil war has already done a pretty good job of doing that, so maybe they are beyond caring," Toby said grimly. "But you've made a good point, and it's one that's worrying our own people. They could launch it against *any* European capital and blame it on the Serbs and Russians, and that would really put the fat in the fire. I simply *have* to get Karras into action to search the island, no matter what it takes. Maybe if we can just scare them away long enough for the Greek navy to move into action it'll serve its purpose."

"What about the people involved? Did you get any names?"

"No question that the ships used are Olympia's, and the name Marolakis has been murmured."

"How about the others?"

He shook his head. "Not a word—it's all so damn nebulous."

"Somebody high up in the Greek government must be collaborating to keep things this quiet. Not a word about the murders has reached Hydra, and that also explains the absence of the media."

"Yes, I *had* noticed that peculiarity," he said stiffly, and gave his whole attention to his steering.

They reached the island in record time and, as they drew

into the pier, saw a police launch ahead of them in which Karras was quietly talking to a small squad of uniformed police. He hailed them as they stepped out of their launch. "Dr. Spring, Sir Tobias—over here, if you please. I am most anxious to speak with you." He waved them into his own launch as the squad of police dispersed. "This place is as good as any to talk—we can't be overheard," he stated. "I have the results of the autopsies for you, and it has helped me to come to a decision . . ."

"What we have to say may alter whatever that is," Toby said quickly, "and it is extremely urgent."

Karras stayed him with a gesture. "All in good time, Sir Tobias. First, the bullet recovered from the head of the Greek seaman was a .38-calibre from a Smith and Wesson—a common American make, as you may know. It was fired at close quarters, indicating that the murderer was known to the seaman, who had no fear of letting him get close to him. Second, both bodies in the cabin were dead *before* the fire started: There was no smoke in their lungs. The cause of death for the Dubois woman has been established as a broken neck—one of her neck vertebrae had been all but severed by a blow: presumably our karate artist at work. As to the male corpse, the charring was so extreme that it is hard to establish the exact cause of death, but his Adam's apple was crushed, so we are pretty certain it was another karate-chop murder. There was no evidence of sexual intercourse in the woman's body, so we presume the bedroom 'scene' was an elaborate setup after the deaths—"

"Was the man Preftakis?" Penny asked.

"From the body itself we still can't be sure, but Ohlsen has identified a rather distinctive belt buckle found in the cabin as belonging to Preftakis. So I'd say, pending the dental check, yes, it is. The exact time of death has yet to be established, but that it was in no sense a rendezvous between Preftakis and Dubois may be surmised from the fact that her partly digested stomach contents indicated she had eaten only an hour or so prior to her death, whereas his stomach was virtually empty. Why the murderer should have bothered with such an elaborate charade is beyond me at the moment, considering the yacht was intended to sink without trace. The means of the explosion has yet to be ascertained, but in the flooded hold we did find three empty gasoline cans of a type similar to those on Theodopolis's launch. Very careless of him, considering all the rest of it, but enough to warrant some action." He tapped his pocket. "I have a warrant for his arrest and interrogation right here."

"And what about Jules Lefau?" Penny choked out, her throat constricted by the horror of it all.

"I think once Theodopolis is in custody, Mr. Lefau will be ready at long last to make a confession," Karras said blandly. "I have allowed him to go to the compound to talk with his son, and he indicated to me that he would clarify some matters if this were allowed."

"Look, this is all very interesting, but there is something far more urgent I have to tell you," Toby broke in. "Something that may well threaten not only the safety of this island but the whole of Greece, and on which action has to be taken *immediately,* both by the police and the Greek navy—so for God's sake listen!"

As Toby rapped out his story, Karras's expression passed from amazement through incredulity to anger. "I shall certainly pass on what you have said, but first things first. I'm going after Theodopolis," he barked.

"But at least damn well search the bloody caves!" Toby roared. "You've got men here. Even if the ship arrives, if it hasn't done so already, just seeing activity about them might scare it off long enough for your naval ships to move in. I *know* I have no concrete evidence to hand you but, damn it, the quickest way to get evidence might be in those caves. The rest can come later."

"I'm sorry but . . ." Karras paused. Jules Lefau was running through the gates of the compound and headed straight for them, his face distraught. "Karras," he gasped, "my son, his wife, Demetrios Pappas—they've all disappeared. The servants and I have searched everywhere for them—they're not in the compound or in the village and there are no boats missing. For God's sake, Major, have your men search the rest of the island immediately. They may be in deadly danger. I'll do anything you want, say anything you want, only please, I beg you, *do* something."

"That does it! No more messing around," Karras said abruptly, and picking up his walkie-talkie, roared into it, "You men watching the yacht, board it and bring Theodopolis in for questioning—oh, and bring those two blond Americans also—at gunpoint if necessary. Bring them to the *Silver Spray* pronto." He turned on Jules. "You're a bit late with your cooperation, Mr. Lefau, but your yacht will, I believe, be the suitable place for a showdown. Shall we go?" He turned to Toby. "I'll radio from the yacht about your concerns, though your worries may be groundless in view of what is now about to happen."

"I'd like to accompany you," Toby snapped. "I have some radio calls of my own that are vital. If the Greek navy won't move, maybe the British navy will."

A constable shepherded Jules on board and down to the saloon; Penny doggedly followed. There Jules sank into a chair and looked up at her despairingly. "Oh God, Penny, what have I done? If anything has happened to Vincent . . ." He choked and buried his face in his hands.

Penny quietly fixed them both a stiff drink and shooed away Ledoux, who had popped enquiringly in from the galley. "Tell the crew to stay out of the way," she whispered to him. "And tell Captain Andersen that Vincent and Melissa Lefau are missing. He and Ohlsen might want to take a tour around the island in the launch to see if they can spot something. *Compris?*"

"Mother of God!" he exclaimed. "I understand. Will do." He disappeared.

Karras returned and settled stony-faced at the head of the table. Toby, equally grim, followed shortly after, just as heavy footsteps overhead signalled the arrival of the police and Theodopolis. As he came down the companionway, Jules looked up at him and choked out, "Kristos, my son and his wife are gone. It's no use, I can no longer keep silent."

Theodopolis's saturnine face tightened slightly, but he nodded and looked over at Karras. "And what is the meaning of this, Major? I don't appreciate being hauled off my ship at gunpoint."

Karras got up and reached in his pocket. "It's no use, Theodopolis, your show's over. I have here a warrant for your arrest on grounds of conspiracy and suspicion of murder." He slapped the paper into Theodopolis's hand.

The billionaire glanced briefly at the taller of the two Americans behind him and gave a resigned shrug. He read the paper and said calmly, "I'm afraid this isn't worth the paper it's written on, Karras. It does not apply. You cannot arrest me."

"What!" Karras roared. "You think you can put yourself above the law of Greece, Kristos Theodopolis? Then *I* tell you, you are very much mistaken."

"No, I do not put myself above any law," Theodopolis returned. "But this warrant is made out for one Kristos Theodopolis—and I'm *not* Theodopolis."

Chapter 18

In the thunderstruck silence that followed this dramatic revelation, Theodopolis turned to the tall man and said, "John, in light of this latest development, I think we have to tell all and just hope that we can salvage something of our mission." He turned back to Karras. "Some introductions are in order, first." He nodded at the tall man. "John Roberts of the United States State Department; and your other detainee is Richard Forbes, an agent for the FBI. You did not round up our CIA man, Silas Green, who is posing as my radio operator. I am Kristos Stephanos, late of Interpol and now of the newly formed 'watchdog' security force of the European Community. For obvious reasons I carry no proof of my real identity, but both Roberts and Forbes can produce theirs." The two men reached slowly into their inside pockets and handed over their identifications. Seeing the total disbelief on Karras's face, Theodopolis went on quickly, "If you will accompany Roberts to the radio room and contact your minister of foreign affairs, he will confirm our identities and the nature of the undercover operation to which we have been assigned. And if that does not satisfy you, he will supply an emergency number at which Theodopolis himself can be reached."

Karras leapt to his feet. "Keep an eye on them," he barked

to his sergeant. "And if they try anything, shoot them. You, Roberts, come with me." He stamped out.

"Theodopolis" looked at Penny and Toby and shook his head sorrowfully. "We thought we had all our bases covered, but we didn't reckon on you two. How much have you found out?"

"Speaking as Stephanos or Theodopolis?" Toby asked drily.

"As Stephanos."

"We know about the arms smuggling, where it came from, and where it went to. What we don't know is if that warhead has reached the island and whether we may all be blown to smithereens at any moment." Toby was testy. "We also know that Preftakis was a plant on Lefau, but we don't know why that poor wretched girl and Kepplik's deckhand should have been murdered as well. Your doing?"

"No, just our very bad slip-up, I'm afraid," Stephanos sighed. "Preftakis wasn't Preftakis either, but he wasn't one of ours. And to put your mind at ease, the warhead hasn't arrived. It was due tonight, but the storm delayed it. Not to worry, though; the ship that's bringing it is being shadowed by a US nuclear submarine. The transfer will never take place now. It's just that we seem to have blown our chance to round up the ringleaders here and elsewhere. All we'll get are the little fish."

"To hell with that!" Jules Lefau suddenly roared. "What about my son and his wife? Why don't you *do* something instead of making speeches? Or are you going to make them sacrifices to your damned mission?"

Stephanos looked at him with compassion. "It's dark now and it would be useless to try and find them tonight. I promise you that at first light we'll have every inch of the island searched. I don't think they've been harmed; if anything, our opponent, in the best terrorist tradition, has taken hostages. Saving Kepplik's yacht from sinking probably caused it."

"And that opponent?" Penny broke her stunned silence.

"Has to be Kepplik, hasn't it?" Stephanos smiled bleakly. "Since 'Theodopolis' is out of it, he's all that's left. Look, it's a very complicated story, so I'd better wait for Karras."

The major shortly reappeared, looking bewildered and angry. "So," he snarled, "now I know who you really are, perhaps you'd explain this whole matter, and particularly the four, possibly five, *murders* it has occasioned."

Stephanos winced. "At the risk of seeming long-winded, I'll have to take it from the very beginning. It starts with the real Theodopolis being approached by a European syndicate with a proposition for rebuilding devastated areas of Yugoslavia and seeking his backing for it—there was money to be made from it eventually, so he went along with it. However, he is a very cautious man and so he sent one of his assistants out to former Yugoslavia to see how the money was being spent. His aide found little to account for the huge outlay and, in his wanderings, came across what appeared to be a large bunker in process of construction at a remote site in the Macedonian mountains. He came back, made his report, and they found that the land belonged to the Marolakis family. Another man was sent out to do further investigating and he disappeared without a trace.

"This alarmed Theodopolis, so he approached the FBI. In the meantime, the CIA had been keeping an eye on this same syndicate for possible violations of the arms embargo on Croatia; they'd learned of Theodopolis's connection with them and were keeping an eye on him. They suggested that he contact Demetrios Marolakis, posing as a prospective interested partner in whatever was going on. This Theodopolis did, only to find that Marolakis was totally unaware of the whole thing and was mightily upset by it. He suggested a meeting to investigate what was happening.

"At this, Theodopolis, who really *is* a recluse, balked, but signified to the Americans that he would not object to them sending a substitute, and would lend them every assistance—including, of course, his yacht and crew. The hunt for a Greek-speaking look-alike was then on and, thanks to the miracle of computer networks, unfortunately they came up with me. A change of hair color and some minor plastic surgery made me sufficiently like him to pass for the subject of any old photos that might still be around."

He paused and grimaced. "*Playing* a billionaire was something else, but I thought I could manage it for a day or two since none of the Marolakis family had ever seen or met me— nor, for that matter, had Kepplik. Then a further complication arose . . ."

Again he paused and looked down at Jules, who sat slumped in despair, his eyes blank and unfocussed. "Marolakis had already made arrangements for the Lefau visit, and we learned that Jules had actually met the real Theodopolis on a couple of occasions. So the State Department got after him, apprised him of some of what was going on, and asked for his cooperation as a patriotic American. As he, too, only anticipated a quick visit to the island, he agreed, and in spite of the ensuing debacle, has kept his promise of silence, much to his own cost."

Stephanos sighed and sank wearily into a chair beside the unheeding Jules before continuing. "Things started to go wrong almost from the start. First Kepplik showed up unexpectedly— the old man certainly hadn't invited him, so it had to have been Georgiou or Olympia Marolakis. Then Demetrios and I were supposed to meet Jules at Epidaurus to get our respective stories straight, but were hampered when Georgiou insisted on coming along also.

"With the benefit of hindsight, it's clear the old man thought his son had to be involved, so he wouldn't communicate in front of him." He looked at Penny. "So, as you know, I made myself scarce in a hurry and only managed a quick word with Jules later to set up a rendezvous and try it again on the island. But by that time it was all too late—Demetrios was dead, probably murdered, while I was waiting to see him upstairs, and the luncheon party was going on downstairs. At this point, I think Georgiou, who had to have been involved—but to what extent we'll probably never know—panicked and, I believe, was on his way to confide in Jules and ask his help when he was intercepted and murdered . . ."

He looked across the table at Karras. "The story of that night that Jules has been so steadfastly telling you is basically true— with one exception. He wasn't with his son that night, he was with me on my yacht, and I ferried him back myself." Jules stirred restlessly in his seat as Penny looked at him questioningly.

"We also know that the man who called himself Preftakis was planted on the yacht when it arrived in Athens. The seaman he replaced was bribed to go away and the real Preftakis, who we discovered is on a freighter bound for India, was also bribed to let his papers be duplicated. If this replacement was not the actual murderer of Georgiou—which now seems unlikely—he was undoubtedly an accomplice in getting the body into that pool. Maybe they hoped Lefau would be well away from the island before the body was discovered; but when it was, and the police were in on the action, well, they had a nice, handy suspect ready."

Stephanos took a deep breath. "As a result, we were all well and truly stuck here, and the only thing left for me to do at that point was to keep on being Theodopolis and to hang around acting suspiciously, in the hopes that Kepplik would believe me to be deeply involved in the arms smuggling— that he would contact me and betray himself in some way. But he has been very, very cautious. He was playing a waiting game with me and made no effort to contact me. Also, no transfer of cargoes had taken place since we had reached the island, and, though we knew two shipments were on their way, we were pretty certain no transfers would be made until the police cleared off. As you know, we did our damnedest to keep the lid on things and to try and get the police off our backs, the media away, and so on, but the police wouldn't be scared off, and then Sir Tobias turned up, doing his own investigating. We tried to turn him off too, but to no avail . . ."

He smiled wanly at Penny and Toby. "Trying to run you off was obviously the wrong tactic, but it was all I could think of. Should have known better, and, considering we thought we had closed all doors, I would be interested to learn how you managed to get so well informed in so short a time."

Karras interrupted him irritably. "This is all very well, but what about your actions on the night of the fire? How the hell do you explain them?"

Again Stephanos winced. "We goofed in a big way. We'd been keeping an eye on Kepplik, still hoping he'd contact me in some way; but when he went off to the compound that night we thought he was there for the night, as he has been several times before. Never dreamed that Preftakis would make for the yacht, or that there was any threat to it. When the fire broke out we were all down in the radio room, helping Green decode the latest input on the warhead and on Sir Tobias and his activities. No one was on deck watch. It was the merest fluke that we got into the action at all. One of Theodopolis's genuine crew got up to take a leak, spotted the flames, and raised the alarm. By the time we got into action, Ribotis was already on the scene. Incidentally, I don't buy his story, either. I think he was worried that his sister was up to something and was keeping a pretty sharp eye on things over here."

Karras was unimpressed. "And how do you account for your gas cans showing up in its hold?"

Stephanos looked at him in amazement. "*My* gas cans? First I've heard of it. In fact, you've done a great job of keeping things hush-hush. Mind telling me now exactly what you did find on the yacht?"

Grudgingly Karras supplied the bare outline. Stephanos looked puzzled. "Strange! It looks as if the bedroom scene was *meant* to be found and the gas cans to implicate me in the fire. So why the explosion? Almost looks like *two* hands involved. But that's beside the point now, as its objective is clear enough—

to keep you busy and to get rid of redundant and possibly trai- torous baggage, while putting Kepplik in the clear and pointing the finger at me. He's doing everything possible to keep you distracted until those two cargoes get through: That warhead might be their grand finale. We think the 'bunker' that Theodopolis's man found was, in fact, the uncompleted silo and launching pad for the completed missile." He looked quizzi- cally at Toby. "Would you agree?"

Toby was noncommittal. "Sounds plausible."

Stephanos sighed. "Anyway, it's all academic now. Nei- ther of those two cargoes will be allowed to reach its destina- tion, and the hunt tomorrow for the young couple will effectively end all hope of them trying the transfer here. So, I'm afraid we've missed our major objective. Kepplik seems to have out- smarted us, so we probably won't nail him, and worse, won't find out the major figure or figures behind him. I can't see any way to bring that about now."

Penny broke her long silence. "I've been sitting here in growing amazement, for in your lengthy explanation I haven't heard a word about Olympia Marolakis's role. Why is that?"

Stephanos looked at her in surprise. "Oh, her. Well, obvi- ously Kepplik's been using her—probably brainwashed her into going along with him because she's crazy about his manly charms. Used her ships, used her money, probably, and used her, period."

Penny looked around at the assembled men, whose faces— with the exception of Toby's, which was studiously blank— mirrored agreement and approval. "That is one of the most sexist and myopic statements I have heard in many a moon," she said. "And I see the consensus of opinion is with you. But let me tell you, not as a woman but as an anthropologist, that I think you are very wide of the mark; and being so far out, you may be missing the only way to get your mission successfully ac- complished."

They gaped at her as she went on. "Let me tell you how I

see Olympia Marolakis. I see her as an intelligent, frustrated, power-hungry woman trapped in the immemorial role of women in Greece, who, despite all protests to the contrary, are treated as second-class citizens and of little account in 'men's affairs.' Despite all her riches and her own abilities, this is what she has faced all her life. Think about it. Always having to play second fiddle to her brother because he is male and automatically 'superior'; second wife to a man who was, in my opinion, her inferior in intellect, who cheated on her flagrantly and openly, and who neglected her, her female child, and his daughter by his first marriage; required to dance to her father-in-law's tune, even to the extent of segregated eating. Frustrated beyond belief by all this, she embraced cause after cause, seeking an outlet that would satisfy her and give her a meaningful role, but found none—*up till now.*"

She appeared to go off on a tangent. "My son is an excellent doctor, and, after talking with her, he came up with some observations that made a lot of sense to me. Granted, Kepplik—probably a lover from her youth—may have, for his own ends, introduced her to the idea of a 'free Macedonia' that could once again emerge as the world power it had been in ancient times. This is an idea that she has not only embraced but become completely wrapped up in. In short, she has become a fanatic, and may even be a little crazy on this issue. And therein lies *your* key."

Toby gave a satisfied grunt, as Stephanos burst out, "What key? I don't see what you're getting at."

"I'm not surprised," she sniffed. "Just tell me one thing. Does Kepplik have any idea that you are *not* Theodopolis?"

He looked mystified. "No, none so far as I know."

"Good, then my plan should stand a chance. It will require a careful setting of scene and considerable acting by you as Theodopolis and you, Major, as the triumphant policeman. Everyone here, with the exception of Jules, who'll be out with the search parties, should be included, as well as all permanent inhabitants of the compound, especially Constantine Pappas. Oh, and it's important that Ribotis be kept away also. Now this is what I have in mind . . ." And in concise detail she went on, finishing with, "If things work out successfully, I think you may get the proofs you've been seeking. And I suggest, Major, that you put the wheels in motion tonight by phoning Mrs. Marolakis and apprising her of this early morning meeting, explaining that you have successfully solved the murder case and that you need her cooperation for a final showdown. That should get them nicely on edge for it tomorrow."

There was a stunned silence; Karras got his voice back first. "It just might work, you know," he said, looking reflectively at Stephanos, who replied, "Well, I'm game for it, though we'll need some heavy rehearsing. It's the longest of long shots, but we don't have any other options that I can see. Yes, it's worth a try."

"Then you'd both better get at it, hadn't you?" Penny said sweetly, getting up. "So we'll leave you to it. Come on, Jules, you'll need all your energy for tomorrow. Toby and I will see you to bed."

After they had steered the submissive and exhausted Jules to his cabin, Toby looked down at her with a grim smile. "Your inspired flights of imagination never cease to amaze me, although I always get the sinking feeling that one of these days they'll be the death of us. Let's hope it's not tomorrow!"

Chapter 19

"I'm thankful this is your show, not mine," Toby remarked as they walked towards the compound gates under a serene sky. "Talk about stirring the pot!"

Penny, who had been bustling about since dawn like an anxious stage manager before a first night, said edgily, "Well, even if it doesn't succeed in its main purpose, at least it'll clear the field for the search parties going after the young Lefaus and Demetrios Pappas. I'm pinning my faith on the villagers rather than the police. Headed up by Zehra's uncle, who seems to be their informal headman, every man, woman, and child is in on the act, and they know every nook and cranny of the place, so the lost must surely be found—alive, I hope, or it will be the finish of Jules."

"I suppose they've been warned there might be gunplay?" he queried.

"Not from the Macedonian guards there won't—they're all penned up in the compound, thanks to Karras; ditto the dogs. Theo . . . I mean Stephanos, was useful in pinpointing the cave apparently housing Marcus's 'pirate.' He thinks a permanent guard was left there between shipments just in case anyone got past the patrols and became too nosy about signs of activity on the beach. They'll leave that cave to the police."

They entered the compound and saw Karras standing with

Ari just out of view of the open French windows, and a crowd of house servants and the uniformed patrol guards milling disconsolately around the swimming pool under the watchful eye of two more policemen. "The police seem a bit thin on the ground," Toby observed.

"Every man who could be spared is out searching, but there'll be a couple more coming with Stephanos," she said. "Now, for God's sake, shut up and look uneasy and upset when we go in."

"That won't be difficult," he said, as they came up to Karras and Ari, who grinned cheerfully at them.

"Wipe that grin off your face," Karras snapped, "and keep your wits about you and your hand on your gun at all times—clear?"

Ari instantly sobered, as Karras took a deep breath and indicated the door. "Well, we're on. In you go."

They trooped into the grand salon, and at the first sight of Olympia a chill went through Penny and her heart sank. Robed in a billowing black-and-gold caftan, Olympia was ensconced in her high-backed chair in serene and queenly glory opposite the open door, Constantine Pappas standing guard at her right hand and Kepplik sitting on her left.

Her first words to Karras as he approached her throne increased Penny's dismay, for they indicated that Olympia was once more queen of the island, and this betokened ill for the missing lovers. "I do not appreciate this extraordinary demand of yours, Major Karras," Olympia stated. "I have only gone along with it because of your assurance that this will be the end of your increasingly unwelcome presence on my island." Beside her, Kepplik stirred uneasily.

As Karras answered her, Penny was impressed by his manner, a nice blend of fawning deference and suppressed triumph. "I assure you, Madame Marolakis, that it is very necessary, and you will shortly understand why. To complete our case against our murderer and his accomplices we have to expose him for the true villain he is, and although you may find what you will hear painful in the extreme, it will also be a relief to you that the affair is over and your husband's murderer in our hands."

Toby had been scanning the cavernous room keenly and murmured in Penny's ear, "Let's sit over here by the bar," steering her firmly towards it so that she missed Olympia's reply. But they were barely seated when Stephanos marched into the room, escorted by two policemen, their guns at the ready.

The minute he saw Karras he started to bluster. "Major, this is an outrage! And one for which I intend to make you pay. My privacy has been invaded; I have been dragged here at gunpoint and been told that I am under arrest. I demand to know what is the meaning of such atrocious treatment. How dare you treat a man like me in this fashion!"

"Kristos Theodopolis, you have been apprised of your rights," Karras roared back. "I am placing you under arrest for the murders of Georgiou Marolakis, Michele Dubois, the seaman called Preftakis, and the seaman Davos. In addition, you are to be charged with sedition against the Greek government and possible illegal arms smuggling."

Stephanos did a convincing instant deflation. "Murder!" he gasped in consternation. "You're insane! I am no murderer." He looked wildly around, his face fear-filled. He settled on Kepplik and seemed to draw himself together. "This has all gone much too far," he stuttered. "I wish to make a statement."

"By all means, Mr. Theodopolis." Karras signalled to one of the policeman, who thankfully holstered his gun, sat down, and whipped out a notebook. "You realize anything you say may be used in court?" He gave Olympia a conspiratorial look. "Please begin your statement."

Stephanos appeared to dither, then pointed a trembling finger at Kepplik. "It's all his doing, all his fault—he's the man you want."

Kepplik sprang to his feet, the picture of outrage. "That's a lie!" he roared.

"Please, Mr. Kepplik, sit down. All in good time," Karras soothed. "Let us hear what Theodopolis has to say first."

"I was approached by some of his partners—rightists, maybe Nazis. Lots of money to be made, they said. Good investment for the future. I'm not a political man, never have been, look at my record," Stephanos gabbled disjointedly. "Had no idea what they were doing. I was told other important financiers were involved, among them the names of Marolakis and Ribotis, so I thought it had to be sound. Got nervous, though, when a lot of money was going out and nothing to show for it. Contacted Demetrios Marolakis. He professed to know nothing of it, but was worried by the use of his name. Suggested this meeting. Hated it, but felt I had no choice. Before we could talk he died. I tried his son—he acted nervous, claimed he knew nothing. Didn't believe him, but then he was killed. Tried Ribotis, he said Kepplik and his partners had been after him for use of his fleet, but he turned them down because he thought there was something shady about their deal. Told me his sister was a stupid woman and easily influenced, always getting mixed up in crackbrained schemes, and that might be where the weakness was, where the names came from."

Penny let out a muffled groan, "Oh, God, no! They're pressing the wrong buttons," as she watched Olympia's hands starting to writhe and twitch in her lap.

"Tackled Kepplik finally," Stephanos gabbled on. "He said to calm down, I was too far into it to get out, so had better keep quiet. That he had everything under control. The final deliveries were just about to be made, and then his Croatian allies would be ready to make their move against the Serbs. Told me they'd got hold of some fanatic group in Macedonia to start up the revolt against the Serbs. Had supplied them with some arms—inferior, of course, because they were expendable, and so the Serbs could wipe them out. While they were busy with that, the Croats would blitzkrieg in from the north with all the heavy stuff, and Yugoslavia would be in their control and there would be rich pickings for us all. Said he'd take care of all the redundant people around here and set up this Lefau man to take the blame, but that he still needed his Mrs. Moneybags, at least for now. He swore he'd keep me in the clear, damn liar that he is!"

Kepplik was on his feet again, his face suffused with rage. "It's a pack of lies!" he yelled. "I never told him *anything!*" He looked wildly at Olympia.

Before Karras could intervene, Olympia leapt to her feet, her eyes blazing as she turned on Kepplik. "So!—*you,* the traitor, *you,* the betrayer," she hissed. "You stupid fool, you'll not succeed. There will be no German Croatia, no *German* Yugoslavia, for Macedonia is ready, Macedonia will rise again. Nothing will stop me, now that I know." As they all stood paralyzed, she whipped out a pearl-handled automatic from the folds of her caftan and, before anyone could move, shot him at point-blank range neatly through the heart. As he started to topple, she whipped the gun around at Stephanos, eyes glaring. "Coward! Betrayer!" she shrieked, and got off a shot at him that spun him around as it caught him in the shoulder, and he collapsed writhing to the floor.

In a second all was chaos; Toby heaved Penny bodily behind the bar and ducked behind it himself, as Ari came to life and trained his gun on the madwoman. Seeing his intent, Constantine Pappas flung himself in front of her with an inarticulate cry just as the shot rang out. It caught him squarely in the forehead, spattering her with blood as he toppled back against her, knocking the automatic out of her hand and sending them both crashing to the floor. The gun went skidding across the polished floor and was pounced upon by the note-taking constable.

"Stop firing," Karras yelled and ran to Stephanos, who was contorted with pain on the floor. "You," he pointed at the note taker, "get the medic by the pool, and you, Constable, get the stretcher from the helicopter and tell both pilots to be ready for immediate takeoff. And give me that damned automatic."

As they raced off, he went over to Kepplik. But there was nothing to be done for him—or for Constantine, who now lay with his head cradled in Olympia's arms, as she crooned, "Oh, my poor, darling Constantine, I must not weep for you, my love, for you will be immortal, you will be the first martyr of our great cause, you will not have died in vain. On our mountain after the triumph I will build your statue."

As they peered over the bar at the macabre scene, Toby looked at Penny's distraught face and said, "I'm sorry, my dear, but this isn't your fault. You mustn't blame yourself. None of us dreamed she was this close to madness or we'd never have gone on with it."

It was small comfort to her, as she looked with pity and a terrible sense of futility at the mad Olympia, who continued to croon and babble over her dead. That Karras was almost as shaken as she was evident when the medic rushed in with his bag and over to the now semiconscious Stephanos, who had lost a lot of blood. Karras said something to the medic, who nodded and produced a hypodermic syringe, which he quickly filled, whispering, "It'll keep her out for hours."

Karras returned to Olympia and gently urged her to her feet and into her thronelike chair. "Madam, let us take care of your fallen hero," he murmured. "You must rest awhile. My man here will give you something to soothe you."

She looked up at him haughtily. "That man . . ." She indicated Ari, who was looking sick and faint after the shootings but still clutching his gun. "He will have to be shot, of course. And . . ." She toed Kepplik's limp body. "Get those two carrion out of my sight—throw them into the sea, they do not deserve burial." She did not appear to notice when the medic plunged the hypodermic into her arm and pushed the plunger in, as she carried on with her commands. "I have taken care of the rest, though Alexander is not dead. No matter, he will do as I say until he is old enough to rule. A good son will do his mother's bidding." A slightly puzzled look came over her deranged face. "And am I not his mother?" She looked up at Karras. "I thought I would have to kill you, too, but with my Constantine dead I must have a new lieutenant to carry out my orders, so will you take his place?" Her words were beginning to slur.

"Assuredly, Madam," Karras soothed. "But should we not have some proofs of these traitors' accomplices to give your people?" His voice became more incisive as her head began to droop. "Kepplik's papers. Did he have any papers?" he said urgently.

"Briefcase. Brought from the yacht. My . . ." and she was asleep.

The wounded Stephanos had been carried out to the helicopter and was already airborne. Karras straightened up from the sleeping woman and barked at Ari, "Pull yourself together, man! Get out to the other helicopter, get the other stretcher for Mrs. Marolakis, and tell the pilot to radio for forensics and the coroner's team. Better bring a supply of body bags. By the sound of it this may not be the end of the victims." He looked grimly at Toby, standing guard over Penny, who was slumped in a chair staring miserably at the carnage. "Sir Tobias, would you go upstairs and see if you can locate Kepplik's briefcase? It may contain what Stephanos was after, but I want it in police hands for now."

"Will you be all right?" Toby asked his dazed partner; she nodded dumbly and he hurried off, thankful for some positive action.

Karras came over and sat down wearily beside her. "So it was Constantine she loved, not Kepplik after all—amazing!" he said.

"Not really," she said bitterly. "Hindsight is such a wonderful thing, if useless. It would have had to be a Macedonian, one of her own, now that I think of it. She must have been using Kepplik just as much as he was using her."

"None of us could have foreseen this violent outcome; you mustn't blame yourself," he said, echoing Toby. "In some ways it's a blessing. Although we may never know for sure who killed whom and all the whys of it, there'll be no trials, no publicity, no international complications. She won't be tried. She'll never see a prison, only an asylum." His tone was bleak.

An eerie silence fell as they gazed upon the slumbering woman on her mock throne, with the dead men prostrate at her feet. Toby came quietly into the room bearing a briefcase, which he handed to Karras. "There's a code book in it that may give you what you want. Your cryptographers should be able to crack it; if not, I know a source that can," he announced. From outside came a sudden hubbub of excited voices and some ragged cheering.

"What the hell!" Karras leapt to his feet. "Good God, there's only one of my men left out there. The Macedonian guards may have started something." He raced out. They followed him, thankful to escape from the death-laden atmosphere, then stood transfixed, torn between fear and hope by what they saw. Advancing around the swimming pool, and accompanied by a small horde of villagers, was Demetrios Pappas, his head swathed in a white bandage, his arm around a beaming Zehra. He was shouldering his way through the excited crowd and heading with determination for the mansion.

As Demetrios spotted them he shouted something in Greek, and Karras and Toby ran forward to meet him, the major motioning the crowd back. Penny stood rooted in anxiety as the three-way interchange went on and on. Finally Toby turned and waved at her. "It's all right, they're alive!" he called. "Groggy, but safe and sound."

Her knees went so weak with relief that she sat down hastily on one of the large urns full of potted shrubs along the wall. She was so busy being thankful that she was only dimly aware of the arrival of the stretcher bearers, the removal of the slumbering lunatic, and the helicopter soaring westwards off the pad. Finally Toby broke away from the group and came loping back to her. "Thanks to the faithful Demetrios, at least we have one happy ending," he announced, settling beside her and groping for the comfort of his pipe. "In a nutshell, the sequence of events was like this . . .

"Vincent and Melissa went for a picnic lunch on the beach. Demetrios was doing his watchdog act at a discreet distance and saw them apparently go to sleep on the beach mats they had brought. Then he saw Constantine creep in and scoop up Melissa to load her into one of the powerboats. He realized something was very wrong, so rushed out and tackled his brother. Constantine tried to pass it off as a practical joke: He was going to put the drugged couple in a boat and set it adrift to give them a good scare. Demetrios wasn't buying it and charged him with trying to murder them. Constantine finally admitted it, but said it had to be done because Olympia had ordered it. Demetrios said she was insane, and that if Constantine tried to kill them, he'd have to kill him as well. They fought, and Constantine knocked him out. When he came to, he found that Constantine had apparently not had the heart to go through with it, but had trussed them all up and stuffed them into one of the smaller volcanic tubes near the mansion. And there they stayed until the villagers found them. Demetrios was afraid the young couple might die of a drug overdose, since they didn't come to until this morning, but they'll be okay. The other police medic has checked them out, and the villagers are bringing them in on stretchers."

"And Jules?" she queried.

"He's with them: furious and out for someone's blood."

"He's a little late for that, isn't he?" she said acidly. "If he has any sense left, which I'm beginning to doubt, he'd better bend his energies to making peace with his own children, who have been thoroughly alienated by his lack of trust in them. Me too."

"Bit hard on him, aren't you?" Toby reproved. "After all,

he was caught between a rock and a hard place with this other business."

"Knowing what he did still didn't prevent him from thinking his own son murdered Georgiou, did it?" she retaliated. "When all he had to do was ask the boy."

"Well, you can tear a large strip off him when he comes in, which should be any minute now; it'll cheer you up no end." Toby tried to lighten her mood.

"I don't even want to see him," she said crossly. "By the way, what of Marcus's pirate?"

"The police got him without a shot being fired. He was asleep in his cave. Apparently one of Kepplik's neo-Nazis. After the Greek police are through with him, I imagine he'll fill in a few more pieces of the picture." Toby looked at her questioningly. "So if you don't want to hang around for Jules, what do you want to do?"

"Get out of here right now!" she cried. "I want to get back to the family and some sanity, and away from all this blood, madness, and intrigue."

"Right, then I'll see to it." He got up smartly. "You go and pack us up, I'll square it with Karras and steal a boat, if I have to, to get us to Nauphlia."

She looked at him in mild shock. "Well, is that what *you* want to do? I mean, if you want to stay, I could get there on my own."

He smiled down at her. "What I want to do is what I should have done in the first place. Instead of being an obstinate old fool, I want to show my grandchildren the glory that is Greece—and to hell with everything else!"

Chapter 20

It took Penny three days in the bosom of her family to return to a stable frame of mind, and this rather neatly coincided with the ban of silence Karras had imposed on them as the price of their liberation from Marolakis. This was reasonable enough in light of all the hushing up and covering up that had to be done about what had really happened on the island, and especially of the two ships en route with their contraband cargoes.

A quiet word from Toby in his daughter's ear on arrival, duly passed on by her to Alex, that they should handle Penny with kid gloves because she had been through a lot, and should curb their curiosity until all could be revealed, was sufficient to quench them and send them into a solicitous dither over her. This duty done, he had then spent most of the day on the phone and finally came off it looking smugly satisfied.

He lured Penny out for a moonlight walk around the quay at Nauphlia and gave her a rundown on the results. "Barham is so delighted that the British government has been kept out of all this mess, and that everything is being resolved without publicity, that he says we may keep the yacht until the end of the month, if so inclined," he related. "So I propose we run up to the Gulf of Corinth tomorrow, stop and see ancient Corinth, and then moor at Itea and do Delphi."

"Sounds fine," she said listlessly.

Undaunted, he went on, "Also, the warhead et al. is no longer headed for Greece but, after a quiet boarding on the high seas, is on its way back to the Ukraine under wraps; we hope it will duly join its defused companions in Russia. The other cargo the Greeks have thriftily confiscated and will add to their own arms store. Stephanos, whom they metamorphosed back to himself on the way to the hospital, is doing fine. The bullet went right through the fleshy part of his shoulder, so no bones were broken; after a transfusion to make up for the blood he lost and a general patching up, he'll be out and about in a couple of days."

She brightened slightly. "That's good."

He went on, "Theodopolis's yacht is already on its way back to home base, ostensibly with him aboard, and no one the wiser. Lefau is on his way to Athens, with Vincent and Melissa recuperating on board. There he'll pick up Juliette and Benedict, and then they'll go off on a reunion cruise, while he mends fences with them all."

She snorted gently.

"And . . ." he went on hastily, "Alexander Marolakis is out of the hospital and will shortly be on his way back to Greece to take up the reins as head of the Marolakis family. He has already been in contact with Lysander, who is understandably very shaken by the turn of events, but they'll act as joint trustees for Olympia's daughter, Cleopatra, after Olympia is declared legally insane."

"Good God!" she exclaimed. "Is the poor child really called that? What a burden to bear through life."

"It *was* the name of Alexander the Great's sister," he pointed out. "Olympia's identification with all this seems to be of long standing and deeply rooted. Anyway, the girl sensibly calls herself Cleo—which isn't that bad."

"Poor Olympia," she sighed, "poor tormented soul. What a waste!"

Wisely, he did not comment on that but said sternly, "Anyway, it's over, and we have to put it all behind us and just get on with our own lives. It's no use brooding."

She looked at him with a wan smile. "I know you're right, but it will take me a while. Bear with me." So he did just that.

On the second day she was sufficiently recovered to talk the whole thing through with him, and by the third, when the ban of silence was lifted, he was confident enough of her return to normal feistiness to leave most of the telling to her. They had reached Delphi by this time, taken a suite in one of its more spectacular hotels—built into a cliff face that dipped down towards the gorge of Itea—and were in the process of exploring the sanctuary precinct of the Phythian Apollo when the ban expired. Toby started the ball rolling by saying, "Well, now it can be told, so why don't you get on with it? I'm taking the children up the hill to see the amphitheatre and racetrack." He promptly set off, flanked by Mala and the eager Marcus.

"Let's sit down. This will take a while," Penny said, and, seated in the shade of one of the great fluted columns of Apollo's temple, Sonya on one side, Alex on the other, she related the sequence of events.

At the end of it Alex leaned back and said smugly, "Amazing, simply amazing! Just shows you what a lethal combination too much money and too much time on your hands is. I'm thankful we'll never be faced with such an awful life."

Sonya looked at Penny and gave her a sly wink. "Oh, I don't know," she mused. "I think it would be simply marvellous—all that money, all that power, all those servants at one's command. Flitting from estate to estate, doing exactly as you please when you please. Sounds wonderful to me."

Penny joined in the game. "Yes, I must say there's a lot to be said for it," she said with a grave face.

Alex straightened up and looked at them in absolute horror. "You can't *mean* that!" he spluttered. "It's against every principle you've ever embraced, ever uttered!"

"Ah, but that was before I had seen the life at first hand,"

Sonya returned. "Now that I have—well, there's nothing to match it!" But she couldn't keep it up and started to chuckle. "Gotcha! Actually one segregated lunch party was enough for me." Penny, for the first time in days, joined in her laughter.

Finally Sonya sobered. "What I still don't see is who murdered whom and why."

"Well, as your father and I have worked it out, I think it went like this," Penny said. "And the first thing he would point out is that, although Olympia did not actually commit the murders herself, she was the cause of them all—I don't agree entirely with him on that, but that's beside the point. The second thing to realize is that, though she and Kepplik were ostensibly working as partners, they had two very different agendas. And her agenda, at least at the start, had motive in its madness: to wipe out the whole Marolakis family and add their enormous fortune to her own. So we are pretty certain that the first murder, that of Demetrios, was by Constantine at her behest, and the method so unusual and unprovable *as* murder that it was passed off as a natural death.

"The second murder, that of Georgiou, was a very different affair—a spur-of-the-moment, snap decision to eliminate him because he had panicked and was about to reveal what he knew to a third party—Jules. Georgiou had been sufficiently intimidated by Olympia to go along with her in delaying the proposed marriage—not knowing it was all too late anyway. But he must have known Olympia hated him and probably felt he might be the next to go. As indeed he was, but this one, I'm sure, was Kepplik's doing. First, by the method used—the same used later on poor Michele and Preftakis—and second, by the fact that Preftakis was *his* plant on Jules, commissioned to see that he did not get close to what was really happening on Marolakis, and who undoubtedly helped Kepplik to plant the body in the pool.

"The hit man who tried and failed to take out Alexander Marolakis was, again, probably Olympia's hireling, but his failure and Melissa's subsequent revelations, seemingly ousting Olympia from power, must also have alerted Preftakis to the fact that a wholesale extermination of Marolakis was in the works, and not just the lucrative arms smuggling—and this was more than he bargained for . . ." She paused to collect her thoughts.

"Not being the real Preftakis," she went on, "he probably felt he could not stand up to any close police scrutiny, so he jumped ship and went to ground, maybe even in the village, and from there undoubtedly put the arm on Kepplik, either for his payoff or for even heftier blackmail. Kepplik was under a lot of stress by this time, what with the imminent arrival of the warhead and Olympia's increasing craziness, so he was desperate to divert police attention away from the island as a *whole* and put them onto another specific target. Preftakis was of no further use to him, and a threat; Michele, ditto. So he decided to eliminate them. He set up a rendezvous with Preftakis on the yacht, but shot the deckhand before he arrived, intending it to look like the work of a desperate Preftakis. Then he murdered Michele and set the stage for the 'lovers' setup. All he had to do when Preftakis sneaked on board was to kill him, put him in the cabin with Michele, douse the ship with gas stolen from Theodopolis's launch, and set up a delayed fuse–type firing mechanism—not difficult to do. He then calmly went off to set up his alibi in the compound for the night. When the fire started, it would look like an attempt on himself, averted by sheer chance, and could be pinned on Theodopolis; this would keep the police occupied until the expected shipment had been safely transferred and was on its way to its final destination . . ."

Again she paused. "Now, this next bit is pure speculation, but I think it makes sense. I don't think Kepplik confided any of this to Olympia, who was already in a precarious mental state, but I think he *did* tell Constantine. He may even have ordered him to light the fuse for the fire. Constantine got to the yacht, saw the setup, and didn't like what he saw; so he added some improvements of his own, rigging an explosion that would effectively sink the ship, but still send the police hot after Kepplik's would-be murderer. Well, of course, that didn't work out as expected, but it succeeded to the extent that the police did pull in 'Theodopolis,' only to find out he was a policeman too—and the rest you know."

"It certainly all seems to fit together," Sonya mused. "A regular old-style Greek tragedy: not only was Olympia the *dea ex machina,* but she was also the cause of her murderous partners being killed." She looked up. "Oh, here comes Father with the kids, so no more murder and mayhem."

Marcus ran panting up to his mother. "That was a neat place. Mala and I ran right up to the top of the amphitheatre three times while Grandpa talked to a man. I beat her."

"No wonder, your legs are longer," his mother said, gazing enquiringly at her father, who looked a little guilty. "Now, why don't we give Grandpa a rest, and your father will take you both to see the Pythian spring down the hill?"

"Great!" Marcus bounced over to his father and pulled him up.

"My legs are tired," Mala announced. "I'm staying here."

"All right," Sonya agreed, "but why don't you pick a nice bunch of pretty wildflowers to put in our hotel room? See, they are growing all around here. Just stay in sight."

The children safely out of earshot, Penny looked sternly at Toby. "All right, out with it—what man?"

"Just a bit of unfinished business." He grinned weakly at them both.

"Such as?" Sonya asked.

He sat down and lit up his pipe. "Oh, all right. I was just passing on some bumph that Barham thought the British government might find useful." As they continued to glare stonily at him, he went on reluctantly, "Er—the contents of that code book."

"But you gave that to the police!" Penny exclaimed.

"Um—not before I had photographed it," he admitted, fishing in a sagging pocket and extracting a miniature camera. "Barham thought this might come in handy."

"Well, move over James Bond, here comes Double-O Eight." Penny was acid.

"In any case, spying appears to be a marvellous cure for gout, doesn't it?" Sonya commented, getting up. "Let's go chase Mala, if you haven't any more cloak-and-daggering to do."

"No, that's the end of it, I promise," he muttered.

"And about time too," Penny said. They wandered off among the ruins, following the lure of Mala's golden head among the spring flowers.

That night, with the happily exhausted children in bed and Sonya and Alex dancing the night away after a luxurious dinner, Penny and Toby sat out on their balcony, looking out over the moonlit gorge under a star-spangled, blue velvet sky. Penny broke their serene silence. "You know, I'm beginning to understand your passion for Greece—it is a magical place, a timeless place."

"Not only Greece, but the Greeks," Toby said. "Oh, I don't mean the Marolakis or the Ribotis. There have always been those kinds throughout its long history, and able though they were and are, they did not make the glory that was Greece. As I see it, that has always rested with men like Demetrios Pappas—steadfast, enduring, and brave. The Onassis, the Niarchos, the Marolakis—they come and they go; but men like Demetrios, they endure forever."

Another peaceful silence fell, until he roused himself. "Considering all the things that might have happened, we didn't come out of this one too badly, did we?"

"I suppose not, but it did convince me of one thing," Penny said. "It's high time we got out of this kind of thing. In fact, the way I'm feeling at the moment—'quoth the Raven, "Nevermore."'"

INSULAIRES

CHRISTIANE LAHAIE

Insulaires

nouvelles

L'instant même

Maquette de la couverture : Anne-Marie Guérineau

Illustration de la couverture : Nycol Beaulieu
La colère de Dieu, *1988*
Acrylique sur toile (102 cm × 127 cm)

Photocomposition : CompoMagny enr.

Distribution pour le Québec : Diffusion Dimedia
539, boulevard Lebeau
Saint-Laurent (Québec)
H4N 1S2

Tous droits de traduction, de reproduction et d'adaptation réservés

© *Les éditions de L'instant même*
865, avenue Moncton
Québec (Québec)
G1S 2Y4

Dépôt légal — 1ᵉʳ trimestre 1996

Données de catalogage avant publication (Canada)

Lahaie, Christiane, 1960-

Insulaires

ISBN 2-921197-63-4

I. Titre.

PS8573.A37494I57 1996   C843'.54   C96-940111-6
PS9573.A37494I57 1996
PQ3919.2.L35I57 1996

Les éditions de L'instant même bénéficient du soutien financier du Conseil des Arts du Canada et du ministère de la Culture et des Communications du Québec pour leur programme de publication.

à Georges

Frederick Ward s'était éteint dans la chambre claire d'un hôpital londonien, entouré de sa sœur et de son beau-frère. On avait incinéré le corps deux jours plus tard. Il avait 68 ans. À mes yeux, ses habits sombres, ses traits flétris et son long sourire chevalin avaient longtemps dressé le portrait vivant de tous les Anglais. De tous les vrais Anglais.

En m'annonçant son décès au téléphone, ma mère me confiait qu'elle venait de perdre un bon ami. Pour ma part, je devais renoncer à la seule parcelle d'Angleterre que j'aie jamais possédée. La porte s'était close sur une cour intérieure au cœur de laquelle je ne pourrais plus pénétrer. Elle serait là, mais on m'en refuserait l'accès pour toujours.

London Leaves

C urieuse ville que cette Londres en ruines après les ra-
vages de l'aube. La première fois que Martha Mansion
y était venue, le quartier sud-ouest abritait un jardin zoo-
logique, et les lions de Trafalgar Square s'étaient exilés. À présent, les fauves de bronze ont reconquis leur socle, et seul le
vent circule entre les cages du côté de Camden Road. Elle se
demande où se cachent maintenant le tamanoir et la taupe, où
se reposent les girafes et leur interminable cou fatigué de tant
de politesse.

Quant aux lions, ils n'ont nullement changé. Démaquillés
sans leur couche de fiente de pigeon, ils auraient pu être
méconnaissables pour n'importe qui d'autre qu'elle. Un soir,
avant Noël, elle avait levé les yeux vers l'un d'eux et lui avait
promis de revenir. Le lion n'avait pas bronché ; il ne l'avait
sans doute pas entendue. Elle est là tout de même, transie dans ce
manteau de fine laine, une véritable peau de chagrin sous la
pluie.

On se bouscule aux portes de la National Gallery pendant
qu'elle grelotte, qu'elle compte les passants sans parapluie et
qu'elle évalue la vitesse à laquelle se doublent impériales
rouges et taxis noirs. Ses doigts parcourent lentement le flanc

11

glacial d'une bête sans souvenirs, tandis qu'elle, elle se souvient de ce qu'un inconnu lui avait dit.

« I'll meet you there. Trafalgar Square. At ten. »

L'ennui, c'est que sa mémoire la trahit souvent. Il avait peut-être dit avant le méridien ou après, avant le sommeil ou plus tard, avant cette vie ou dans la prochaine. Ce qu'il lui reste de l'homme, c'est surtout le reflet d'un réverbère sur sa chevelure blafarde. Ses yeux ne lui appartiennent pas ; il les a gardés pour lui seul. Et sa voix lui parvient, étouffée, comme amortie par un oreiller de duvet. Ses paupières relâchent leur étreinte, s'étendent sur ses iris et, chaque fois, elle en meurt. Tous les matins, elle ressuscite, étonnée de voir le soleil luire à travers les branches des sycomores et d'entendre la pluie à sa fenêtre.

Elle a froid. Ses dents claqueraient si elle ne serrait pas tant les mâchoires. Toute cette rage qu'elle refoule, qu'elle ravale, qu'elle exècre. Que fait-elle là ? Pourquoi attendre alors qu'il ne viendra pas ? Elle referme son col, le tient si fort que ses jointures lui font mal. Elle soupire au lieu de respirer. Un *bobby* l'observe du coin de l'œil. Elle baisse les yeux pour ne plus voir ce visage étiré, ces lèvres charnues et cet air triste qu'elle connaît bien. Il se tient là depuis un bon moment. Comme elle, d'ailleurs. Si elle ne quitte pas la place, il finira par venir s'enquérir de ses desseins, pour ensuite lui intimer gentiment, mais fermement, l'ordre de circuler.

Elle ne dérange personne. Elle ne fait qu'attendre. Elle ne sait qu'attendre l'homme qui ne vient jamais. Elle contourne son hôte à la crinière d'airain et s'éloigne. Les pigeons s'écartent sur son passage en battant des ailes, en hochant la tête, en trottant comme de vieilles dames affolées.

Elle traversera la rue jusqu'au *tube* et s'engouffrera dans un wagon sale et bruyant comme un pub anglais mal tenu. À moins qu'elle ne s'attarde dans une librairie et ne revienne à son poste plus tard ? Une autre factionnaire l'a remplacée à la droite du lion de bronze. Elle attend, elle aussi. Elle attend peut-être le même.

Pour le moment, les voies souterraines de la ville sont encore dégagées. Chaque fois que Martha Mansion met les pieds dans le métro londonien, elle pense à cette jeune femme plutôt grosse et plutôt blonde qui, à l'heure de pointe, avait somnolé, debout à côté d'une porte automatique. Dans ses bras potelés, elle tenait mollement une boîte métallique. Chocolats ? Gaufrettes ? La boîte menaçait à tout moment de tomber, et son contenu, de s'étaler sur le plancher bringuebalant du wagon. Martha Mansion était descendue avant que le pire n'arrive et se demande encore si les friandises avaient fini écrasées sous des centaines de semelles pressées de retourner à la banlieue.

Londres est hors de prix. Encore heureux que Martha Mansion ait déniché cette pension tout près de Hyde Park. La propriétaire, une fausse rousse aux joues cramoisies, ne tient pas à savoir ce qu'elle fait de ses journées. Elle se contente de lui servir tous les matins des œufs tièdes, du bacon un peu cuit, du café faible, du pain grillé et de la marmelade aux trois fruits. Martha Mansion n'en demande pas plus. En fait, elle n'en demande pas tant.

Tout ce qu'elle veut, c'est le retrouver, lui. Prendre sa main longue et dure, la tenir contre sa joue, la mordre, la rattraper, la serrer, la palper longtemps, comme si elle l'avait tirée d'un lac étrange, stagnant, bordé de nénuphars et peuplé de brumes d'où elle aurait surgi, armée d'une épée transparente.

Elle descend à Paddington. Il y aura eu un attentat, un appel à la bombe, une agression. On a rempli la gare de *bobbies* aux aguets. D'habitude, les terroristes choisissent la fin de l'après-midi. S'ils se mettent à frapper à toute heure, eux aussi, où allons-nous ?

13

Et où va-t-elle, maintenant ? Hyde Park est à deux pas, sa pension aussi. Mais elle n'a pas envie de rentrer. Il ne viendra pas la rejoindre dans cette chambre mal éclairée ; ses lèvres n'ont rien à voir avec l'obscurité, sa bouche crache des novas et sa langue luit comme une flamme folle.

À l'entendre penser, on pourrait croire qu'elle est fascinée par cet homme. En réalité, elle l'est tout à fait. Elle se déteste de tant le vouloir ; elle s'en veut de tant l'aimer.

Que fait-il, de son côté de l'univers ? Quel trottoir arpente-t-il avant la nuit ? Où déjeune-t-il et avec qui ? Sur quelle étoile, dans quelle caverne, à la table numéro 13 de quel restaurant de Leicester Square ? À quel moment traverse-t-il la City ? Est-ce que ses yeux violets se posent parfois sur la désolation du nouveau port, sur les eaux savonneuses de la Tamise, sur les déracinés des guettos pakistanais qui ont la chance de le croiser sur leur chemin ?

Ses facultés affaiblies l'empêchent de bien le voir. Les murailles de sa mémoire s'écartent, se referment, s'affaissent. Elle a peur d'avoir oublié l'essentiel. Non pas le grain de sa peau, la carrure de ses épaules ou la lenteur de sa démarche, mais la courbe de sa hanche. Une hanche liquide, veloutée, presque visqueuse. Les larmes d'une armée de bannis ne sont rien en comparaison de cette coulée de lave tiède.

Elle ira s'asseoir sur un des bancs du jardin italien. Elle pourra méditer dans le tumulte de ses heures perdues. L'eau des fontaines viendra l'éclabousser si le vent se lève un peu. Mais pleurer, elle ne sait plus. Elle commence à oublier cela aussi. Il fut un temps où il lui suffisait d'improviser un petit mélodrame pour provoquer la débâcle de ses deux rivières. Elle a perdu ce précieux talent ; elle ne saurait même plus s'en servir pour le manipuler, lui, à supposer qu'elle le retrouve, qu'il honore son rendez-vous aux pieds des lions. Il a peut-être fait comme chacun à Londres : il sera parti pour le week-end. À moins qu'il n'ait pu remonter dans le temps, jusqu'à elle.

La pluie a cessé, mais le banc de bois n'est pas encore sec. Elle sera encore plus détrempée qu'avant. Plus tard, elle marchera peut-être jusqu'au Flower Walk ; le prince Albert y a son monument par là. Lui qui voit les amants passer à cœur de jour, sans doute saurait-il lui expliquer pourquoi il n'est pas revenu à Trafalgar Square, pourquoi il n'a pas cherché par tous les moyens à la revoir, pourquoi il n'est pas là depuis tout ce temps ? Elle ose à peine envisager la réponse la plus logique : il en a eu assez. Ou la plus romantique : il est mort de chagrin. Elle deviendra folle, à la fin, si elle ne le retrouve pas ! Mais comment faire dans une ville surpeuplée, aussi discrète qu'un champ de mines sous la neige ?

Elle parie qu'il n'y aura plus de neige sur Londres. Elle parie qu'elle n'a pas peur du froid, ni d'être seule ou de périr sous une couche de glace bleue comme les veines gonflées de son cou. Elle donnerait sa main à couper qu'il ne l'entend pas penser à lui, qu'il se moque de sa hargne et qu'il regarde, serein, vers la lune ou Jupiter.

Le temps passe, il passe tant qu'elle se lève bientôt pour retourner sous la terre. Elle s'enfonce encore une fois dans les entrailles de Londres-la-grise. Le jour va tomber ; il est presque cinq heures. Mais elle ne dit rien. Elle se fera bousculer par des étudiants enjoués, par des hommes taciturnes, fermés comme des huîtres. Elle toisera ceux qui la toisent. Elle se fera menue sur la banquette, les yeux levés vers le tapage publicitaire d'une paroi étouffante, vers le panoramique filé qu'on projette sur ses murs concaves. Béatrice Dalle ou Sade Adu, les Stones, encore eux, ou les *Bomb Alerts*.

Au moment précis où elle émerge d'un macadam encore grouillant, Big Ben carillonne. De l'autre côté de la rue, il est là. En train de régler sa montre. Un pan de son pardessus sombre flotte un instant puis retombe sur sa jambe. Dans sa main, un bouquet de rudbeckies. Il lève le bras. Disparaît dans un *black cab*. S'enfuit. S'éloigne dans le fracas des klaxons et le crissement des pneus sur la chaussée mouillée.

Martha Mansion réprime un sanglot, puis étouffe un hurlement de dépit. Il ne lui reste qu'à s'en retourner. À moins qu'elle ne prenne place sur un banc, au pied de l'horloge, en face du palais de Westminster, sous un ciel couvert, entre deux rendez-vous manqués, après la lumière. Le temps que ses artères se calment, que ses doigts cessent de trembler, que ses yeux s'imprègnent à jamais de cette vision déjà ancienne... Il n'a pas changé d'un iota.

Trafalgar Square reste aussi le même. On l'a reconstruit, il y a quelques années, mais sa faune demeure. Nelson aussi. Et Martha Mansion attend. Aucune excuse, cette fois. Il a réglé sa montre. La montre qu'il a au poignet. Le poignet de son bras. Son bras qui tient à son épaule, son épaule fixée à son torse, à son corps, son corps à sa tête et sa tête à lui. Lui entier. Celui-là même dont elle a tout inventé.

Avant de visiter l'Angleterre, j'ai passé de longues soirées à imaginer les ponts de Londres, les piétons et les automobilistes distraits circulant du mauvais côté de la voie. Des journées entières, j'ai feint d'écouter le vent siffler entre les monolithes de Stonehenge. J'ai miré mon visage dans les eaux qui ceinturent Avalon, un morceau de terre et de brume où le roi Arthur pansa ses plaies. Mon regard a erré le long des murs d'un château en ruine, couvert d'efflorescences et de champignons. J'ai arpenté lentement des jardins où les roses, rouges et blanches, se côtoyaient sans qu'on ne songe à les décapiter. À présent que mon roi a quitté ces lieux, tout ce qui m'y rattache ressemble à la pluie, au brouillard. Je refuse de voir les grèves sauvages qui rongent mon Angleterre, les centrales nucléaires hideuses qui poussent en son sein et tous les terroristes qu'elle abrite, à son corps défendant.

Bridge over the River Cam

Ils ont choisi la nuit. Les petites heures du matin, peut-être. Comment savoir, et quelle importance ? Ils sont remontés à la surface comme deux bouées inutiles, l'un sous le pont, l'autre un peu plus loin, sous les barques. L'homme a le torse perforé ; un *punter* l'aura pris comme point d'appui, entre deux énoncés savants, croyant toucher une souche pourrie. On jurerait que la jeune femme sourit, brisée, bleuie, presque transparente. Elle a les yeux ouverts sur quelque souvenir fluide. Ses longs cheveux lui collent à la figure. Ils courent sur ses lèvres violacées, entre ses dents de marbre. Je voudrais découvrir entièrement son visage lunaire avant qu'on ne l'enferme dans un sac de vinyle, mais je n'ose pas. Après tout, je suis là pour travailler auprès du médecin légiste, pas pour m'attendrir.

Nous traverserons Cambridge sous bonne escorte ; les cyclistes perplexes s'écarteront sur notre passage. Dans ce dédale de rues étroites, on cherchera à comprendre, on se perdra en conjectures sur ce qui a bien pu pousser deux jeunes gens à s'enlever la vie, car se noie uniquement qui veut dans la rivière Cam. Elle peut paraître profonde par endroits, mais ses berges sont rarement désertées : professeurs émérites en vacances, amoureux distraits, noceurs en promenade, chercheurs

19

en mal de sujets, rien ne lui est épargné. Alors, comment expliquer le drame ? Le professeur aura-t-il regardé ailleurs, les amoureux se seront-ils embrassés plus longuement, les noceurs auront-ils effacé toute trace de pas dans l'herbe ? Quant aux chercheurs, c'est bien connu, ils préfèrent chercher à trouver.

Mais je raisonne encore. Je m'illusionne aussi. Tandis que nous approchons de la morgue, j'essaie de capter le regard du policier, là, dans le rétroviseur. Ses yeux pers, un peu écartés mais très beaux, évitent la visée des miens comme la peste. Je n'apprendrai donc jamais à garder mes distances. Il serait temps, je le sais. Il serait sans doute temps aussi de démissionner. Je n'arrive pas à croire qu'il faudra charcuter ces deux cadavres rien que pour confirmer ce que tout le monde sait déjà : mort par asphyxie. Accident. Noyade. Une fin pure et simple, à l'image de l'élément qui a envahi leurs bronches, dilaté leur ventre, entrouvert leur bouche. La purification ultime par l'eau, le dernier baptême, le seul véritable sacrement, avec le mariage.

La camionnette s'est immobilisée. Le chauffeur descend aider les brancardiers. Je m'étonne que l'air arrive encore à se frayer un chemin jusqu'à mes poumons. Je m'extrais du véhicule à mon tour, partageant ma conscience entre la honte et le dégoût. Je regarde ailleurs pendant qu'on emporte les corps, de ridicules enveloppes sans dignité, sans âme. Plus jamais elles ne se dévêtiront seules, plus jamais elles ne pousseront de soupirs impatients ni de cris rauques. Une dernière bulle a éclaté à la surface de la Cam. Elle est montée, chargée d'une haleine inquiète, et s'en est allée loin, de l'autre côté de quelque part. Et ce quelque part ne ressemble nullement à cette salle frigorifiée, aveuglante et stérile. Du moins est-il permis de l'espérer. On ouvre deux grands tiroirs. On les referme. On m'abandonne là, au milieu de tous ces morts en transit.

J'ai l'impression de partager le sort de tous ceux qui m'entourent, de vivre à côté de ma chair, de ne sentir que le froid, dans le noir, entre quatre cloisons provisoirement étanches. Ce qui viendra ne sera ni beau à voir ni agréable à entendre. Rien que le silence du ver qui creuse lentement la terre, rien que le bruit de la pourriture qui craquèle le bois verni, rien que la rumeur de la cendre qui cherche à s'échapper de l'urne. C'est pour cela que j'ai voulu profaner les corps, les découper, les ouvrir et les refermer. Je veux prouver que la mort ne règle rien, qu'elle n'arrange pas les choses, qu'elle ne nous fait pas oublier les vivants.

Tout à l'heure, cet homme en blouse blanche viendra, armé de son scalpel, de ses yeux indécents, de ses doigts agiles et pervers. Mais il ne trouvera rien. Rien que de l'eau de sang, rien qu'une coupe de vin rosé dans leur bouche béante, rien que la froideur rigide d'un objet qu'on a déjà cru animé, doué de raison, de sentiments, de sensations. Il voudra enfoncer ses ciseaux dans cette peau livide, palper les viscères, évacuer tous les liquides, assécher les organes et les membres. Moi, je prendrai des notes, je ne broncherai pas quand il parlera d'enflure des parois, de saturation des tissus, d'éclatement des veines. Je me terrerai dans le silence d'un formulaire vierge et dans la tristesse d'une longue pluie. Au bas de la page, on inscrira la date de l'autopsie, de même que le jour et l'heure présumés du décès. On supposera qu'ils ont voulu mourir ensemble, mais lui aura rendu l'âme un peu avant elle, car il aura coulé plus vite à cause du pourcentage de gras moins élevé chez l'homme. Puis nous signerons, tous les deux.

Ce qu'on ne connaîtra jamais, c'est le motif qui me poussera, à la tombée de la nuit, à enlever les deux cadavres pour les rendre à la rivière. Je les attacherai l'un sur l'autre et, à leurs pieds, je nouerai juste assez de cailloux pour qu'ils flottent à la

21

dérive, entre deux eaux. Je respecterai leur dernière volonté. Ils n'auront pas lutté en vain. Et si les corps s'obstinent à jaillir, je serai là pour les faire caler de nouveau, jusqu'à ce qu'ils soient emportés par le courant et qu'ils se perdent au large.

Quand j'irai les rejoindre, ils ne formeront plus qu'une seule chair déchiquetée que je pourrai réintégrer, dans laquelle je pourrai me perdre et oublier. Oublier que je les ai précipités dans un gouffre aqueux, oublier que je les aimais tous les deux et qu'eux s'aimaient sans moi. On ne mettra pas la main sur mon corps. Quand j'aurai enjambé le pont, il se dissolvera dans la Cam comme le métal dans l'acide sulfurique. Il ne restera rien de ce cœur aride, rien qu'un galet dans le lit de la rivière, un galet que la mer rejettera sur une plage, en d'autres parts où je pourrai enfin me réfugier sous la plante d'un pied ferme, chaud et nu.

« All this affection wasted on a cat ! »

L'exclamation, émise à voix haute par un jeune homme guindé, m'a tirée de ma rêverie. J'aimerais bien me rappeler où j'ai déjà entendu cette phrase, cet accent cassant et fier. Le jeune Anglais, assis de l'autre côté de l'allée, a des gestes d'impatience qui n'amusent que moi. À bord d'un Lougheed L-1011 en direction de Heathrow, j'observe les passagers qui circulent, s'arrêtent, repartent ou font la queue en soupirant. Je voudrais me reposer, les jambes enserrées dans une longue couverture de laine, mais le jeune homme me regarde avec trop d'insistance. Ses yeux d'un bleu de glace soutiennent longtemps les miens. Il s'incline, puis se détourne pour regarder les étoiles à travers le hublot. Je baisse la tête pour ne plus voir ce visage allongé, ces lèvres charnues et cet air triste que je connais bien. Frederick. Il ressemble à Frederick.

York's Bars

Il vaut mieux ne pas pénétrer à l'intérieur des murs d'Eboracum dont les fondations remontent à la conquête romaine et qui, bien plus tard, devint York. C'est du moins ce qu'apprit Montana Malone. C'était avant qu'elle n'atteigne l'âge de raison, un âge qu'elle n'aurait sans doute jamais. Elle n'en avait franchi les limites qu'une seule fois. Elle n'en était pas ressortie. Cela s'était passé du côté de Bootham Bar. À cause d'un homme aux traits familiers, qu'elle avait entrevu en train de se promener sur la muraille de York. À cause d'une silhouette élégante et noire, aperçue alors qu'elle s'apprêtait à passer son chemin, sans même se retourner, au cas où, ce faisant, elle s'engagerait dans une vaine entreprise. Pourquoi s'attacher aux vivants, puisqu'ils sont encore plus têtus que les morts et mille fois plus cruels ? On pleure les autres, mais les uns nous font pleurer. Et Montana Malone refusait de verser une larme ; personne ne lui ferait épouser Loth.

Mais quand elle vit cet homme, elle eut soudain envie de caresser son visage parfait, de mordre dans ses lèvres charnues, de se blottir contre son torse, solide comme le marbre. Elle avait besoin de sombrer dans ses bras grand ouverts. Il lui fallait retrouver ce qu'elle avait perdu, il y avait de cela une vie, peut-être deux. Il s'appelait Mike ou Nigel.

Aussi, tenta-t-elle d'abord de suivre l'homme à distance, bien qu'il lui arrivât de le perdre au hasard d'une meurtrière ou d'un arbre trop plein du bruissement de petites mains, vertes et luisantes, prêtes à applaudir à la moindre brise. Puis le marcheur reparaissait, impassible, sa tête avançant au-dessus de la muraille comme celle d'un guillotiné en exil, son corps disparaissant entre deux créneaux érodés par la pluie d'avril. Il redevenait ensuite entier puis, à nouveau, rien que sa tête, puis rien que son corps. Comme si on ne pouvait arriver à percevoir les deux à la fois. Comme si les deux n'existaient que séparément. Elle le fila longtemps ainsi, le perdant et le retrouvant, à travers le crachin glacé d'une matinée encore jeune.

Elle rallia Mickelgate Bar, l'une des portes de York, et voulut entrer, lorsqu'elle vit un grand gaillard au crâne rasé, chaussé de sandales de cuir. Il tenait son lourd javelot appuyé au sol, la pointe tournée vers le ciel, de manière à bloquer le passage. Elle fit un pas en avant, mais il l'arrêta aussitôt : elle ne pouvait pas pénétrer dans Eboracum !

Eboracum. Il avait dit Eboracum. Il plaisantait ! York n'avait pas porté ce nom depuis des siècles. Et puis, que faisait-il, habillé de la sorte ? Montana Malone avait peut-être affaire à un illuminé, ou pire, à un de ces néo-nazis en quête de pouvoir. Elle haussa les épaules et voulut contourner le javelot, mais le jeune garde recula pour obstruer à nouveau la voie. Puis, il répéta la litanie qu'on lui avait apparemment imprimée dans la tête à coups de serments d'allégeance à un dieu de carton-pâte. Montana Malone commençait à s'énerver, d'autant plus que Mike, ou Nigel, s'éloignait rapidement. Elle sollicita le droit de passer, d'une voix neutre, prétextant un rendez-vous urgent. Sans succès. Le jeune homme se montrait poli, mais ferme. Intimidée, Montana Malone se rendait bien compte qu'il la considérait d'un œil attentif aux moindres détails : les traits de son visage, ses cheveux fins qu'elle refusait de nouer, sa peau transparente comme de la porcelaine.

Tout vient à point à qui sait attendre, dit-on. Mais Montana Malone n'avait pas appris à attendre. Elle ne savait pas non plus à qui elle avait affaire. Il valait mieux ne pas insister. Elle tourna le dos au jeune légionnaire et se mit à courir vers le sud-est. Avec un peu de chance, elle entrerait par Walmgate Bar, de l'autre côté de la ville.

Le fugitif avait pris beaucoup d'avance ; elle arriva péniblement à sa hauteur, encore haletante et fébrile. Il allait comme un somnambule, plutôt nonchalant, mais constant dans sa progression. Puis, tout à coup, elle le perdit complètement de vue. Les murs de la cité s'interrompaient juste avant le pont de Skeldergate. À l'horizon, le château de York, du moins ce qu'il en reste — c'est-à-dire les donjons — se dressait telle une sentinelle de pierre au regard myope. Montana Malone se traînait, maintenant, cherchant des yeux celui qui, peut-être, mettrait un terme à cette quête absurde. Trop tard. Mike, ou Nigel, était retourné au néant.

Avec lassitude, elle franchit le pont de Castle Mills. Elle n'éprouvait même pas l'envie de se mirer dans l'eau à peine agitée de la rivière. Ses yeux scrutaient inutilement l'horizon. Au loin, les clochers de la cathédrale crevaient les nuages, qui avaient commencé à battre en retraite. Le vent soufflait, mais pas assez pour que s'effondrent York, son château et sa muraille interminable. Il aurait fallu, pourtant, puisque tout cela séparait Montana Malone de Mike, ou Nigel.

Nigel Manly. Il s'appelait Nigel Manly.

Parce qu'elle venait de rendre son nom à un fantôme, Montana Malone crut tout à coup qu'elle avait encore une chance de rejoindre l'inconnu qui marchait sur les murs. Même s'il s'était évaporé comme un parfum rare dans cet air humide.

Bien que le *barbican* de Walmgate Bar s'avançât pour l'engloutir, telle une gueule de dragon, Montana Malone s'y rua. Peine perdue. Un étrange *gentleman*, vêtu de noir et coiffé d'un melon, lui pointa un parapluie rouge et blanc sous le nez. Il lui demanda où elle comptait aller, comme ça... Avait-elle l'intention d'entrer dans Eorforwic ?

Montana Malone s'immobilisa, étonnée que York ait encore changé de nom. Elle pria tout de même l'homme de la laisser passer. Il réitéra son refus en lui disant qu'elle n'avait rien à faire à Eorforwic. Montana Malone voulut savoir pourquoi, quand le garde, qui la braquait toujours avec son parapluie, se mit à parler d'une triste génération qui ne voulait rien comprendre, qui ne savait pas quand persévérer ni baisser les armes au moment opportun. Il scrutait le ciel délavé, comme s'il y cherchait un signal, un appel de détresse, ou le visage de Montana Malone.

Intriguée par ce sermon, la jeune femme restait là, à toiser cet être bizarre qui la tenait en joue. Elle pensait surtout à celui qui avait rappelé Nigel Manly à sa mémoire, lorsqu'elle l'aperçut, dans l'embrasure d'un créneau. Son profil fluide se tournait vers le nord. Aussitôt, Montana Malone s'élança, laissant la vigile anglo-saxonne à son curieux soliloque. Au bout de quelques minutes, elle se mit à crier, à agiter les bras pour attirer l'attention de l'homme. Il fallait qu'elle y parvienne. Sinon, elle devrait se rendre jusqu'à Monk Bar. C'était encore loin et Montana Malone commençait à être fatiguée. Ses souliers prenaient l'eau. Elle était transie.

Quant à celui qui ressemblait à Nigel Manly, il ne paraissait pas l'entendre ni la voir. Il allait, silencieux et secret, sans accorder la moindre importance au monde, tant et si bien que Montana Malone le perdit encore.

Le long de Foss Islands Road, elle se mit à pester contre sa propre stupidité, contre cet entêtement qui la faisait courir après ce qui n'était pas pour elle. Elle se détestait et ne trouvait pas de mots assez crus pour décrire un tel aveuglement. Il ne suffisait pas de persévérer. Encore fallait-il savoir quand le jeu en valait la chandelle. L'homme au melon n'avait peut-être pas tort, après tout. Montana Malone ne savait pas avoir raison.

Il fallait pourtant trouver un moyen d'investir York. Il fallait que ce soit possible. Autrement, personne ne serait jamais entré dans Eboracum. Dans Eorforwic. Dans York, enfin ! Mais comment faire ? Soudoyer le garde ? L'injurier ? Le séduire ? De toute façon, elle essaierait quelque chose à Monk Bar. Elle tenterait sa chance. Cet homme, la doublure de Nigel Manly, ne serait peut-être plus là, mais elle devait essayer quand même.

Il s'y trouvait ! Juste au-dessus de l'entrée de Monk Bar. Il se tenait tout droit, comme s'il regardait au loin devant lui. Il dominait la ville, du haut de son promontoire de pierres médiévales, et semblait évaluer l'étendue de son royaume. Toute tremblante, elle courut vers lui, mais il avait tourné les talons et s'éloignait.

L'entrée de Monk Bar était surveillée par un type plutôt costaud, à la chevelure rousse et longue, qui lissait sa barbe. Montana Malone s'en approcha. Lui parla de la pluie, mais surtout du beau temps qui s'annonçait. Elle lui offrit de l'argent, sa montre, tout ce que contenait son sac à main. Le seul résultat tangible qu'elle obtint fut un sourire sur le visage de l'imposant individu dont la main droite serrait le manche usé d'une massue de bois noueux. Il la considérait avec une sorte de pitié, comme déchiré entre son devoir et son envie de combler cet être fragile, à bout de souffle et inquiet, qui l'implorait du regard. Il lui dit, enfin, qu'elle aurait tort d'entrer dans Jorvik.

Encore autre chose. Montana Malone soupira, puis expliqua qu'elle devait entrer dans York au plus vite. Sinon, elle risquait de perdre la trace de quelqu'un pour toujours. Elle lui demanda aussi combien de temps durerait cette mascarade. Elle voulait bien se raisonner, graver une croix sur son propre corps s'il le fallait, mais là, elle commençait à perdre patience. Elle n'avoua pas qu'une petite voix gémissait en elle, comme si on l'avait emprisonnée sous la pierre, l'albâtre ou l'acier. Elle craignait de ne jamais pouvoir accompagner l'homme des murs dans sa marche sereine.

Le Viking, c'est du moins ce à quoi il ressemblait, interrogea Montana Malone sur ce qu'elle venait chercher à Jorvik. Il avait parlé, les bras croisés sur son large torse. Mais ses yeux trahissaient un sentiment plus doux. De la sollicitude. De la tristesse même. Une expression qu'on ne devait pas voir souvent dans les yeux immenses des conquérants. Quant à Montana Malone, elle était plus désespérée que jamais. Toute cette course l'avait épuisée ; toute cette vie la brisait. Plutôt que de discuter davantage, elle s'enfuit en courant. Elle n'avait pas le choix. Cette folle croisade devait se terminer à Bootham Bar où, elle le savait à présent, un quatrième larron l'attendrait.

Le dernier garde était affublé d'une cotte de mailles et d'une épée qui, du haut de sa hanche, se balançait en éraflant le pavé. Une balafre sur son visage fit d'abord reculer Montana Malone, mais il était sa dernière chance de déambuler à l'ombre de Nigel Manly. Comme prévu, le chevalier sans monture se mit en travers de son chemin, en lui refusant l'accès à York. Eboracum-York. York-Eorforwic. Jorvik-York. Exaspérée, Montana Malone se mit à inventer des charades et à débiter des insanités dans une langue macaronique, rien que pour embêter le garde. Puisqu'elle avait déjà tout essayé. Ou presque. Le preux homme hocha la tête, sincèrement désolé. Sans grande conviction, il lui dit qu'il était préférable qu'elle n'entre pas dans York. À ce moment, Montana Malone sentit qu'il allait se plier à sa requête. Il allait céder. Il le fallait. Elle venait d'apercevoir la réplique exacte de Nigel Manly. Il était là-haut. Il la regardait. Il l'avait donc vue.

Montana Malone porta la main à ses lèvres pour les sceller, pour retenir un cri de joie. Sans doute avait-elle peur d'enfreindre un code connu d'elle seule. Quand elle s'avança pour franchir le seuil de la ville, le garde n'éleva pas l'épée et s'écarta. Une ligne rouge à l'horizon laissait présager du soleil pour le lendemain. Mais quand Montana Malone eut gravi les marches de pierre qui menaient au sommet de la muraille, elle ne trouva personne.

Elle ne se rendit pas compte qu'elle pleurait. À la vérité, elle n'éprouvait plus la moindre sensation. L'eau dans ses chaussures. Le froid entre ses reins. Tout avait été oblitéré. Elle tourna le dos au crépuscule et, sans jeter le moindre regard derrière elle, se mit à arpenter les murs de l'ancienne cité de York.

Ce midi, je prends mon déjeuner dans un pub. L'atmosphère bruyante et chaude des lieux m'isole sur un îlot de sommeil. Je pense à ce vieil homme rencontré hier. J'étais restée seule dans mon coin de wagon, jusqu'à ce qu'il vienne s'installer près de moi. Tandis que les bornes et les maisons défilaient rapidement de l'autre côté de la fenêtre, je compris qu'il m'observait. J'eus beau cacher mon visage derrière une revue, ses yeux collaient à moi comme une odeur suspecte, puis il daigna enfin s'intéresser à son journal. Au-dessus de sa tête d'un blond cendré, je remarquai une affiche où une cigarette était écrasée sous un gros X rouge. Je songeai à Frederick, à cette mauvaise habitude qui avait fini par l'emporter. Cette douleur aiguë dans son poumon gauche, ce drain qui émergeait de ses côtes, l'eau et le sang qui se mêlaient, ses membres décharnés et livides. J'avais dû verser une larme, car l'étranger s'était avancé et me tendait un mouchoir. Je le pris et m'essuyai les joues. Elles étaient sèches. Je fermai les yeux une seconde. Il n'en fallut pas plus pour qu'il allonge la jambe et me caresse doucement la cheville. Je me redressai brusquement et le dévisageai. J'étais si furieuse que je n'arrivais même pas à prononcer la moindre injure. Il sourit.

« If you were a little bit older, I would marry you. »

Je savais qu'il me dirait quelque chose de ce genre. Je savais que Frederick parlerait par la bouche de cet homme-là. Je quittai le wagon à la hâte, mais je laissai ma honte sur la banquette.

Men of the Moors

A près des heures de désespoir et d'attente, il ne me restait pour unique compagnon que le reflet givré de la lune. Une lente brume silencieuse rampait sur la lande avec la patience d'un fauve prêt à engloutir sa proie endormie. L'eau avait commencé à me traverser de part en part ; je n'arrivais plus à dégager mes jambes de la fange où elles s'étaient enlisées. Mais je ne pouvais pas leur en vouloir : elles n'avaient fait qu'obéir aux forces obscures de ma volonté. On m'avait dit qu'il ne fallait pas s'aventurer seul dans la lande du Yorkshire même si, en cet automne avancé, la bruyère avait fleuri et s'étendait à perte de vue en ruisseaux violacés. La pluie des derniers jours avait détrempé ce tapis de mousse noire et l'avait transformé en éponge avide de voyageurs égarés. On s'y enfonce, m'avait-on dit, comme dans des sables mouvants desquels on ne saurait s'extraire sans l'aide de bras secourables. Et dans le désert de ma lucidité absente, j'avais entrepris l'impossible voyage. Toute cette longue stagnation pour une gerbe de fleurs dégoulinantes que je ne rapporterais nulle part. Rien que le vent qui effleurait les pétales baignés de rosée, rien que le brouillard qui m'enveloppait de ses longs bras fluides.

Longtemps, j'ai hurlé, dans l'espérance qu'une âme bienveillante entende ma plainte. Je me prenais pour Catherine, enfermée dans son corps malade, et loin d'un bâtard aux yeux assombris par la haine. Mais personne ne me répondait des hauts de hurlevent et je dus me taire. La gorge endolorie, je n'osais même pas interpeller les grands moutons à la jeune toison nauséabonde qui s'aventuraient de mon côté. Je ne me faisais pas d'illusions, car on ne viendrait récupérer ces bêtes qu'à la fin de l'hiver. C'est là qu'on me découvrirait, penchée comme une ancolie morte, entre deux collines durcies par le froid. Je m'étais éloignée de la route ; impossible qu'un automobiliste aperçoive ne serait-ce qu'une vague silhouette en train d'agiter frénétiquement les bras. J'étais seule avec le vent. Il ne me restait que son insistance à effacer doucement mes larmes, une à une. J'aurais sans doute sangloté, n'eût été cette étrange lassitude qui envahissait mes membres meurtris par l'humidité. Le temps n'était plus de ce monde et je me disais que j'irais le rejoindre tôt ou tard.

Mes paupières lourdes s'apprêtaient à se refermer pour une dernière nuit quand je vis une forme mouvante à l'horizon. On aurait dit une aquarelle à l'indigo, liquide et changeante, qui se déformait et se reformait sans cesse devant mes yeux affaiblis. Je la distinguais si mal qu'il me fallut attendre qu'elle soit à proximité avant d'appeler au secours, ce que je fis avec le filet de voix qu'il me restait. L'homme qui s'approchait était coiffé d'un chapeau dont le rebord dissimulait son visage. Je voulus tendre les mains vers lui, mais une crainte sourde m'en empêcha : l'étranger était suivi d'une douzaine d'individus vêtus comme lui. Leurs longs manteaux sans couleur balayaient le sol, et leurs pieds, enserrés dans de hautes bottes noires, foulaient à peine la bruyère qui, stoïque, ne paraissait pas vouloir les engloutir comme elle l'avait fait avec moi. Je pris peur.

J'étais à la merci de ces inconnus et, dans cette contrée perdue, nul ne se soucierait de ma disparition. J'imaginais le pire quand ils m'encerclèrent sans dire le moindre mot. J'entendis la bruyère craquer mollement derrière moi et de puissantes mains gantées me saisirent sous les bras pour m'arracher à mon piège spongieux et glacial. Puis, alors que je titubais encore, l'un d'eux vint se placer devant moi et me fit signe de mettre mes bras autour de ses épaules tandis qu'il serrait mes cuisses contre ses hanches. Comme une enfant démunie qui n'a d'autre choix que de s'en remettre à l'adversité, je m'abandonnai à ce dos ferme, anonyme et étonnamment chaud.

C'est sur cette curieuse monture que je visitai la lande, transie mais apaisée. Je ne connaissais pas ces hommes, ni leurs noms ni leur destination, pas plus que je n'entendrais le son de leurs voix. Ils m'avaient rescapée du désastre. Pour le moment, cela me suffisait. J'ignorais où ils m'emmenaient ou ce qu'ils entendaient faire de moi. Je n'avais pas la force de protester, de me débattre ni de simplement parler. Je me contentais de leur présence obstinément silencieuse. Leurs pas froissaient à peine la bruyère et seules les gouttes de pluie qui se relayaient sur leurs épaules voûtées leur prêtaient un semblant de matérialité. Ils allaient comme des fantômes occupés à arpenter les quatre coins d'un royaume défunt. Rien ne les pressait, rien ne les atteignait. Ils restaient si muets que le vent dans mes oreilles paraissait volubile, bavard, agaçant même. Pendant tout ce temps, ils marchaient à travers une brume de plus en plus épaisse, me portant tour à tour.

J'éprouvais une curieuse sensation à me sentir serrée, soudée à ces corps apparemment interchangeables tant ils se ressemblaient. Ils avaient tous à peu près la même taille, le même tour d'épaules et de hanches, la même odeur de camphre et de clou de girofle mêlée à la sueur baptisée de leur front. Ils marchaient d'un même pas qui, sans être alerte, me semblait régulier, assuré, presque mécanique.

Nous nous enfonçâmes plus avant dans les terres, la lune nous devançant de quelques foulées, enroulée dans son étole de brouillard, pendant que mes craintes se dissipaient lentement, à mesure que défilaient les bancs de bruyère de part et d'autre de notre cortège muet. Après tout, si ces hommes avaient voulu abuser de moi, ils l'auraient fait immédiatement, dans cette lande où ils étaient les maîtres. À présent, j'éprouvais une totale confiance à leur endroit. Leur présence, comme celle d'un ami multiplié, arrivait à me faire croire que le vent se calmerait à l'approche de l'aube. Mais je ne vis pas le soleil se lever puisqu'ils m'emmenèrent sous terre, dans ce qui semblait une grotte aux murs phosphorescents et dont le suintement dégageait une odeur fétide et douceâtre, comparable à celle d'une source au printemps. Parvenus à une sorte de voûte faiblement éclairée qui devait leur servir de salle commune, ils m'allongèrent sur un lit de granit. Il faisait chaud dans cette grotte aux parois lumineuses et je ne sentais sur mon visage qu'une brise timide.

L'un après l'autre, comme s'il s'agissait d'une cérémonie souvent répétée, ils retirèrent leurs vêtements qu'ils suspendirent çà et là, près d'un feu qui semblait brûler depuis toujours et qu'ils se contentèrent de ranimer d'une longue bûche de bouleau blanc dont l'écorce se mit à se tortiller dans les flammes. Une légère fumée s'éleva, pour s'échapper par un orifice pratiqué à même le roc. Je préférai me concentrer sur la forme en constante mutation de ses volutes plutôt que de regarder les corps nus et ruisselants de mes hôtes. Je ne savais pas si je devais les imiter ou les ignorer, feindre le sommeil ou l'apoplexie.

Leur peau, comme encroûtée par le soleil et le froid, brillait d'un éclat mat sous la lueur orangée du brasier.

Sur mon lit de pierre, j'hésitais à esquisser le moindre geste, paralysée devant l'étonnant spectacle dont j'étais témoin, car tous ces hommes n'avaient plus de visage ; ils avaient tous été défigurés par quelque violent coup, fil d'une lame ou brûlure intense. Leurs corps, sûrement beaux à l'origine, étaient maintenant couverts de cicatrices, d'anciennes plaies et de marques rougies ou sombres comme du sang séché.

Ils s'affairaient autour du feu à faire cuire des herbes, des rutabagas et de la viande dont le fumet rappelait l'agneau. Je voulus me lever, quand je constatai que mon manteau alourdi par la pluie me collait froidement aux os. Aussi commençai-je tranquillement à m'en défaire. L'un des hommes, dont une balafre noircie découpait le visage en trois, vint vers moi et prit les vêtements que je lui tendais. Taciturne et impassible, il les mit à sécher. Nul ne parut remarquer que je me dénudais ; nul ne parut s'émouvoir devant la blancheur lisse de mes bras, devant les rondeurs de ma poitrine aux mamelons durcis, devant mes longues jambes effilées. Je m'approchai des flammes et, pendant que leur chaleur venait lécher la courbe incertaine de mes hanches, je bus à la coupe qu'on me donnait. Je m'appuyai à une épaule nue et je fermai les yeux pour m'assoupir, sans bruit, sans heurt, sans regrets.

Quand je repris conscience, je gisais au bord de la route, dans des vêtements secs qui n'étaient pas les miens. J'avais chaussé de longues bottes noires et sales ; un long manteau grisâtre me protégeait du froid humide de la lande pourtant inondée de soleil. Dans mes bras, je tenais une gerbe de bruyère sèche, nouée par un bout de corde grossièrement tressée.

En échange d'indications routières plus ou moins confuses, un automobiliste me ramena à l'auberge où j'avais réservé une chambre. Personne ne fit de cas de mon étrange tenue. Et quand je revins m'attabler, personne ne me demanda où j'avais passé la nuit.

S'il m'arrive parfois encore de rêver que de longues mains brûlées et meurtries me caressent en silence, je sais que la journée sera belle. Je sais que les hommes de la lande ne m'ont pas oubliée, que la bruyère retient leurs larmes et que leurs pas liquides ne s'égarent jamais.

Pour oublier le vieil homme du train, je visitai les lieux les plus pittoresques de la capitale : des boutiques d'antiquités, Trafalgar Square, Nelson et ses lions, Saint-Martin-in-the-Fields... J'aurais aimé déambuler le long des allées fleuries de Hyde Park avec sérénité. J'aurais voulu y rencontrer quelqu'un qui n'ait pas de beaux yeux clairs, bleus et tristes.

« *The Soviet Union and the United States are like two naughty boys... We should bang their heads together !* »

J'étais certaine d'avoir entendu ces paroles quelque part, mais elles ne venaient pas de ce quadragénaire vêtu de noir qui serrait le bord d'un chapeau melon entre de longs doigts marbrés de taches de son. Il m'avait saluée et avait souri en arborant de grandes dents immaculées. Je marchai vite, aussi vite que je le pus, sans courir. Chaque pas m'éloignait de l'étranger, tandis que je sentais le poids de son regard sur moi. Je m'éloignai jusqu'à ce que la distance ait raison de lui et de sa vision que je devinais aussi perçante que celle d'un faucon. Je préférais encore marcher seule que de l'avoir, agrippé à mon poing.

Down and Out in Edinburgh

Une brume épaisse s'attardait encore sur Calton Hill et la rosée matinale me collait aux semelles. Je me sentais comme une de ces grosses gouttes ; j'hésitais entre la possibilité de m'évaporer dans l'air froid de l'aube et celle de m'enfoncer dans le sol pour aller à la rencontre d'une jeune racine de houx. Je me dirigeais vers Princes Street dans l'espoir de trouver un café où je pourrais prendre le petit déjeuner, entre la nouvelle cité et l'ancienne, à mi-chemin entre le passé noir et sanglant d'Édimbourg et son présent aux façades blanchies. Bientôt trois mois que j'étais sur la trace du jeune Alec Stirling, un adolescent issu d'une bonne famille, qui prenait la fuite de temps à autre. Mais cette fois, il n'était pas rentré au manoir après quelques jours de bacchanale, et son absence prolongée avait suscité tout un émoi chez ses parents. D'abord, ils alertèrent tous les corps policiers de Grande-Bretagne, puis ils firent une sortie dans les médias. En désespoir de cause, ils eurent recours aux services d'un détective privé, et ce privé, c'était moi, Elmer Crane, de Crane et Allison, Birmingham, Angleterre. La filature d'Alec Stirling m'avait mené un peu partout déjà, mais je ne croyais pas qu'elle m'entraînerait jusqu'ici, jusqu'aux collines escarpées d'Édimbourg, à cette heure où les travailleurs se font rares, où les impériales sombres roulent presque vides, mis à part quelques jeunes gens au crâne tatoué.

En Écosse, l'aube a cette propriété d'émousser les contours acérés des toits et d'aiguiser le flou de l'horizon. J'avais eu l'occasion de le constater ; depuis quelques jours, je me levais tôt dans le but de surprendre Alec en flagrant délit d'errance. Là-bas, la longue aiguille du monument à Sir Walter Scott s'enfonçait doucement dans un renflement de nuage, à la recherche d'un peu de pluie. En vain, cependant. Il n'était pas tombé un brin de cette manne transparente depuis que j'avais mis les pieds au royaume de Bonnie Prince Charlie. Le ciel restait pesant. Les collines demeuraient muettes, désormais privées de l'ubac et de l'adret, comme refermées sur elles-mêmes. C'est par là que je regardais quand j'aperçus Alec pour la première fois.

Sa longue chevelure avait attiré mon attention, mais pas autant que ses vêtements bariolés, sortes de retailles sorties tout droit des tiroirs de quelque vieux Britannique au goût douteux. Son apparence aurait repoussé le simple quidam. Mais moi, j'étais précisément à la recherche de quelque chose d'original, d'inattendu ou de carrément déroutant. On m'avait décrit Alec comme un excentrique discret, ce qui m'avait paru plutôt contradictoire, je l'avoue. On m'avait dit également qu'il lisait beaucoup et qu'il vouait une admiration sans bornes aux poètes et à leurs élucubrations. J'avais donc pris le train pour Édimbourg après qu'un collègue, moyennant un chèque à la somme assez rondelette, m'eut signalé l'apparition intempestive de graffitis lyriques, disséminés à travers la ville. S'il s'agissait d'Alec, il avait, selon toute vraisemblance, une mission à remplir, une mission assez importante pour qu'il coure le risque de se faire prendre et d'être contraint de rentrer chez lui. Je tenais assurément mon bonhomme.

*I'm truly sorry man's dominion
Has broken Nature's social union,
An' justifies that ill opinion
    Which makes thee startle
At me, thy poor, earth-born companion,*

J'avais lu à haute voix les vers encore dégoulinants que le jeune homme venait de transcrire à gros traits, à même le monument de Burns, un mausolée auquel des colonnes doriques conféraient un air à la fois grandiose et ridicule. Alec s'était brusquement retourné vers moi. Ses cheveux en broussaille, et gris comme le temps, lui masquaient presque entièrement le visage. Il les écarta d'un geste saccadé, d'une fine main blanche, tachée de rouge. Il me considéra d'abord avec méfiance, mais mes souliers aux semelles décousues et mes frusques râpées lui firent probablement croire que j'étais de la même allégeance que lui. Il prit donc son pinceau, sa peinture, et acheva son travail. Puis il s'éloigna : démarche fière et droite, vêtements flottant au vent tels des fanions défraîchis.

J'avais ri sous cape. Encore un fils de bourgeois égaré, instruit jusqu'aux yeux et révolté jusqu'à la moelle. J'aimais bien le tableau : je m'y reconnaissais. Je lui emboîtai le pas rapidement, car il dévalait déjà la colline, et le rejoignis au moment où il s'engageait dans Calton Road. Il enfouit son matériel sous un arbuste et poursuivit son chemin. Il ne semblait pas étonné que je le talonne ; j'eus même l'impression qu'il ralentissait. En quelques enjambées, j'étais à ses côtés, mi-amusé, mi-intrigué par cette jeune arrogance un peu désabusée.

La semaine précédente, Alec avait eu le temps de peindre quelques vers sur les murs du palais de Holyroodhouse avant que des gardes en kilt n'accourent pour l'arrêter. Il leur avait sans doute échappé de justesse, s'évanouissant derrière les talus en fleurs. Je reconnaissais la patte du jeune fugitif et je pouvais affirmer qu'il avait déjà plusieurs sites profanés à son actif : l'édifice du Parlement, une paroi de la tour d'observation de Calton Hill, l'entrée de la gare de Waverley de même qu'une crête de Castle Rock. À vrai dire, seuls le monument à Scott et le clocher de la cathédrale Saint-Gilles avaient été épargnés. Mais on n'arriverait pas à le prendre. Sans domicile fixe, on n'existe pas. On s'évapore avec la brume et on réapparaît avec le vent. C'était là le secret de son étrange réussite. Hier, il squattait sans doute sur la place Moray ; aujourd'hui, il dormirait dans un hamac de fortune, quelque part dans les jardins de Princes Street. Mais, malgré le fait que mon enquête m'avait permis d'évaluer l'ampleur de la tâche qu'il accomplissait dans la clandestinité, je restai longtemps dans l'ignorance de ses véritables motifs.

Ce jour-là, je le suivis à travers la ville. Je le vis voler quelques pommes au marché, subtiliser quelques pinceaux à un quincaillier complaisant, s'abreuver à la fontaine publique et s'assoupir sur un banc de parc. J'en profitai alors pour lui glisser un billet de vingt livres dans la poche, ainsi qu'un poème de William Blake que j'avais copié en vitesse à la bibliothèque de l'université d'Édimbourg. Ma missive le priait de transcrire le poème sur le transept nord de Saint-Gilles où il n'avait pas encore frappé. Puis je m'éloignai tandis qu'il roupillait toujours. Je risquais de perdre sa trace ; c'était peut-être de la folie.

J'attendis avec impatience. Deux semaines, environ. Puis vint une aube où il prit la cathédrale d'assaut et transcrivit les dernières lignes de *London* à la faible lueur d'un lampadaire encore allumé. Je n'attendais que ce signal pour me manifester. Quand je le hélai, il se tourna vivement dans ma direction et je crois qu'il me reconnut, car il ne semblait pas effrayé outre mesure. Il savait que je lui avais tendu un piège et il avait accepté d'y sauter à pieds joints. D'une voix rauque, comme celle de quelqu'un qui a l'habitude de se taire, il me demanda qui j'étais. Son accent me parut dur et chantant. Je répondis à sa question, lui confiant que ses parents payaient une fortune pour le retrouver et qu'ils étaient en train d'assurer à eux seuls mes vieux jours, juste pour lui mettre le grappin dessus. Il sourit et me fit signe de le suivre. Se débarrassant de ses outils dans la première poubelle venue, il voulut savoir pourquoi je ne l'avais pas coffré tout de suite. Je lui répondis que je n'avais pas intérêt à clore l'affaire trop rapidement. À cela, il sourit encore.

En fait, je lui mentais. J'avais longtemps caressé le rêve de répandre moi-même les vers de ce poème très noir sur les murs de quelque bâtiment. J'avais toujours cru qu'on devait déclamer les poèmes aux coins des rues et pas seulement dans les bistrots pour intellectuels blasés. Et puis, je voulais savoir ce qui poussait un jeune homme à quitter un foyer cossu pour mener la rude vie des itinérants. J'avais laissé une famille aigrie, pauvre et orageuse, mais lui ? Pourquoi cette errance alors que tant de possibilités s'offraient à lui ? Évidemment, je n'osais pas poser directement la question, de peur de paraître naïf ou dépassé. Je me disais qu'il s'agissait d'un malentendu entre lui et ses parents. Il avait voulu devenir poète, son père le voyait médecin, ou alors, il rejetait en bloc toute l'opulence de sa race, parce qu'il se sentait coupable et qu'il en avait assez d'une existence qu'il jugeait étriquée. Mais il était plus probable qu'il préférait mendier, ou voler des inconnus plutôt que ses proches et, dans sa dignité d'indigent qui a choisi de l'être, il ne demandait pas, il prenait.

Nous déambulions dans High Street en direction du château où la vigilance de Robert the Bruce et de William Wallace, tous deux fondus dans le bronze, ne se démentait jamais, quand je m'approchai de la vitrine d'un café plutôt chouette. Alec acquiesça, et je me demandai soudain si l'odeur que dégageaient ses hardes ne nous forcerait pas à quitter prématurément les lieux. La serveuse, une dame corpulente au visage cramoisi, nous dévisagea, mais ne dit rien. Si j'avais retrouvé mes habits propres de privé en devoir, Alec arborait toujours son allure désolante, et ses ongles, tachés de rouge, complétaient joliment le portrait. Je commandai deux petits déjeuners copieux. Alec accepta de partager ce repas avec moi, me dit-il, parce qu'il voulait des nouvelles de ses parents. Je lui en donnai, mais je ne savais pas grand-chose à leur sujet, sinon qu'ils tenaient à revoir leur fils vivant. Il parut d'abord satisfait de cette réponse, puis s'assombrit. Il observait une clocharde qui avait collé son visage creusé d'innombrables ridules contre la vitre et qui s'était éloignée en clopinant. Il sanglota soudain très fort et versa une toute petite larme qui coula longtemps sur sa joue maigre. Tous s'étaient tus dans le café. Je ne saurais dire s'ils étaient dégoûtés ou émus. Leur mutisme parut s'éterniser pendant qu'Alec s'essuyait le nez du revers de sa manche, déjà passablement souillée. Quand il se fut calmé, c'est-à-dire deux œufs frits, quelques lisières de bacon et quelques muffins plus tard, je me risquai à lui demander ce qu'il cherchait. Il ne répondit pas, absorbé par un tourment que son regard trahissait, et termina son café sans plus relever les yeux vers moi.

Je compris que notre entretien était terminé. Alec avait choisi son clan ; il savait de qui il préférait être solidaire. Quant à moi, il y avait belle lurette que j'avais mis une croix sur tout ce qu'il représentait. D'ailleurs, je n'avais fait que le précéder dans le renoncement. Tôt ou tard, lui aussi aurait à remiser sa couleur et ses vieux pinceaux. Enfin, l'homme raisonnable et calculateur que j'étais devenu ne viendrait certainement pas à bout du silence presque serein qu'il avait retrouvé, lui.

En sortant du café, Alec me demanda de saluer ses parents, ce que je ne pouvais évidemment pas faire sans m'attirer leurs foudres ou perdre mes gages. Je le laissai partir. Il pressa le pas, fixant le sol comme s'il avait peur de trébucher ou de ne plus reconnaître son chemin. Je lui fis un signe de la main ; il ne le vit pas et disparut au tournant d'une avenue bondée. Midi sonnait. J'étais convaincu que je le reverrais et que, ce jour-là, il baisserait les armes.

Quelque temps plus tard, je désertais Édimbourg, non sans avoir aperçu un hamac habilement dissimulé entre les branches d'un chêne de Princes Street. Sur la façade ouest de la pension où je logeais, on s'affairait à nettoyer des graffitis peints en rouge, frais et inachevés. Je reconnus les premiers vers du *Auld Lang Syne*. J'aurais voulu tourner le dos à toute cette triste besogne, marcher vers le nord, vers les Highlands et la mer, sans laisser ni adresse ni souvenir à qui que ce soit, sauf à un jeune vagabond en quête de paroles éparpillées. Mais il faut bien vivre.

Un jour, je devrai cueillir Alec avant sa majorité et le ramener au nid. Pour le moment, rien ne presse. Blake et moi avons encore besoin de tout ce sang factice qu'il verse au pied d'un volcan refroidi. En outre, j'estime que ses parents ont les moyens.

Tout le reste de la journée, j'eus l'impression que l'homme au melon me suivait. Je ne le voyais pas, mais c'était comme si ses yeux avaient laissé leur empreinte sur mes épaules et que je n'arrivais plus à m'en défaire.

Ce midi, le boudoir de l'auberge me suffit pour prendre un peu de repos. Je ferais n'importe quoi pour me changer les idées, mais j'hésite à m'aventurer au dehors. Il n'y a que deux projets auxquels je n'ai pas encore renoncé : assister à une représentation de Macbeth et visiter le cimetière où on a inhumé les cendres de Frederick. Le patron est venu vérifier le contenu de ma tasse. Je n'ai presque rien avalé ; il s'en retourne sans dire un mot. Il n'insiste pas. Ici, tout est ambre et amer : le thé, la bière, les humeurs. L'aubergiste s'adresse à sa cuisinière, qui s'apprête à partir.

« You're the only friend I have who knows how to cook ! »

Je déglutis avec peine. Le malaise m'a reprise, aussi sournoisement que la première fois, aussi brutalement que la deuxième, que la troisième... Je me lève, me dirige vers le hall d'entrée. Je m'arrête un instant au petit comptoir derrière lequel un jeune serveur, dont je devine la couleur des yeux, me souhaite une bonne journée. Je sors précipitamment pour me perdre dans la foule qui retourne travailler. Je ne suis en sûreté nulle part.

Monks of Melrose

L'incident avait dû se produire une bonne dizaine de fois. Elle lui disait blanc, il comprenait noir, et une querelle sans fondements s'ensuivait. Cette fois, Melany Rowan était allée trop loin. Elle avait eu la mauvaise idée de faire l'éloge d'un homme qui n'était pas celui qu'elle avait épousé. Ce dernier, rageant, s'était mis à l'insulter, à la traiter de garce, de fille perdue et d'obsédée. Sa crise de jalousie prit une telle ampleur que, bientôt, il quitta l'autoroute 68 en direction des Highlands et, sur l'accotement d'une route secondaire, lui ordonna sèchement de descendre. Mariés depuis sept ans, ils avaient joué cette scène à répétition, *ad nauseam* ; elle refusait toujours d'obéir. Mais cette fois, à cause du regard obscurci de l'homme, ou en raison du filet de salive qui lui collait à la lèvre inférieure, elle ne dit rien, prit son grand sac avec fébrilité et s'extirpa de l'habitacle surchauffé de leur modeste voiture.

Les pieds délicats de la femme avaient à peine foulé le gravier que la voiture redémarrait en trombe et s'éloignait plus vite que toute limite de vitesse ne le permettait, jusqu'à ce que Melany Rowan ne perçoive plus qu'un point bleuâtre à l'horizon. Une bourrasque la happa, soulevant avec impatience la jupe fleurie qu'elle avait acquise la veille dans une boutique huppée d'Édimbourg. D'un geste empreint de fatigue, elle l'empoigna et la tira vers le bas, vers le sol que jonchaient de minuscules cailloux gris et roses.

Elle n'eut d'abord aucune réaction apparente : ni pleurs, ni cris, ni apitoiement sur le sort qu'elle avait choisi. Elle ressentait plutôt une indicible lassitude mêlée à un profond désarroi. Il n'y avait rien à ajouter à de tels actes. Rien sinon que leur mariage, comme tant d'autres, voguait à la dérive. En fait, le leur avait plutôt tendance à *courir* à sa perte, mais cela ressemblait déjà à une autre histoire.

Elle soupira, puis soupira encore, se tourna vers le nord, puis traversa la route pour s'approcher d'un panneau de signalisation qui ballottait au vent : Melrose 2. C'était donc Melrose qu'ils venaient de contourner à toute allure. Et cette rivière qui coulait en bas, tout en bas du vallon, c'était la Tweed. De gros points blancs incrustés dans l'herbe semblaient se mouvoir avec une lenteur désespérante, tandis qu'elle marchait vers le village, encore saoule d'une sorte de rage contenue qu'elle éprouvait souvent. Aveuglée par des larmes retenues sous ses paupières, elle mit du temps à comprendre qu'il s'agissait de paisibles moutons en train de paître. Penchée au-dessus d'eux, tout en haut d'une falaise taillée dans l'émeraude, elle se prit à envier leur destin, infiniment plus morne, certes, mais plus simple que le sien. On ne leur demandait pas d'être beaux, spirituels ou attentionnés, seulement d'être ce qu'ils sont : des machines à laine qu'il faut nourrir et tondre de temps en temps. Sa laine à elle, on lui demandait de se l'arracher pendant qu'on l'abreuvait d'injures et de vaines promesses. Sans compter qu'on lui faisait payer cher le moindre écart de conduite, et que les chiens qu'on envoyait à ses trousses ne se contentaient pas d'aboyer. Elle marcha longtemps, souhaitant presque que l'homme se calme et revienne la chercher, mais il n'en fit rien.

Peut-être avait-il enfin décidé de mettre un terme à leur épreuve de force. Peut-être avait-il voulu lui donner une bonne leçon, à défaut de pouvoir lui frapper la paume des mains à coups de baguette.

Le soir venait déjà quand elle atteignit Melrose. Calme et déserté, le village l'accueillit avec une certaine indifférence. Seuls quelques regards curieux, derrière des vitrines couvertes de lettrage clair, la considérèrent un moment, puis tout un chacun retourna à sa *lager*, à son plat de *mutton pie*, à son *Earl Grey* refroidi.

Melany Rowan avait les pieds endoloris, l'épaule usée par le poids de son sac qu'elle avait porté en bandoulière, et le cœur pareil à un morceau de quartz. Le soleil ne l'aveuglait plus ; ses rayons qui déclinaient rapidement avaient disparu derrière les collines. Seule l'abbaye en ruines dressait ses arches brisées contre le vent apaisé du soir. La femme décida d'aller dans cette direction, comme si elle eût espéré y trouver une âme généreuse ou un baume. Elle avait lu quelque part que, dans les jardins de cette abbaye cistercienne, on cultivait des herbes médicinales. En réalité, ce qui l'attirait là, c'était le refuge solitaire qu'elle comptait trouver parmi ces pierres roses que le couchant enluminait de silence.

Bientôt, elle contourna deux larges stèles de grès posées à angle droit, un peu comme une pierre tombale, et s'assit avec précaution. Elle ferma les yeux. Elle n'avait ni faim ni soif. L'estomac noué par la colère, elle n'aurait pas pu avaler la moindre bouchée. L'air se rafraîchissait vite, et elle dut se couvrir d'un épais lainage. Elle s'appuya contre son dossier improvisé et s'endormit.

Au milieu de la nuit, la femme s'éveilla en sursaut. On s'activait autour d'elle. Légèrement voilée, la lune n'offrait que peu d'aide à Melany Rowan dont les pupilles dilatées scrutaient l'obscurité avec acharnement. Quelqu'un, tout près, soulevait des objets, s'avançait péniblement, haletait, l'épiait peut-être. Elle demeurait interdite, immobile, osant à peine emplir ses poumons d'un air froid et humide. Il était revenu. Il la cherchait, sans doute prêt à la saisir au collet ou à la bousculer pour un oui ou pour un non...

Mais elle ne reconnaissait pas sa démarche ample et pesante ; le bruit léger de riches étoffes qui se frôlaient n'avait rien de commun avec le cuir dont il aimait se parer. Non, cela ne lui ressemblait pas. Et puis ces murmures qu'elle croyait entendre, transportés par une brise hésitante, finirent par la rassurer. Dès que le fantôme de son époux se fut estompé dans son esprit, la lune, étrangement, devint plus brillante et elle les vit distinctement, en train de transporter des blocs de grès et de s'affairer autour de l'abbaye. Des moines, courbés par le temps et l'effort, semblaient soudain surgir du sol et se dirigeaient lentement, tels des pèlerins aveugles, vers un transept, puis un autre, déplaçant des pierres, les fixant sur leurs socles, redressant des arcs, en érigeant d'autres. Encapuchonnés, leur soutane balayant le sol, les moines ne laissaient rien voir de leur visage.

Elle songea d'abord à s'enfuir, mais elle restait fascinée par la scène étonnante dont elle était témoin. Ils se déplaçaient avec une patience infinie, sans se plaindre et sans hésitation. Ils étaient précis, méticuleux. Chacun de leurs gestes semblait réglé, sûr, serein même. Elle eût bientôt envie de les rejoindre, de faire comme eux, ou de découvrir leur front et de l'éponger. Elle voulut leur trouver à manger, à boire ; elle voulut les forcer à s'asseoir et faire le travail à leur place. Mais elle ne parvint qu'à rester muette comme une statue de bronze, jusqu'à ce que la lune disparaisse derrière un nuage épais. Elle eut tout juste le temps de voir, érigée devant elle, l'abbaye de

Melrose telle qu'elle avait dû exister quelques siècles auparavant. Trapue et glaciale, à nouveau désertée et silencieuse, elle élevait ses murs vers un ciel sombre, changeant et parcouru de coulées de lait bleuté.

Melany Rowan s'approcha doucement d'une porte basse et pénétra dans une sorte de chapelle. Les murs lisses de la pièce ne lui renvoyaient aucun écho ; le bruit de ses pas, absorbé par la pierre, s'obstinait à ne pas lui revenir. Elle flottait, comme emportée par le temps, entre les parois suintantes qui semblaient se refermer sur elle pour l'expulser. Ses mains cherchaient à s'y agripper, mais ne saisirent qu'une substance visqueuse dont l'odeur rappelait l'eau et le sang.

Elle quitta abruptement le seuil de la chapelle et courut vers l'aube qui pointait au loin. Derrière elle, les pierres de l'abbaye glissèrent une à une vers le sol, jusqu'à ce que les arches fussent démantelées, les murs, fissurés, et le parterre moussu du jardin, jonché de morceaux de grès rose prêts à retomber en poussière.

Melany Rowan se mit à pleurer. Elle ne savait pas vraiment pourquoi, mais elle le faisait tout de même. Elle sentait que cela était bon. Peut-être qu'elle aussi tentait de reconstruire quelque chose en vain. Quelque chose qui, jour après jour et quoi qu'elle fasse, ne retrouverait jamais la beauté du crépi frais.

Quand elle reprit la route, une voiture rouge s'arrêta à côté d'elle, juste à la sortie de Melrose, sans qu'elle ait levé le bras comme le font les auto-stoppeurs. Cela suffisait pour qu'elle y monte. Et derrière elle, elle laissa tout son bagage.

La fenêtre de ma chambre donne sur une rue parallèle à Fleet Street. La circulation automobile est rare, mais les piétons abondent. Je reste là, à regarder la pluie qui coule en lentes dégoulinades le long de la vitre. J'ai laissé le temps filer, et il ne me reste qu'une heure pour me vêtir, appeler un taxi et me rendre à Picadilly Circus. J'ai vérifié mon billet une dizaine de fois. The Shakespeare Company. The Tragedy of Macbeth. A Play in Five Acts. *14th of October, 1986. Je le remets dans son enveloppe. Je lisse mon veston de lainage noir, mon foulard de soie. J'espère pouvoir me glisser jusqu'à mon siège sans que personne ne se rende compte de mon véritable statut. Je ne veux pas qu'on me perçoive comme une touriste ; je suis venue ici tant de fois ! Et je reviens pour visiter un ami. Quelque chose, ici, m'appartient. Ces étrangers que je vois partout me connaissent. Je rêve à eux et ils rêvent de moi.*

Je scrute mes traits dans la glace et l'image qu'elle me renvoie m'effraie. Mes jeunes rides, mes cernes, la couperose sur ma joue. Je dors mal. Ces hommes, cet homme. Ils me suivent. Ils sont plusieurs. Ils ne sont qu'un. Je voudrais savoir ce qu'ils veulent et, en même temps, je refuse de leur parler. Je les évite, comme on évite l'amant qui veut partir. On connaît ses intentions, ses sentiments, l'odeur de ses bagages, défaits et refaits. On voudrait que tout cela ne soit jamais formulé. Que tout reste indicible. Les actes sont déjà bien assez.

Je vais à la rencontre de l'aubergiste. Je lui demande d'appeler un black cab. *Mes cheveux trop longs cachent la moitié de mon visage. Je les ai déliés justement dans ce but. Pour qu'on ne puisse pas vérifier mon identité. Plus qu'une journée et je quitterai cette ville étrangère, ce méconnaissable pays.*

Loch Ness, Past and Present

Pour ne pas perdre de vue la vie qui est en train de me filer entre les doigts, je compte les vagues qui viennent clapoter contre la coque du bateau-mouche. Les derniers passagers ont quitté ce ridicule autobus sur lequel un gigantesque serpent de bandes dessinées, coiffé d'un bérêt de tartan, ondoie en arborant un large sourire. Ils viennent de s'installer à bord et ils n'attendent que moi, leur guide. Bientôt sept ans que je fais ce trajet aller-retour, entre Inverness et ce qui reste du château d'Urquhart. Dire que, pendant des siècles, cet amas de pierre vitrifiée a fait l'objet des convoitises les plus sanglantes, passant de main en main, de Robert the Bruce à quelque Highlander occupé à repousser les Jacobites.

À présent, seules quelques fondations, quelques parois s'élèvent encore face au vent du loch Ness. On ne songe même plus à habiter la région, et ceux qui s'y aventurent le font pour six livres de la Banque d'Écosse, croisière sur le loch Ness et visite des ruines comprises. Moyennant un léger supplément, on peut se rendre ensuite au musée de Drumnadrochit, modeste établissement consacré à Nessie, le monstre du loch. En fait, tout ce qu'on y trouve se résume à quelques présumées photos sous-marines de ce qu'on croit être un animal préhistorique bien conservé. Nessie exerce une fascination durable sur tous les hommes, profanes comme savants : sondes, sonars, bathyscaphes et autres appareils plus sophistiqués encore s'y côtoient dans une même inutilité. Ils n'ont su que se heurter aux fonds escarpés de cette ancienne vallée glaciaire. Nessie garde jalousement son mystère et se contente d'attirer les touristes en mal de sensations fortes. N'allez surtout pas suggérer que le monstre n'existe pas ! On vous accuserait aussitôt d'hérésie, de lèse-majesté et de blasphème devant les dieux de la mer. En somme, vous seriez un vrai rabat-joie.

Jusqu'à l'an dernier, je n'avais pas la plus petite raison de croire en cet animal aussi fabuleux que millénaire. Je me souviens que c'était un matin clair comme celui-ci, avec un vent frais, sec et subtilement parfumé. Une dizaine de touristes de tous âges avaient pris place à bord du rafiot qui nous servait alors d'embarcation. Ils étaient tous étonnamment silencieux, comme si, sur les eaux sombres du loch Ness, ils venaient en pélerinage pour délivrer un saint, prisonnier du temps et de fidèles jaloux et hystériques. Deux vieilles dames se tenaient la main en regardant par les fenêtres panoramiques. Deux jeunes gens en blue jeans se tenaient aussi par la main, mais se regardaient dans les yeux. Une femme maigre et agitée consultait systématiquement une série de dépliants sur le loch, tandis que trois hommes d'âge indéterminable accompagnaient un adolescent à la peau crevassée.

Enfin, il y avait lui. Vêtu de noir. La trentaine, pas vraiment grand ni petit, les yeux d'un vert d'algues échouées sur la grève. Les lèvres pleines mais serrées, la chevelure brune, un peu ondulée et généreuse, qui tombait sur des épaules à la fois délicates et musclées. Ses grandes mains noueuses s'étaient refermées durement autour d'un journal, comme s'il avait voulu l'étrangler, et ses pieds battaient la mesure d'une musique qui jouait dans sa tête.

Alors que le bateau avançait lentement sur les eaux agitées du loch et que nous étions ballottés doucement, il fixait le vide, droit devant lui. Mais la plupart du temps, il plongeait, tête première, dans mes yeux qui fuyaient son regard. Il arrivait à l'occasion que certains touristes prennent cette attitude avec moi, comme pour vérifier si leur charme opérait toujours. Cette fois-là, je sentais que je n'avais pas affaire à un de ces séducteurs ordinaires qui ne connaissent ni vacances ni respect d'autrui. Celui-là ne tentait pas de me séduire, il agissait plutôt comme si j'étais déjà conquise et qu'il ne lui restait plus qu'à me mépriser. Pendant que je débitais le boniment d'usage sur les nombreux assauts qu'avait subis le château d'Urquhart à cause de sa position stratégique sur le loch, il haussait les épaules, soupirait d'impatience, ricanait doucement ou me prenait tout entière avec ses yeux de rapace affamé. Non seulement je le trouvais impertinent, mais il me paraissait même bizarre, et inquiétant. Il me rappelait ces époux qui raillent les efforts de leur femme pour sortir de l'anonymat, voire de l'aliénation dans laquelle elle se confine à force de nettoyer la moquette, de ranger les jouets d'enfants égoïstes.

Un enfant égoïste, voilà ce à quoi il ressemblait, avec ses vêtements chic et sa coiffure savamment défaite. Quand nous eûmes complété le trajet qui nous séparait du château et accosté en contrebas de ses ruines teintées de rose, bien découpées et lumineuses sur fond de ciel pur, il se leva le premier et passa devant moi, non sans me jeter un coup d'œil torve, presque lubrique. Je lui souris, parce qu'il me dérangeait, parce que son odeur de chèvrefeuille musqué me troublait et que sa démarche ondulante m'invitait à le suivre entre ces murs éparpillés derrière lesquels la sueur et le sang avaient coulé d'une commune mesure.

Les autres passagers lui avaient aussitôt emboîté le pas, comme s'il eût été naturel de marcher sur ses traces et de fendre l'air en singeant le rythme de ses bras ballants. Quand tous l'eurent imité et se furent massés au pied du château, je les invitai à se disperser, à visiter les lieux à leur aise, à monter dans la tour pour regarder du sud vers le nord, à admirer le majestueux point de vue qu'elle offre, à humer la brise venue des collines et des conifères, bref, à se comporter comme des touristes dignes de ce nom.

Quant à mon étrange voyageur, il ne se fit pas prier et eut tôt fait de disparaître parmi les restes de gloire ancienne qui jetaient leur ombre sur moi. Il me parut vibrant, véritable et vivant au milieu de tout ce passé, de tous ces relents de guerre érigés en mythe et de cette troupe muette et morne, semblable à un amas de pierres tombées au fond du loch. On eût dit qu'il pouvait m'arracher à moi-même et m'entraîner ailleurs. Il échappait au temps comme on nargue la mort. Aussi, je lui tournai le dos, effrayée par le trou noir qu'il avait creusé entre ma vie d'alors et moi. Il me rappelait ces amants que j'avais eus, jadis, à une époque où rien ne comptait pour moi que le frottement d'une peau inconnue sur la mienne, où rien ne me procurait autant de plaisir qu'un souffle saccadé sur ma bouche offerte en prime. J'avais renoncé à cela, à cela, à l'amour et à tant d'autres choses. Je n'avais conservé que le souvenir vague d'une hanche aux muscles saillants, que les contours flous d'une poitrine, que la couleur indéfinissable d'un œil indifférent, que la spirale tordue d'une oreille endormie.

Le vent se leva bientôt et je consultai ma montre. L'heure avait sonné où une partie du groupe, en compagnie d'un collègue, devait gravir la côte en haut de laquelle un autre autobus les attendait pour les mener à Drumnadrochit, à la rencontre du monstre et seigneur incontesté des lieux. Ils n'y trouveraient finalement qu'une créature de latex, semblable à un dinosaure aux pattes palmées et d'à peine dix pieds de long, attachée à un pieu, au milieu d'un petit étang.

Les trois hommes et l'adolescent, de même que la femme émaciée, remontèrent à bord, et je soupirai de soulagement quand je constatai que l'homme ne viendrait pas se joindre à nous. Je fis signe à notre capitaine de pousser les machines et de nous ramener à Inverness où m'attendrait un nouveau groupe de pèlerins.

J'avais à peu près réussi à retrouver mon calme au terme de notre bref voyage, mais ma sérénité ne dura pas. Une jeune fille, très jolie et très blonde, en proie à une grande agitation, vint me demander où était resté un certain M. Blake, qui devait la rejoindre là. Je l'ignorais, bien sûr ; je n'avais pas l'habitude de demander le nom de mes passagers. Elle me le décrivit et je reconnus là l'homme qui m'avait tant remuée. Je la toisai longuement, me disant qu'elle était probablement sa petite amie. Dix ans de moins que lui, au bas mot.

Je la rassurai et lui offris de téléphoner au musée de Drumnadrochit où il se trouvait sûrement. Elle acquiesça et me suivit comme un chiot apeuré suit sa mère. Sa nervosité s'accentua quand elle apprit qu'il n'avait pas mis les pieds au musée, et je n'étais pas loin de partager son sentiment. Je ne savais quel lapin cet homme avait voulu poser, ni à qui, mais, chose certaine, j'avais perdu un passager quelque part le long du loch Ness et je devais le retrouver. Je fis patienter les touristes qui se pressaient sur le quai et j'appelai l'agence pour qu'elle me déniche rapidement une remplaçante, puis je contactai la police. Si cet homme avait toute sa tête, il devait apprendre à mieux s'en servir ; s'il ne l'avait pas, moi j'avais des témoins. Les agents arrivèrent, nous montâmes en voiture et je dus écouter toutes sortes de questions auxquelles je ne pouvais répondre. La jeune fille blonde, qui nous accompagnait, parlait du comportement bizarre dont M. Blake avait fait preuve ces derniers temps. Il lui avait paru distant, absorbé. Cette façon qu'elle avait de l'appeler M. Blake m'horripilait, car personne n'était dupe de la passion qu'elle éprouvait pour lui. Un policier lui demanda avec le plus grand tact si l'homme avait déjà tenté de se suicider, s'il était dépressif ou s'il avait l'habitude de disparaître, comme ça. Interdite, elle ne répondit pas, puis éclata en sanglots. Prévisible. Je me demandais seulement quand elle craquerait.

Parvenue à la colline qui surplombe le château, je vis que deux autres équipes de policiers avaient déjà commencé à ratisser le secteur. On dut même annuler toutes les visites, cette journée-là, et je me souviens que je m'étais sentie comme Sganarelle à la mort de Dom Juan. J'avais l'impression que je ne reverrais jamais les gages pour lesquels j'avais pourtant travaillé. Les recherches se poursuivirent pendant de longues heures ; il ne faisait pas de doute que M. Blake avait disparu, et certains commençaient à reluquer les eaux noires et glaciales du loch. La jeune fille blonde — elle s'appelait Amanda — s'effondra de désespoir et on dut la reconduire chez elle, à Nairn.

Quatre jours s'écoulèrent avant qu'on ne retrouve le corps de M. Blake, nu et brisé, sur la berge du loch, à quelques milles en aval du château d'Urquhart. Étant donné qu'Amanda, apparemment minée par le chagrin, refusait d'identifier le cadavre, on me dépêcha sur les lieux pour que j'accomplisse cette étrange besogne. Quand on ouvrit l'enveloppe translucide et que je vis la dépouille blanche comme l'albâtre de M. Blake, je ne bronchai pas. Je regardai un bref instant le visage. Son expression hagarde. La bouche entrouverte. Un policier m'attira à part et je lui dis ce qu'il voulait savoir. Mais pour le reste, je me tus. Je ne lui parlai pas de ce tatouage sur l'épaule gauche, une épaule dans laquelle j'avais déjà mordu, à laquelle je m'étais déjà accrochée en hurlant. Je ne mentionnai pas ces bras puissants que je reconnaissais, ni ces cuisses qui avaient enserré les miennes. De cet homme, je n'avais connu que le corps, un soir, dans l'obscurité, il y avait de cela une éternité, je crois. Et dans le noir, quand je l'avais prié de s'en aller et de me laisser dormir, il s'était levé en jurant de me faire payer cet affront un de ces quatre. J'avais trouvé ces menaces bien anodines et cet orgueil, plutôt suranné. Tout indiquait que M. Blake n'avait pas eu le temps de mettre son plan, quel qu'il fût, à exécution.

Je navigue toujours sur le loch Ness, entourée de touristes indolents ou curieux, et j'essaie d'oublier. À quelques détails près, j'y parviendrai sans doute avec le temps. Quant à l'origine de cette large plaie dont je notai la présence sur le torse livide de M. Blake, je laisse aux policiers, au loch et à ses eaux vivantes le soin de la découvrir.

« False face must hide what the false heart doth know. »
Macbeth vient de quitter la scène. Sa longue cape a remué la poussière des planches, et les projecteurs s'éteignent, l'un après l'autre. La foule observe un silence religieux entre le premier et le deuxième acte. Elle semble suspendue entre ciel et terre, entre un rêve qui refuse de s'estomper et une réalité beaucoup trop pâle pour qu'on puisse bien la saisir. Dans la demi-pénombre, deux jeunes gens viennent s'asseoir, l'un à ma gauche, l'autre à ma droite. Je me résigne, moi qui espérais jouir du confort que procurent les sièges vides autour de soi : on s'appuie comme on veut, personne ne vous embarrasse, et vous n'embarrassez personne. Je deviens de plus en plus méfiante, irritable, surtout. Comme les trois sorcières de Macbeth, j'aimerais pouvoir mijoter l'avenir des gens dans une profonde marmite, m'y baigner moi-même et faire peau neuve. Guérir Frederick, le rajeunir, lui trouver une compagne digne de ses bonnes manières.

Underground Glasgow

Je me demande comment j'annoncerai la nouvelle à Kyle. Il me tuera, c'est sûr ! À moins qu'il n'ait pitié de moi et me console. Ça m'étonnerait. Heureusement, Anna est partie et ne reviendra pas, à moins d'un miracle. Le wagon arrive à la hauteur de Kinning Park. Trois grosses femmes viennent de monter. Elles parlent fort. Elles parlent toutes en même temps. Pas question d'écouter les autres. Elles vont s'asseoir plus loin, sur la banquette la moins usée, évidemment. Moi, ça m'est égal d'être ici ou ailleurs. Tant que je ne suis pas face à Kyle et à ses yeux mouillés de colère. J'enfouis mes mains sous mes cuisses. J'ai honte du cambouis qui me noircit les ongles. J'ai beau les laver, les brosser, les couper au point de m'écorcher le bout des doigts, il reste toujours de cette graisse nauséabonde.

Les wagons du métro s'ébranlent, cette fois en direction de Shields Road, West Street, Bridge Street puis St. Enoch. C'est là que les trois pies vont descendre. Elles iront se pavaner sur Argyle Street et dépenser quelques centaines de livres dans ses grandes bijouteries. Moi, je ne porte pas de bijoux. Mes doigts sont trop forts, trop courts, trop sales. Je connais le quartier de réputation, mais je n'y vais jamais. Il est réservé aux touristes, aux richards et aux politiciens. Ces temps-ci, j'ai le privilège de côtoyer la bonne société, moi qui, d'habitude, me contente de la mauvaise.

C'est à cause des taxis. Ils font la grève dans toute l'Écosse. Tout le monde doit prendre les wagons rouges de la Circle Line ; tout le monde étouffe comme moi. On est tous entassés dans le ventre d'un reptile qui creuse des trous sous les terres gaspillées de Glasgow. On n'a pas le choix. Il n'y a qu'une ligne pour relier tout le périmètre de la ville. Mais ça décrit un cercle difforme qui évite les beaux quartiers. Le métro a été construit pour les travailleurs ; il n'y a qu'eux d'assez fous pour s'enfermer dans ses wagons trop étroits, aux plafonds trop bas et mal éclairés. Tout dans cette longue boîte de métal me donne l'impression de tourner en rond : un wagon rond, un tunnel rond, un trajet en rond.

Tourner en rond. C'est exactement ce que je fais depuis une éternité. C'est l'effet que ça produit, un congédiement. L'horloge s'étrangle et le temps s'arrête. On reste sonné, abasourdi, puis on enrage et on claque la porte. J'ai dû laisser du cambouis sur le cadre ou la poignée. Bien fait pour eux. Ils engageront quelqu'un pour nettoyer jusqu'à la plus petite trace de mon passage. J'aurais dû faire un détour par les cabinets pour en boucher quelques-uns. Trop tard pour y penser, maintenant. Je pense trop, d'ailleurs. À force de regarder mes mains sales, j'ai oublié de descendre à Buchanan Street.

J'aurais pourtant dû me douter de ce qui m'attendait au tournant. Deux nouvelles machines, plus ou moins intelligentes, mais habiles et capables de visser les boulons à ma place. Au diable mes quinze années de loyauté au service de la Gallaguer & Tyle. Je vérifie le travail pendant un temps, juste assez longtemps pour ajuster ces belles mains de métal, plus précises et plus propres que les miennes. Je l'ai fait sans me plaindre. Je n'ai pas posé de questions. J'ai accepté de devoir me tourner les pouces. J'ai même remonté le moteur de la voiture de Kyle, juste pour me prouver que j'étais encore capable, moi, Midge McLeod, de remplacer une bougie ou de sceller un joint.

Puis, ce matin, on m'a convoqué dans le grand bureau tapissé du patron. J'avais compris ; pas besoin de me faire un dessin. Ils n'avaient pas à prendre cet air morose ni à s'excuser ou à me donner tant de tapes dans le dos. J'avais compris. C'est seulement que ça me faisait mal d'y croire. Il faut toujours prendre son temps avant de mourir.

Si Anna était encore avec nous, elle réagirait probablement encore avec une fausse résignation : elle hausserait les épaules. Puis elle me regarderait dans les yeux pour s'assurer que je ne blague pas. Ça ne me ressemble pas, de faire de l'esprit, de toute façon. Je n'en suis pas totalement dépourvu — il faut bien vivre —, mais je garde ça pour les copains de l'usine. J'ai souvent tenté de la dérider, Anna, mais elle est grave et timide. On se casse la figure contre son sourire éteint. Alors, on renonce à tout ça et on cherche du côté des larmes.

Le métro ralentit pour s'arrêter à Hillhead. J'ai une envie folle de soupirer. Je me cale dans mon siège et j'attends. Quelques punks enrobés dans le cuir et les clous s'entassent sur la banquette, juste devant moi. L'un d'eux me sourit : il n'a presque plus de dents. J'incline la tête pour le saluer. J'ignore si ce qui me reste pris dans la gorge est un grand rire ou un sanglot. Je me détends. Je pose mes mains noires sur mes genoux écartés. Mon voisin d'en face passe son bras maigre autour du cou blanchâtre de son amie, une fille décharnée avec un long nez pointu et une crinière rouge comme les parois du wagon qui nous tient tous prisonniers. Ils s'embrassent. Ça dure longtemps, longtemps. Je suppose qu'ils trouvent ça bon. Je croise les bras à nouveau et je baisse les yeux vers le sol. Quelques chiffons

de papier. De vieux emballages de chewing-gum. Les semelles boueuses de deux longues bottes lacées. Je parie
que ces épouvantails à corneilles étudient à l'université de
Glasgow. Eux seuls ont les moyens de se payer des guenilles
de ce genre. Le genre usé avant le temps. Ils quitteront le
wagon à Govan, ou à Ibrox. À moins qu'ils ne poussent jusqu'à Cessnock.

Je ferme les yeux ; je voudrais dormir. J'ai une bonne
raison de ne pas descendre à Buchanan Street. Je n'ai pas encore eu le temps de trouver les mots justes pour convaincre Kyle
que tout n'est pas perdu. Qu'un nouveau boulot m'attend. Bref,
je vais devoir mentir. Et mentir avec fermeté. Il faudrait lui dire,
par exemple, que nous finirons par surmonter le départ d'Anna.
Que sa contribution au loyer n'était pas si importante. Qu'il y
a une vie après elle, même si ça n'a rien d'évident. Il serait
préférable, aussi, que je devienne subitement aveugle et que je
ne sois pas obligé de regarder Kyle dans les yeux. Kyle, mon
petit frère, nous n'avons pas de chance mais, tu sais, la chance,
c'est comme ce damné métro, ça tourne.

Le wagon s'immobilise, mais je n'ai pas la force de me
lever. Je reste seul, parasite collé à la chair d'un autre parasite
en train de se nourrir à même les entrailles de Glasgow. Je
regarde vers la rame. Je suis las. Un mince visage inquiet se
tourne vers moi. Les portes mécaniques se referment et les joues
blêmes de la femme disparaissent à toute vitesse, derrière un
mur de béton.

Quelque chose vient de se pétrifier entre mes côtes. Anna
m'a vu. Elle était venue m'attendre, peut-être. Mais comment
aurait-elle su ? Elle vit loin, maintenant, dans un autre quartier, avec d'autres gens, des imbéciles sans doute, riches mais
imbéciles. Affalé sur une banquette de métro avec cet air de
condamné en sursis, je ne peux plus mentir. Elle a sûrement

tout lu dans mes yeux rougis, tout vu, même mes épaules tombantes. Je me dégoûte. Je vais descendre, et m'expliquer avec Anna si elle est encore là, puis avec Kyle, qui doit bien commencer à s'inquiéter. Dès que la ligne complétera un autre tour.

La nausée me gagne lentement. Je me demande si c'est à cause du roulis que je supporte depuis près d'une heure, ou à cause des quelques pintes d'ale que j'ai avalées avant de gagner le guichet. J'ai envie d'uriner. C'est atroce. Je devrais descendre, me soulager dans une ruelle et rentrer. Je suis quand même chanceux de ne pas avoir à me tenir debout.

Kelvinbridge. C'est la quatrième fois, ce soir. Je n'ai qu'une chose à faire. Descendre et me perdre dans la ville. Avec un peu de veine, je ne retrouverai pas le chemin du retour. Kyle dénichera quelqu'un d'autre pour partager le loyer. Anna nous oubliera. Tous les deux. Je croyais même qu'elle l'avait déjà fait. Qu'est-ce qu'elle pouvait bien faire à Buchanan Street ? C'est loin de chez elle, et trop près de chez nous...

Et si je retournais aux études ? Je pourrais mettre Kyle à la porte, ou mieux, lui payer un appartement dans un autre pays. Je pourrais revoir Anna, nettoyer mes ongles pour de bon et passer toutes mes nuits avec elle. Je serais parfait pour la consoler, pour lui acheter des lierres en pot et de la marmelade d'oranges de Séville. Je pourrais même lui offrir un voyage en Grèce ou à la Martinique. Mais avec quel argent ? À la limite, mon oncle de Cornwall pourrait m'avancer les fonds nécessaires... Eh ! merde, à 37 ans, je n'ai déjà plus le goût de refaire ma vie.

Anna, elle, n'a pas eu peur de recommencer à zéro. Elle ne traîne pas ses revers comme un boulet de fonte. Elle a trouvé du travail et s'occupe d'adolescents drogués ou alcooliques, quelque part du côté de Gallow Gate. Au début, j'ai méprisé les types qu'elle soignait. Maintenant, je les envie. Et je l'admire, elle. Moi, Midge McLeod, je n'ai jamais fait quoi que ce soit gratuitement. Je paie chaque goutte de bière ingurgitée au pub et je ne vois pas pourquoi je ferais des cadeaux. Mais pour Anna, c'est autre chose.

St. Enoch encore une fois. Je devrai me résigner à quitter mon cocon d'acier. La Circle Line n'a rien à voir avec le réseau souterrain de la capitale. Là-bas, une correspondance ratée veut dire de longues minutes d'attente sur une rame inconnue. Ici, rien du tout. Je suis un cowboy déchu qui loue sa monture, et mon serpent de métal articulé ne me perdra nulle part. Ma plaine est circulaire et mes bottes, usées. Si je me cache derrière une colline ou au fond d'un ruisseau, Kyle, ou Anna peut-être, enverra les policiers à mes trousses. Je verrai rapidement se pointer quelques casquettes à damier. Je n'aurai qu'à me rendre, mes mains souillées levées au-dessus de la tête. Non, pas de ça. Il vaut mieux quitter les lieux de mon propre chef. Conserver ce qui me reste de dignité.

Buchanan Street. Anna m'attend toujours. Elle se lève soudain et court vers mon wagon pour s'y engouffrer, mais les portes se referment juste à temps. Je suis sauvé. Je ne veux pas d'elle ici. Ni d'elle et de son beau courage, ni de Kyle et de sa paresse maudite.

Je fais semblant de leur en vouloir. Je sais bien que je suis plutôt furieux contre moi-même. Je quitterai le sous-sol de Glasgow à la prochaine station. St. George's Cross, plutôt Cowcaddens. Je vais trouver un cabinet de toilette, calmer ma vessie, laver mes mains et courir jusqu'à Buchanan Street. J'espère qu'Anna attend encore. Je vais la prendre dans mes bras, l'embrasser sur la bouche et l'emmener avec moi. Je trouverai mieux que ce travail de demi-portion. Je vais devenir quelqu'un qu'on ne remplace pas facilement. Quelqu'un qu'on n'a pas le droit de trahir. Quelqu'un qui vaut plus cher qu'un sourire embarrassé et un papier rempli de petits caractères. Je serai quelqu'un de bien. Comme Anna. Quelqu'un dont les ongles sont clairs et pointus.

À Cowcaddens, je reste assis. Mieux vaut repasser plus près de chez moi. Encore un tour, et un autre. On dirait que ce wagon m'aime. On dirait que je tiens à lui. Et puis, il ne me demande rien. Je regarde une de ses parois ; je la caresse. Je me concentre sur le plan de la Circle Line de Glasgow. Si j'arrive à le mémoriser, je deviendrai peut-être enfin quelqu'un. Je pourrai participer à un *quiz* et gagner le gros lot. Et je répondrai à la dernière question, celle qui paie le plus. Je le leur dirai, à tous, que la Circle Line de Glasgow n'a pas de terminus.

« Upon my head they plac'd a fruitless crown, and put a barren sceptre in my gripe, thence to be wrench'd with an unlineal hand, no son of mine succeeding. »

Frederick n'a eu qu'une fille et pas de fils pour lui ressembler. Les tableaux se suivent, mais je n'assiste plus vraiment à la représentation. J'entends des vers, de belles paroles dont le sens m'indiffère. Je suis là sans être là. Comme Macbeth qui, dès le premier acte, n'est plus maître de son destin, j'ai l'impression d'être victime d'un complot dont je ne connais pas les buts, d'une sorte de machination dont j'ignore la vraie nature.

White Sun of Blackpool

Airport : Scheduled, charter, helicopter and pleasure flights, flying lessons, parachute school, public enclosure, bar, restaurant, information desk, duty free shop and Vulcan Bomber exhibit.

J'avais pris place dans un vieux Beechcraft, plutôt fragile, à la limite de la vétusté. À cette époque, je n'avais pas peur de grand-chose. Le petit avion s'était même posé sur la piste comme sur un matelas. Cela m'avait étonné. Je crois que j'allais là-bas pour la Medco ou la Pharmex, une des firmes de produits pharmaceutiques que je représentais. J'allais souvent à Blackpool vendre mes sirops et mes onguents. Les touristes américains étaient de gros consommateurs. Car il y a deux choses à Blackpool : le tourisme et le mauvais goût. Et les deux marchent main dans la main. On dirait Rio de Janeiro, la chaleur en moins. Rien à envier à sa cousine brésilienne, cependant : côté quartiers kitsch et ruelles mal famées, notre Rio des mers britanniques se défend bien. Les sirènes qui y retentissent la nuit m'avaient vite fait comprendre qu'il valait mieux rester confiné à ma minuscule chambre de Church Street. À cause de la Blackpool Tower, une manière de tour Eiffel sans la base, il y avait trop de lumière et, pour arriver à fermer l'œil, je devais garder les rideaux tirés. J'étouffais encore davantage, car je fais partie de ceux qui ont tellement peur de vivre qu'ils refusent de respirer à fond.

Art Gallery : Queen Street.

J'avais visité une galerie d'art en espérant trouver un peu de beauté dans une ville où tant de couleurs s'affichent sans la moindre harmonie. J'avais perdu mon temps. Je n'y avais vu que des croûtes : le littoral achalandé de Blackpool, sa tour, dessinée à gros traits. Je crois qu'il y avait aussi de ces portraits de clowns souriants. Ils me font pitié, ceux-là. Je suppose que je me reconnais dans ces visages mi-gais mi-tristes, trop humains, en quelque sorte. Puis une femme, grave et longue, était entrée. Enveloppée dans un ciré gris. Ses cheveux roux tombaient en chignon lâche sur sa nuque. J'en avais eu le souffle coupé. Sa peau blême et légèrement fardée. Son expression de déception et de dégoût. Elle allait tourner les talons et ressortir quand je l'avais interpellée. Elle s'était tournée vers moi. Elle paraissait étonnée. Pas autant que moi, je suppose. Encore aujourd'hui, je me demande où j'ai trouvé le courage, plutôt le culot, de m'adresser à elle. Et de façon aussi cavalière. Mais si je ne l'avais pas fait, je m'en serais longtemps voulu.

Beach : Seven miles flat sandy beach.

Maureen O'Hara, c'est bien ainsi qu'elle s'appelait, était aussi de passage à Blackpool. Je crois me rappeler qu'elle effectuait des recherches sur l'architecture des églises anglaises. Elle s'était arrêtée quelques jours sur la côte. Elle n'avait visiblement jamais entendu parler de Blackpool qu'elle avait prise pour une station balnéaire tranquille. Elle avait vite déchanté à la vue de ces rues bondées et bruyantes, de ces casinos grouillants de vacanciers obèses, bref, de cette fausse ville-lumière.

Nous avons passé beaucoup de temps ensemble, à marcher le long de la plage, à la marée basse. Nous avions trouvé un peu de solitude, à condition de nous éloigner de la jetée nord. Avec ses grands piliers, elle ressemblait à un monstre condamné à hanter la mer d'Irlande. Un monstre criard et vibrant. Je laissais des empreintes profondes dans le sable humide. Les siennes étaient toutes délicates. Elle évitait soigneusement les gros vers marins entortillés dans les algues mortes. J'avais parlé de mes souvenirs d'enfance. Elle m'avait raconté des anecdotes du temps des collèges. On grandit toujours trop, et trop vite. Et puis, je crois que je lui ai tout dit. Je n'avais pas peur de souffrir devant elle. J'étais si certain qu'après Blackpool, il y aurait le déluge et que je ne la reverrais jamais.

Churches : List available on request.

Nous nous étions trompés. Tous les deux. Dès le lendemain, je fis la tournée des églises de Blackpool. Je voulais voir Maureen. Je désespérais. Après une demi-journée de marche, j'étais éreinté. Je m'étais arrêté pour manger un morceau dans un restaurant de Central Drive. Du poisson pané un peu rance et des pommes frites dans un cône parafiné. Mais je n'avais pas tellement faim. Je faisais des calculs. Je ne savais plus dans quel sens orienter mes recherches. Il ne me restait pas plus de deux jours pour la retrouver. C'était complètement fou. Totalement absurde. Mais j'étais obsédé par cette femme. Elle ne voulait pas être consolée. Cela me blessait. Et puis, j'avais envie de son parfum dans mon visage. J'enrageais parce que j'avais oublié le son de sa voix. Et j'étais dur comme de la craie.

Coral Island : Indoor leisure complex — 1000 seat Bingo Hall, two restaurants, Shades Disco, Flagship Cabaret Lounge, Astrojet Flight Simulator. Yellow Brick Road children's play area and the latest amusements.

Maureen avait lu *Le magicien d'Oz* qu'elle avait, elle aussi, préféré au film. Sans les couleurs et les chorégraphies, on arrive à mieux saisir le sens de cette histoire. On aime ces personnages qui cherchent ce qu'ils avaient déjà. Maureen prétendait s'être reconnue dans ce lion peureux. Dans cet épouvantail aux facultés insoupçonnées. Dans cet homme de ferblanc qui pleurait un cœur absent, sans savoir d'où viennent les larmes. Elle disait qu'on peut mettre toute une vie à comprendre qui on est et ce qu'on veut vraiment. Je m'étais demandé si j'avais terminé ma propre quête. Maureen avait souri. Si je ne cherchais plus, c'est que j'avais de la chance. J'avais trouvé le pays d'Oz.

Greyhound racing : Three times per week. Princess Street Stadium.

J'avais revu Maureen quelques heures avant de quitter Blackpool. Je l'avais reconnue derrière ses jumelles. Elle avait un foulard de soie autour du cou. Ses couleurs délavées flottaient au vent. Le vent venu de la mer et qu'un soleil de plomb ne peut pas calmer. Elle avait paru contente. Elle avait insisté pour que je parie sur la prochaine course de chiens. J'avais brandi un billet de dix livres au guichet. Mais dans ma tête, je pariais sur moi. Et sur elle.

Illuminations : The Greatest Free Show on Earth — five miles of spectacular lights and Tableaux — Annually Early September to late October.

J'avais gagné 30 fois ma mise. Maureen jubilait. Nous avions quitté le stade. Il fallait trouver un endroit digne de ce gain inespéré. Ma chance venait de tourner. Je le croyais. J'avais pris d'assaut la main délicate et froide de Maureen. Je suis brusque et maladroit. Elle n'avait rien dit. Elle avait même semblé moins triste. Sur Hornby Road, j'avais hélé un taxi.

Librairies : Central library, Queen Street, Branch Librairies operate special Visitors Services.

Nous avions passé une heure à bouquiner. Elle me proposait des livres. Je voyais des noms défiler. Mais je ne les lisais qu'avec mes yeux. Je regardais surtout les seins discrets de Maureen. Je me concentrais sur la sensation que me procurait son épaule contre la mienne. J'étais en sueur. Mon sexe était gonflé. J'avais espéré qu'elle ne remarque rien. Puis, plus tard, à l'aéroport, quand le dernier appel avait retenti pour les passagers du vol 045 à destination de Londres, j'avais plongé. Je m'étais rué sur ses lèvres. J'avais collé mes cuisses contre les siennes. Mes mains tremblaient. C'était ridicule. J'avais glissé mon adresse entre les pages d'un roman que je venais de lui offrir. J'ai oublié le titre. Il parlait de garennes inondées et de lapins prophètes.

Radio Lancashire : B.B.C. The Voice of the County on 855 Khzs 351 metres. M.W. 95.5 VHF. 103.9 VHF/FM. 1557 Khzs. M.W. and 104.5 VHF.

Puis j'étais retourné auprès d'elle, à Blackpool. *Brazil* jouait en sourdine quand je m'étais réveillé. La fenêtre panoramique donnait sur la Promenade. Le soleil avait commencé à descendre. Il allait se noyer. Je soupirais constamment, le nez enfoui dans ses épais cheveux roux. J'étais heureux. Non. Pas heureux. Plus que cela.

Elle m'avait appelé. Elle m'avait donné rendez-vous au milieu de la semaine. J'avais dû remettre deux importantes rencontres. Ma voix m'avait trahi. Ou mes yeux. L'un de mes patrons — Herbert probablement — avait souri. Un petit sourire moqueur et vaguement envieux. Je lui aurais mis mon poing dans la gueule s'il m'avait refusé cette faveur. Il avait compris. Et moi, je ne dormais plus. Je rêvais de cette femme. Je la prenais de toutes les façons. Elle voulait ; je voulais. Je pleurais, seul dans mon lit, la main souillée à force d'avoir prononcé son nom. Ce soir-là, Maureen dormait profondément et de la regarder me suffisait.

Stanley Park : 256 acres of formal gardens, conservatories, lake, new recreational facilities, trim trail.

Le lendemain, nous avions parcouru le parc de long en large. J'avais fini par me décider à lui avouer : je l'aimais. J'en devenais fou. Et de savoir qu'elle m'aimait aussi m'avait effrayé. Puis j'avais compris qu'avoir peur et aimer, c'est la même chose. Nous étions rentrés, moi à Londres, elle à Belfast. Je voulais lui écrire, mais elle avait refusé parce qu'elle s'absentait souvent pour ses travaux. Elle avait accepté de me téléphoner à intervalles réguliers. J'avais voulu lui rendre visite. Elle avait fait non de la tête. Elle disait que la ville était trop dangereuse. À ce moment, j'aurais dû savoir. Un orage d'été se préparait et je l'avais quittée trop vite. J'étais inconscient. Triste, heureux et dévasté.

Tide : Half mile ebb, twice daily.

À bord de l'avion qui me ramenait chez moi, j'avais pleuré. Je sentais encore un poids sur mes hanches. Celui de Maureen. L'odeur âcre de son sexe humide. J'entendais encore le cri de rage qu'elle avait poussé quand j'avais joui violemment en elle.

Elle s'était jetée sur le côté pour cacher son visage. J'étais étourdi. Je ne disais rien même si je savais qu'elle retenait ses sanglots. Je ne savais pas quoi dire.

Winter Gardens : 4 1/2 acres of entertainment and conference facilities consists of Empress Ballroom, Planet Room, Pavilion Piazza and Restaurant. Spanish and Baronial Hall, Opera House.

Je ne l'avais revue qu'à la fin de l'automne. On avait déserté la plage de Blackpool et fermé la plupart des attractions touristiques. Elle portait un manteau de drap noir. Ses belles mains étaient dissimulées dans un manchon de fourrure. De la zibeline, je crois. Elle m'avait convoqué d'urgence. Quand je l'avais aperçue, là-bas, sur la Promenade, elle avançait comme une âme perdue. J'avais couru vers elle. J'avais ouvert les bras. Elle paraissait lointaine et refermée sur elle-même. Une fois près d'elle, j'avais eu l'impression que ses yeux m'avaient atteint en plein visage. Elle avait retiré sa main gauche de son manchon et l'avait posée sur ma joue inondée. J'avais juste eu le temps d'apercevoir l'anneau qu'elle portait à l'annulaire et qu'elle avait oublié de retirer, cette fois. Je n'avais rien trouvé de mieux à faire que de me taire. Cela m'était égal. Elle n'aurait pas voulu divorcer, je le sais bien. Mais cela m'était égal. Je la voulais, pour moi seul. Je la méritais. J'avais le droit de lui dire que je l'aimais quand même. Que je l'aimais encore plus, sachant cela. Et, au lieu d'écarter le silence pour la prendre contre moi, j'ai regardé la mer.

Come see us soon ! Reservations preferred.

Harry Malvin laissa tomber le dépliant publicitaire dans la corbeille à papier. Après tout ce temps, il valait mieux ne pas retourner là où Maureen ne reviendrait jamais. Puis il se leva et marcha péniblement jusqu'à la fenêtre. Il pensa à cet autre soleil. Celui de Blackpool. Celui qui n'éclairerait plus la mer où a sombré l'Irlande.

Macbeth s'est écroulé. Un silence opaque plane sur l'assistance et rien ne bouge. Mes yeux n'arrivent plus à se détacher du visage du comédien qui gît, étendu de tout son long, sur les planches lumineuses de la scène. Son front se plisse lentement. Son nez se déforme. Ses lèvres minces se gonflent, pâlissent, s'allongent dans une expression d'étrange sérénité. Sa bouche s'entrouvre et ses yeux, immenses et brillants comme de la glace craquelée, se referment. On le soulève, on l'emporte vers les coulisses. Autour de moi, on maugrée parce que je dérange, parce que je veux quitter la salle avant la fin de la représentation, parce que je cours et que je ne veux pas m'arrêter. Ils regardaient ailleurs. Moi, j'ai tout vu. Même la main blafarde de Frederick qui a bougé juste avant de disparaître derrière les rideaux.

Walls of Wales

Préposée à l'entretien ménager, Samantha Smith n'avait pas l'habitude de s'immiscer dans les affaires d'autrui mais, ce matin-là, elle éprouva l'envie subite de ranger ses principes dans le placard. Armée de son aspirateur sans fil et de sa serpillière effilochée, elle avait refermé la porte derrière elle et mis le loquet. Puis elle avait décidé de trier (c'était plus fort qu'elle) et de consulter (une fois n'est pas coutume) la correspondance abandonnée qu'elle venait de découvrir dans la corbeille à papier. On avait libéré précipitamment la chambre ; elle était restée dans un désordre extrême, au grand dam de Samantha Smith. Le grand jeune homme blond qu'elle avait croisé quelques jours auparavant lui avait pourtant semblé si soigné, si frêle et si poli.

Toutes les enveloppes étaient estampillées. Elles avaient été ficelées pour former un petit paquet portant la mention « Parti sans laisser d'adresse ». Visiblement, elles ne s'étaient rendues nulle part. En tout cas, pas entre les mains d'une certaine Chris Marshall, de Londres, à qui les missives étaient destinées. Samantha Smith s'assura une seconde fois qu'elle avait bien verrouillé et s'installa à l'étroite table de travail qui occupait le coin le plus éclairé de la pièce. Émue, elle ouvrit la première lettre d'une main à la peau fissurée par l'âge et le phosphate.

Cardiff, le 24 mai 1986

Dear Chris,

Je suis arrivé au pays de Galles après trois heures d'un voyage calme et sans histoires. J'étais presque seul dans le wagon de 1re classe et j'ai pu terminer La modification. J'avais espéré qu'une telle lecture me fasse oublier ce que nous venons de vivre. Cependant, l'angoisse de ce personnage écartelé entre la réalité et l'illusion n'a pas cessé de me renvoyer à mes propres interrogations. Pour le punir, je l'ai laissé sur la banquette du train. Tu comprends, j'en suis sûr.

La gare de Cardiff m'a paru un peu terne et n'annonce en rien les beautés de la capitale galloise. Il faudra que tu la visites un jour. Cette fois, je me suis installé dans un petit hôtel de Cathedral Road. Ma chambre n'a rien de vraiment coquet, un tapis vert olive, un couvre-lit de chenille beige et des rideaux de mousseline jaunis par le soleil et la fumée de cigarettes. Mais je ne me plaindrai pas. Je suis trop content de pouvoir m'isoler entre quatre murs anonymes et réfléchir à ce que nous deviendrons.

La femme de ménage en Samantha Smith promena un regard inquisiteur autour d'elle. Elle n'avait jamais porté une attention particulière au décor des chambres qu'elle nettoyait. Elle cherchait les nids de poussière et les dégoulinades à récurer. Elle ne s'arrêtait jamais aux motifs de la moquette ; elle ne prenait pas le temps d'apprécier les teintes des draperies. Pour elle, la vie se résumait à des gestes sans cesse répétés, toujours précis, et dont on ne pouvait jamais douter du bien-fondé. Elle n'avait pas choisi sa carrière ; elle avait pris ce qu'on lui offrait et, depuis, pas une tache ne résistait à ses assauts. Elle tenait à bien faire les choses, si modestes soient-elles. Tant que tout était propre, elle n'en demandait pas davantage. Elle aurait seulement apprécié qu'on ne jette pas la soie dentaire dans le lavabo, ni les cotons-tiges dans les cabinets.

Mon hôte est indien d'origine ; il a le regard sombre et le même sourire énigmatique que toi. Son épouse, une magnifique rousse taillée au couteau, se lève toujours après lui et, pendant qu'il sert le petit déjeuner, elle fait la belle. Ils ont l'air d'un couple harmonieux. J'envie beaucoup leur candeur quand ils se regardent et se touchent.

Samantha Smith poussa un lent soupir et hocha la tête. Il avait raison. Mme Rhamlha avait de la chance. Ses draps étaient parfumés et, sur sa table de chevet, il y avait des fleurs coupées ou un pot-pourri à la pêche. Sur sa table de toilette, on pouvait compter une trentaine de petits flacons et de parfumeuses irisées qu'il fallait passer au plumeau toutes les semaines. Dans sa penderie, il y avait de la soie, du cachemire, du cousu main. Et sur sa commode, une brosse à cheveux au dos nacré qu'il fallait toujours débarrasser de ses longs fils de cuivre fin.

Demain, j'irai tracer quelques esquisses du château et du mur qui l'entoure, celui dont je t'ai parlé, avec ses animaux de pierre grise.

La femme sourit. C'était sûrement l'Animal Wall, autour du château de Cardiff... Le reste de la lettre mentionnait d'ailleurs un certain nombre de sites de ce genre, puis on avait signé « Love, Kenneth ». Le jeune artiste transportait donc des croquis dans sa grande valise aux coins usés... Elle leva un instant les yeux vers les rideaux qui empêchaient la lumière du jour de percer jusqu'à elle ; ils étaient sales, en effet. Elle replia la lettre et en ouvrit une autre, en date du 25 mai, qu'elle parcourut rapidement jusqu'à ce qu'elle se bute à un court passage où on la mentionnait.

J'ai rencontré la femme de ménage. Une drôle de créature toute maigre, à la silhouette bancale, à la peau noire et grise, comme du chocolat pur qui aurait eu froid.

La femme de chambre n'eut aucune peine à se reconnaître, bien qu'il lui en coûtât d'admettre que le portrait était fidèle. Vaguement contrariée, elle poursuivit sa lecture.

J'ai réussi à reproduire la petite lionne de l'Animal Wall et, pendant que je l'observais, j'ai eu l'impression qu'elle se penchait sur mon dessin pour mieux le voir. Elle paraît si vivante, même si elle est juchée là-haut depuis cent ans. Après tout ce temps passé à se laisser scruter par des visages curieux, elle en aurait probablement long à dire sur les hommes. Parfois, j'ai le sentiment que ma vie se résume à cela : ne rien dire et regarder passer le temps, voir les autres pleurer ou se réjouir, sans jamais arriver à pénétrer tous ces petits mondes. On dirait que je ne sais faire que des projets, dresser des croquis et des plans, pour ne jamais les fixer dans la couleur ou le marbre. J'ai beau cerner les contours ondoyants d'un corps, essayer de peindre les nuances infinies d'un épiderme luisant ou vouloir emprisonner la lumière sur une fausse pupille, je ne parviens pas à reproduire la vie. Mes personnages ne respirent pas, ils ne bougent pas, leurs mains ne s'agitent pas dans le vent et leurs paupières ne tremblent jamais quand je les reluque, emmuré dans mon silence. J'ai beau les aimer, ils ne me rendent pas ce qu'ils me coûtent de souffrance et de doute. Quant à cette petite lionne de pierre, perchée sur un mur, je sens qu'elle pourrait briser son moule et bondir pour déchiqueter sa proie et la traîner entre ses dents, jusqu'à son repaire de basalte. La matière ne l'arrête pas. Pas un mur ne la retient.

Suis-je déjà mort pour que mes mains ne parviennent plus à faire jaillir la moindre étincelle de tout ce qu'elles touchent ? Chaque fois que je prends un pinceau, de la glaise ou du bois, j'ai l'impression de les dépouiller de leur essence, de leur soutirer leur force et de les laisser choir, vidés de leur substance. Le minéral s'effrite entre mes doigts tant je le pétris. Plus je cherche à le modeler à mon image, moins il me ressemble. Le végétal se crispe, s'émiette et s'éparpille à mes pieds. Moi qui voulais tellement créer, il me semble que tout ce que j'approche n'aspire qu'à être détruit. Il n'y a que toi qui...

Samantha Smith sentit le sang affluer à ses joues mates. Quand elle comprit qu'il commençait à être question de cuisses, d'une bouche et d'une langue, d'étreintes intermittentes et de cris sauvages, elle voulut ranger la lettre avec la première. Mais la curiosité l'emporta. De toute façon, elle avait déjà forcé une porte, déjà pénétré une intimité. Elle lut jusqu'au bout.

Elle n'aurait jamais cru qu'on pouvait écrire de telles saletés. Les penser, peut-être. Les faire, à la rigueur. Mais les écrire, cela dépassait largement le seuil si étroit de la décence. Et Samantha Smith avait outrepassé cette limite avec un étrange plaisir. Avec délectation même. Elle prit la troisième lettre et entama sa lecture, les mains tremblantes et la gorge sèche.

Cardiff, le 26 mai 1986

Dear Chris,

J'espère que tu ne t'ennuies pas trop. Quant à moi, j'essaie d'oublier que Malcolm est mort, lui aussi ; j'essaie d'oublier que la déchéance physique nous guette tous et que je cours après un temps qui se dérobe à chacun de mes pas. J'espérais qu'en venant ici, je ne verrais plus ses membres meurtris et décharnés, je souhaitais qu'une promenade le long du

103

canal de Bristol me ferait du bien et qu'un vent lointain me redonnerait le goût des choses belles et vraies, mais ma solitude me ronge encore plus que n'importe quelle maladie. Enfin...

Je crois que je passe trop de temps à jouer les bravaches. À présent que la maladie rôde, je ne trouve rien de mieux à faire que d'user de faux-semblants. Je rampe dans la boue en espérant que la pestilence souffle au-dessus de ma tête. J'ai eu tort de te quitter, alors que tout ce qui me rattache à la vie a sa source en toi. Je passe mes journées assis devant un mur glacé, à dessiner des animaux de pierre, tandis que je devrais être à Londres, à tes côtés. Je me cache derrière un mur qui ne me protège ni de ma lâcheté ni de mon amour pour tout ce qui te ressemble.

Le reste de la lettre était très chaste et si larmoyant que Samantha Smith la chiffonna et la jeta au panier. Elle sortit un mouchoir empesé d'une des poches de sa robe à grosses fleurs et essuya ses yeux rougis. Elle hésita longtemps avant de lire la dernière lettre, puis elle se dit qu'au point où elle en était, tout scrupule devenait risible. Finalement, elle ne contenait rien de spécial, si ce n'est que le jeune homme annonçait son retour imminent à Londres. Il réitérait ses sentiments à l'égard de sa destinataire et concluait par un timide « Je t'aime tant ». La femme de ménage plia la feuille de papier en deux et, la joignant aux autres, jeta le tout dans son grand vide-ordures. Elle se penchait pour vérifier la doublure de la corbeille quand elle aperçut une toute petite enveloppe, à moitié cachée dans un repli.

Elle était adressée à Christopher Marshall, à Londres.

Samantha Smith n'ouvrit pas la lettre. Elle la glissa parmi les autres. Une demi-heure plus tard, au moment où elle quittait la chambre nettoyée, elle se jura de ne plus se mêler de ce qui ne la regardait pas. Elle poussa un soupir de soulagement lorsqu'elle entrouvrit la porte de la chambre suivante. Dans la corbeille à papier, il n'y avait rien.

J'ai laissé mes valises en consigne à Heathrow. Je serre un bouquet de marguerites entre mes mains. Le contrôleur du train me signale que nous sommes presque arrivés. Le brouillard est si épais que c'est à peine si on voit le nom des gares. Il fait un temps froid et mouillé ; mes os sont déjà glacés. Dès que nous aurons atteint Stowmarket, dans le Suffolk, je descendrai, trouverai l'endroit où on a enterré les cendres de Frederick, puis je retournerai chez moi, dans le Nouveau Monde.

From Oxford, with Love

Anita Jones contemplait avec lassitude les plis que ses bas de soie synthétique s'obstinaient à tracer sur ses chevilles. Bien qu'elle les étirât constamment vers le haut et jusque sous sa jupe de flanelle grise, ils avaient toujours tendance à redescendre et à s'affaisser. Elle craignait que les étudiants ne le remarquent et qu'ils ne se désolent devant tant de disgrâce, car leur bibliothécaire avait la taille épaisse, les doigts jaunis par la cigarette, les joues luisantes et les cheveux ternes, et la voix chevrotante, et les mains rugueuses et sèches à force de dépoussiérer les livres dans lesquels ces enfants gâtés enfonçaient leur joli petit nez qu'elle enviait. Elle les détestait tous, tous autant qu'ils étaient avec cet air de supériorité qu'ils lui servaient comme un plat de poisson refroidi. Il ne lui restait plus alors qu'à se réfugier dans le réduit qui lui servait de bureau, entre les recueils de jurisprudence et les traités de sciences naturelles.

Depuis trente ans, elle tournait en rond entre les murs de la Radcliffe Camera, à servir tous ces fils et ces filles de bourgeois trop nourris, imbibés de bière et remplis de bœuf au cari ingurgité à la hâte dans un pub de Cornmarket Street. Oxford pullulait de ces jeunes universitaires anglais aux poches

pleines et au cœur sec. Anita Jones les avait côtoyés assez longtemps pour savoir qu'on les avait bien dressés et qu'ils avaient
compris que n'importe quel diplôme rapporte davantage que
tous les sourires de la terre mis bout à bout. Elle avait la certitude que très peu d'étudiants se souciaient d'elle, de ce qu'elle
pouvait éprouver lorsque, grimpée sur une échelle, elle entendait des rires étouffés. Elle avait tenté d'expliquer à Oliver Ash,
le directeur et son patron, qu'elle aurait préféré porter des
pantalons, qu'elle en avait assez d'être la cible de calembours
faciles et de propos scabreux, mais l'homme autoritaire qu'était
Ash, et qu'elle soupçonnait d'être encore plus libidineux que
n'importe quel collégien, avait rétorqué que la vieille fille, sans
doute un peu aigrie, voyait des problèmes là où il n'y en avait
pas. Il lui avait ensuite expliqué que la tradition à Oxford
voulait qu'elle conserve son uniforme, qui lui allait très bien,
et qu'une femme paraissait beaucoup plus jolie en jupe et
bonjour à vous et patati et patata.

Or, être femme pour Anita Jones ne signifiait plus rien
depuis qu'un amant l'avait quittée pour une autre, une autre
qui possédait une vraie bouche rouge, une femme dont les hanches ondulaient même quand elle marchait droit, qui avait des
seins fermes et ronds comme des boules de boulingrin, une
femme qui avait autre chose à offrir que de l'érudition et un
sourire intellectuel. Anita Jones ne savait même plus si le
duvet qui encombrait sa lèvre supérieure était le simple fruit
d'un désordre hormonal bénin ou la preuve que son organisme
tout entier niait sa propre féminité.

Souvent, le soir, une fois le soleil couché sur les nombreux
clochers d'Oxford, une fois rangés tous ces romans, ces recueils
de textes, ces dictionnaires et toutes ces revues scientifiques,
Anita Jones longeait les murs silencieux de son fief, puis
s'enfermait. La gorge nouée par la rage, elle tentait de pleurer,

mais elle ne parvenait qu'à gémir comme une chatte prise au fond d'un puits asséché. Ensuite, elle se calmait un peu et grillait une cigarette malgré l'interdiction de fumer dans l'enceinte de la bibliothèque. Personne ne venait frapper à sa porte pour la consoler, pas même le jeune homme qui l'avait remerciée si chaleureusement un matin d'octobre, alors que les cours commençaient à peine et qu'une nouvelle année s'annonçait, avec son lot de frustrations à venir et de colères qu'il faudrait refouler. Il lui était reconnaissant parce qu'elle avait réussi à identifier et à dénicher *Elsa* de Louis Aragon ; il ne se souvenait que de deux vers, mais elle les connaissait. « Nous étions faits pour être libres, nous étions faits pour être heureux. » Il rayonnait quand elle lui avait remis le recueil, un signet lui indiquant la page. Il avait paru si doux, si aimable, si beau, en fait, qu'Anita Jones s'était soudainement crue capable de se réconcilier avec tous ses bourreaux, à commencer par elle-même.

Par la suite, il l'avait saluée avec respect chaque fois qu'il franchissait le seuil de la bibliothèque circulaire que tant de jeunes enviaient aux diplômés d'Oxford. Elle se retenait pour ne pas le suivre dans les allées, pour ne pas tourner les pages de son livre, lui prendre la main ou se pencher sur son épaule afin de respirer l'odeur épicée qui émanait de sa peau fine. Il n'avait pas plus de 20 ans. Anita Jones savait qu'elle se couvrait de ridicule chaque fois qu'elle s'approchait d'une fenêtre et qu'elle parcourait le campus d'un regard inquisiteur. Qu'elle se tourne vers le Sheldonian Theatre ou qu'elle scrute l'horizon, par-delà Merton College, elle n'avait d'yeux que pour la longue silhouette d'un jeune, très jeune homme à la voix feutrée, dont l'accent lui rappelait celui de Plymouth ou de Penzance. Dans sa bouche, il y avait de nombreux voyages, de la pluie chaude et des embruns.

Bientôt, elle se prit à le désirer si violemment qu'à sa simple vue, elle devait fuir et se cacher, tant ses membres tremblaient. Puis elle s'était mise à rêver de lui. Parfois, ses songes demeuraient très chastes ; elle et lui se contentaient de se tenir la main en contemplant les nénuphars à la surface d'un étang tranquille. Mais il arrivait qu'il l'entraîne dans un coin retiré de la bibliothèque, pour lui retrousser la jupe, baisser sa culotte, la pénétrer et la chevaucher en poussant des soupirs de profonde jouissance. Elle se mettait alors à sangloter, à se débattre et à hurler, tandis que les traits du jeune homme se durcissaient et qu'ils prenaient cette expression hagarde qu'elle avait si souvent vue sur le visage d'Oliver Ash. Anita Jones se réveillait alors, remplie de dégoût et saisie d'une panique que le reste de la nuit ne suffisait pas à dissiper. Elle était amoureuse ; elle ne pouvait plus le nier.

Ce sentiment, qui aurait dû la combler, ne lui apportait que désarroi, surtout depuis qu'elle avait surpris le jeune homme entre les bras d'une fille à la chevelure rutilante et aux jambes magnifiques. À compter de ce matin-là, Anita Jones ne connut plus qu'un long vertige, comme si le sol s'était ouvert sous ses pieds et qu'elle pouvait basculer dans le vide à tout instant, un vide qu'elle souhaitait dur comme le roc, pour qu'elle se fracasse les os et que cesse enfin sa souffrance. Elle aurait volontiers arraché les yeux bleus de sa jeune rivale pour les enfoncer dans ses propres orbites. Elle ne parvint qu'à se mordre les doigts jusqu'au sang, dans l'obscurité de son alcôve.

Un soir, juste avant la fermeture, Anita Jones dévala l'escalier central de la Radcliffe Camera, quelques vieux bouquins sous le bras et la tête couverte d'un mouchoir aux couleurs de l'université. Quelques étudiants qui s'attardaient encore s'étonnèrent de la voir circuler si vite, elle qui normalement avançait avec peine, le dos courbé. Au rez-de-chaussée, elle avait pénétré dans la réserve des professeurs où s'entassaient quelques milliers d'articles savants et d'ouvrages spécialisés mis à la disposition des étudiants les plus avancés. Elle déambula un instant entre les rayons et, sans sourciller, frotta une allumette qu'elle jeta au loin, droit devant elle. Des feuillets se mirent à flamber et, en un rien de temps, les flammes se répandirent, emplissant la pièce d'une fumée dense et noire.

Anita Jones toussait beaucoup quand on se mit à crier derrière la porte et qu'on l'enfonça, mais elle ne souffla mot quand on l'entraîna à l'extérieur et qu'on la mit sous surveillance, en attendant l'arrivée des policiers. Quand on l'escorta pour traverser le quadrilatère en direction d'un fourgon, sous les yeux de jeunes gens abasourdis, elle ne chancela ni ne versa la moindre larme.

Elle ne vit pas qu'un jeune homme avait relevé le col de son manteau parce qu'un violent frisson l'avait parcouru. Elle ne sut jamais, non plus, que cette nuit-là, il s'enferma dans la tour de l'Observatoire pour chercher dans quel coin du ciel une étoile venait de s'éteindre.

Je pousse une barrière de métal et franchis le seuil d'un vaste cimetière. Je circule rapidement, cherchant des yeux le nom qui me délivrera de ma longue quête. Tous les patronymes et les pierres tombales se ressemblent. Au bout d'une allée, je me penche sur l'une d'elles. Non. Pas celle-ci. Tout à coup, j'aperçois une silhouette — qui disparaît aussitôt, comme happée par la brume. Mon cœur se met à battre la chamade. Je serre le bouquet contre ma poitrine et continue d'avancer, les yeux rivés au sol. Elizabeth Smith — 1900-1968 — William Baley — 1889-1957 — Mary Ann Stuart — 1905-1973 — Frederick Ward — 1918-1986.

Reading, the Signs

Q uand on trébucha derrière moi et que j'entendis un homme jurer entre ses dents, je compris qu'il fallait que je garde mon sang-froid. Je savais que je courais un risque en circulant sur le campus à cette heure où la lune n'avait pas encore commencé sa course lente à travers le ciel charbonneux de Reading. Là-bas, dans les champs qui me séparaient de la résidence où j'espérais pouvoir me réfugier à temps, il y avait des taches blanches et grises qui gambadaient, une queue de coton entre leurs petites jambes musclées. N'importe qui eût été rassuré à la vue de ces familles entières de lapins sortis de terre pour brouter l'herbe mouillée du soir, mais pas moi. Moi, je luttais contre une violente envie de courir ou d'appeler à l'aide. Je m'étais mise à marcher très lentement afin de m'assurer que l'homme me suivait bel et bien et que je n'étais pas victime de mes mauvaises lectures. J'espérais surtout qu'il ne fasse que passer dans ma vie. En fait, lui seul avait un pouvoir sur ma destinée : ou bien il se faisait oublier, ou bien il gravait son visage à jamais dans ma mémoire.

Instinctivement, j'avais plongé la main dans mon sac : allais-je lui donner mon porte-monnaie ou déclencher mon alarme personnelle ? Tout dépendait de cet étranger et de ses

117

besoins du moment. J'avais beaucoup de mal à contrôler le rythme de ma respiration. Derrière moi, l'homme soufflait de plus en plus rapidement. Je me demandais ce qui m'avait poussée à m'arrêter à la procure de la Student's Union. Je voulais acheter des livres, mais tout était encore fermé. Mon impatience m'avait d'ailleurs nuit à maintes occasions ; je faisais toujours tout trop vite. Je ne savais même pas pourquoi j'avais choisi cet endroit déprimant pour mes études. Si j'avais pris le temps de visiter la ville un dimanche matin et si j'avais eu l'occasion d'attendre l'autobus en face d'un de ses nombreux *take-out* chinois, j'aurais probablement opté pour Cambridge ou Oxford. À la fois si proche et si éloignée de Londres, je me sentais prisonnière de cette misère sourde qui lacérait les cœurs et grugeait les visages. Et puis, je n'aimais pas ces distances démesurées entre les pavillons et les résidences d'étudiants.

J'aurais voulu pouvoir me retourner et cracher à la figure de l'homme qui me suivait, lui balancer mon sac à la tête et détaler derrière un talus. J'aurais aimé enfoncer mes ongles dans ses joues et le traiter de brute et de maniaque, le projeter contre le sol et le rouer de coups dans les parties. Mais je n'arrivais plus qu'à courir au ralenti et à déglutir avec peine, car la salive ne venait pas jusqu'à ma bouche. Je me détestais. Je me haïssais encore plus que je ne pouvais le haïr, lui. Il avait au moins la lâcheté de son désir débridé. Moi, je n'avais rien que cette révolte que j'enfouissais au plus creux de mes entrailles vierges. Je n'avais jamais pu me faire à ces regards de fauves affamés, à cette façon qu'ils ont de nous redessiner avec leurs yeux qui ont des mains, de nous remodeler à volonté et de finir par ne plus désirer ce que nous sommes, mais uniquement ce qu'ils veulent. J'étais fatiguée de lutter, épuisée de n'éprouver que de la peur, lasse de ce régime de terreur incessant, justifié par des siècles de bêtise et de droits acquis par la force.

Quand je parvins à Whitenights Road et qu'il me restait encore quelques centaines d'enjambées à parcourir, je sentis que l'étranger ralentissait et qu'il prenait ses distances. Peut-être était-il si sûr de lui qu'il ne se donnait plus la peine de me talonner. Peut-être détectait-il si bien ma peur qu'il ne doutait plus de son emprise sur moi.

Je pressai le pas davantage. Je savais qu'il l'interpréterait probablement comme un geste de panique. Il jouait au chat et à la souris avec moi ; il n'attendait peut-être qu'un faux pas de ma part pour bondir et me déchiqueter. J'avais tort de montrer ma crainte. J'avais tort de faire preuve de faiblesse alors que j'aurais dû passer à l'offensive et lui arracher les yeux. Je tremblais tellement que j'avais du mal à avancer sans que mes souliers ne se heurtent aux pavés inégaux du trottoir.

Lorsque je passai la barrière et que les murs de Foxhill se profilèrent devant moi, je me sentis plus vulnérable que jamais. L'homme comprendrait que j'étais en mesure de lui échapper et qu'il ne lui restait qu'une étroite marge de manœuvre. Je résolus donc de courir, de courir et de courir encore, sans me retourner, mais il était un peu tard : l'étranger avait saisi mon bras et m'avait forcée à le regarder en face. J'eus tout juste le temps d'apercevoir la courte cicatrice qui zébrait son cou. Ses yeux, très beaux, très noirs, étaient écarquillés, mais ils ne semblaient pas me voir.

Un renard était sorti d'un buisson de houx et nous regardait à distance, le museau humide, les oreilles droites. J'en profitai pour m'échapper et, en courant, j'appuyai si fort sur le bouton de mon alarme qu'elle se brisa sans émettre la moindre note. Le son horriblement aigu qui transperça l'horizon ne sortait pas de cet objet que j'avais jeté au loin, mais de ma gorge dénouée par la peur et la rage. Quand je fus dans ma chambre, la porte verrouillée, je saisis toute l'importance de ce que j'avais confié aux bêtes nyctalopes de Foxhill. Je ne pleurai pas, tant mon cri m'avait libérée ; je ne dormis pas, tant la nuit me parut éternelle et noire.

Le trimestre débuta enfin. J'eus envie de partir, de me terrer quelque part ; on refusa de me rembourser ce que j'avais versé pour me loger et apprendre à me battre. On déplorait le regrettable incident ; on compatissait. Toutefois, ceci ne suffisait pas à justifier le remboursement de tant de livres sterling.

Mais quand les traits d'un de mes professeurs me parurent familiers, quand l'expression hagarde de ses yeux assombris n'atteignirent plus seulement mon cerveau, mais mon âme, je retournai dans la capitale. Je savais qu'il me faudrait beaucoup d'espace pour réparer et polir mon armure ; j'aurais besoin de plus de temps encore pour parvenir à la retirer.

Frederick Ward. 1918-1986. Ma gorge se noue. La tombe est jonchée de fleurs magnifiques : roses, lis, magnolias, orchidées bleues... De quoi auront l'air mes marguerites ? Derrière moi, des pas. Le jeune homme de l'avion ou le passager du train ? L'étranger du parc ? Eux tous ? Je m'accroupis devant la tombe de Frederick, comme si j'espérais qu'il intervienne.

Puis, plus rien. Sauf la rosée et le vent. Le brouillard et ses bras fluides.

Whispers in my Room

Isaac Lear tremblait quand il alluma le lampion. Dès qu'il eut enfoui à nouveau sa main dans la poche de son manteau, la petite flamme se mit à sautiller, comme pour prendre la relève. Le jeune homme se concentrait sur la lumière diffuse et hésitante qu'elle projetait autour d'elle ; il n'entendait pas tous ces chuchotements. Même les chants qui flottaient dans la cathédrale Saint-Paul n'arrivaient pas à se frayer un chemin jusqu'à ses oreilles rougies par le froid. Ces lentes mélopées ne l'atteignaient qu'après avoir franchi un banc d'épais brouillard dans lequel Isaac Lear s'était réfugié depuis longtemps. Il s'ennuyait. L'ennui lui collait à la peau comme des anémones de mer à un rocher. Il vivait seul entre les murs d'un bel appartement où il ne lui arrivait jamais de changer les tableaux ni de laisser se briser la moindre faïence sur le carrelage. Ses pantoufles l'attendaient chaque soir, l'une près de l'autre, sur la carpette de l'entrée, dans la position exacte où il les avait laissées le matin. Seuls le philodendron et l'oxalis réclamaient son attention et quelques gouttes d'eau versées à la surface d'un terreau craquelé, une fois la semaine.

Il avait passé des années à chercher une femme. Il savait qui il souhaitait rencontrer, mais ignorait où la trouver. Il attendait un signe ; du ciel ou d'ailleurs. Il passait ses rares temps libres chez des amis, fréquentait les bistrots chic, les salles de cinéma obscures de Leicester Square et les boutiques de Bond Street. Il assistait aussi à des vernissages, à des lancements de campagnes de financement ainsi qu'à toutes sortes de happenings. Toujours en vain. Pas même une ombre qui puisse ressembler à celle qu'il avait dû s'inventer au fil des ans, à défaut de la côtoyer vraiment.

Il y avait des nuits où Isaac Lear sombrait dans un désespoir sans fond, et des jours où il se disait qu'il ne fallait pas renoncer. Il lui arrivait aussi de prendre le *tube* jusqu'à St. Paul's et, une fois enfermé dans l'enceinte de la cathédrale, une fois dominé par ses dômes vivants et ses vitraux ternis, il allumait un autre lampion et faisait un vœu. Toujours le même. Il ne déposait son obole qu'ensuite ; il lui arrivait même de l'oublier. Mais il ne l'oubliait pas, elle. D'ailleurs, il n'avait même pas songé à essayer. Bien que la vie lui parût absurde, il demeurait convaincu qu'il fallait s'accrocher à une vision. D'elle, il avait appris la patience. Il était aussi devenu sensible à des choses anodines : la pluie qui trace des sillons tortueux le long d'un carreau fêlé, l'haleine froide de l'aube, l'âge qui s'incruste dans l'écorce des arbres et la compagnie taciturne des hommes et des femmes de bronze qui peuplent les places et les squares. Avec ses cheveux clairsemés, son nez trop long et sa minceur inquiétante, Isaac Lear se disait que c'était là la seule intimité à laquelle il pût rêver. Après trente-trois ans de solitude transparente, il aurait souhaité que les pas de cette femme viennent résonner devant sa porte. Mais celle qu'il imaginait souvent, marchant vers lui, n'avait eu le temps de croiser son chemin qu'une seule fois.

Il passa un moment à méditer devant le regard lumineux et multiplié des lampions, puis il s'éloigna. Il alla s'asseoir sur une chaise, tout près de la chorale muette, et ferma les yeux. Il se coupait ainsi du monde, de tout ce qui pouvait le faire souffrir davantage, tout ce qui n'avait ni la peau blanche ni les yeux de bête apeurée de sa chimère.

Il ne vit pas qu'une femme lui avait emboîté le pas ; il ne l'entendit pas l'appeler en silence. Elle s'était trouvée là chaque fois qu'Isaac Lear avait allumé un lampion et, chaque fois, elle avait fait un vœu, elle aussi. Elle croyait que, lorsqu'elle obtiendrait la faveur demandée, la mèche s'éteindrait toute seule, comme par magie, emportée par le temps, par une subite raréfaction de l'oxygène ou par des doigts invisibles qui viendraient l'écraser et la réduire en cendres. Elle croyait également que des esprits habitaient la cathédrale et que, du haut de la galerie des Murmures, ils exerçaient leur sacerdoce en répandant dans l'air des mots qui n'étaient pas ceux des vivants, mais ceux des morts. Elle se disait que sa parole à elle s'était tue depuis si longtemps qu'elle ne pourrait pas faire autrement que de rejoindre celle d'Isaac Lear. Elle avait besoin de coller son oreille à la paroi convexe de la galerie, et de l'entendre, lui, de reconnaître le timbre brisé de sa voix et l'étrangeté de son élocution, en provenance de l'autre côté de la coupole, d'un autre hémicycle, d'un autre monde. Elle marcha le long d'une allée latérale jusqu'à l'escalier en colimaçon qui la mènerait là-haut, au-dessus de l'autel et de ces ondes cristallines dont les vibrations fragiles et instables tenteraient de flotter jusqu'à elle.

À mi-chemin de son ascension, la femme s'appuya contre la rampe et souffla un peu. Quand elle parvint à la galerie, elle s'approcha de la balustrade de métal ouvré et regarda dans le vide. Là, elle vit Isaac Lear, celui qu'elle aimait sans le dire, celui dont elle n'arrivait plus à s'éloigner. Il était celui qui avait failli effacer ses propres traits dans la glace, des traits creusés de l'intérieur, comme irrigués par des courants souterrains.

Une violente émotion la transperça de part en part, tandis qu'elle se penchait sur lui, cet homme minuscule parmi la foule. Il avait rouvert les yeux et regardait droit devant, comme s'il refusait d'imiter ses voisins, distraits par tant de sons et de beauté. La femme hésita avant de tendre la main pour attirer son attention, puis laissa tomber des paillettes d'or et d'argent qui se mirent à virevolter, du haut de la galerie jusqu'aux pieds d'Isaac Lear qui semblait recueilli, les mains jointes et le regard perdu. Bientôt, une rumeur allant croissant s'éleva de la foule, et tous se tournèrent vers la coupole, Isaac Lear y compris.

Le jeune homme avait toujours été trop occupé pour suivre la lune dans sa course empesée à travers le dôme éteint de la nuit. Il ne l'avait jamais vue se lever. Aussi avait-il la certitude qu'elle surgissait de l'horizon pour s'accrocher à sa toile de feutre criblée de trous. Quand il aperçut la femme dont la main coupable s'agitait encore, il eut la certitude qu'il ne s'était pas trompé. Il eut même l'impression qu'il était témoin d'une éclipse lunaire projetée en accéléré : un visage rond, laiteux, puis coupé en deux par une frange noire, le toisait depuis le ciel. Il poussa un cri rauque tant il se sentit transporté. Mû par une allégresse soudaine, il se leva si vite qu'il faillit s'affaler sur le sol glacé de la cathédrale et courut vers l'escalier qui menait à la galerie des Murmures.

Tout en haut, la femme n'osait plus bouger. Elle ne savait pas encore ce qu'elle dirait à Isaac Lear. Elle ne savait que son nom et ne connaissait que son visage qu'elle avait vu à l'endos d'un livre. Mais elle savait qu'il avait trouvé ce qu'il cherchait. Elle avait compris que le jour où ils s'étaient croisés tout près d'un lion de Trafalgar Square, Isaac Lear n'avait plus oublié son visage, ni sa démarche saccadée et rapide. Quant à elle, elle l'avait suivi partout, à distance, notant ses déplacements, épiant ses gestes. Elle connaissait cette habitude qu'il avait de jeter de rapides coups d'œil à sa montre, comme pour s'assurer qu'elle tenait toujours le temps. Elle savait tout de ces mains agiles et déliées, de ces yeux brillants et de cette voix qui, rarement, brisait le silence.

Isaac Lear gravissait l'escalier en courant ; il n'avait plus ni maux de dos ni élancements dans les jambes. Ses muscles se tendaient comme la corde d'une arbalète, et ses semelles, à peine posées sur le plat d'une marche, volaient aussitôt vers la suivante. Au terme de son périple en spirale, il n'eut pas la force de se ruer sur ce corps qu'il avait imaginé tant de fois contre le sien. Il leva les mains, esquissa un geste très bref, puis les croisa sur sa poitrine. Elle traça dans l'air les mots d'une phrase, très courte et très belle.

Elle le regardait en face, sans bouger, bien qu'elle eût envie de serrer ces mains, de palper tout ce qui pouvait palpiter sous ces étoffes sombres. Elle n'avait plus sur la langue ce goût de fiel qu'elle avait longtemps pris pour sa propre salive. Elle voulait cet homme. Elle voulait redescendre cet escalier à côté de lui, avec juste assez d'espace entre eux pour que le vent y grave des airs durables, comme les contours des montagnes anciennes.

L'homme était étonné d'entendre son cœur battre à tout rompre. Et quand elle s'approcha de lui, il entrouvrit la bouche pour émettre des sons discordants et criards, les seuls dont il était capable. Elle posa un doigt sur ses lèvres ; il sourit.

Près de la sortie, alors que les fidèles s'en retournaient à la rumeur constante de la ville, tous les lampions s'étaient éteints, soufflés par une brise soudaine venue du dehors. D'une mèche encore brûlante s'éleva un filet de fumée bleue qui s'enroula sur lui-même, avant de se dissiper dans l'air renouvelé de la cathédrale presque déserte.

Au retour, le contrôleur n'ose pas me demander mon billet, tellement je pleure. Je le lui remets tout de même ; il le vérifie et acquiesce. Puis il pose sa main sur mon épaule.

« *Do you need any help ?* »

Je fais signe que non. Dans les yeux de l'homme, il y a un reflet bleu et pur que j'ai appris à aimer. Il me sourit. Je m'empresse d'essuyer mon visage, tandis qu'il s'éloigne sans bruit. Je respire. Me voilà rassurée, moi qui croyais que je n'avais plus d'ami en Angleterre.

NOTICE BIBLIOGRAPHIQUE

Les nouvelles suivantes ont déjà paru sous une forme différente : « Liminaire » dans *L'horreur est humaine*, Québec, Le Palindrome, 1989, sous le titre « Mes amis d'Angleterre » ; « Bridge over the River Cam » dans *L'Écrit primal*, n° 16, mars 1994 ; « London Leaves » dans *Les Cahiers Œuvres ouvertes*, n° 7, printemps 1994.

Dans la même collection :

Meurtres à Québec, recueil collectif
Légendes en attente de Vincent Engel
Nouvelles mexicaines d'aujourd'hui, recueil collectif
L'année nouvelle, recueil collectif
    (en coédition avec Canevas, Les Éperonniers et Phi)
Léchées, timbrées de Jean Pierre Girard
La vie passe comme une étoile filante : faites un vœu
    de Diane-Monique Daviau
L'œil de verre de Sylvie Massicotte
Chronique des veilleurs de Roland Bourneuf
Gueules d'orage de Jean-Pierre Cannet et Ralph Louzon
    (en coédition avec Marval)
Courants dangereux de Hugues Corriveau
Le récit de voyage en Nouvelle-France de l'abbé peintre
    Hugues Pommier de Douglas Glover
L'attrait de Pierre Ouellet
Cet héritage au goût de sel de Alistair MacLeod
L'alcool froid de Danielle Dussault
Ce qu'il faut de vérité de Guy Cloutier
Saisir l'absence de Louis Jolicœur
Récits de Médilhault de Anne Legault
Аэлита / Aélita de Olga Boutenko
La vie malgré tout de Vincent Engel
Théâtre de revenants de Steven Heighton
N'arrêtez pas la musique ! de Michel Dufour
Et autres histoire d'amour... de Suzanne Lantagne
Les hirondelles font le printemps de Alistair MacLeod
Helden / Héros de Wilhelm Schwarz
Voyages et autres déplacements de Sylvie Massicotte
Femmes d'influence de Bonnie Burnard